DEATH WILL BE BRIEF

VOLUME ONE

BY

RANDALL J. FUNK

ALSO BY RANDALL J. FUNK

Death is a Clingy Ex

Death Lives Across The Hall

Death Wears a Big Hat

Death is Sleeping with My Wife

Published in the United States by Ghost Light Press, LLC

www.randalljfunk.com

ISBN: 978-0-9978277-7-4

Cover design by Ann McMan

First Edition

Special thanks to:

Steel Toe Brewing in St. Louis Park. The majority of this book was written during my Sunday beer and writing sessions there. Thanks to Chelsea, Matt, Casey, Luke, April, Nick and Jane for making me feel so welcomed.

Zach Curtis, for providing the name of this book.

Samantha Papke, for her assistance in preparing the manuscript.

Ann McMan, for her terrific cover design.

Kris and Ben, for their patience and love.

Everyone who has bought *Death is a Clingy Ex*, *Death Lives Across The Hall*, *Death Wears A Big Hat* and *Death is Sleeping with My Wife* and has helped me start this adventure.

For my aunt, Bonnie Walker, who read all my Joe Davis short stories when I was a kid. Thank you for your never-ending support and encouragement. This wouldn't be possible without you.

DEATH IS MY LITTLE BROTHER

I'll be honest: I've always found family to be a lame reason for doing anything.

Now, there are some who remain strictly loyal to their families. "Nothing counts so much as blood" and that sort of thing. But they never stop to consider it's just blind loyalty. Like rooting for the local sports team or voting Republican. You do it without thinking.

Personally, I have a good relationship with my parents. Yes, there are times when my father doesn't know what to make of me and my mother thinks all my problems would be solved if I find the right girl. But on the whole, our relationship is very solid. My brothers, on the other hand, are close enough to my age that the relationship we shared growing up bordered on the murderous. As we've become adults, it's faded into an understated mutual contempt. I know I'm supposed to love and be loyal to these guys, but what have they done to earn that? I didn't choose to have them as brothers. How much loyalty have they really earned?

My name is Joe Davis. I get paid to write stuff like that.

I'm not sure why I'm thinking of family. It's mid-January and I managed to get through the holidays relatively unscathed. My mother asked about my romantic prospects and my older brother Kevin repeatedly offered to loan me money as if I'm a charity. But otherwise, I was able to hole up in my old room or watch the occasional bowl game with my father until I could safely make my escape.

Apparently, I'm desperate for material, though that's not usually the case. I'm a thrice-weekly columnist for *The Daily Bugle*, an indie newspaper that ditched the paper thing a while back and became a website only. My column (*Cup o' Joe*) covers all topics of interest (to me, at least). Politics, entertainment, social questions, sports and the like. The same stuff with which I've wearied many a friend, but now make a living (or something similar) doing.

The view out of the three arch windows at the front of my apartment doesn't inspire creativity. It's a sunny, but bitterly cold, January day. My desk is stuffed into the corner of my one-bedroom apartment. There's very little activity on Summit Avenue; formerly the home to St. Paul's wealthy elite, but now something a little closer to an artist's quarter. My own apartment is located across the street from where F. Scott Fitzgerald wrote his first novel. Pretty heady digs for a guy who writes glorified poop-and-fart jokes for a living.

The door buzzer goes off and I let out a groan. The buzzer and I have a difficult relationship. I don't like being interrupted and the buzzer facilitates just such a thing. I'm debating whether to answer it when the buzzer goes off several more times. Clearly, someone is desperate to see me. Could be a deranged fan. Then again, while my fans are certainly deranged, they don't tend to leave the house. I decide to see who it is.

"Yeah?" I say, pushing the intercom button with more force than required.

"Joe? Joe, it's Owen. Can I come up?"

I've got to admit: I'm floored. I've been living in this apartment for five years and I don't think my younger brother Owen has even been to my neighborhood, let alone my front door. I'm surprised he found the place. I stare at the buzzer for longer than I intended.

"Joe? Joe, are you there?"

I snap out of it and press the intercom button. "Yeah, I'm here. Come on up."

I press the buzzer and a few seconds later there's a knock at the door. I open it and, sure enough, there's Owen in all his stocky, needle-nosed glory. He looks past me, into the apartment.

"I'm, uh, I'm not interrupting anything, right?" he says.

That's a thing about my family. If my friends Mike or Lars or Carol had said such a thing, I would toss it off with a light laugh. They know my work habits well enough to know they're not interrupting anything I couldn't get back to. With Owen, though, I'm irritated at his assumption that my life is so empty and meaningless, there's nothing to interrupt.

"Actually, I'm working on a column," I say, "I'm kind of busy."

Okay, the first part is true. The second part is an utter lie. A column generally takes me about two uninterrupted hours to write. My daytime schedule can always accommodate an interruption. But I don't want Owen to know that. He wipes his feet on the mat and waits for me to invite him in. If I didn't, he'd rat me out to my parents. I step aside and throw out an arm, welcoming him to my humble abode.

Owen paces my living room, hands jammed deep into the pockets of his black overcoat. At first, I think he's just cold, but there's something fidgety in his movements. And Owen doesn't fidget.

"Can I get you something?" I ask, "Tea, coffee, Quaaludes?"

Owen runs a hand through his sandy blonde hair. "No, I'm fine. I just, uh…I'm fine."

I step over to my desk and pick up my coffee. Owen doesn't look fine, but I'm not in the habit of drawing him out (or performing any other act of conversation with him) so I'm not sure what to do. Finally, he lets out a breath and sits on my futon couch, his back still ramrod straight.

"Okay, here's the deal," he says, "I need your help."

"With what?"

"Somebody's after me."

I nearly laugh, given the absurdity of the statement. Then I remember Owen's in my apartment, where he's never been or shown any inclination to go, let alone show up unannounced. Absurdity rules the day.

"You care to explain that?" I say.

Immediately, Owen is on his feet and again pacing the room. My cats peer out from the bedroom, questioning the presence of this rank stranger. The cats are litter-mates and they run my household. One is Lenny, a handsome butterscotch tabby with the subtlety of a Sherman Tank, and the other is Squiggy, the former runt of the litter whose black-and-white coloring reminds me of a butler. Squiggy looks at me and I picture an English-accented voice asking: "Sir, do you require assistance with this ruffian?" Meantime, there's a little sweat on Owen's upper lip. With his needle nose and the general lack of lips, it's not a good look for him.

"I'm in town for a convention," he says, "Pipes and shit. Boring stuff, but these pipe guys know how to party."

"That's the word on the street."

"Anyway, last night, I decided to go out with some of the guys from Tool Town. We went bar-hopping, kicked back. I don't remember about half of it."

"Typical convention."

Owen stops. "How would you know?"

"Dad used to tell stories. The ones he could remember anyway."

"Well, they're all true. As far as I know. Anyway, I wake up this morning. Got a mother of a hangover. I go down to the hotel restaurant, figure I'll get rid of it with some bacon and eggs. I'm sitting at my table, minding my own business, when these two guys come up to me and want to know where the papers are."

"What papers?"

"That's what I asked them," Owen says, "They get real pissed off at me, like I'm fucking around with them. They keep asking and finally I raise my voice. That's when hotel security comes over and wants to know what's going on. These two guys say it's all cool and back off."

"I'm guessing that's not the end of the story."

Owen shakes his head. "I go to a couple events at the convention this morning and I see these guys following me. Finally, I pretend I'm going back to my hotel room, get off on a wrong floor, sneak out of the hotel and decide to come here."

That fills in a few of the gaps. For those scoring along at home, I should explain a few things. My father runs a hardware store in my hometown of Porter's Bay. He's owned it for as long as I can remember. In the manner of many small businessmen, he hoped to pass the store along to one of his sons. My older brother Kevin was ruled out when he met a girl from San Francisco and decided to move out there and become a lawyer. I was ruled out when I started making a living as a writer. Owen was more than happy to become my father's heir apparent. Since Dad is approaching retirement, Owen has been handed more and more of the responsibilities, such as going to the Twin Cities and attending boring-ass conventions. This one, however, doesn't sound so boring.

"You have no idea who these guys are?" I ask.

"None. And I have no idea what these papers are, either. All I know is that they want answers real bad. And I don't have any to give them."

"So you came to me. What can I do?"

That seems to genuinely flummox Owen. He opens his mouth a couple of times, but nothing comes out. Finally, he shrugs and says, "You were the only person I could think of."

Yeah, the brother you didn't bother to let know you were in town. I'm tempted to tell Owen he's being paranoid and turn him back out into the cold. I swing my chair toward the arch windows, trying to find the perfect phrasing for such a request, something my mother would consider unimpeachable. As I do this, I see a couple of guys who, near as I can guess, are not indigenous to my neighborhood.

"Hey Owen," I say, "These two guys who were following you. What did they look like?"

"You remember The British Bulldogs?"

For the uninitiated, the British Bulldogs were a pro wrestling tag team back when Owen and I were kids. They were a couple of fireplugs with almost-freakish quickness and the ability to throw large bodies through space. I should have known Owen would go to a wrestling reference. Thing is, I'm just as big a fan.

"Yeah, I remember them," I say.

"They looked like those guys. Only about a foot taller."

And that would perfectly describe the two guys I'm looking at. Tall and muscular with ill-fitting suits and no overcoats. They're coming up my front walk when they're approached by Lars, my downstairs neighbor. Lars is salting the sidewalks; one of the rare times he performs his duties as building superintendent. He engages the muscular guys in conversation.

Owen finally realizes what I'm talking about (quick on the uptake, our Owen). He glances out the window and immediately goes into full retreat. "Holy crud," he says, "That's it. That's them. They followed me here."

"Take it easy. I don't think they're—"

And before I finish that thought, things on the front walk get ugly. One of the guys, the one with the slightly receding hairline, grabs Lars by the over-sized parka and starts shaking him. The other guy, the one with the lantern jaw, grabs his partner, as if trying to hold him back. Lars accidentally backhands Lantern Jaw and now Lantern Jaw takes a turn at shaking Lars. The shaking causes Lars to slide out of his parka. He runs up the front walk. The guys slip and slide as they try to run after him (Lars does a for-shit job of salting the sidewalks.) Lars disappears into the building.

"What are they doing now?" Owen asks, "Are they coming in here?"

"Well, I don't think—"

And I only get that much out before there's a knock at the door. Owen runs down the hallway toward my backdoor, scattering the cats as he goes. I jump out of my chair and wave my arms, trying to get control of my house.

"It can't be them," I say, "They're still out front. It's probably my superintendent."

"Will he help?"

"No. But he'll certainly hinder."

I flip open the front door and Lars sweeps into the room, tracking snow all over my hardwood floors.

"There's trouble out front," he says, jerking a thumb toward the window.

"So I saw," I say, "What's going on?"

Lars runs a hand through his quasi-pompadour and waves his pipe-cleaner arms about. "The hell if I know. They said they were looking for some guy named Owen Davis. I told them nobody by that name lives here. They wanted to come in and look around. I told them that wasn't possible. And then they got downright unfriendly." Lars finally takes notice of my brother, who's cowering in the corner nearest the TV. Lars throws a hand out. "Don't believe we've met. I'm Lars."

Owen takes the hand, tentatively. "Owen Davis."

Lars' eyes get wide. "Owen Davis? Same name as the guy they were looking for. Quite the cowinky-dink."

I roll my eyes. "Yeah, quite the dink, indeed. Did they say *why* they were looking for Owen?"

Lars shakes his head. "It was left unsaid. But I don't believe the intentions were friendly."

That seems to be the prevailing opinion. If their treatment of Lars means anything, they're not collecting for the March of Dimes. Since I don't feel like being the next guy to get strong-armed, I make a snap decision.

"We're getting out of here," I say.

Immediately, I'm at the hall closet, collecting my pea coat, stocking cap and a pair of gloves. My snow boots are waiting by the backdoor. Owen follows me down the back hallway.

"This is the way out?" he says.

"Yeah," I say, "My car's in the parking lot."

"The stairs are safe?"

"As long as the super remembered to salt them, they should…y'know what? Just assume they're not safe."

A few seconds later, Owen and I are heading out the backdoor. My apartment has a small deck joined to an erector set of stairs, decks and walkways that are not native to the building (some past owner's idea of a fixer-upper). My car, a black Saturn Ion, sits in a tiny parking lot near the bottom of said erector set. As we skid across the deck, I'm dismayed to discover that Lars, his hands lodged in his armpits, has decided to join us.

"Lars, what are you doing?" I say.

"I'm going with you."

"No, you're not. This thing, whatever it is, doesn't concern you and, well, since I'm pressed for time, I'm going to have to be candid: you're utterly useless in a crisis."

Lars' head snaps back. He's stung. "I had no idea you felt this way."

"Actually, I tell you that on an almost-daily basis."

"I thought that was just banter."

"Doesn't make it any less true. Now, if you'll excuse me…"

Owen and I make our way down the stairs, which takes far longer than the situation requires. We only narrowly avoid going ass-over-teakettle. When we finally get to the bottom, Owen surveys the parking lot.

"Which one's yours?" he asks.

We don't have time, but I can't help myself. "For crying out loud, Owen, you don't even know what car I drive? We just saw each other three weeks ago!"

"I've got a lot on my mind."

"You can memorize seventy-eight varieties of wall screws, but you can't remember a car you just saw a month ago?"

"Do we have to do this now?"

The fact he's right only adds to my irritation. We take a few steps before we're each grabbed by a set of beefy hands.

"You're going to talk to us, sunshine," a voice behind us growls.

Owen and I are spun around and come face to face (well, face to chest) with the goon squad. The guys are as large as advertised and a short chase through the cold has done nothing to improve their attitudes. Owen's chest puffs out. But he looks at me and the fight goes out of him. I can follow his line of thinking. Owen went to college on a wrestling scholarship. He can handle himself in a fight. But I'm utterly worthless, unless Owen picks me up and uses me as a weapon.

Lantern Jaw, apparently, is the designated spokesman. "All right, we're done fucking around. Where are the papers?"

"What papers?" Owen asks.

Receding Hairline grabs Owen's tie and pulls him close. "We already talked to your girlfriend. Now we're talking to you. You gonna play dumb, numbnut?"

"I'm not playing!"

I shake my head. "I've been telling you that for thirty years. *Now* you confess?"

Lantern Jaw shoves me away. "Nobody's interested in what you have to say, fucknut." He focuses on Owen. "Last time I'm asking nicely: where is it?"

Before Owen can answer, the roar of a car engine fills the air. It can come from only one source: Lars' piece of crap Buick. It's roughly the size of an aircraft carrier and was built sometime during the Nixon administration. The muffler has always been treated as a luxury item, meaning Lars gets noise complaints from as far away as Chicago every time he heads out to get groceries. We were so preoccupied, we didn't notice him sneak down.

The Buick mounts the curb and chugs down the small patch of lawn, shoving its way through the snowbanks. It's headed right for us. Receding Hairline shoves Owen away and gives the Buick his undivided attention. He looks ready to throw a roundhouse right at the damn thing, but Lantern Jaw pulls him out of the path (apparently, he does both the talking and the thinking). Lars swings past them and throws open the passenger door (without bothering to stop.)

"Get in! Get in!" he shouts, as if we needed prompting.

In a second, Owen and I have barreled into the Buick. I struggle to close the door as Lars shoots past the carriage house that encloses our parking lot and into the alley beyond. Two quick turns, a pedestrian near-miss and a middle finger later, we're on Summit Avenue heading east. The goon squad is not visible behind us.

I lean my head against the dash. "Okay, at least I know you're not blowing this whole thing out of proportion."

Owen, ensconced in the backseat, sits up. "What do you mean? You really thought I was blowing this out of proportion?"

"Because that's unheard of, right?"

"Hey, screw you—"

Lars shouts at both of us. "Boys! Knock it off and act like adults!" It has the effect of quieting both Owen and me. Even Lars seems surprised. "What?" he asks.

"Nothing," I say, "Just that for a second there, you did a stunningly good impression of our mother."

Owen nods. "Eerie, actually."

Lars allows himself a moment of satisfaction. I turn my attention to Owen.

"These papers they're looking for," I say, "You have any idea what that's all about?"

Owen slumps back against the seat. "No."

"Does it have anything to do with the convention?"

"Joe, it's a pipe manufacturer's convention. How much cloak-and-dagger you think goes on there?"

"There wasn't *anything* out of the ordinary? Anything you can remember?"

Owen folds his hands in his lap and looks down. His deep-thinking pose. When he looks up, he tilts his head to one side. "I remember talking to a guy named Alan. One of the Tool Town guys. We spent most of the night bar-hopping. If all this is related to last night, Alan would've been there, too."

"Where do we find Alan?"

"At the hotel. The Ambassador Suites. You know it?"

Lars gives him a thumbs up and angles the car down Ramsey Hill. "Big hotel on the edge of downtown. I used to drive a shuttle for them."

My eyebrows go up. "When was this?"

"A few years ago. It ended after the, uh, the incident."

"What incident?"

"It was nothing. The ban from the United Arab Emirates hasn't affected me in the least."

That's probably a story I'd love to hear over beers. But now is definitely not that time. I turn to Owen, to ask him more about this Alan guy, when something catches my attention. A car is following us, coming up fast as we go down Ramsey Hill.

"Lars..." I say.

He's looking in the rearview mirror. "I see it. I don't think they—"

And that's as far as he gets before the car crashes into us. It's not horrific, but it's certainly more than a love tap. The Buick, despite its girth, fishtails on the icy road. Given that Ramsey Hill is so steep it nearly goes straight up and down, this is more than disconcerting. Lars gets control of the Buick, just in time to get another shot from the trailing car.

"They found us mighty quick," Lars says, swinging the wheel about.

"Just keep us on the road," I say.

"And get us out of here," Owen says.

There's a stoplight at the bottom of the hill and a few more beyond that. Fortunately, the first light is green, but it will take a miracle to run all of them. And that only increases the odds of crashing into something coming the other way. The car behind us doesn't seem willing to back off.

"You got a plan?" Owen asks, leaning toward Lars.

Lars, ever the fatalist, seems largely unconcerned. "I'll just keep the pedal down and I'm sure everything will work out as it should."

Owen and I look at each other, not at all convinced. We'd be better off getting into the other car and taking our chances. The Buick blasts through the stoplight at the bottom of the hill and follows the street over Highway 35E. Another stoplight comes up near United Hospital. It's going yellow. Lars doesn't slow down. Neither does the car behind us. This is about to get hairy.

And, of course, Owen's cell phone rings. He glances at the screen. "Not now."

"Who is it?" I ask.

"It's Dad. I've got to take this."

"Are you kidding? Let it go to voicemail."

"I can't. I told him I'd call him first thing this morning. But I didn't 'cause I was a little…"

"Hungover?" Lars says.

Owen nods. "Yeah, that. And Dad goes nuts when I don't answer. He'll keep calling."

He's right, of course. Owen might be a thirty-year old man with a wife and a child, but in my father's eyes, he's still a kid. Leave him alone in the big city and all hell's likely to break loose. That my father is completely right about the situation should not be considered relevant.

"Hey Dad," Owen says, working to affect a nonchalant tone, "How's it going?"

We've cleared two stoplights, but the third is red as a monkey's ass. Worse, someone's taking roughly three months to make a left-hand turn. They're going to wind up right in our path. And there doesn't seem to be room in the other lane.

"No, no, it's going great," Owen says, looking behind us at the trailing car, "Really productive."

Lars shoots through the red light and swings into the oncoming lane. Another car comes right at us. I manage to avoid crying out. Lars throws the Buick back to the right and threads the needle between the oncoming car and the one making the slow left. We're in the clear.

"That?" Owen asks, "Oh, that was nothing. You know how these pipe guys are."

The car following us has managed to clear the intersection as well. It's coming up fast again. Lars is facing another stoplight at West Seventh, this one is also red and the intersection is as busy as hell.

"You going left into downtown or straight into Irvine Park?" I ask.

"My preference is Irvine Park."

"Doesn't matter. There's no way you're going to Frogger yourself through there."

"Probably not."

Owen waves for us to be quiet. "Oh, that's just a couple of salesmen. You know how it is. Always be closing. Yeah, the one guy does sound a lot like Joe. Heck of a shame for him."

I'd give Owen the finger, but it's low on the priority list. Lars keeps his foot on the accelerator as we head toward the intersection. I grab the dashboard, bracing myself.

"What are you going to do?" I whisper, drawing another annoyed wave from Owen.

"I'm going through the intersection," Lars says, looking supremely unconcerned, "The universe will tell me where to go from there."

"Is it going to give *me* a heads up?"

"Unless your attitude changes in the next two seconds, I doubt it."

The Buick flies at the intersection. Even Owen has taken his attention away from his phone call. The car behind us isn't backing off. The light is still red. I close my eyes and await the inevitable screeching of tires and crunching of metal.

When I open them about a second-and-a-half later, the Buick is past the intersection and heading for Irvine Park.

"What happened?" I ask.

Lars shrugs. "The light changed, we got through it. It was meant to happen."

Owen is bug-eyed and frozen against the backseat. The phone is still clasped to his ear. "Wouldn't have believed it if I hadn't seen it," he mumbles. Something on the other end of the line gets his attention. "What? Oh, the deals, Dad. You wouldn't believe the deals if you didn't see them."

The car trailing us has also managed to get through the intersection. I'm wondering how they pulled it off. I'd love to hear Lars explain how the universe has determined this.

"What now?" I ask.

"We'll see how they handle the ice," Lars says.

Owen snaps out of his stupor and regains his air of forced joviality. "When am I coming home? Well, that's kind of, uh, kind of hard to say. There might be, uh…" He looks back at the trailing car. "Other factors involved."

The street ends in a T stop a few blocks after West Seventh. A right-hand turn is out of the question. The street only leads back to West Seventh and more trouble. If we go left, we have a shot at downtown St. Paul or Shepard Road and a possible get away. The question of how long we can keep this up is more of a mystery.

Lars wheels through the stop sign at the T stop and slides through a left-hand turn. I look out the back window while the car trailing us nearly overcooks the turn. As soon as we're past Forpaugh's Restaurant (an upscale eatery that used to be home to a prominent St. Paul resident), Lars throws the Buick to the right. Irvine Park itself is right in front of us. It's a square park with a lovely gazebo in the center. The streets form a square around it. It's not more than a city block (and a small one at that). It's also largely enclosed.

"What the hell are you doing?" I say. Owen gives me another frantic wave, as I'm apparently drawing more questions from my father.

"Nothing, Dad," he says, "Some guy waiting to use the restroom."

"Time to test their handling on the ice," Lars says.

Immediately, Lars begins swinging the car around the turns, fishtailing every one like he's driving a stock car on a dirt track. It's not a pleasant experience for the passengers. The scenery is whirling past like we've gone to warp drive. There's no chance to turn my head and see how the trailing car is doing. The G forces simply won't allow it. It's like someone threw a hangover into a blender.

Owen sprawls across the backseat, eyes wide. "Listen, Dad, this is a little off-topic, but in case I don't see you again…"

There's a loud crash behind us. Lars straightens the car out. The car trailing us has crashed into a stone ledge. Smoke billows from the now-crumpled hood. Owen stares out the back window.

"I'll see you soon, Dad," he says, hanging up.

A minute later, Lars has us out of Irvine Park and heading for the Ambassador Suites. I slump against my seat and try to resume normal breathing.

"Nice driving," I say.

Lars flits a hand. "The universe unfolded as it should. I was simply behind the wheel."

"I'll have to figure out a way to thank the universe."

"You could live a better a life."

"I was thinking more along the lines of a fruit basket."

Five minutes later, we pull into the parking lot of the Ambassador Suites. It's a ten-story hotel on the edge of downtown. Not quite the glamor of the St. Paul Hotel, but several cuts above a Motel 6. Lars finds a parking space and Owen leads us inside.

"All right, how are we going to find this Alan guy?" I ask, "You got a room number?"

"No," Owen says, "We met at the convention, started hanging out at the hotel lounge."

"Then maybe we should start in the hotel lounge," I say. I'll admit: the possibility of getting an adult beverage might have played into that suggestion.

We go through the revolving door and survey the small lobby. The hotel lounge is on the left and the front desk is on the right. Owen and I head for the lounge. Lars hangs back.

"If you don't mind," he says, "I believe I'll have a chat with that lovely young lady at the front desk."

Beauty, of course, is in the eye of the beholder. But even I'm wondering if Lars is talking about the mousy clerk with the pulled back hair and the mole. Lars hunches his shoulders, straightens a tie he's not wearing and sashays off.

"Don't wait up," he says over his shoulder.

Owen looks to me for an answer, but all I can do is gesture toward the lounge. "Your friend Lars is weird," he says.

"And you've only known him twenty minutes. Think how I feel."

The lounge is nice enough, what with the mahogany bar and the brass rail. There's a handful of high-top tables and booths along the walls. The bartender is a bald guy whose gut is ready to push his white shirt through his black vest. He tosses some cardboard coasters in front of us as we sit down.

"What can I get you gentlemen?" he asks, his voice a smoker's growl.

Owen starts to ask a question, but I interrupt. "Two pale ales," I say. The bartender heads toward the tap

"What are you doing?" Owen asks, "I don't want a beer."

"The guy's going to be more inclined to chat if we bring him some business. Make sure you give him a nice tip."

"I don't even want the beer! I'm supposed to pay?"

"If I remember right, you came to me for help and brought a couple murderous goons with you. The *least* you can do is buy me a beer."

Owen tries to keep his voice down. "If you want one, fine. But the last thing I need is a beer. I think I had enough last night."

The bartender sets the beers on the bar. "Yeah, I gotta agree with you there," he says, "Pardon my saying, but you were a little lit."

Owen shoots the guy a startled look. "You were here last night?"

"Yup. Late shift followed by an early shift. My least favorite time of the week. I'm not surprised you don't remember me. You and your friend were weaving pretty good."

I can't help chuckling, prompting a dirty look from Owen. It's one of the ongoing issues I have with my brother. Once upon a time, Owen was fun. Irritating, but fun. A guy who'd hoist a drink or do a bare-ass slide in the locker room shower or be a general wiseass to teachers. There was a good possibility we could become friends as adults. Sadly, by the time Owen got out of college, I was living in the Cities and he was getting involved in my dad's business. Owen's sense of humor was replaced by a stick up his ass that was roughly the length and diameter of a Sequoia. Hearing he let down his hair is delightful. Knowing he doesn't share my delight is even more delightful.

"What friend was this?" Owen asks.

The bartender starts cleaning a glass. "Guy's name was Alan. You're Owen, right?"

"Right."

"Yeah, then it was Alan. You were having a good time, though. That's what counts. I'm just glad you didn't go through with cannonballing the duck pond. Management gets a little touchy about that kind of thing."

Now I'm laughing out loud. Owen starts knocking back his beer. It takes me a few seconds to regain control.

"Have you seen this Alan guy today?" I ask.

The bartender shakes his head. "Not in the bar. I think he's still in the hotel. He said something about staying here through Sunday. Said he had something big going down with his bosses at Tool Town. He was going to put the screws to them. I don't think he pardoned himself for the pun."

Owen and I look at each other. Owen does the talking. "Did he say what this deal was?"

"No. I think he was just making conversation while you were over at that table, hitting on the pretty blonde."

Owen goes white. My brother has been happily married for the past eight years to a girl he originally dated in high school. Mary's a lovely young lady, but if she found out Owen was cheating on her, she'd systematically remove the portions of his anatomy that facilitated the activity. Owen downs the rest of his beer.

"I, uh, I didn't, uh…I didn't get…anywhere with this girl. Did I?"

"Unless you call getting a drink thrown in your face *getting somewhere*, no."

Owen can't look at me. Given the shit-eating grin I'm sporting, it's probably for the best.

"Any idea what room Alan's in?" I ask.

The bartender starts wiping down the bar. "Sorry, guys. Can't give that information out. Management would have my ass."

"Even if I'm a guest?" Owen says.

"You can ask at the front desk, but you're not going to get much out of them."

I finish my beer and we head out. Some interesting information about this Alan guy, but snake eyes on finding him. Owen is out ten bucks for the beer, but he's much richer in embarrassment. Lars is waiting in the lobby. I give him a quick update. When I'm done, Lars waggles his eyebrows.

"It's good you brought me along," he says, "Because I got Alan's room number. And a date with that little she-devil over there."

The she-devil in question is the same mousy desk clerk we saw when we walked in. Even now, she focuses on a computer screen and gives off waves of frigid air. She glances up and gets a conspiratorial finger wave from Lars. She looks back at the screen without returning the wave.

"You sure you aren't being punk'd?" I ask.

Lars leads the way to the glass elevators at the edge of the lobby. "Oh no. She's a blaze of mouse brown fire, that one."

The elevator ride to the eighth floor is silent. We follow Lars to a room in the corner. He knocks. Several seconds later, the door cracks open and a beady eye looks out.

"Yes?" a deep voice says, slowly.

Owen steps forward. "Alan? I'm Owen Davis. From last night?"

A moment and then: "Yeah, I remember you."

"I want to talk. Some strange stuff is going on. I'm wondering if you can help me out."

The door shuts. A lock is thrown and the door pops open. Alan is a dumpy, middle-aged guy with glasses and a weak chin. He doesn't make eye contact with Owen.

"You brought friends," Alan said.

"This is my brother, Joe and his friend Lars. They gave me a ride down here."

Alan steps back. "Come on in."

Owen leads the way, followed by me and Lars. The door clicks behind us. I start to turn and then Lars cries out.

"Ow! What the hell?"

Lars is on his knees. Alan stands over him, wielding a squash racket. He reaches back for another blow. I grab the racket. We struggle. There isn't much to Alan, but he's surprisingly strong. Owen runs over to help me. Alan throws out a foot and it connects with Owen's balls. Owen drops to his knees, swearing.

Lars dives toward Alan but gets a knee in the face. This is embarrassing. Three young and relatively healthy men getting taken out by a single middle-aged dude. We have to get our act together.

I drop to the floor, taking the racket with me. Alan holds on and I flip him across the floor. He lets go of the racket and tumbles into the bathroom. I get to my feet. A second later, Alan emerges from the bathroom. I step toward him, prepared to offer an olive branch. Unfortunately, I'm holding the racket and wielding it like I'm going to hit him. So maybe I deserve it when he raises a can of shaving cream and shoots me in the eyes.

I'm able to avoid most of it, but you don't need a lot of shaving cream in the eyes for it to sting like a motherfucker. I drop the racket and frantically try to wipe the crap off. There's a pounding of feet and some struggling. A lot of swearing. When my vision mostly clears, I see Owen and Lars have tackled Alan. A dog pile is developing, so I hop on. Alan cries out.

"All right, all right! Will you idiots get off me!"

Owen does the negotiating. "Fine. But no more squash rackets or shaving cream or kicks to the nuts. Understand?"

"Understood."

Slowly, we all get off Alan. Lars picks up the squash racket and holds it like a samurai sword. Alan slumps against the table; a spent force. Owen gingerly walks around, fighting off the pain in his swelling nuts.

"Okay, you want to tell me what in the blue hell all of that was?" Owen says.

"I thought you were going to turn me in," Alan says, "Are you?"

"Turn you in for what?"

"You don't know?"

"No!" Then something occurs to Owen. "I, uh, I had a little too much to drink last night."

Alan lets out a barking laugh. "You're telling me? I thought for sure that cop was going to haul you in. You don't call someone *Paul Blart* repeatedly and get away with it."

Owen puts a fist to his head. I tamp down my mirth. "What are we supposed to turn you in for?" I ask.

Alan looks from one of us to the next, getting more confused as he goes. "You guys really don't know?'

"No," I say. I give him the shorthand account of Owen showing up at my door and the merry chase with the goons that led us downtown.

Alan stares at the floor. "I didn't think they'd go after you, Owen. If I did, I never would've blamed you."

Owen stops pacing. "Blamed me for what?"

"Stealing the spreadsheets."

I look at Owen and we silently contemplate which of us is going to beat answers out of this guy. Lars gently places a hand on Alan's knee.

"Maybe you need to tell us what the fuck you're talking about," Lars says.

Alan takes a breath. "It's some information I came across. You guys know who Jeff Greenwald is?"

Lars has no clue and the name sounds only vaguely familiar to me. Owen, however, is all ears (and nose, but he hates when I make that joke).

"Jeff Greenwald?" he says, "The guy who owns Tool Town?"

"The very one," Alan says.

Now the name is familiar. "I remember him. He's the one who ran for Congress, right?"

"And just missed winning," Alan says, "I know he's, technically, my boss, but there's a lot of people who can't stand him. Small business owners, mostly. If Tool Town hasn't put them under, they're worried it's going to. That's what those big box stores do."

I've heard that same assessment from my father. Dad's gotten lucky, in that Porter's Bay values its old hometown tourist appeal and figures big box stores will detract from that. So, Davis Hardware has remained in its relatively unthreatened position on Howard Street lo' these many years. Other stores in other towns haven't been as lucky.

"Okay, so what about this guy?" I ask.

"Well, there were some rumors going around that Greenwald siphoned some of his campaign money into Tool Town, to help build new stores in the Cities. And one of my co-workers, a guy named Edgar, he, uh, he had proof."

My eyebrows go up. "Proof?"

"A couple of financial spreadsheets. One that showed money going out of Greenwald's campaign fund and one that showed the money coming in. Edgar made copies. But he got cold feet, didn't want to do anything with them. So I, uh, I got a hold of them."

"In other words, you stole them."

"Pretty much, yeah."

I pinch the bridge of my nose. Owen looks ready to kick Alan's ass, but we've had quite enough of that. I hold up a hand, backing him off.

"When did you steal them?" I ask.

"Last night. Just before we all went out. I think Edgar got suspicious. I was maybe saying more than I should have. He must have figured out the spreadsheets had been stolen. He started asking me about it. I got nervous. Because I had the spreadsheets on me."

Owen shoots a look at Alan. "And what did you tell Edgar?"

"That, uh, that you stole them."

He makes a move toward Alan, but Lars and I cut him off. Alan drops below the table, putting his hands over his head.

"I'm sorry, Owen!" Alan says, "I didn't want to do it. But you were there. I needed an easy mark!"

Owen struggles for the right word to say; the most appropriate crusher. All he gets out is: "Fuck you!"

"I know! I know! Fuck me. I don't blame you. It was a panic move. I didn't mean anything by it."

Owen stops struggling. He paces the room while Lars and I stay situated between he and Alan.

"And that's why these goons are after me?" Owen says, "Because you panicked? Me, my brother, his friend. We almost got killed because you're greedy and gutless. Thanks a shitload!"

Owen stalks into the bedroom, mainly to pace. I squat next to the table. Alan looks like he's lost his best friend. I'm not sure that would make Owen feel any better.

"Where are the spreadsheets?" I ask.

"I ditched them. I was getting scared and didn't want any part of them."

"Where did you ditch them?"

"I don't know." Responding to the look on my face, he says, "I don't! We were drinking and I wasn't thinking straight. I just knew I had to get rid of the spreadsheets and blame somebody. But I don't remember where I ditched them."

I fall back on my haunches. "Do you have *any* idea where they might be?"

Alan thinks about it. "There are a couple of places. One of the salesmen had a room at The Plaza. We were doing some partying over there. And there was that little waitress down in the bar."

Lars and I look at each other. "What about her?" I ask.

"I, uh, I went back to her place. For a while. I might have left them there."

"But you don't know for sure where it is?"

"No. Sorry."

I let out a cluck of disgust. Yes, it's frustrating. On the bright side, if we find the spreadsheets, we'll be able to neutralize the hired goons and their boss. I turn to Lars.

"Listen, we need to keep Chumley here safe, in case the goons come looking for him," I say, "You know anybody who could do the job?"

Lars nods. "I believe Old Man Albertson owes me a favor."

I cock my head to one side. Old Man Albertson lives on the first floor of our building. He's a crusty war veteran and a shut-in. More by choice than necessity. "What favor does Old Man Albertson owe you?" I ask.

"I stopped bothering him about getting out of his apartment. He said he owed me one."

I'm not sure that's the kind of favor Old Man Albertson was talking about. But he's a stand-up guy, so I'm betting he'll keep Alan safe. I authorize the plan and help Lars get Alan out from under the table.

"What are you guys going to do?" Lars asks.

"The Plaza's only a couple blocks away," I say, "We can start there. Maybe we'll get lucky."

"May the Force be with you."

I step toward the bedroom. "Owen? Let's go."

Owen stalks back into the room and glares at Alan. He makes a half move, more to startle Alan than anything. It works. Alan grabs his coat and scurries out of the room. I clap a hand on Owen's shoulder.

"Easy, big fella," I say, "You can cool off on the walk."

The Plaza's another luxury hotel, not unlike The Ambassador Suites. At first, Owen and I seem inclined to make the whole trip in silence. Of course, you can only go so long before the cold starts to get the better of you and you want a little distraction. And that leads to conversation. We small talk about the cold, but don't stay on the subject.

Owen, without looking at me, says, "Sorry I didn't let you know I was in town."

"It's all right."

"I was just here for the convention. I didn't think you'd be interested."

"You can always invite me out for a beer."

Owen shrugs. "I didn't think of it. Before last night, I don't remember the last time I went drinking."

"That's probably for the best. Sounds like you're terrible at it."

He shoots me a look, then cracks a smile. A second later, we're both laughing. Not gut-busting, but enough to take the edge off. Owen gazes up at the buildings.

"I always figure you and Kevin look down on me," he says, "Because I stayed in Porter's Bay."

"It's a nice town. Just not where I wanted to live."

"And I always figured Dad would have rather you or Kevin took over the store. Y'know, if either of you had hung around."

I stop and stick my gloved hands in my pockets. "Listen, Dad's always been honest. Honest with other people, honest with himself and honest about his kids. I think early on he knew Kevin wasn't interested in running a hardware store. Kev's too..."

"Arrogant?"

"I was going to say ambitious, but they're pretty much the same thing. And he knew I wasn't cut out to spend fifty or sixty hours a week in the store. Hell, he had a hard-enough time keeping me focused when I'd help out on weekends. So I think he was hoping all along that you'd be the one to take over the place. And I'll bet he's pretty happy about that."

Owen still doesn't look at me. But there's shadow of a smile on his face. "You really think that's the case?"

"Yeah, I do. I mean, he still likes me best, but—"

"Shut up."

We make it to The Plaza and con our way past the front entrance. The maids are working on the room when get there. Owen stops in the hallway.

"What do we do?" he asks, "We can't just barge right in there."

"We take a page out of my buddy Mike's book. Follow my lead and don't say anything."

The maid, a heavy-set Latino woman, looks startled when we walk in. She quickly regains her composure and says, "Yes?"

"Hotel security," I say, "We just need to give the room a quick going over."

"For what?"

"I'm afraid that's classified."

The maid debates this, then shrugs. "Close the door when you go."

She leaves and Owen shoots me a stunned look. "You do this a lot?" he asks.

"Usually, I leave it up to Mike. And I wouldn't say I do this a lot, but…I do this."

"You got some interesting friends."

"You have no idea."

Owen and I take a quick look around, but it's much ado about nothing. The spreadsheets are nowhere to be found. We slip out of the room and head down to the lobby, where we sit at a glass table. Owen runs a hand through his hair and lets out a long breath.

"What do we do now?" he asks.

"I suppose we should check out the waitress' place. We could probably get her address from Alan. We just have to figure…"

And something occurs to me. Something that the goons said when they came to my door. Owen notices my thinking.

"What's going on?" he asks.

"How did you guys get around last night? When you were bar-hopping?"

"A rental car."

"Yours?"

"No. Alan's."

Immediately, I'm up and pacing. "You remember what the goons said? Something about having talked to your girlfriend?"

"Yeah." Then it hits him. "That was the waitress, wasn't it?"

"It had to be. If the goons were over at her place, they must have been looking for the spreadsheets. And if they came looking for you—"

"Then they didn't find them." Owen kicks the table leg. "That means the damn things aren't in either place. We're screwed."

I wave that off. "Not necessarily. Think about it. Alan's room, the girl's place and your hotel. What's the one thing that connects all three?"

Owen snaps his fingers. "Alan's rental car."

I take out my phone and call Lars. He quickly puts Alan on the phone. "Where did you ditch your rental car last night?" I ask.

"I think I left it over by The Saints' stadium."

CHS Field is the home of the minor league St. Paul Saints. It's about a chilly ten-minute walk from The Plaza.

"Where are the keys to the thing?" I ask.

"I have them."

"Tell Lars to get back down here. Meet us at your rental car."

I ring off and lead Owen out of the lobby. Ten minutes later, we're outside of CHS Field. It's across the street from the St. Paul Farmer's Market and kitty-corner from my buddy Mike's apartment building. It's a nice place, built in such a way that it seems to slip quietly into the neighborhood. (Would that the new Vikings' stadium could say the same.) The rental car is an unassuming little blue Hyundai, so small that Owen could probably pick it up and carry it back to the hotel.

"How many guys were you bar-hopping with last night?" I ask.

"Four or five."

"Must have looked like a clown car when you came rolling out."

Lars hasn't arrived and it takes about six seconds for the cold to get to us. Owen tries the door and, sure as shit, the damn thing's unlocked.

"I'm guessing Alan's not a big one for security," I say.

"Not the sharpest knife in the drawer, no."

We start a hard-target search for the spreadsheets. There's a lot of discarded wrappers, an empty food bag ("White Castle, Owen? Really?") and some receipts. Finally, Owen finds something in the glove box.

"Bingo," he says, pulling out some folded sheets of paper.

I lean over from the backseat. It's exactly what Alan described. A lot of dry numbers on a few pages, but enough to bring down Jeff Greenwald. And get my brother out of trouble.

"I think you're in the clear," I say, gazing over the papers.

Owen, though, has his eyes on other things. "I wouldn't go that far."

He points out the front window. The guys who visited him this morning are heading our direction. And, not surprisingly, they don't look any happier than they did when we last saw them. Quite the opposite, really.

"Son of a bitch," I mutter, "Those guys don't quit."

"I think they're paid not to."

Owen and I quickly set about locking the doors. We've just finished the job by the time the goons arrive at the car.

Lantern Jaw slams his fists down on the hood. "Get out of the fucking car!"

Owen shoots me a helpless look. "What do we do?"

"Well, I wouldn't recommend getting out of the fucking car," I tell him.

Lantern Jaw reaches for the driver's door, but finds it locked. Receding Hairline moves to the other side and tries the passenger door. He gets the same thing. The car is now secured. Well, as secure as a crap box stalked by two homicidal goons can be. Receding Hairline starts throwing kicks at the passenger side window, looking for an alternate way in. Lantern Jaw throws elbows at the driver's window, aiming for the same effect. Owen looks at me, desperate.

"We are in deep fucking trouble," he says, as if I somehow wasn't aware of that.

"And we aren't staying here!"

I throw open the rear-passenger door. Receding Hairline is so wrapped up in his kicking, he doesn't immediately react. It's enough to let me get clear by a step or two. Receding Hairline makes a dive at me, but I slip under him. His momentum takes him past me and the unsteady footing causes him to wind up on his ass. Meantime, Owen throws open the driver's door, knocking Lantern Jaw to the snowy ground. We start hauling ass up Broadway Street. We don't set speed records, what with the uphill grade and the ice, but we're a step ahead of the goons.

"Where are we going?" Owen asks.

"I don't know. We can flag down a cop. A passing car. Santa Claus. Somebody."

Of course, this being downtown St. Paul, there's no sign of anyone. Or any kind of life, really. Owen tucks the spreadsheets into his coat. I try to think of a way to get the goon squad off us. Turns out, I don't have to think of a plan.

I'm trailing Owen by half-a-step when I feel a hand on the collar of my pea coat. I'm yanked back into the grasp of Receding Hairline. He gives me a good shake and draws back a fist the size of a ham. The future structural integrity of my face is in serious doubt. The punch never lands.

Receding Hairline gets tackled before the punch gets anywhere. Owen was a good linebacker in high school and he hasn't lost his form. He hits hard, grabs Receding Hairline's legs and deposits him in a snowbank. Unfortunately, there's one other goon after us. Lantern Jaw shoves me out of the way and goes after Owen. By the time I'm back on my feet, the two of them are facing off. Owen takes a swing at Lantern Jaw but misses by an area code. Owen ducks a roundhouse right and backs toward me. He arrives just as Receding Hairline has made his way out of the snow.

"You give me those spreadsheets," Lantern Jaw growls, out of breath, "Or I beat you into the sidewalk."

I'm not convinced. "If we give you the spreadsheets, you're still going to beat us into the sidewalk."

"Yeah, but I won't enjoy it as much."

Owen looks at me. "Negotiation isn't really your thing,"

"Doesn't appear to be his, either."

Lantern Jaw steps forward. "Shut up! Now give me the fucking spread—"

And he only gets that far before the cavalry arrives. A familiar Buick hops the curb. Lantern Jaw's ass bounces off the front fender, hurling him across the sidewalk. Receding Hairline spins out of the way, only to have the passenger door fly open and crack him upside the head. Receding Hairline drops to the sidewalk, stunned.

Lars retracts his foot from the passenger doorway and pops his head out of the driver's side window. "The cops are on the way. Didn't look like you had time to wait."

Owen, for one, isn't waiting. Sensing an advantage, he boots Receding Hairline in the face, sending him tumbling further down the sidewalk. He turns back toward Lantern Jaw, who's gingerly picking himself up off the sidewalk. Lars tosses Owen a tire iron and Owen buries the damn thing in Lantern Jaw's gut. He tosses it back to Lars, who stashes it in the car just as the cops come wheeling around the corner.

Owen is smiling. "I've wanted to do that all day."

***

About an hour later, Owen and I are back in my apartment. The goons and the spreadsheets are in the possession of the cops. The goons broke quickly and were immediately willing to talk about their boss. Both they and the spreadsheets could create the beginning of a very interesting investigation into Jeff Greenwald and Tool Town. For the moment, though, my brother is perfectly safe, which is the most important thing.

"That's what I get for drinking," Owen says, finishing a cup of coffee.

"Really? You sure it isn't worth killing the bug up your ass every now and again?"

"Don't start with me."

I raise my hands in mock surrender. There's plenty of time for the two of us to bicker and banter. Besides, I owe him for saving me from the goon. (Well, saving me from a goon he brought to my front door, but still…)

Owen sets his coffee cup in the sink and heads for the front door. "I should probably get going. I can salvage some of the convention before I head home."

"I think Dad would appreciate that."

Owen puts on his coat. "I'm probably going to have to come back down to the Cities at some point. Testify against Jeff Greenwald. I'll, uh, I'll give you call when that happens."

"I'd like that."

He stops at the front door and sticks out a hand. "Thanks, Joe."

I take it, quickly. "Least I could do."

Owen gives my hand a few quick pumps, then breaks off and opens the door. "Thank your friend Lars for me. Good guy. Little strange, but…"

"Believe me, I know."

He's halfway out the door when he stops. "Listen, uh, life would be a lot easier for me if Dad didn't know anything about this."

I hold up a hand. "No worries. I won't tell him a thing."

"I appreciate that. Take it easy."

The door is nearly shut before I add, "I didn't say anything about not telling Mom, though."

DEATH PLAYS BROOMBALL

For guys, much of our lives are spent in dick-waving contests. This could be traced back to man's ancient role as hunter/gatherers and our need to establish dominance over the tribe. Personally, I think it's because we're morons.

I'm not aware of any other species in any other corner of the globe that will turn the most mundane activities into a competition. In the heat of battle, all perspective is lost and a pickup game of basketball played by a bunch of middle-aged fat guys becomes a death struggle to see who can still lay claim to his youth. My brothers and I are all in our thirties and yet our parents have banned us from playing Monopoly because we still go at it with the murderous intensity of a mob war. Afterwards, we can take a deep breath and say to ourselves, "Man, that really got out of hand. I mean, did I really have to make such a big deal simply because that filthy son-of-a-bitch bought Park Place when I already had Boardwalk! *That pile of puke!" And then the whole thing starts again.*

And yet men make up eighty-five percent of our armed forces. That should keep you awake at night.

My name's Joe Davis. I get paid to write stuff like that.

I'm working on this little missive when my friend, Mike, the living embodiment of male pettiness, comes stalking into the bar. While I generally work out of my apartment, every now and again I grab my laptop and take my show on the road. Most often, it's over to Glacier's coffee shop on Selby. Today, though, I decided to hit The Tav, our local watering hole. The Tav is a combination pub and sports bar, featuring a lot of quaint decorations, high-top tables and big-screen TVs. Picture windows look out on Selby and other parts of the Cathedral Hill neighborhood I call home. Since it's a sleepy Wednesday afternoon and we're getting a light snow, I thought I would work best at a high top, enjoying a Peppermint Patty (hot chocolate and a bit of peppermint schnapps, topped with whipped cream). The sort of peaceful calm a writer needs. Except, of course, when Mike's on the scene.

He brushes the snow off the nest of black hair sitting atop his big bulldog head and says, "We gotta kick a guy's ass in broomball."

I close the laptop. There's no point telling Mike I'm in the middle of something. Once Mike has the floor, no one's getting it back. He and I have been best friends since about five minutes after we got to college. He grew up the only child in a military household and was smothered accordingly. Once he discovered his freedom, he conducted himself like Charlie

Sheen on spring break. His self-control has never quite recovered.

"Okay," I say, "I get kick a guy's ass. I get broomball. How do these things go together?"

Mike lets out an impatient breath. It would be so much more efficient to do a Vulcan Mind Meld and bring me up to speed. But, lacking that, he's forced to use his words.

"Okay, you know Selina?" he says, "This girl I'm dating?"

"I have met the young lady. Yes."

"Before we started going out, she had made the mistake of dating a guy at her office."

"Oops." Not that I've ever had an office job. But I know a bad scene when I hear one.

"Apparently, the guy's not happy about Selina dating someone new. He keeps making smartass remarks around the office, bothering her for information, shit like that."

"Okay." I know there's a connection between this and broomball somewhere on the horizon. I just have to be patient.

"So, Selina's office had a little lunch get-together today, kind of an informal thing. She invited me to drop by. And that's when I met the ex-boyfriend. Troy. Doesn't that sound like a typical shithead ex-boyfriend name?"

"It's got a little Cobra Kai in it."

"And you want to know the worst part? He doesn't even live up to the name. He's some dumpy, balding pile of shit. He's not even close to being in Selina's league."

Truthfully, Mike isn't in Selina's league, either. As I recall, she's a tall, willowy blonde with big blue eyes, terrific cheekbones and a smoky voice. Unless you're George Clooney, you're not really in Selina's league.

"I'm guessing you and the ex-boyfriend didn't hit it off," I say.

"Not remotely. He kept giving me the stink eye, muttering under his breath every time I opened my mouth. Just a complete assclown."

Clearly, Mike's going to need a little kick in his get-along if we're going to get to the point. "And how does this relate to broomball?" I ask.

"I mentioned the broomball league to Selina. Selina, mind you. Because *that's* who I was fucking talking to. And then this Troy idiot pipes up about how he's part of a kickass broomball team and there's nobody even close to matching them. Well, there was no way I was going to put up with that."

I should explain. Mike and I, along with some college buddies and a few others, play in a broomball league during the winter. It's not quite as big a deal as the annual All-City Touch Football Tournament, but we still take a certain amount of pride in our team (The Bluejackets). We are, after all, the defending third place champions (in a four-team league).

"And so…" I say, coaxing Mike along.

"And so this Troy asshole and I get into it about our broomball teams. I tell him we have an open date a week from Saturday and if he's got any sack, he'll bring his fucking coffee klatsch to the rink and put his money where his mouth is."

Great. I should have known Mike couldn't confine a dick-waving contest to his own dick. "You sure the rest of the guys will go along with this?" I ask.

"Why wouldn't they? We can't let this Troy asshole run his mouth. You think the guys are going to put up with someone saying his team is better than ours?"

"You mean like the two teams that finished ahead of us last year? Or the three that are ahead of us this year?"

Mike's jaw tightens to the point of implosion. "So what? We give this asshole a pass? Is that what you're saying?"

"Hey, hey, relax, Fredo. I'm sure the rest of the guys will go along with it."

"Good! Good. That's exactly what I'm hoping for. Troy. Yeah, fuck you, Troy. We'll see what kind of broomball your ladies' tea party plays." He slaps the table. "I'm getting wound up. Maybe I need a drink."

"Maybe you need six."

Mike throws an order of a whiskey, beer back, to the bar (at the moment, the bar's informal enough that we can just shout out orders). "This guy, Joe. This guy is going to regret the day he met me."

"I know the feeling."

***

Sadly, Mike's able to talk the rest of our broomball team into this ridiculous pickup game. There are eight guys on the whole team. I only needed two to join me in vetoing the whole stupid thing. But they all fell in line, one by one: Robbie, Stoner, T.J., Moose, Rex and Frankie. Every last one of them. (I thought Stoner at least would hold out for money, but he agreed to do it pro-bono.) So now we're forced to practice for this idiocy.

Normally, we don't spend a lot of time on practice. If the weather's decent, we'll go for most of an hour. Otherwise, it's ten minutes of running around the ice before somebody (usually Robbie) will shout out, "Fuck this nonsense. Let's grab some beers." However, Mike's determined to win this game. So, we're on an outdoor rink at Highland Park, running around under the lights, doing the same stupid drills we never execute properly. All so Mike can show off in front of his girlfriend. (Although this is stretching the definition of *showing off.*)

"All right," Mike says, whistle dangling around his neck (prompting the rest of us to wonder who the hell gave Mike a whistle), "Let's run that play again."

"Which play?" Robbie asks, "The one where we all run down the ice and whack at the ball or the one we say 'Fuck this shit' and go grab a beer?"

"The, uh, the first one."

A round of groans go up. Although, truthfully, it's not like any of us are working our asses off. Stoner and Robbie keep trading insults. T.J. keeps checking his watch because his wife will kill him if he gets home late. Moose stands in nets doing his usual workmanlike job of not falling over. Rex checks out the female joggers out for a winter evening's run. And Frankie…I don't even know what the hell Frankie's doing.

Mike slams his broom on the ice. "C'mon, you guys! What the hell?"

"Can we take five?" Robbie asks.

"Fine. But let's hold it to five."

Mike glides over to me, standing near the boards. Selina, who's been watching practice, slinks toward us. I've got to admit: she's sexy as all hell. I'm not really allowed to say that, given her status as Mike's girlfriend. But as a guy with a pulse, I'm allowed to think it.

Mike, however, ignores his girlfriend's approach. Something on one of the other rinks has his attention. I try to scan it, but I'm not seeing anything unusual. Mike points that direction with his middle finger.

"You see those guys over there?" he says, "That's our opposition. The balding fat ass in the middle is Troy."

Much as I don't want to validate Mike's irrational anger, Troy fits the description. If he were about a foot taller, he'd be a robust, outdoorsy sort, what with the full red beard and the crooked nose. Instead, he's kind of short; his gut pushing against his white jersey. (I'm too far away to tell, but I'm guessing there are some yellow sweat stains in the armpits.) He doesn't exactly resemble an arch criminal and yet here we are, practicing on what's normally an off-day, so we can beat this guy and a bunch of his henchmen. It's like reading a Batman comic featuring The Cluemaster. Sure, there's some entertainment value, but really, doesn't it feel like a waste of everybody's time?

Selina gives Mike a kiss on the cheek. He brushes some sweat away from his massive forehead and tries to look presentable.

"What do you think of practice?" Mike asks.

"Looks like you guys had fun," she says.

Mike's brow knits. "*Had* fun?"

"Yeah. Isn't it over? Your team is leaving."

Mike looks toward the parking lot and sure enough, the rest of the team is heading to their cars. He runs along the boards, shouting to get everyone's attention.

"Hey! Hey, where are you guys going?"

Robbie looks over his shoulder but keeps walking. "We're going over to Moose's place. Play some video games."

Moose waves his hand. "Nah, man. No can do. Game system finally went south."

"Oh. In that case, we're just leaving."

Mike starts jumping up and down. "You were only supposed to take five."

Robbie shrugs. "We're taking five *days*. You weren't real specific."

Mike dissolves into shouting obscenities, none of which are likely to get the guys to come back. Selina's probably wondering what she's gotten herself into.

"Mike's kind of intense," she says.

"Only if you consider George Patton intense."

"Who?"

"Never mind."

Mike slides back to Selina and me. "Can't believe those S.O.B.s took off like that," he says, banging his broom against the boards, "How are we supposed to win this game if they're not going to practice?"

"The way we win all other games," I say, "Blind luck."

"Not good, man. Not good."

Selina coughs, politely. "I think you might have a bigger problem."

Mike's head swivels her direction. "What bigger problem is that?"

She throws a glance toward the other rink and lowers her voice. "Troy said something at the office today, to one of our co-workers. He's bribed one of the guys on your team to throw the game. You don't stand a chance."

Mike and I look at each other. He hangs his head. "Guess there's no point in practicing."

***

While Mike's lived in Minnesota for most of his (I hesitate to call it an) adult life, his early days as a military brat were spent in a number of warm weather states. Thus, he doesn't put up with the cold as well as someone like me, who's grown up in this climate. (Although why I keep living here is more of a mystery.) Hot chocolate may not be a solution, but it certainly doesn't add to the problem.

I put a mug down on the breakfast bar in front of Mike. He's quick to snatch it up. "I can't believe it," he says, "Somebody on our team is a damn Judas. It shakes your faith in humanity."

"And you didn't have much to begin with."

"I did not."

I sit across from him, sipping my own mug of hot chocolate. "I guess you want to figure out who the traitor is."

"You're damn skippy, I do. I'm not going to let that son of a bitch Troy beat us without a fair fight. And even then, we can't let that son of a bitch beat us."

Yep. There's no talking him out of this. "Okay, fine," I say, "Let's figure it out."

"Great, good." He and his hot chocolate pace the room. "Okay, eight guys on the team. You and I are clear."

"You think so?"

"Joe!"

"Sorry."

"Robbie's hyper-competitive. He'd never lose on purpose. T.J.'s too honest. Frankie, well, nobody who's watched our team for more than six seconds would bribe Frankie. Who's that leave?"

I tick them off on my fingers. "Stoner, Moose and Rex."

"All right, we're getting somewhere. Three possibilities. Who do you think's most likely?"

"Stoner."

"Oh God, yes. Completely."

In our defense, we'd say the exact same thing if Stoner was here. And he probably wouldn't be offended by it. Stoner's venal and corrupt, but he's honest about it.

"What about Rex?" I ask.

"I don't know much about Rex. Or Moose, for that matter. They played on Robbie's old team. We'll start with Stoner, though. If he's pulling something, we'll break him."

Ah, that's cute. It's like he's never met Stoner.

***

Mike and I first stumbled across Matthew Riley Stone during our freshman year in college. Stoner was acting as Robbie's manager and bookie for various drinking contests around the dorm. He eventually parlayed those winnings into funding a floating poker game. By the time we graduated, Stoner's criminal organization was profitable enough to pay back his student loans. Law enforcement agencies the world over can be relieved that Stoner lacked the ambition to continue his criminal ways after college.

We find Stoner hanging out at The Tav, enjoying an early happy hour. He gives us a wave from a corner table as we walk in. Mike turns to me.

"Okay, remember," he says, "The old good cop/bad cop."

"How is it the *old* good cop/bad cop? We've never done it before."

"What did I say about bogging me down with details?"

"Sorry."

We sit on opposite sides of Stoner. He quickly picks up on the seating arrangement and seems amused (then again, that shit-eating grin is permanently affixed to his face).

"How's it going, Stoner?" Mike says, adding a little edge to his voice.

"Why, I'm fine, Michael," Stoner says, hoisting his large glass of beer, "Just enjoying a bit of happy hour. Yourself?"

"Funny you should ask. We're a little tense about the game. Aren't we, Joe?"

It's all I can do not to roll my eyes. "Yes, Mike. We are indeed tense about the game."

Mike leans close to Stoner. "Why do you think that is, Stoner?"

"Because your girlfriend has the hots for Rex?"

Mike recoils, his eyes zooming back and forth between me and Stoner. "What do you mean she has the hots for Rex?"

"At practice, she was watching Rex more than you. Can't say I blame her. Rex is a good-looking guy."

Mike is thrown completely off his game. He stares at the table, probably wondering how he could have missed such a thing. There's half a chance Stoner is lying. Of course, that's the deadly part of dealing with Stoner: he could be telling the truth as well. He certainly isn't going to tell you which it is.

Mike tries to get the bad cop vibe back. "That's not what we're concerned with. There's a bigger issue here. A thing called loyalty. You know what loyalty is, don't you, Stoner?"

"Of course, I do. You remember that time you propositioned Joe's girlfriend? I didn't say anything about that, did I?"

I shoot a look at Mike. "What girlfriend was this?"

Mike slaps the table. "It didn't happen. He's making that up!"

Stoner rubs his chin. "What was her name? Carrie?"

"Carly," Mike says. Then he hangs his head and adds, "Shit."

As I glare at Mike, Stoner says, "Carly. That's right. She was a sweet girl. Nice enough to turn Mike down. Although you did make out a little at Robbie's party."

"It was at T.J.'s," Mike says. Then he hangs his head and adds, "Goddammit."

Clearly, this is not going well. Not only is Stoner working Mike like a speedbag, I'm not exactly feeling *good cop* at the moment. Mike, though, is not dissuaded.

"We're not here to talk about any of that, okay? We wanted to talk about the team." Suddenly, his tone is like Robert De Niro in *The Untouchables*. "You see, Stoner, a team is only as strong as its weakest link."

He nods. "So, you?"

"No, not me."

"Well, that's what Joe said last week."

"I did not!" I say.

"What about that own-goal Mike scored?"

"Yeah, well, that was just fucking stupid," I say. Then I hang my head and add: "Dammit."

Mike punches me on the arm. "I told you that wasn't my fault. I was distracted."

"By what?" I ask, "Tripping over your own damn feet?"

Stoner holds up a hand. "Boys, boys, boys. I don't think you came here to fight. Is there something you want to talk to me about?"

Mike's still glaring at me. If this nonsense doesn't end soon, we'll be demanding armed satisfaction. I turn toward Stoner.

"Yeah, Stoner," I say, "Did you take money to throw the broomball game?"

Stoner's eyebrows go up. "Who's offering money to do that?"

"Troy. The guy Mike's got the issue with."

Stoner muses on this. "That's not a bad plan. I wish I'd thought of it. But no, nobody bribed me to throw the game."

Mike lets out a sigh of relief. "I'm glad to hear that."

"I can't say I wouldn't do it if somebody offered, though."

"How much would it take to bribe you?" Mike asks, nearly stammering.

"Oh, I don't know. If someone put a couple hundred on the table, I might listen."

"A couple hundred to throw the game? You'd actually do it?"

"For three hundred dollars, I'd have to consider it."

"Okay, fine," Mike says, "I'll give you five hundred to stay loyal."

Stoner toys with his drink. "If it's just about money…"

"Five hundred dollars and free oil changes for three years. I know a guy."

"Oil change isn't much good without a tire rotation."

"I'll make sure he throws those in, too."

Stoner lets out a long sigh. "Well, we've been buddies a long time. You can't put a price on that kind of loyalty. I'm in this with you come hell or high water. And five hundred dollars, three years of free oil changes and Marie Downey's phone number."

Mike dutifully takes out his phone and looks up Marie Downey's phone number. "You're a hell of a guy, Stoner. You can't buy this kind of loyalty."

This is why nobody ever plays cards with Stoner. You'd wind up going home wearing only a barrel…that he's renting to you.

"Always a pleasure, Mikey," he says, putting the number in his phone, "You gentlemen have a good evening."

With that, Stoner finishes his beer and heads out. Leaving Mike and me to pay the check.

***

"This better work," Mike says, pacing the floor of my apartment, "I'm losing patience."

We're T-Minus three days to the broomball game and I'm wondering if Mike's going to make it. There are bags under his eyes, telling me he hasn't been sleeping. His face is red and there's a vein I never noticed before sticking out from his gargantuan forehead. His fists are clenched so often, I'm afraid to hand him one of my coffee cups. My cats, Lenny and Squiggy, have known Mike all three years of their existence and yet they've started to avoid him whenever he comes over. I'm thinking of joining them. It's a little difficult to be sympathetic. Mike talked the team into more practices and he's been driving us crazy. He even yelled at Frankie. Then again, none of us are certain Frankie has any sort of sensory apparatus known to man, so Mike gets a pass on that one.

"When did Lars say he'd be here?" Mike asks.

"In a couple of minutes. He's just finalizing his report."

"He wrote up a report?"

"We'll be lucky if there isn't a power point presentation."

Lars was assigned to follow Moose and report any suspicious activities. Even though I'm sure the report is going to be a shambles, it would be preferable to dealing with Herb Brooks over here. Right on cue (assuming I ever give him a cue) Lars bursts through the door, a thick file under his arm. Oh, joy.

Lars faces us like he's Winston Wolf from *Pulp Fiction*. "All right, gentlemen, should we get right to it?"

"That would be helpful," I say.

Mike sits at my desk chair (even though I've told him a hundred times that nobody is allowed to sit there but me). Lars takes center stage in my living room. He opens the folder and ignores the twenty papers that immediately fall out.

"Okay, so my job was to follow this Moose person," he says, "Subject is a six-five, African-American male. Former football player, I'm given to understand?"

Mike nods. "When he was in college. Yeah."

Lars consults the file. "Currently plays goaltender for your broomball team."

"Because he can block most of the net without moving," I say.

He makes a note of that in the file. "I encountered the suspect last evening. I followed him from his residence in south Minneapolis to a tavern called Tiffany's on Ford Parkway in the Highland Park neighborhood of St. Paul. While there, the suspect sat at a table with a number of friends and watched a college basketball game. I took a seat at the bar where I could observe the suspect. While at the bar, I ordered a pale ale from Grand Brewing. It was well-balanced, with a mild hop bite and a good mouthfeel—"

"You want to skip ahead a bit?" Mike says.

Lars is thrown off. Clearly, he's been practicing this presentation. He fumbles through the file, spilling more paperwork. "Okay, so the suspect watched a basketball game with his friends. Several pitchers of beer were consumed—um, you're going to want me to skip my guesses on what kind of beer it was—and the suspect left the venue with said friends. I continued my pursuit."

"How drunk were *you* at this point?" I ask.

Lars takes a handwritten slip of paper out of the file. He studies a list of figures until he finds what he's looking for. "Rather."

"Glad we cleared that up," I say.

Mike waves a hand at me. "Joe, will you stop interrupting this idiocy?"

"My apologies to the idiot."

"It's all right," Lars says.

Mike puts a hand on Lars' shoulder. "You remember that guy Troy we were telling you about? Was he one of the friends?"

"As a matter of fact, I have a surveillance photo right here." He pulls it out of the file and hands it to Mike.

Mike's face goes red. "Lars, he's on the toilet."

"Yes, my notes indicate that was due to several Buffalo wings and the beer."

"Son of a bitch," Mike mutters, handing me the photo.

"Yes, that was not pleasant," Lars says, "Fortunately, I was able to put my camera over the top of the stall, so I wasn't compromised."

"Which is more than you can say for Troy," I say, tossing the photo aside.

Lars goes back to the file. "From there, I followed the suspect back to his house in south Minneapolis, keeping a safe distance between myself and the suspect's vehicle. The house was entered by not only the suspect and his friends, but a group of young males described by one witness as *suspicious*."

"Who was your witness?" Mike asks.

"That would be me," Lars says, "I parked my car across the street from the house. Through the front window, I was able to view the suspect and his friends gathering various firearms. Clearly, they had unlawful intentions."

Mike and I look at each other. Moose is one of the nicest, most happy-go-lucky dudes we know. He's the last guy on the team I could imagine committing any kind of armed robbery. And I'm including myself on that list.

"So what did you do?" Mike asks, "Call the police?"

"No, I felt it more expedient to affect a citizen's arrest."

My head drops to my chest. "Oh dear God."

Lars continues. "Fortunately, I keep a remarkably simulated firearm in my vehicle for such emergencies. And, uh, some, some other stuff. I didn't really put it in the report."

Mike clenches his fists. "And so?"

"I crossed the street, approached the door and proceeded to kick it open. Well, I made an attempt to kick it open. Several, actually. The door proved to be quite sturdy. Excellent craftsmanship. Finally, one of the suspect's friends opened the door and inquired…" He consults his notes for the exact quote. "'Dude, what the fuck?' At that point, I waved the simulated firearm and announced that everyone in the room was coming with me."

Mike looks ready to throw up. "Then what?"

"By my count, there were nine males, ages ranging from twenty-five to forty. All of them dropped to the floor and covered their heads. The male who answered the door crouched down and began crying. At least one of the males voided his bladder."

"What about their guns?" Mike asks.

Lars clears his throat. "They were not actual firearms. It turns out they were simulations designed to accompany a home entertainment system. A top of the line system. They were indistinguishable from the real thing. Of course, the orange coloring should have been a tip-off."

I take over before Mike starts crying. "So—and I hesitate to ask this—what happened next?"

"A few of them were willing to give up their wallets. I didn't feel that was necessary. So I just walked out the door."

Lars closes the file with a flourish, spilling more of the paperwork. Mike rubs his temples. "So as far as finding out if Moose is being bribed to throw the game..." Mike asks.

"That's inconclusive."

I move Lars to the door. Mike heads for the liquor cabinet. Lars looks back and says: "I'll send you my bill."

I shove Lars out the door before Mike can chuck a vodka bottle at him. I start picking up the paperwork. (I try to keep my apartment as clean as an operating room. Orderly place, orderly mind. That's what I need to write. And my friends generally fuck that up.)

"That was beautiful," Mike says, swilling his vodka rocks, "Try to find out about Moose, wind up with a home invasion."

"It's like asking your superintendent to do a repair. It'll get done. But done competently might be too much to ask."

Then I remember Lars is the superintendent of my building. I think I need a vodka, too.

***

"Maybe we can just win on our own," Mike says, "Even with Troy messing around. Practice was pretty good today, right?"

I take a sip of my beer. "In the sense that we all showed up, yeah, it went swimmingly."

It's strange to see someone as perpetually gloomy as Mike try to be optimistic. The game is tomorrow and we've made no progress in finding out who Troy bribed. And our practices haven't been a study in clockwork efficiency. Or civility. Normally, everybody on the team comes to our after-practice gathering at The Tav. But Mike's Genghis Khan routine has gotten so old that only he and I have shown up.

"Robbie was just kidding, right?" Mike says, "About slashing my tires?"

"Robbie gets a little bombastic."

"Of course."

"Right before he slashes someone's tires."

Mike's about to challenge that point when he spots something over my shoulder. Selina is approaching our corner booth and her presence seems to lift Mike's spirits (an effect only Selina and vodka have these days). She slides in next to Mike and gives him a peck on the cheek.

"Are you guys ready to go for tomorrow?" she asks.

Mike updates her on our practice, though factually, it resembles Kim Jong-Il's golf score. Fortunately, he's good at the art of disinformation (the CIA really dropped the ball in not recruiting Mike). Selina pats the table, anxious to share some information.

"I think I've got a way to help out," she says, "I'm getting together with Rex."

Mike's face falls, but he quickly covers. "With Rex? For, uh, for what…with Rex?"

"We're having coffee," she says.

Mike's smiling, but his face is getting red. "Having, having coffee."

"I told him about Troy throwing bribes around. He seemed interested. If he's guilty, maybe I can get him to confess."

"Sure. When, uh, when did you talk to Rex?"

"On the phone last night. I gave him my number at practice the other day."

Mike struggles to get the words out. His mouth seems to have gone dry. "When, when are you getting together?"

"Tonight. I'll call you tomorrow morning. Let you know how it went."

Mike sets his beer down, misses the table and nearly dumps it on the floor. I grab it from him. His determined smile remains in place.

"Tomorrow. Okay, that, that sounds great. Good, uh, good thinking. Honey."

"Thank you."

Mike wipes some sweat off his forehead. "Meantime, who wants to do shots?"

***

Mike and I are surprisingly good at stakeouts. This is largely due to our ability to talk for hours without really saying anything. However, that's contingent on Mike's willingness to chat with me. Otherwise, it's just a lot of sitting around, planning your next piss break.

Besides, there's something fundamentally wrong with sitting in a car, sipping coffee, and staking out a *coffee* shop. Yet here we are, parked across the street from Jitters, a little coffee shop on Lyndale Avenue in Uptown. We're staring at a picture window that gives us a look at everything except the kitchen and the bathrooms.

"I thought you trusted Selina," I say.

"I do. It's Rex I don't trust. What if Selina drags the truth out of him? What if he realizes he's busted and gets desperate? She might need help."

"And what are we supposed to do? Call for some?"

"Just shut up and let me concentrate."

Jitters seems cozy enough, with the low lighting, the wooden tables and the dude playing acoustic guitar in the corner. I'd love to be in there right now. We've been staking the place out for only fifteen minutes, but I'm already bored and cold.

"Will you at least start the car?" I ask.

"No. We don't know how long they're going to be in there. Sit in a running car too long and people will think we're up to something."

"We *are* up to something."

"Besides, it's bad for the environment. Don't you give a rat's ass about global warming?"

"Do you?"

"Not as such, no. But I'm not turning on the car."

A few minutes later, a red Chevy Cruze parks in front of the place. Rex gets out of the driver's side and Selina out of the passenger. They stroll into the coffee shop. Mike grabs a pair of binoculars.

"When did Rex get the new car?" Mike asks, "What happened to that piece of shit Toyota he used to drive?"

"I don't know," I say, "But that car is nice."

Mike grimaces. "Too nice."

Rex and Selina approach the counter to order. "They came together?" I ask, "Why didn't they just meet here?"

"Could be a lot of reasons. Maybe it's more convenient." Mike lowers the binoculars and chews a corner of his goatee. "I think she's wearing makeup."

I take the binoculars from Mike and give it a looksee. Selina certainly appears wearing makeup. Mike, though, is already in damage-control mode.

"It's nothing," he says, "A little refresher after work. You know how women are."

"Of course." I hand the binoculars back to Mike. "She looks nice, though."

"Yeah. I think that's the same sweater she wore on our first date."

We sit there for more than two hours, watching Selina and Rex in conversation. Well, Mike watches them in conversation. At some point, I give up and use my phone to cruise the internet. I'm considering either downloading *Paradise Lost* or setting fire to the accumulated trash on Mike's front seat for warmth when Selina and Rex finally emerge from the coffee shop.

"About damn time," Mike growls.

"Selina must have gotten information by now."

They crawl into Rex's car and as soon as they pull out, Mike's in hot pursuit.

"Where are we going?" I ask.

"I'm going to call Selina when she gets home," he says, "I can't do that until I know the coast is clear."

We follow them through Uptown and back to Selina's apartment building, located near Lake Bde Maka Ska. Mike ditches his car a half block away. Selina and Rex get out of the car. They *both* head into the building.

Mike hustles toward a restaurant across the street. I'm forced to follow. He runs around to the back and climbs up the fire escape. The restaurant has a patio that offers rooftop dining. Since this obviously isn't needed in February, it's unoccupied. Mike finds a hiding place near the edge of the roof. I plunk down next to him, making a mental note to check the internet for hypothermia symptoms.

Selina and Rex have settled down on the couch. She's opened a bottle of wine and is pouring a glass for each of them. There are no candles lit, but I get the sinking feeling soft music is playing. Mike looks ready to chew off his goatee. He takes a couple of deep, cleansing breaths.

"You know what this is?" he says, waving his hand toward the apartment, "Selina's working Rex for information. Give him a glass of wine, loosen his tongue."

I'm certain there's going to be tongue involved, but I keep that thought to myself. Mike seems to believe everything's on the up-and-up. It's a nice thought, so I go along with it. I once believed in Santa Claus, too. We sit on the damn rooftop and watch them chat for another forty-five minutes. Not only am I certain that pneumonia is setting in, but Mike keeps making remarks like, "Wow, she's really doing a job on him." Seriously, how many of those am I expected to let pass without comment? Eventually, I give up watching. I'm considering heading back to the car when Mike's play-by-play gets interesting.

"Looks like they're wrapping things up," he says, taking out his cell phone, "I'll call Selina as soon as Rex leaves. Maybe she'll invite me over."

"How are you going to explain the icicles in your beard?"

Mike ignores me. "They're at the door. She's giving him a good night hug. A really long good night hug. I'm, uh, I'm not sure this is still a hug."

I glance across the street. Unless Congress has redefined hugging, no, this is not just a hug. Mike stays on the play-by-play.

"Okay, that, uh, that looks a lot like making out. Now he's got her shirt off. And…there goes the bra." He lowers the binoculars and can only say: "Rats."

I drop a hand on Mike's shoulder. "Maybe we should get going."

"Maybe it's not…" He looks through the binoculars again, but quickly lowers them. "Holy shit, she told me she wasn't into that kind of thing."

"Let's go, big fella."

I lead Mike across the roof. He stares at his feet. "I thought she liked me."

"I thought that, too."

He stops. "Thought she liked me or thought she liked you?"

"Apparently, she likes a lot of people."

***

So, it's the day of the big game, although I can't for the life of me figure out what it is we're playing for. But since I haven't heard the game is off, I show up at the rink at the appointed hour, along with the rest of the team.

Including Mike.

We're gathered against the boards when Mike stalks up. He storms past us and goes out on the rink to warm up. I'm the only one who tries to catch up with him.

"I've got to ask," I say, "Is there a reason we're still playing this game? I'm guessing you and Selina are history. There's nothing to actually prove to this Troy guy."

"Bullshit. Just because Selina turned out to be a treacherous snake woman doesn't mean I'm gonna let Troy run his mouth. We need to take him down a notch."

Mike glides away, whacking his broom against the ice. He glares at Troy, who doesn't help matters by smirking back at Mike. I run back to the team. As it happens, the first guy I run across is Rex. He perches his chin on his broom.

"Something up with the boss?" he asks.

"He's upset. He knows about what went on with you and Selina."

Rex doesn't seem remotely bothered. "Got his undies in a twist, does he?"

"Well, you stole his girlfriend."

"What do you mean? I didn't steal her. I just had sex with her. He's welcomed to keep dating her if he wants."

"Mike's not built on the soundest moral foundation, but even that's a little much to ask."

"His loss. I mean, 'cause in the sack, she's really—"

"Why don't we stop there?"

Rex shrugs and strolls away. I move back toward Mike, who's glaring at Troy's team. I tap him on the back with my broom.

"Please tell me you're not going to go full-on Tasmanian Devil today," I say.

"I'm in the mood to do some damage." He throws a dark look toward Rex. "No matter who it is."

"If you want to win, we need Rex. You cannot cause him grievous bodily harm."

"How do we know he isn't the one selling us out? Guy who'd steal another guy's girlfriend, he might be capable of anything."

"If it makes you feel any better, he just wanted to sleep with her. He doesn't want to date her."

The look Mike gives me is half-murderous, half-incredulous. "Joseph, how in the blue fuck is *that* supposed to make me feel any better?"

"Sorry, that was dumb."

"For starters."

The game gets going a few minutes later. There are two twenty-five-minute periods. Our league has assigned the referee while Troy's team is required to provide the ball. Everything's fair and equal, save for the possibility that someone on our team has been bought off.

Troy's team, truthfully, is no more impressive than ours. They all seem to equal Troy in girth and talent deprivation. The goalie has roughly the size and perspicacity of a Wookie. However, they have one dude, a skinny little prick with blonde hair, who's clearly the most talented player on the ice. Doesn't take much for him to motor through everyone else and outmaneuver Moose. He does this three times in the first five minutes, reducing Mike to an apoplectic state.

"What the fuck are you guys doing?" he screams, "It's one guy. He's making us look like idiots."

"We don't need him for that!" Robbie shouts. And that becomes our rallying cry.

For all the good it does. By the end of the first half, the skinny dude has totaled six goals and the rest of his team has two more. Mike and Robbie have two goals each, so we're at least keeping it respectable. That's little comfort to Mike.

"Eight to four," he says, spitting the words out, "What the hell are we supposed to do?"

"Demand a recount?" Stoner says.

Robbie nearly cross-checks Stoner with his broom. "Fuck you, Stoner!"

Stoner, who's impervious to irritation from every source on the planet except Robbie, has to be restrained. Although Robbie hasn't artfully stated it, we all share the sentiment. Stoner's normally a very efficient defenseman, but he's let the skinny dude get by him on four of the six goals. A very un-Stoner-like performance.

"Hey, hey, fellas, take it easy," Rex says, gliding between the two of them, "Let's remember the real enemy."

Mike doesn't give Rex much more than a dirty look, though his arms are quivering from holding the broom abnormally hard. If Mike suspects Rex of selling us down the river, he's justified. Rex has botched several passes, and on defense, hasn't gotten within an area code of the skinny dude.

"C'mon, you guys, knock it off!" Moose shouts, tippy-toeing toward the two of them.

If we were on dry ground, there's no doubt Moose would toss both of them around. However, the ice has neutralized him. Moose isn't the greatest goalie on God's green earth, but he hasn't put up much of a fight with the skinny dude. Two of the goals were unforgivable. One was a slow roller that went right between Moose's legs. The other went in without Moose so much as blinking. It's clear that, beyond the skinny dude, someone is hurting our chances. Mike has picked up on this.

"This friggin' sucks," he says, "The whole game is a waste of time. The fix is in!"

"We'll figure it out," I say, "But we're going to need to stop that skinny dude."

Robbie's been listening to the conversation. The notion of the fix being in has gone past him, but he grasps the idea of taking out the skinny dude. He pats Mike on the shoulder.

"Don't worry," he says, "We got this." He looks over at Stoner. "The Crunch?"

Stoner nods. "I believe that is what the situation calls for. Yes."

I'm actually the one who named The Crunch. I originally called the move *The Malachi Crunch*, after the legendary Malachi brothers on *Happy Days*. Since neither Stoner nor Robbie has ever heard of the Malachi brothers or *Happy Days*, they simply call it The Crunch. It's not a particularly complicated move. Send an opposing player between Robbie and Stoner and, while they pretend to go after the ball, they inflict an unreasonable amount of blunt force trauma. It's a move we do only when the game is in jeopardy and we can handle the legal fees.

As we head back onto the ice, Mike glides up next to me. "We still don't know who's throwing the game," he says, "What are we going to do?"

"I'll figure it out."

"You've got twenty-five minutes. Maybe less."

Great. I never do my best work when I'm up against a deadline. Rex, Stoner and Moose. One of them has to be guilty. And all of them have been playing terribly. Could be a coincidence. But probably not.

The second half starts and the skinny dude immediately goes to work. He gets the ball and slips past Mike and Rex. He heads toward Stoner, ready to move around him. Stoner gives him a bit of room and the skinny dude winds up between

Robbie and Stoner. A second later, the skinny dude's carcass is on the ice, staring at the cloudy sky.

The game is temporarily stopped as Troy's team howls in protest. The referee, however, tells them he didn't see anything wrong. Troy lobs an ill-advised threat at Robbie, who has to be held back. Troy scrambles away while Robbie runs through a truly impressive string of threats. Stoner slaps Robbie on the back and makes no effort to hide his shit-eating grin.

Mike slides past me. "I guess we can rule Stoner out."

"Seems to be doing his job," I say.

"It must be Rex. Please, please, please let it be Rex."

After the shouting has settled down, the game resumes. The skinny dude doesn't seem ready to come back into the game. We take advantage by getting a few quick goals, courtesy of Rex. He seems to be off the hook until he's too lazy to get back on defense. Troy nearly scores, but Moose makes his first nice save of the game. Things go back and forth for another ten minutes. The skinny dude makes a reappearance, but he's a shadow of his former self. He's either still feeling the effects of the hit or he's afraid to be in the same five-state region as Stoner and Robbie. Either way, he's been neutralized.

Mike scores and bring us within one goal. But Troy gets it right back with another weak roller between Moose's legs. Mike smacks his broom on the ice.

"Dammit! We get this close and Moose screws up!" he says, "What the hell was he doing?"

Frankie stops picking his nose. "He was up late, playing video games."

Mike lets out a cluck of disgust. "I should've sent Lars over for another home invasion."

But I already have a thought. I look to Mike. "Where did Moose get the new system?"

"What do you mean?" he asks.

"Remember last week, at practice? Moose said his game system died. Where did he get the money for a new one? The man works at a liquor store. Part time. How the hell does he afford a new gaming system?"

Mike looks across the rink at Troy, who's looking at Moose. Moose seems determined not to make eye contact. Mike shakes his head.

"I wanted it to be Rex," he says, "Was that too much to ask?" He smacks the boards with his broom. "Okay, what do we do about it?"

"Think Stoner and Robbie could figure out another way to do the Crunch?"

A smile crawls across Mike's face. "Won't know until we ask them."

It takes only a brief conversation with Stoner and Robbie. Neither of them is happy. Robbie hates being betrayed. Stoner hates it when someone beats him to the punch. They nod in agreement.

The next time the action comes toward our net, Robbie and Stoner are quick to get back on defense. So quick, in fact, they wind up hitting Moose with The Crunch. It costs us another goal, but sometimes you take a step back to take a step forward. When the dust clears, Moose is deemed too woozy to continue. Any doubts we had about Moose's innocence disappear when we get a look at Troy, who seems like he's about to swallow his tongue.

But it's not all sunshine and lollipops. We're down ten to seven and there's eight minutes left. We're forced to put Frankie in goal (a clear violation of our *Never let Frankie on the ice when the game is on the line* policy). Troy's team may have done enough to win the game.

Mike gets the ball, runs over the skinny dude and scores a quick goal. Seven minutes left and we're down by two. Stoner and Robbie do their best to keep Troy's team away from the goal. Rex swats a long shot into the net and brings us within one. Just five minutes left. Troy's team manages to get past Stoner and Robbie, but Frankie blocks a shot with his face. He doesn't seem bothered by it. (Frankie falls into the *No Sense, No Feeling* category.) Rex gets the ball and weaves past everyone on Troy's team. He throws a shot at the net, but it gets stopped.

Mike's comes in right behind and slams it past the goalie. Three minutes left. Game tied.

"We got this!" Mike says, smacking his broom against the boards, "We're all the way back! We got this!"

Moose leans toward Mike. "I think I can go back in."

"You can go to hell, you turncoat bastard!" Mike says, "You sold us out for a fucking gaming system!"

Moose hangs his head. "I'm sorry, man. I ain't got cable. Video games are all I got."

"Well, tough shit."

"We still getting beers after the game?"

"Yeah, of course. No hard feelings."

We get back on the ice. Troy's team seems shell-shocked and okay with playing for a tie. Our team keeps attacking. Mike is like a man possessed. He cross-checks Troy, maybe hoping to get *some* satisfaction out of this game.

The other team suddenly goes on the attack. Troy gets past Mike and slips through Stoner and Robbie. He's all alone on Frankie, who's staring at the light posts over the rink.

"Ah fuck," Mike says, summing up the situation.

Troy fakes left (unnecessary since Frankie's not paying attention) and moves right. He's got the whole net open to him. He casually flips the ball toward the open goal.

It never gets there.

Frankie snaps out of whatever reverie he's in and makes a beautiful slide across the net. He boots the ball into the corner. Mike's broom drops to the ice.

"Holy shit," he says, "Who the hell knew he had that in him?"

"I'm not sure Frankie knew," I say.

Less than a minute to go. Stoner collects the ball and slaps it up the ice to me. Two guys converge on me, but I'm able to get the ball to Mike. He slips a defenseman and runs in all alone on net. Rex is coming in fast as well. The goalie moves toward Mike, giving him a bad angle. The smartest play is to pass the ball to Rex, who'd have a wide-open net. The only question is whether Mike will do it.

Mike glides to one side, causing the goalie to move along with him. With a sudden flick of the wrist, Mike lifts the ball off the ice. It whistles through the air and bounces off Rex's face. Rex falls over backward as the ball trickles past the goalie and into the net.

We lead!

Mike walks past Rex's prone body. "Hell of a goal, Rex."

Rex rolls on his side, hands to his face. "I think you broke my nose."

"Way to take one for the team," Mike says. Then he whacks Rex in the ribs with his broom.

The game only goes a few more seconds before the referee blows the whistle, signaling the end. He suggests the two teams shake hands, but the closest we get is Mike and Troy giving each other the finger. Rex stuffs two Kleenex up his nostrils and walks off, head tipped back. He walks past Selina, who's just shown up. She sashays toward Mike.

"Looks like you won," she says.

"No thanks to your friend Troy," he says.

She gives Mike a kiss on the cheek. "Congratulations. Are you guys going for drinks?"

Mike nods toward the team. "They are. I've got a date."

Selina's eyebrows go up. "A date?"

"Girl named Marie Downey. Old girlfriend. Sexually uninhibited. Willing to do most everything. We're going to do it this afternoon, in fact. No time to hang around. Sorry."

Selina takes stock of Mike, then kicks him really hard in the shin and walks off. Mike goes down to one knee, but comes up smiling.

"It was worth it," he says.

Mike puts a hand on my shoulder and I guide him toward the car. There are beers awaiting. Robbie, Stoner and Moose pile into one car. Frankie wanders off and I genuinely wonder if we'll ever see him again.

"I'll buy the first round," Mike says, "You guys deserve it. You kicked ass."

"I appreciate that, but it wasn't all us." I say, "We were lucky the referee missed a few of those calls."

"Oh that." Mike dismisses it with a flit of his hand. "That wasn't luck. I paid him off two days ago." He slaps me on the back. "Let's go raise a glass to sportsmanship."

DEATH GOES MISSING

I understand people being frustrated with politics. Unfortunately, it's the best system we've thought up so far.

It's hard to believe that when looking at various talking heads shouting at each other about policies they've demonized without bothering to understand them. And it's hard to look at a political ad that might have been made by the producers of Saw and think this is what the Founding Fathers envisioned. But consider the alternatives.

Back in the Middle Ages, all wealth was controlled by elites who had no interest in sharing it with the general public. They would grudgingly give a bit of money to the government, but only to curry favor. The servant class had nothing to look forward to but a life of eking out a meager living while covered in feces. Today, it's...it's...um...well, we don't have the feces.

Yet.

My name's Joe Davis. I'm a member of the servant class.

Not that I feel that way all the time. I'm employed by an independent newspaper turned independent website. I'm not getting rich, but I'm living as close to free and easy as I'm likely to get. (As my parents are fond of reminding me.) And my friends fall largely into the same category.

Even if that requires literally serving from time to time.

In this case, we're talking about my buddy Lars. He has a caterer friend who requires help occasionally. This usually happens when Lars is short of money. Sort of a win-win deal. (Assuming anything involving Lars can be termed a *win*.)

"You feel out of place here?" Carol asks, sipping a Cosmo.

I fish an olive out of my martini. "I feel out of place everywhere."

The place in question is the Union Depot station in downtown St. Paul. We're attending an event that's announcing a plan to return trolley service to St. Paul. Five-year old Joe rejoices at the prospect of trolleys in his city. Thirty-three-year old Joe resents hobnobbing with the fat cats who will make it happen. Still, it's a decent excuse to hang out at the Depot. The place was built in 1913 and can still be found in its original cavernous marble glory. Each of my friends has a task at this gig. Lars is serving food. Carol's an ad writer and her agency has been hired to work P.R. I'm technically covering this for *The Daily Bugle*. (I might get a column out of it. Might.) And Mike is gate-crashing. A place for everyone and…

Carol brushes her dark hair away from her face and focuses her laser-like blue eyes on the party. "Lars seems to be in his element."

"That's what frightens me," I say.

Carol and I are in a quiet corner, sipping heavily-watered down drinks. Lars glides our direction, wearing a white shirt and black tie and waving a platter of some kind of puff pastry. He gives us a slight bow.

"Cream cheese ball, sir?" he says, then with a glance toward Carol, "Or madam?"

I wave him off. "I think there's enough cheeseball going around."

Carol elbows me in the side. "This is a good cause. And Dr. Palmer is speaking. That alone is worth the price of admission."

I'm tempted to remind her that the price of admission is free, but I'm not going to dampen her enthusiasm about Dr. Palmer. Because I share it. Barbara Palmer has been a professor of political science at the University of Minnesota for the last twenty years. She's frequently called upon by news agencies for her brilliant analysis and cool voice of reason. Recently, Dr. Palmer has abandoned her analytical position to take an active role in shaping policy. Rail travel is a favorite cause of hers.

Even Lars, not exactly a political animal, is aware of the evening's significance. "I'm hoping to talk to Dr. Palmer," he says, "I've got some ideas to boost the state's commerce."

I shudder at what those ideas might be. Lars' thinking usually runs to impractical get-rich-quick schemes. I'm not certain the state needs those kinds of ideas. Not that various Republican administrations haven't tried…

Mike slides into the conversation, toting a cheap beer. "How much longer is this thing going on?"

Carol rolls her eyes. "Dr. Palmer is going to give a speech. When that's over, there'll be some socializing. Then you're free to go."

"I'm not worried about going," Mike says, "I'm making time with that cute blonde over there. I'm wondering how much time I have left."

Before we can think up a way to chastise Mike, Dr. Palmer steps up to speak. Everybody listens with rapt attention.

Dr. Palmer is not, at first glance, an imposing figure. She's a slight and small woman, inclined to dress in tweeds and neutral colors. Her hair is pulled back into a severe bun and her large white eyes stand out against her dark skin. But her voice is instantly arresting. Deep, rich and ringing. It draws the listener in and makes them hang on every precisely-spoken word. Clearly, this is someone who's commanded audiences for years. The speech is on the merits of trolleys; how they will provide an affordable, fuel-efficient way to connect neighborhoods to the Twin Cities' increasingly large rail system. The crowd responds with appreciative applause.

Dr. Palmer is replaced at the podium by a middle-aged guy with thinning gray hair. With his calm eyes and placid face, he exudes the same kind of decency as Dr. Palmer, but in an even quieter way. It's Cal Smith, President of the St. Paul City Council and a possible candidate for Mayor. And a close ally of Dr. Palmer's. Smith and Dr. Palmer exchange a few words. Dr. Palmer seems anxious to get off the stage. Lars zooms past us, hoisting another tray of hors d'oveurs. Carol rests her chin against the rim of her glass.

"She makes some good points," Carol says.

"Rare in any politician," I say.

Mike sneaks into the conversation, still holding his beer-flavored mineral water. "You guys going to hang around? I think I might be getting somewhere with this chick."

I glance past him. "You mean the one who's leaving with the metrosexual dude?"

Mike spins around in time to see his prospective date strolling out with a guy who's one part hair gel and three parts moisturizer. Mike takes a half step that direction, then stops and lets his shoulders fall.

"Crud," he mutters.

Mike lives only a few blocks from the Union Depot, but I get the feeling it will be a long walk home. Meantime, Carol finishes her Cosmo and sets it on a nearby table.

"You think we can take a second to talk to Dr. Palmer?" she asks.

I glance toward the good doctor. "Assuming Lars doesn't beat you to it."

Carol shoots a look that direction. Sure enough, Lars is knifing through the crowd, making his way toward Dr. Palmer. Carol grits her teeth.

"Once he gets there, the waterhole will be poisoned," she says, "We'll be lucky if she wants to talk to *anyone* after that."

The sight of someone as goofy as Lars chatting up someone as classy as Dr. Palmer takes the air out of Carol. She drops into a seat at one of the tables. Lars is quickly squeezed out of his conversation with Dr. Palmer as the crowd whisks her out of the room. Lars straggles back to us, looking a tad dazed. Carol gives him the atomic stink eye.

"How was your chat with Dr. Palmer?" she says, bitterness dripping from every syllable.

Lars screws up one corner of his mouth, the way Carol often does when she's thinking. "It was fine. She's a nice lady. The conversation was a little weird."

"Weird how?" Carol asks.

"She said she hoped to see me again and shoved a note in my hand." He waves a small slip of paper.

Lars hands the note over to me. It reads *I'm going to the Kiefer Hotel. Help me.* I turn the note over, hoping there's a *j/k* or something on the other side. No such luck.

"You got this from Dr. Palmer?" I say.

"I did. Personally, I would have been okay with an autograph."

Carol and Mike press forward to look at the note. Carol glances around the very large room. "I don't see her," she says, "You think that note's on the up-and-up?"

"Kind of hard to imagine it's a practical joke," I say, "I mean, I've heard worse, but…"

Carol grabs my arm and runs toward the exit. Mike and Lars are a step behind. A few seconds later, we're out the front door and into the perfectly pleasant May evening. There's a limo parked on Sibley Street, next the light rail station. The crowd has dissipated, and we get a glimpse of Dr. Palmer. She's surrounded by three guys who, except for the suits, would look right at home on the Vikings' defensive line. They seem to move her along faster than she'd like. Lars runs toward the limo, the rest of us shambling after. Dr. Palmer sees us coming. We're not going to get there before she's put in the car. She makes eye contact with Lars and mouths a single word.

Help.

The limo's heading down the street by the time we get to Sibley. We stand there, dumbfounded. As usual, Carol is the first one to come to her senses.

"What should we do?" she asks. (Remember: I said *Come to her senses,* not *Provide a helpful solution.*)

"We talk to the cops," I say, "There's plenty of them around. We'll give them the note and let them handle it."

Lars looks in the direction of the departing limo. "You sure that's a good idea?"

"Yes, it is. When we *don't* involve the cops, that's the bad idea."

I march back to the Union Depot, not bothering to see if the Three Stooges are following me. Judging by the wheezing and complaining, they must be right behind. Fortunately, there's a cop just inside the Depot. Unfortunately, the cop is an Officer Bukowski. When my apartment was broken into not long ago, Bukowski was the guy who answered the call. In the sense that he showed up and pretty much told me there was nothing he could do. Despite my misgivings, I approach him and tell him that we think Dr. Palmer might be in some trouble. To the shock of absolutely no one, he looks a little skeptical.

"You saw her getting into a car?" he says, "That makes you think she's in trouble?"

"Well, no, not just that," I say, "There's the note she gave Lars. Lars, hand me the note."

And he'd probably do that. If he was here. I look around quickly and ask: "Where's Lars?"

Carol and Mike glance behind them. They are, by turns, annoyed and confused.

"He was here a second ago," Mike says.

"Try his cell phone," Carol says.

Mike, as he usually is in cell phone situations, is quick to dial. After a second, though, he slips the phone back into this pocket. "Straight to voicemail."

Carol and I each give it a shot but get the same results. By this time, we've taxed what little patience Officer Bukowski had in the first place.

"Listen, you guys have a good night," he says, "Let me know if Santa Claus or The Boogey Man show up, okay?"

With that, Officer Bukowski waddles away from us. Mike points toward Bukowski, using his middle finger.

"Somewhere," Mike says, "A mall missed out on one hell of a cop."

I'm starting to panic. Lars is missing. Dr. Palmer may have been grabbed. And we've got no one to help us. Carol rummages around one of the tables, looking for an abandoned drink.

"What do we do?" she asks, "Where could Lars have gone?"

I take the note out of my pocket. "The note says they're taking Dr. Palmer to the Kiefer Hotel. I guess we know where to start looking."

Mike and Carol rarely agree on anything, but in this case, they're joined by their lack of enthusiasm for this idea. But they don't say anything. They just fall in line behind me as I rush out the door

Anybody order a round of *The Blind Leading The Blind?*

***

The Kiefer Hotel was built in the early 1900's and is known for its Old-World charm and luxury. Or so I'm told. I've never gotten past the lobby. The building sits in the heart of downtown St. Paul. It's a boomerang-shaped place wedged into the general landscape. It's been home to its share of politicos, celebrities and gangsters over the decades. Not the kind of place losers like us can stroll about with impunity.

The first order of business is to get past the front desk. Maybe during the day, when there's a bit more foot traffic, we could access the place relatively unnoticed. In the shank (if shank is really the word I want) of the evening, however, the front desk staff eyeballs us the minute we come through the revolving glass doors. We huddle together.

"How are we going to get past the front desk?" Carol asks.

Mike attempts to smooth his brush of hair. "Don't worry. I got this."

Before we can stop him, Mike strides to the front desk. The clerk, a gentleman in his forties with slicked back-black hair and beady eyes, nods to Mike, who slaps his hands on the marble countertop.

"Good day to you, sir," Mike says, "I believe you have my reservation."

The clerk stares at Mike, dubious. "And your name please, sir?"

"My name? Certainly. It's Thompson. Hunter Thompson."

The clerk gives Mike another in his Catalogue of Suspicious Looks before punching the name into the computer. After a few seconds, he turns back to Mike.

"I'm sorry, Mr. Thompson, we don't have a reservation under that name."

Mike throws his hands out. On the subtlety scale, it's somewhere between Don Knotts and a circus clown. "Don't have my reservation? This is an outrage. I made it several months ago."

"Do you have a confirmation?"

"Confirmation? I'm far too important to deal with such trifles. Do you know who I am?"

"Yes. You're Mr. Thompson."

By all rights, the clerk's tone should have stopped Mike cold. But nothing short of an elephant gun will stop Mike when he's on a B.S. run. He places his palms down on the counter and fixes the clerk with his most intimidating glare.

"Am I to understand," Mike says, "That this hotel—whose reputation is known far and wide—has lost my reservation and will do *nothing* to make the situation right?"

The clerk is unmoved. "That, of course, assumes you had a reservation in the first place. Without a confirmation, we have only your word. I'm afraid there's nothing we can do"

"I'd like to speak to a manager."

"You're speaking to him."

Mike bobs his head, like an actor struggling to figure out his next line. From where Carol and I are standing, it's over. Mike, though, pulls out his wallet.

"Okay, how much is it going to take?" he says.

The clerk raises an eyebrow. "Excuse me?"

"Please, let's not play games. What are we talking? Ten? Twenty dollars?"

"I'm going to have to ask you to leave."

"I won't go higher than thirty."

"Please don't make me call security."

Mike slaps the wallet shut. He uses it to point at the clerk. "You're making a big mistake, my friend. I am a powerful man. I hate to sully—Joe, is sully the word I want?"

"It'll work."

"Sully the Kiefer Hotel's reputation, but you leave me no choice. Unless, uh, unless, of course you want to give me a room."

The clerk turns away. "Have a good evening, sir."

"This isn't over," Mike turns on his heel and stalks back to us. "Well, that's over. What do we do now?"

Lacking an answer and being subjected to the clerk's stare, leaving the lobby seems our best option. Once we're street side, we look up at the hotel, towering some twelve stories above. I'm sure there are multiple ways into the place, but they all lead back to the lobby. Desperate times, though, call for desperate measures. Only one guy I know is great at desperate measures.

"Mike," I say, "We've got to break into this place."

He looks relieved. "Why didn't you say so? What's all this assing around, trying to talk our way in there? Follow me."

Carol gives me a pained look but doesn't object. Mike leads the way around to the back of the hotel. There's a large black door set into the brickwork. Mike takes up position near a streetlamp and keeps an eye on it. Carol and I try to play it cool, though Carol's scowl makes that a little difficult.

After about ten minutes, a couple ladies come out the door. If I had to guess, they're kitchen staff for the Lawler Grill, the restaurant located in the hotel. Mike glides over to the ladies and bums a cigarette. He immediately strikes up a conversation. It seems friendly enough, but I have no idea what the purpose is. Finally, the ladies head back inside. Mike lingers by the backdoor and says his final goodbyes.

"What the hell is he doing?" Carol asks, "We're supposed to get inside. He's over there bumming cigarettes and trying to get laid."

I'm not going to disagree. Mike leans against the wall with a dopey grin on his face. He frantically waves us over. When we get there, he points down to where his foot is wedged in the door, holding it open.

"You want to hurry up?" he says, "Before somebody notices this or my foot falls asleep?"

Mike leads the way inside. We find ourselves in a back hallway, leading past the kitchen for the Grill. Mike strides confidently while Carol and I hover over each of his shoulders.

"What if somebody stops us?" Carol asks.

"Be cool and nobody will," Mike says.

"What if somebody asks what we're doing here?"

"We say we're with Walter."

"Who's Walter?"

"The guy we're with."

The hallway winds back toward the lobby. Mike slows as we pass what looks like an oversized cloak room. Navy blue blazers line coatracks along the walls. Mike ducks inside.

"What the hell are you doing?" I ask.

"We need some cover," he says, "Heinrich Himmler at the front desk will spot us if we don't fit in."

Mike searches the racks until he finds a jacket that fits him. He slides it on and holds his arms out, as if looking for approval.

"You look like hotel security," I say.

"Good," he says, "Find a couple coats and let's get going. Time's a-wastin'."

Within a minute, Carol and I are both outfitted like Mike. We quickly go back to prowling the hallways.

"Where do we look?" Carol asks.

"I think our only option is to walk around and keep an eye out," I say, "If they're here, we'll find them someplace."

"Or get thrown out," she says.

The best plan, though I'm not in love with it, is to split up. There are twelve floors to the place, so each of us can take four. Mike gets the bottom four floors. I get the middle floors. Carol gets the top floors. We stay in touch through our cell phones. I'm not optimistic. We're not brilliant as a team, but we're even less effective individually.

Each floor largely looks like another. There's an elevator in the middle and staircases on both ends. I'm dressed as a security guard, but still feel like I'm skulking about. I take my time checking each floor, walking slowly past the doors, hoping to overhear something of interest. But I get nothing (beyond a couple tete-a-tetes that *really* weren't meant for public consumption). After four floors of nothing, I text Mike and Carol and arrange a meet on eighth floor. They come off the elevators a few minutes later. Neither of them looks happy.

"Nothing," Carol says.

Mike shakes his head. "Nada."

"Maybe they're not here," Carol says.

I shake my head. "The note said Dr. Palmer was going to be brought to the Kiefer. If Lars was trying to follow her, this is where he'd come."

"Then where is he?" Mike asks.

"I don't know," I say, "I'm starting to lose hope."

Mike and Carol hang their heads. The whole thing suddenly seems an incredible boondoggle. Lars is out there by himself. And there's nothing we can do about it.

So, it's probably good Lars walks right past us.

At first, I don't even notice him. It's so natural to see Lars strolling around that I forget I'm looking for him. Carol and Mike join me in a double take. Lars doesn't pay any attention. He marches down the hall. We're off in hot pursuit.

I call to him, but he doesn't even look back. I swat him on the arm. "Lars, what the hell is going on?"

He speaks out of the corner of his mouth. "Not the greatest time."

I look to Mike and Carol, but they don't seem to know what's going on either. I join Lars in talking out of the corner of my mouth. "What do you mean this isn't the greatest time?"

"I've got somebody following me." I look around, but don't see anybody. Lars taps me on the arm. "Don't look," he says, "You shouldn't even be talking to me."

Carol catches up to us. "Who's following you?"

"He's back there." Lars says, adding a barely perceptible nod toward the way he came.

I throw a more subtle look, but I'm still not seeing anything. "Okay, I give," I say, "Who's back there?"

"The guy Cal Smith sent."

I stumble, both vocally and physically. "Cal Smith? Cal Smith, the President of the City Council? That Cal Smith?"

"The very one."

Carol elbows me out of the way and takes pole position next to Lars. "Why does the President of the City Council need a guy to follow you around?"

"To make sure I find the evidence."

I take another glance back. A large guy has come around the bend in the hallway. He looks not unlike someone stuffed a gorilla into a cheap suit. Lars picks up the pace.

I grab at Lars, but he eludes me. "Are you going to tell me what the hell is going on?"

Lars doesn't break stride. "Joe, I'm going to ask all of you, in the nicest way possible, to get the fuck out of here."

Lars puts on a burst of speed (he's perilously close to dork-walking right now) and gets clear of us. Carol, Mike and I come to a halt. The big guy shoves past us.

"Stay the fuck out of the way," the guy growls, "This ain't got nothing to do with you." The goon adds a dirty look but otherwise shows no further interest. He continues to follow Lars.

"What the hell is going on?" Carol asks.

Mike chews on his goatee. "You think Lars is working with the people who took Dr. Palmer? Like he's been some sort of super villain the whole time?"

I let out a breath. "Not unless the Legion of Doom's made some serious budget cuts."

"What do we do?" Carol asks.

"I guess we follow him," I say, "See what the hell is going on."

Mike grabs my arm. "Um, did you hear the very large and potentially homicidal man? He doesn't want us following him. I think we should respect his wishes."

I start down the hall anyway. "We'll keep our distance. But we can't let Lars out of our sight. Something's going on."

Lars stops at the last door on the left. He takes out a room key and heads inside while the goon stands in the hallway. We find a nearby hiding place to observe the proceedings. Lars emerges a minute later.

"It's not in there," he says.

The goon gives the wall an open-handed slap. "That's bullshit. It's got to be there."

"I'm telling you it's not," Lars says.

The goon grabs Lars by the throat and lifts him slightly off his feet. "I think you're bullshitting me."

"Frankly, I think that would be a lousy plan on my part," Lars rasps.

The goon shakes Lars like a ragdoll. I run down the hallway with Mike and Carol a step behind. There's a lovely vase of flowers on a little table, about five steps from the goon. I scoop up the vase and, with a leap, bring it down on the goon's head. The vase shatters, as planned, depositing shards all over the green carpeting. The goon remains standing, not as planned, shards peppering his black suitcoat. He turns to me, weaving slightly. He stares down his hawk nose and the look on his face tells me I'm in extremely deep sewage.

Lars, amazingly, comes to my rescue. He produces a small souvenir baseball bat and brings it down on the goon's head. The goon staggers and Lars hits him two more times. The goon slumps to the floor.

"Guess that souvenir from the Saints' game wasn't such a bad idea after all," Lars says. He squats down over the body. "Help me get him into the room."

Mike steps away. "To hell with that. Just leave him there and we'll call it a day."

"No!" Lars is exceedingly annoyed. "Someone will spot him and those guys will know."

"What guys?" I ask.

Lars holds out his hands, exasperated. "Cal Smith and his men. Have you not been paying attention?"

Dealing with Lars is like watching an Andy Kaufman routine. I wonder what everyone else is seeing and why I'm missing the point. Or maybe I'm being conned and that *is* the point.

"Let's get him into the room," I say, "We can stash him there."

It takes all four of us to get the goon into the hotel room. We drop him into the bathtub and close the shower curtain. It won't be impossible to find him, but it's a cut above leaving him in the hallway. The four of us converge in the main room to get our breath back.

"Now that we've helped you with goon disposal," I say, "Maybe you can tell us what the hell is going on?"

Lars nods, conceding the explanation he owes us. "I'm trying to save Dr. Palmer from Cal Smith."

Embarrassed confession: I don't know a hell of a lot about Cal Smith. I see his name pop up in the news and it's generally acknowledged that he wields greater influence over the City Council than anyone (including the mayor). And he's popular and well-liked. I don't really know why he'd be a threat Dr. Palmer. Still, Lars seems one hundred percent sincere.

Carol takes the lead in getting answers out of our goofy friend. "What does Cal Smith want with Dr. Palmer?"

"That I cannot tell you," Lars says.

Mike perks up. "State secret?"

Lars shakes his head. "Not as such. Although, that would be cool, wouldn't it? But the fact is, I genuinely don't know. I need to find some information to save Dr. Palmer."

Carol looks at me, helpless in the face of this Abbott and Costello routine. I take Lars' arm and guide him over to the window, figuring a one-on-one chat might be more useful (and if all else fails, I can just push him out).

"Okay, let's backtrack," I say, "Dr. Palmer was grabbed and brought here. I'm assuming Cal Smith's behind that?"

"You would be right."

"And you came here looking for Dr. Palmer?"

"No. I was grabbed. By the same men. Because Dr. Palmer passed me that note. They figured they couldn't take any chances."

They were probably right. But I don't want to appear to be empathizing with the possible crooks. "So now the big question: *why* did they grab Dr. Palmer?"

"Dr. Palmer has some information that Cal Smith wants. She must have stashed it here at the hotel, but she won't tell Smith where it's at. Since they had me, they ordered me to find it or they'd do something to Dr. Palmer."

I'm guessing *something* isn't *play Scrabble*. "Okay, so what is it you're supposed to be looking for?"

"A manila envelope. Kind of thick. With some papers inside. That's all they'd tell me."

"And it's somewhere in the hotel?"

Lars nods. "Apparently, Dr. Palmer had it earlier. And she stashed it on her way out, when she was going to the event. She won't tell them where it's at. So, they sent me to retrace her steps and find the thing."

"Accompanied by the one-man goon squad."

"Yep. In case I got any ideas about grabbing the information and trying something. Which I wouldn't. I mean, I wouldn't want to put Dr. Palmer at any kind of risk."

I decide not to break this to Lars, but if Dr. Palmer has something Cal Smith needs, she's already at significant risk. Finding the information isn't going to change that. But I'll bet Smith didn't plan on Lars' friends showing up, so there's at least a wild card in this deal.

"Okay, so we need to find this envelope," I say, "Where are we supposed to look?"

"Well, Dr. Palmer stayed in this room," Lars says, strolling the floor, "And she left here and went to the event tonight. Smith knows she didn't have the envelope when she left the hotel. So, it's somewhere between here and the front entrance."

Clearly, Lars is going to need help in finding this thing. Carol's on board, but Mike looks skeptical (civil service has never been his strong suit). Still, he doesn't raise an objection.

"Where is Dr. Palmer being held?" I ask.

"Cal Smith has a suite on the top floor," Lars says.

"What do you know about Dr. Palmer's route?"

Lars rubs his chin. "She was in this room and she went out the front door. She didn't use the elevator, because Smith saw her coming out of the stairwell when she got to the lobby."

"Was anybody with her?"

"Nope. Just her."

Eight floors between here and the lobby. This is going to be like looking for a piece of hay in a giant stack of needles. The only thing in our favor is that there are four of us (granted, it's *us*, but still…) We can cover the ground in a short amount of time.

"We better get moving," Mike says, "I think Clthulhu in there is stirring."

Sure enough, a small groaning from the bathroom indicates Cal Smith's goon is coming around (at least, I hope that's what the groan represents). We *really* don't want to be here when he stumbles out. Mike grabs a chair and jams it under the bathroom doorknob.

"Probably won't hold him long," Mike says, "But every second counts, right?"

We troop out into the hallway and make our plan. Each of us will take two floors. Again, it doesn't produce much. Searching my two floors doesn't take long, but I do what I can. Check around the trashcans, check the little desks, look behind the mirrors and the vending machines, peek into the utility closets. I don't have access to any of the rooms, but then neither did Dr. Palmer. I come up with bupkus. Judging by the looks I get from Lars, Carol and Mike when we return to the eighth floor, they weren't any more successful. Lars seems particularly agitated.

"I don't know what we're going to do," he says, "If I don't find that envelope, Smith will do something to Dr. Palmer."

Lars paces in small circles. I'm getting one of those desperate feelings, like I have to do something but have no idea what. (I sometimes get that while writing a column, particularly when I'm up against a deadline.) I take a deep breath and find what passes for my Zen.

"You were in the room with Smith and Dr. Palmer," I say, "Did you hear anything that might help us? Anything useful?"

That's an uncertain way of gain, to be sure. Lars' whole life is built on a solid foundation of uselessness. But he gives it the old college try (for a guy who dropped out of college). He stares at the floor in deep concentration.

"Smith said something about the money," Lars says, "Dr. Palmer didn't seem impressed. She said it was nothing but trash. She actually looked at me when she said that."

"Did she say anything else?" I ask.

"She was arguing with Smith about money. Then she looked at me and said, 'This project could be delayed up to seven years.' And she nodded to me and said, 'Seven years.' I'm not sure why she did that. I think trolleys are neat, but I don't consider myself much of an expert."

A thought is niggling its way into my brain. "Did she say anything else?"

"Just that she hoped people like me would be free to enjoy it. And she nodded again."

The idea is crystalizing. "Dr. Palmer was giving you marching orders of her own."

Lars' eyebrows go up. "Marching orders? No, you see, I got my marching orders from Cal Smith. I don't know if I made that clear. See, he's the bad guy in this whole thing…"

I draw back to punch him, but somehow resist. "I know that, you idiot. I'm saying Dr. Palmer was giving you a code. She was telling you where to look for the envelope." Mike and Carol swing their heads toward me. Neither of them is quite on my wavelength yet. I start ticking the reasons off on my fingers. "Freedom. Seven. Trash. If you get free, look in the trash on the seventh floor. *That's* where she put the envelope!"

Carol doesn't seem convinced. "Didn't you look in the trash on the seventh floor? That was your section."

"Well, I looked *around* the trash. Inside? That's icky."

Lars seems supremely unconvinced. "I seriously doubt I would have missed a clue that obvious. If anyone is tuned into what people are thinking, it's me."

"You getting anything from me at the moment?" I ask.

"You think I'm an idiot."

"That's not fair. I'm *always* thinking your idiot."

Mike steps between us. "Hey look, we could stand here trading insults—and don't get me wrong, I'd be totally down with that—or we can check the trash on the seventh floor."

Huh. Mike is a lot of things in our little group, but the Voice of Reason is almost never among them. Reflexively, we look to Carol, who usually plays that role. She shrugs.

"Let's do what the man says," she tells us.

Less than a minute later, we're on the seventh floor. We've got a one-in-three shot of finding the trashcan we're looking for. There's one on each end of the hallway and one sitting in the middle. Mike, as he often does in trashy situations, takes command.

"I'll look at this one," he says, "Lars, you take the one in the middle. Joe and Carol…ah, you guys are too prissy to search a trash can. Go to the end of the hall and wait for us."

Carol starts to protest, but realizes Mike is right. She gives him a dirty look and follows me. Carol more or less justifies Mike's opinion by looking on with distaste as he and Lars take apart the two trash cans. Lars is particularly thorough, which seems to nauseate Carol and, if I'm going to be honest, me. The more nauseating part, though, is that neither of them comes up with anything. They join us, looking frustrated and smelling like homeless dudes at high tide. Carol slides behind me and grabs her nose as they approach.

"We only got one left," Mike says, "Hope for the best."

Mike and Lars start in on the final trash can. They work with reckless abandon and it's only a handful of seconds before they strike pay dirt.

"Got it!" Mike says, brandishing the envelope, "She taped it just under the liner."

Lars takes the envelope and nods, impressed. "She's a clever woman. I'll give her that."

Before we can look inside the envelope, though, a shadow falls across us. And I don't mean a metaphorical shadow. I mean a literal giant fucking shadow descends, emanating from the large goon we left unconscious in the bathtub. He throws out a hand.

"Give me that damn thing," he says, "Or I'll beat you to death."

He drives a hard bargain, I'll give him that. But we didn't come this far just to hand the damn thing over and call it a day. Lars, in possession of said damn thing, bolts for the door to the stairwell.

"Hey motherfucker!" The goon shouts.

But the motherfucker isn't listening. Neither are his friends, because we're just a step behind. And the goon, sadly, is a step behind us. Time to put my cardio work to the test.

Lars darts down the stairs and toward possible freedom in the street. Mike quickly peters out (smoking hasn't done wonders for him) allowing me and Carol to move ahead of him. Still, I give Mike credit: he's in good enough shape to outpace a woozy, oversized goon.

Turns out I've given him too much credit.

I'm rounding a flight of stairs when I hear something that most closely resembles *Glurk!* I look back and see Mike in the grasp of the goon. He's getting lifted up by his neck.

"You give it here," the goon says, "Or I snap his neck."

The rest of us freeze in position. For a few seconds, nobody's sure what to do. Lars throws his hands out and lets them drop to his side. "It's okay," he says, "I'm sure Mike can get himself out of this mess."

Mike momentarily forgets about the hindrance to his breathing and looks genuinely pissed off. Even the goon's a little taken aback (not enough to let go of Mike's neck, but…)

"Lars, you prick!" Mike croaks.

The goon shakes Mike like a baby's rattle. "Hey, I ain't shitting around here. I will snap—"

And he doesn't get any further. Because Mike has brought his heel up full force into the goon's groin. The goon goes bug-eyed and lets Mike's feet return to the floor. But he keeps his hands on Mike's neck.

So Mike kicks him in the balls again.

This one brings a gasp and a slight stoop to the goon. His grip on Mike's neck slackens, but he doesn't let him go.

So Mike kicks him again.

That's enough to take down the goon. His hands go from Mike's neck to his own precious noogs. Mike steps free and follows us down the stairs.

Just to be on the safe side, Mike goes back and kicks the goon in the balls one more time.

Lars slips off the stairway when we get to the fourth floor. He ducks into an alcove with vending machines and an ice machine. We crowd in as he opens the envelope.

"You sure you should be doing that?" Carol asks, "That could be classified information."

Lars waves that scruple away like a mosquito. "If we're going to save Dr. Palmer, we need to know what's in here. Besides, there's such a thing as freedom of information. I have a right to know. It's my duty as a citizen. And a giant buttinski."

He opens the envelope and extracts a series of papers: budgets, reports, projections, etc. They all relate to the trolley project. Fairly dry reading, even by budgetary standards. It's when we get to a green cover page marked *ACTUAL PAPERWORK* that stuff gets interesting. The remainder of the paperwork mirrors the earlier stuff, but there's a radical shift in where the money's going. Rather than the trolley project, a large chunk of the funds appears to be going into a slush fund for Cal Smith.

"Suckling at the public teat," Lars says.

Carol nods. "In the fine tradition of politicians throughout the ages."

I take the paperwork from Lars. "Dr. Palmer must have gotten ahold of this. Smith couldn't risk anything until he knew where the evidence was located."

"Meaning," Mike says, "That Dr. Palmer's life expectancy is only as long as the time we can keep this paperwork from Smith."

Lars takes the paperwork, stuffs it down the front of his pants and uses his shirt to cover it. I look to Mike and Carol.

"Well, nobody's going to want it *now*," I say.

Lars wags a finger at me. "This is just a stopgap. We need to get Dr. Palmer some help."

"We can go to the police," Carol says, "*Now* we've got something they'll listen to."

However, Lars is not on board with a common-sense plan. "We may not have time. Once that goon gets back up there and lets them know we've got the paperwork, they'll get desperate."

I take Lars' arm in my most gentle, grandfatherly way. "If this paperwork holds water, Cal Smith is in a world of hurt. The *only* thing he could do to make the situation worse is do something to Dr. Palmer. He doesn't need to add murder to graft, theft and kidnapping."

"I wish I could believe you," Lars says, "But I've got a bad feeling about this guy. I've dealt with people who have nothing to lose. You can't predict what they'll do."

Which would mean Lars has had nothing to lose for the entire five years I've known him. He pushes past us and heads to elevator. Common sense will have to wait for another day. When we reach the top floor, Lars pulls us into a huddle.

"Here's the deal," he says, "I'm going to distract Smith while the three of you get Dr. Palmer out of the room."

"How are we going to do that?" I ask.

Lars looks exasperated. "Joe, I can't hold your hand through this entire thing. At some point you're going to have to take ownership."

With that helpful bit of advice, Lars marches to the door of Smith's room. He gives the rest of us a knowing look and grandly knocks. There's a moment's silence before a gruff voice comes from the other side.

"What do you want?"

"We need to talk to Cal Smith," Lars says, "I've got something he wants."

The door opens a crack. I don't get much of a look at the person on the other side, but he amply fills the crack in the door. "You the asshole we sent to find the paperwork?"

"I am that asshole," Lars says, "And I've brought it back. But I'll only directly deal with Cal Smith."

The door is whipped open. The guy is holding a gun on us. He steps back and nods into the room.

"Get in here. Quick."

Lars leads the way. The guy doesn't seem too impressed with the presence of Carol, Mike and me. Not that he's got a lot to worry about. The room is sizable enough, but a lot of space is taken up by the two other goons in Smith's employ. (One of them is the goon Mike tried to separate from his noogs. That's going to make this situation awkward. Well, *more* awkward.) Smith stands next to a sofa. Dr. Palmer, seated on the sofa, turns to get a look at us. She seems a little relieved at the appearance of Lars and a little confused at the appearance of the rest of us. Frankly, that's something we all have in common.

Smith gives Lars a smile. "Good to see you again," Smith says, in a voice that's clipped and high pitched, "I was afraid you'd run off on us."

Lars folds his arms. "I'm not going anywhere without Dr. Palmer."

"You know my price."

"I do. And there's no deal until I know she's safely out of the hotel."

Smith chuckles. "Sorry, no. I get the paperwork and then I let Dr. Palmer—and you—go. A deal's a deal."

Mike scoffs. "Don't think you're the one to be talking about how a deal's a deal."

The goon Mike booted steps toward him, ready to go to Smith's defense. Mike strikes a judo pose (which is doubly ridiculous, because Mike doesn't know judo). The goon's hands instinctively go to his groin. The other goons surround us. Smith keeps his focus on Lars.

"One of your friends has a big mouth," Smith says.

"If you get to know him," Lars says, "You'll realize he has a very big mouth."

"I don't plan on getting to know him."

"Your loss. He's a very interesting—"

"Shut the fuck up!" I was wondering how long it would take Smith to lose his cool. "I want the goddamn envelope and you're going to give it to me. You understand?"

Lars holds his hands out. "Maybe I don't know where it is."

Smith's face turns red. The goons look ready to crack either their knuckles or someone's skull. Even Dr. Palmer is sitting rigid. Lars is the one cool customer in the room.

Smith speaks in a murderously low voice. "I want the envelope. You wouldn't be here if you didn't have it. So quit jacking around and give it to me."

Lars scratches his head and does his best James Dean. "I don't think we're making any progress here. See, I know where the envelope is, and you don't. That means you're going to have to follow my lead. And that requires—Ow! Oh my God, the envelope sliced me! I've got a papercut on my wang!"

On the downside, the ruse that we don't have the paperwork has gone completely out the window. On the upside, Lars has brilliantly—if unintentionally—executed the distraction he hoped to create. He's got the attention of the entire room, Smith in particular. And since Mike, Carol and I are used to seeing Lars act like an idiot, we recover quicker than anyone else.

I take three giant steps across the room and grab Dr. Palmer's hand. We start toward the door. Mike and Carol are heading there as well. Lars is still hopping around, trying to separate the edge of the paperwork from his Johnson. Dr. Palmer and I aren't halfway to the door before Smith gets his bearings.

"Stop them!" he shouts.

Immediately, three goons are in my path. I let go of Dr. Palmer's hand. Mike and Carol move into position next to me. If this is a showdown, it's a mismatch on the level of *Bambi vs. Godzilla.*

"Now," Smith says, "Give me the goddamn envelope."

Mike, Carol and I scatter in three different directions. Lars finally extracts the envelope from his pants and holds it above his head as he dances around the room. Smith is in hot pursuit of him. The goons are in hot pursuit of the rest of us. Dr. Palmer is completely lost in all this.

I duck under the grasp of the goon in charge of kicking my ass and dart toward the door. He swings out a foot and trips me. I wind up in the entrance to the bathroom. I grab the doorknob and pull myself to my feet. The goon closes fast.

Out of instinct, I swing the bathroom door closed. It doesn't quite close, because it stops at the guy's skull. He looks at me, surprised and a bit offended. Then his eyes go crossed and he slumps to the floor. A second goon lumbers toward me. He suddenly stiffens and hits the floor. Carol has hit him with a judo chop to the neck. (Forgot to mention: one of us *does* know judo.) When the dust clears, there's a third goon on the floor, curled into a fetal position at Mike's feet. It's the same guy who went after us earlier.

"What happened to him?" I ask Mike.

Mike shrugs. "I kicked him in the nuts. Self-defense really isn't the dude's strong suit."

But we can't celebrate just yet. Lars is struggling with Cal Smith. Though Lars has a height and youth advantage, he's also a crappy fighter. Smith has Lars by the throat and looks to be trying to choke the life out of him.

Before any of us can make a move, the air goes out of Smith, his eyes roll up into his head and he hits the floor. Dr. Palmer stands behind him, still holding the lamp she clocked him with. Lars gets to his feet, holding his throat. Dr. Palmer looks at Smith and sums up what all of us are thinking.

"Asshole."

***

A few hours later, we're in the hotel bar, enjoying a well-earned drink. Dr. Palmer has joined us, which is an honor, but also makes everyone uncomfortable (we're not used to having people of substance in this group). We've given her what amounts to the head of the little table we've commandeered. Lars is on her right, the man of the hour.

"I should have known Cal was up to something," Dr. Palmer says, staring into her gin and tonic, "He'd spoken out against rail travel for years. There's no way he was going to pivot on it unless he'd found a way to line his pockets."

"He's always had a pretty good reputation," Carol says.

"To the public," Dr. Palmer says, "This is politics. Nobody's ever what they seem to be."

A sobering thought. But after the events of tonight, we're not going to disagree. I take a healthy gulp of my beer.

"I know it sounds trite," I say, "But it seems like we need a few more honest people in politics."

Dr. Palmer sighs. "Good luck finding a decent person who wants to get their hands dirty."

Carol adopts a sly grin. "There's an opening on the City Council now."

Dr. Palmer holds up a hand. "I've had enough of politics for a while. Maybe a lifetime"

Lars props a bony elbow on the table. "Y'know, I think what this city really needs is a visionary. Someone who can think outside the corrupt box. A champion of the people."

I sincerely wish he was talking about Dr. Palmer, but judging by that faraway look in his eyes, he's not. This idea is going to take a hold of him and we'll watch him fumble around with it for weeks and months to come. And everyone but him will realize it's going to eventually come to nothing.

"Lars, I don't think—" I start to say.

"No, Joe, I've got to consider this," he says, "Maybe I've been going down the wrong road all these years. Maybe what I really need is to be the champion of the people. Maybe I'm *exactly* what the City Council needs."

I'm not sure how to talk Lars out of this. Mike and Carol know him well enough to not even try. Dr. Palmer toys with the stir stick in her drink.

"You may want to think about this," she says, "It's a lot of work."

"I'm not afraid of work."

"It's a lot of glad-handing and wheeling-and-dealing."

"I've got hands and wheels."

"It doesn't pay for shit."

"I…oh. Well, forget the whole thing."

And for the second time tonight, Dr. Palmer has saved the city of St. Paul from graft and incompetence.

DEATH, YOU MAGNIFICENT BASTARD

When I was kid, my gang of friends and I were caught throwing snowballs at cars. The whole idea was Bob Sunde's and nobody would ever confuse Bob with a Rhodes Scholar. When a particularly meaty snowball crashed into the windshield of Mrs. Walker's truck, Bob was the only one she managed to collar. Bob didn't waste time ratting out the rest of us. When Mrs. Walker was done haranguing my father, he immediately began haranguing me. When I pleaded that Bob Sunde was the mastermind of this idiocy, it led to this exchange:

DAD: So, if Bob Sunde wanted to jump off a bridge, would you jump off a bridge, too?

ME: (After a disquietingly long pause) Which bridge?

The three-weeks grounding I received allowed me time to reflect. And I realized how susceptible we are to our friends. See, when we're younger, there's safety in numbers. The last thing we want is to stand out, thus leaving us to the mercy of thugs and dullards. The second-to-last thing we want is to be cast out for the unpardonable crime of going against the herd. If the group is benevolent enough, you'll be okay. If the group has other things on its mind, however…

My name is Joe Davis. When I was younger, I belonged to one of the latter groups.

Strangely enough, I didn't belong to this group when I was in high school. It was in college, rather, that I hung with a crowd that did its fair share of carousing. So much so, that we forged lifelong bonds over nothing more than the ability to survive our own idiocy.

Many of those guys are still in my sphere of influence. Mike, of course, has remained my best friend. Robbie, Stoner and T.J. are part of my fantasy football league, as well as participating in touch football and broomball. The only exception is Wayne. Until recently, I believed Wayne was incarcerated or a fugitive from justice. Thus, it was a bit of a surprise when he called Mike out of the blue.

Said call interrupted our usual night at The Tav. Wayne didn't say much other than asking us to meet him at King's Bar on Nicollet as soon as possible. King's is a shithole, but Wayne was part of the old gang. Loyalty goes a long way.

"What kind of trouble do you suppose he's in?" Mike asks on the drive over.

"Knowing Wayne?" I say, "Deep."

While Wayne was part of the group, nobody's quite sure how he got there. He didn't have a close friend within the group (like me with Mike or Robbie with Stoner) and nobody had a shared history with him. Nobody saw him in a class or a club. To this day, we're not completely sure Wayne even attended Adams College. He started hanging with us at a freshman party and was with us for the next four years. Which means he's with us for life.

King's is a hole in the wall; so thin the tables on one side are only feet from the bar on the other side. The place isn't busy. The bartender, a bored-looking college-age kid, doesn't look up from his phone when we enter. Wayne is at a table near the back. He's slumped over a lowball glass containing the dregs of what I'm guessing is *not* his first drink of the evening.

When we were in college, we did a lot of barhopping with Wayne. Not because we liked barhopping, but because Wayne got us thrown out of every place we went. So, you'll understand our hesitation regarding him and booze. Mike orders us a couple beers of reasonable price and dubious quality. Wayne doesn't notice us until we're right at the table.

"Hey, pull up a chair," he says, thickly, "I'd get up, but…fuck it."

It's been six years since I last saw Wayne. He's a few pounds heavier and there are fewer brown follicles on his nearly-shaved head. But the malignant blue eyes and the thin, broken nose are still there. The wan smile reveals the crooked teeth. He's the same Wayne we used to know, for better or worse. Largely worse.

"What's going on, Wayne?" Mike asks.

"I'm fucked," he says, "And I need your help."

Wayne downs the watery remains of his drink and snaps his fingers for a refill. He pushes the empty to the side.

"How can we help?" I ask, "Vis-à-vis the, uh, fuckery?"

The bartender puts a new whiskey in front of Wayne and collects the empty. Wayne tosses most of it back. He doesn't even grimace. (Guessing most of the dude's esophagus was burned away years ago.) He slumps back in his chair.

"I got some guys coming after me," he says, "And they're going to fucking kill me."

Mike and I look at each other. This situation calls for alcohol or a reasonable facsimile. We knock most of our beers and get matching sour expressions on our face (they match the quality of the hooch).

"Maybe we need a little explanation here," I say.

Wayne stares at the tabletop, trying to marshal his thoughts. After a few seconds, a sort of clarity comes over him. Or at least a willingness to focus. (This could also be a prelude to him throwing up.)

"Here's the deal," he says, "I've been working at this place called Icon Express. You heard of it?"

"Delivery company, right?" Mike says, "I've seen the vans out and about."

"Yeah, that's us. We move all sorts of shit. Like UPS, only a hell of a lot smaller. Anyway, I been doing it about a year. It's monkey work. You pick up the packages, drive your route, call it a day. If the weather's decent and the traffic's not bad, it's a pretty good gig."

That's good to hear. Wayne used to go through jobs at a rate of one every couple months, depending on how much customer service was involved and how much of a douchebag he assessed his boss to be.

"So what happened?" I ask.

"All right, there's this chick in the office. Name's Denise. We get together every now and again, have a few beers, go back to her place. Fuck. You know how it is." Wayne always had a touch of the poet about him. "So, one night, we got to talking and she told me about some of the stuff we've been moving: iPads, gaming systems, laptops, shit like that. It's decent merch." He stifles a belch. "Denise tells me Icon has a delivery rate of about ninety-five percent. Means some packages just never get where they're going. Shit happens, right? You want tracking and that shit, you go to FedEx. You want to save a buck, you come to us. So, if you look at it one way, there's about five percent wiggle room to, uh, make a profit. You get what I'm saying?"

"Of course," I say, "It's called theft."

"It's not…well, yeah, I guess that's what you call it. Anyway, Denise had this plan. I could miss a delivery every now and then, maybe just go *Whoops* with some fairly high-end stuff. And then she starts talking about how she knows a guy, can maybe move stuff like that."

Here comes the other shoe. "When you say *move*," I say, "You're not talking from retailer to consumer, are you?"

"No. Well, kinda. But not the retailer and consumer it was supposed to be moved to." Wayne knocks back the rest of his whiskey and snaps his fingers for another. "I started thinking about what Denise had to say. The only thing I didn't like about Icon was that the pay is for shit. At least they have their own vans. Because if I had to use my car, I wouldn't be making anything. The thought of making more money sounded good. Especially coming from Denise. I mean, the woman could blow you, leave you cross-eyed for a year. She does this thing where—"

"And what happened with the stuff?" I ask.

"Okay, the guy Denise was talking about was more a friend of a friend. She never actually met the guy. Denise tells me she can cook Icon's books. Cover our tracks."

Mike gives me a brief look. He finally understands that *disappointed with the kid* feeling I get every now and again when I deal with *him*. (Not that Mike's going to let it govern his future behavior. But at least he understands.)

"Okay, what happened that you're totally fucked?" Mike asks.

Wayne puts his elbows on the table and nearly misses. "Well, first part went okay. Me and Denise, we got a whole bunch of stuff. Didn't take all that long, either. We sold it to this guy. I handled everything. Looked like the start of a great enterprise. And then we, uh, found out something about Icon." Wayne clears his throat. "Icon Express isn't, uh, completely legitimate. We're moving product, sure. But where the money's coming from might not be, strictly speaking, y'know, *legal*."

While Wayne has his fair share of drawbacks, being obtuse has never been one of them. It takes me and Mike a second to realize what he's driving at.

"It's a front company," Mike says, "For money laundering."

"Yeah, that's the case. I stole from a bunch of thieves. Fuck of a deal, huh?"

Mike and I look at each other, stunned. Sure, we knew this was going to be bad. But we were thinking it was of the *My old lady's pissed off and wants to garden shear my wang* variety. We didn't realize it was *Criminals want my ass dead*.

"Who *are* these guys?" Mike asks.

Wayne scratches his ear. "From what I gather, if you go far enough up the food chain, you'll find a bunch of Chechens out of Boston. Guys running Icon are pretty much subcontractors, but they answer to the Chechens, so..."

"You should be shitting your pants," Mike says.

"I'm well on my way. Yeah."

Holy fuck. I don't know a lot about Chechen gangsters, but I know enough to know crossing them doesn't lead to a long life-expectancy. No wonder Wayne looks like he's trying to drink himself to death. It would be the better fate. Another drink arrives and Wayne downs it in one gulp. Mike grabs the bar napkin and shreds it as he thinks.

"I'm still not seeing how we can help you out with a bunch of Chechen gangsters," Mike asks, "It's not exactly our specialty."

Wayne waves toward the bar, requesting another drink. I turn as well and try to wave the drink order off. The bartender pours it anyway. Money talks.

"Here's the deal," Wayne says, "I know where the stuff is. And I know who bought it."

"And who's that?" I say.

"A guy named Frankie Ace. Works over on Rice Street. I explained the whole thing to him. And he basically told me to go fuck myself."

"What did he say?" I ask.

"*Go fuck yourself.* Didn't I explain the part?"

"Sorry," I say.

"Point is, the guy won't give the stuff back. He hasn't even moved it yet. Just says *A deal's a deal* and that's that. And Denise has disappeared, so I can't even get her to talk to him."

"Disappeared?" Mike asks, "You got any idea where she's at?"

"No. I think she's running scared. But if we can get the stuff back from Frankie, I can get it where it goes and nobody's the wiser. Especially the Chechens."

Mike swirls the beer in his glass. "What kind of time frame we looking at?"

"Maybe two days."

Okay, Wayne needs a favor. That's clear enough. But there's one giant part of this that needs clarity. "Why did you call us?" I ask.

Wayne's whiskey arrives. The bartender ignores the look I give him. (I guess he's dealt with worse than a mildly annoyed humor columnist.) Wayne ignores the whiskey, temporarily.

"This Frankie, he's got a whole crew he runs. It ain't going to be a simple smash-and-grab. I can't do it by myself." Suddenly, Wayne is, for the first and only time I've known him, close to tears. "I didn't know who else to ask. You guys—all of the old gang—you're the only people I trusted in my entire life. If I couldn't ask you for help…"

Wayne clears his throat and downs his whiskey. I look to Mike, who holds up his beer in a mock toast.

"Okay," Mike says, "I guess we're getting the band back together."

***

Any plan that's bound to gruesomely fail and probably get us all killed needs a mastermind. If I was going to nominate someone to come up with a plan that *wouldn't* get us killed, it would be Stoner. (Of course, Stoner is also smart enough not to get involved with this foolishness, so…)

Mike and I track down Stoner at his day job. Despite his relative brilliance and ruthlessness, Stoner's settled comfortably into a life of managing a branch of the Artist Formerly Known As Kinko's. We get there in time for his coffee break, which he's more than happy to take at the Caribou Coffee next door. As long as we're buying.

"Wayne needs us to save us his life, huh?" Stoner says, looking at us over a Turtle Mocha big enough to have an undertow, "I'm surprised he's lived this long."

"We all are," I say, "But are you willing to help him?"

Stoner runs a hand through his mop of brown hair (naturally, it falls right back into position). "I don't know. A plan's only as good as the crew working it."

Mike looks vaguely offended. "What's wrong with us?"

Stoner holds up a hand. "Hey, don't get me wrong. Back in the day, we might have been able to pull this off. But we're all domesticated now. T.J.'s not allowed to leave the house. Robbie's got a kid. Mike and I have day jobs. Joe, you've got a couple of cats. Are we really going to risk everything—even if the everything is kind of pathetic—to help *Wayne?*"

Funny how Stoner can be caring and insulting at the same time. Nevertheless, he's thrown down the gauntlet; one that Mike is only too willing to pick up.

"We can do this," Mike says, "Just a matter of you thinking up a decent plan."

There's no point in baiting Stoner. The man's every success in life (in areas such as broomball, gambling, fantasy football) is attributable to his refusal to let insignificant things such as emotion or any discernible moral compass affect his decision-making. He's more amused than offended by Mike's challenge.

"All right, I guess we're going to do this," he says, "Just a matter of coming to terms."

"Terms?" I ask.

"You can't expect me to do a thing like this for free."

Mike puts a hand over his forehead. We've known Stoner long enough to know he would pull something like this. And yet, we're still surprised by his venality. (It would be touching if it weren't so annoying.)

"You're expecting to get paid?" I say, "For saving Wayne's life?"

Stoner isn't moved. "Like my dad used to say: 'Stoner, nothing in this life is free.'"

"Your dad called you 'Stoner'?" I ask.

"Where do you think I got the nickname?"

I look to Mike, but he just shrugs. Come to think of it, neither of us did know the origin of Stoner's nickname. I guess we've solved that mystery. Which is nice.

"What are we supposed to pay you with?" I ask.

Stoner checks out a blonde in a gray business suit who's just walked in the door. "Payment can come in many forms. I'd be willing to do this for the low-low price of Robbie loaning me his car for a night."

"You have a car of your own," I say.

"If you want to call that rolling crapbox a *car*, then technically, I do. But Robbie has that lovely Camaro and I just need it for an evening. Unfortunately, he's been rather…recalcitrant on the subject."

Mike nods. "He told you to go fuck yourself."

"The man gets to the point in a hurry. You can't deny him that."

Stoner continues to check out the blonde in the gray suit. She places her order and finds a table near the espresso bar. She makes eye contact with Stoner as she opens her laptop and gives him a little smile. We no longer have Stoner's undivided attention and will shortly have *none* of his attention.

"What are you going to use Robbie's car for?" I ask.

"You probably don't want to know that."

Yeah, I really don't. Unfortunately, Robbie will. But there's no moving Stoner off this. We could appeal to his sense of decency, but it would be like appealing to Donald Trump's sense of decorum.

Mike has already doped this out. "So we get you Robbie's car for a night and you're in?"

Stoner stares at the blonde. "That is the deal. Oh, and I'll need the payment in cash."

Mike and I look each other. "What payment?" I ask.

"The two hundred dollars. I'll need half up front."

"When did we agree to this?" Mike asks.

"C'mon, guys. *Nothing in life is free.* All of that? Follow the conversation, would you? It needs to be cash only, by the way." He slips on his shades. "Now if you'll excuse me, I've got to get back to work."

Stoner makes a beeline to the blonde's table, bringing her the beverage she ordered in the process. She smiles as he sits down. Mike looks at me.

"He better come up with one hell of a plan."

***

We finagle a visit with Robbie while he's on his lunchbreak from work. Robbie sells medical supplies for a living, so whatever charm he turns on for clients, he balances by being a miserable prick off the clock.

"Fact is, I never liked Wayne," Robbie says, plowing his way through a burrito bigger than his already-bulbous head, "Why am I supposed to save him from a bunch of Russian gangsters?"

"They're Chechens," I say.

"What's the difference?"

"To be honest," I say, "I don't know."

Mike takes a furtive look around the food court. He's not comfortable discussing the finer points of theft or scamming eastern European gangsters with a bunch of suburban soccer moms hovering nearby. He lowers his voice.

"Wayne's one of the gang," Mike says, "We can't leave him hanging. Like him or not, these guys will kill him."

Robbie looks unimpressed. "They won't kill him. Maybe maim him a little. Okay, a lot."

Just as we should have seen how negotiations with Stoner would play out, we should have known there'd be some palaver with Robbie. Compassion's never been his strong suit and he's being truthful when he says he and Wayne never got along. Both were alpha males and there could be only one in the group. If we're going to get Robbie's help, we need to try another tactic.

"Stoner's going to work out the whole plan," I say.

Robbie snorts. "Stoner? How much are you guys paying him?"

"What makes you think we're paying him?" I ask.

"Fifteen years of knowing the guy. If you asked Stoner to donate a kidney, he'd want two in return."

"There's some cash involved," Mike says, "And, uh, something else he's looking for."

Robbie immediately picks up on what it is. "No. I am not loaning that fucker my car."

Mike sets aside his sandwich. "It's just for a night. Besides, you know Stoner's not going to trash the thing."

"Doesn't matter," Robbie says, "It's the principle. Stoner can upgrade that shitbox of his—"

"Please," I say, "He prefers *crapbox*."

"He's always asking to borrow my car. Forget it, man. Count me out of this whole wackadoo business."

Son of a bitch. A perfectly good half-assed plan and it stalls on Robbie's stubbornness. I don't know how we can get through to him. Fortunately, Mike does.

"What *would* it take to get you involved in this whole wackadoo business?" Mike asks.

Robbie opens his mouth to dismiss the idea. Then he stops and stuffs some burrito into said open mouth. When he finally swallows, he's come to a conclusion.

"You guys got T.J. on board?" he asks.

"He's our next stop," I say.

"I'm guessing Teej still has that uncle who works at Club Vieux?"

"The one who books the acts?" I ask, "I suppose he does. Why?"

"You heard of that band, The Jehovah's Witness Protection Program? They're coming to Club Vieux. I got a girl who's into them. I'd love to bring her to the show. Only one problem."

"You can't afford the tickets?" Mike asks.

"Oh, I can afford them. But free is *more* affordable. You get Teej's uncle to get me free tickets to that show and I'm in."

I'd love to tell Robbie he's a cheap, petty son of a bitch and give him detailed directions to where, exactly, he can put his request. But no Robbie means no Stoner means no plan means no Wayne. Our hands are tied.

"Fine," I say, "We'll talk to T.J. See what he says."

"Good," Robbie says, "Just let me know when it's going down. And where I can pick up the tickets."

Robbie wraps up his burrito, tucks it under one arm and wishes us a good day. (His exact quote is, "Smell ya later.") When he's gone, Mike and I push our lunches aside.

"You think T.J.'s uncle will come through?" Mike asks.

"He will if T.J. asks him," I say.

"Tough part is getting Teej to ask."

"No," I say, "Tough part is getting to T.J. When we have to go through his wife."

A shudder runs through the two of us. If we had any option at all, we'd leave T.J. out of the plan. Unfortunately, he's become the linchpin.

Maybe we can leave *us* out of the plan.

***

The key with T.J. is to catch him before he gets home. Once he's there, he's rarely out of sight of the lovely Mrs. T.J. They've been married for nearly ten years and have two wonderful children. Mrs. T.J. is part of the Parent-Teacher Organization at their kids' school and does volunteer work through their church. She's family-oriented and civic-minded.

She'd also make Rhonda Rousey shit her pants for a cowardly soul.

Fortunately, there's a small window where we can get T.J. alone. He works in an office building in Roseville, a first-ring suburb north of St. Paul. Mike and I stake out the building, waiting for T.J.'s work day to end.

"You realize there's no guarantee he's going to talk to us?" I say.

"All we can do is ask," Mike says, "It's not like we can threaten him. His wife is a fate worse than death."

From previous experience, we know T.J. gets out of work at five. He strolls through the glass doors of the lobby. Mike and I are out of the car as soon as we see him. We intercept him (and probably lead his co-workers to believe we're kidnapping him) just as he's dug his keys out of his pocket. He nearly drops them when he sees us.

"Hey guys," he says, straightening his glasses, "What are you doing here?"

"We need your help," Mike says, "You got a minute?"

"Uh, I don't, actually. Hunter's expecting me home in about twenty minutes." Yeah. His wife's name is *Hunter*.

Mike hops over to T.J.'s Camry. "Not a problem. We'll ride with you."

T.J. doesn't seem thrilled with the idea. But he's never done well standing up to personalities more forceful than his (and that group is *mighty* large). He plucks at the front of his polo shirt and his eyes flick back and forth between me and Mike. I step over to the rear passenger door, reinforcing Mike's gambit. T.J. rattles his keys and sighs.

"Okay, fine," he says, "But you're going to have to get out before you get to my place. Hunter doesn't like strangers riding in the car."

"We've known you longer than her," Mike says, "How are we strangers?"

"Well, you don't talk much to Hunter."

We don't, but it's more out of a sense of self-preservation than any wish to offend Mrs. T.J. Still, I'm okay with whatever gets this lunacy moving. T.J. unlocks the car and Mike and I climb in. I leave the talking to Mike, who deftly lays out Wayne's conundrum. T.J.'s face tightens up so much that his resemblance to Napoleon Dynamite is uncanny.

"Wayne did something that stupid?" T.J. asks.

Mike looks back at me. "Ah, that's cute. It's like he's never met Wayne."

T.J. raises his fingers off the steering wheel, surrendering the point. "Why are you coming to me? You must be able to find another wheelman."

The universe answers our question by presenting someone who takes a left at a stoplight without signaling. T.J. deftly threads the needle and gets around the jackass without coming close to creating an accident. Since I won't be able to speak until I can unlock my hands from the armrest, Mike continues the pitch.

"We're not going to find a wheelman like you," he says, "And you know that."

While T.J. is a dweeb of Hobbiton proportions, he's also a man of surprising talents. Looking at him, you'd never guess he had more college girlfriends than anyone in our group or that poking out of the right sleeve of that aqua blue polo shirt is a cannon arm that almost carried us to the All City Touch Football title or that he's a wheelman who would make Dale Earnhardt Jr. eat his steering wheel out of sheer envy. Sadly, it's the Hobbit we're dealing with right now.

"You're going to have to find another wheelman," T.J. says, "There's no way Hunter's going to let me to do this."

"It's more than just being a wheelman," Mike says, "We need your uncle to get Robbie some tickets to a concert."

Mike lays out the daisy chain of events that brought us to T.J.'s doorstep. Again, T.J. goes full Napoleon Dynamite. (You never want to go full Napoleon Dynamite.)

"You're kidding me," he says, "You want me to risk my life for *concert tickets?*"

"It's not just the tickets," Mike says, "Robbie could get laid in the deal."

"And you're saving Wayne's life," I add.

As with all our friends, this last appeal leaves T.J. cold. "The truth is, I never liked Wayne. I didn't understand why you guys hung out with him."

"I thought it was your idea," Mike says.

T.J. nearly drives off the road. "Me? I couldn't stand Wayne. Remember how he'd punch me in the back of the head every time he got drunk?"

Mike chuckles. "Yeah, that was great." Then realizing that's not the mood of the room, he switches to a *tsk-tsk*. "Yes, Wayne should have known better. That's a form of abuse."

"And Hunter doesn't want me to have *anything* to do with him. Not since he headbutted our wedding DJ and puked all over his equipment."

Mike waves that off. "Hey, in Wayne's defense, that headbutt took a lot out of him." Responding to a look from T.J., Mike adds: "No, I, I suppose that isn't really a defense."

T.J. executes a hairpin turn off the main drag, smooth as silk, only one hand on the wheel. "There's absolutely no way Hunter's going to agree. And I'm with her on this."

That conveys the seriousness of T.J.'s resistance. Normally, his acquiescence to Hunter's wishes seems to come from a man whose balls are in a vice (and I'm not ruling out the possibility that this really happens from time to time). The time to negotiate has arrived.

Mike again takes the lead. "Okay, let's approach this from another angle. Stoner wants something. Robbie wants something. Is there anything *you* want?"

T.J. starts to dismiss this but stops. His eyes narrow. We might have an opening here. He slows the car down, as if buying some time.

"Maybe there is," he says, "I'm just not sure you guys can deliver it."

Mike gives this an airy wave of his hand. "Name it."

"I need a doll."

Mike looks at me, as if I'm supposed to know what the hell T.J. is talking about. Mike returns his attention to T.J.

"A doll?" Mike asks, "You mean like a blowup doll?"

"No!"

"Because that's really not a problem—"

"I don't mean a blowup doll, you perverted moron! I need an actual doll. A kid's doll."

Mike seems crestfallen. He really could have delivered the blowup doll. Since we're out of Mike's area of expertise, I take over the negotiations.

"What kind of doll?" I say.

"You heard of the Susie Madison doll?"

"T.J., I'm trying to be polite here," I say, "But what fucking frame of reference would I have to know what a Susie Madison doll is?"

T.J. holds up a hand, conceding the point. "It's a children's doll. It's got red hair, looks fashionable and glamorous."

"Like Barbie?" I ask.

"Yeah, except…well, it's exactly like Barbie. Yeah. Anyway, my daughter Allie had one of those. She loved it. Problem was, Allie's lousy about keeping her room picked up. I mean, *really* bad. Mike's dorm room was the only thing I ever saw that was worse."

"And so?" Mike says, annoyed.

"And so, I went into Allie's room to look for something and without realizing it, I stepped on her favorite Susie Madison doll. Crushed its little face. It was horrible. I tossed the thing in the trash before Allie got home from school. It's been a couple of days and she hasn't said anything. But it's just a matter of time. I need to get a new Susie Madison doll. And they aren't easy to find. Not the edition Allie has."

"Which edition is that?" I ask, "The *Five Thousand Dollars or I Tell Your Wife Where You've Been Spending Your Lunchbreaks* edition?"

T.J. throws a nasty look over his shoulder and, when he faces forward again, narrowly avoids someone's dog. "It's not in the stores anymore and every time I try to get one on EBay, some dickhead snipes me. If I don't get the doll back, Allie's going to have a major meltdown and I don't know what Hunter will do to me. I don't want to know."

The pit of my stomach drops. This whole dipshit house of cards is about to come crashing down. I can't think of a way

Mike and I are going to be able to get ahold of a somewhat rare Susie Madison doll. Mike, however, does not share my pessimism.

"Not a problem, Teej," Mike says, tapping the dash, "I'll have that thing at your house tomorrow night."

T.J. has the good sense to be suspicious. "How are you going to pull this off?"

"Don't worry about that. I have connections. You just think how happy Allie will be when she gets her doll back."

"She doesn't know it's gone."

"But on some level, she'll know how much her daddy loves her. I'm assuming. I consider kids a fate worse than death. But you seem happy. So there's that."

T.J. pulls to the curb and throws an anxious glance up the street. As I recall, we're about a block from his place. He rests a hand on the wheel and lowers his voice.

"If you can get me that doll, I'm in," he says, "I don't know what I'm going to tell Hunter."

"You'll think of something," Mike says.

Mike and I get out of the car and T.J. takes off with nary a wave back. Mike gives me a satisfied smile.

"There we go," he says, "We got the band back together."

"Yeah? How are you going to get that doll?"

"Easy. You remember Renee? The chick from Duggan's Bar? I've got a standing invitation for, as the French say, a booty call. Renee's got a curio cabinet full of those Susie Madison dolls. Bet you anything she's got the one we're looking for."

"And she'll just give it to you?" I ask.

"No. But I know where she keeps the key to the curio cabinet."

There are times in life when you look around and wonder how the hell you got where you're at. You can piece it together, step by step, and still be amazed at how you managed to get to this fucked up state of affairs. Right now, I'm tempted to retrace my steps and figure out how Wayne's life has come to depend on Mike stealing something from a woman he's taken advantage of. But I think that process would be too depressing.

Meantime, we realize we're temporarily stranded, since my car is back at T.J.'s work. We're supposed to get a bunch of stolen goods out from the under the nose of a career criminal...and we can't even get ourselves out of Roseville.

What could go wrong?

***

"All right, we start with the most dangerous shit," Stoner says, solemnly addressing the whole room, "T.J., when does your wife get home?"

T.J. flicks a look toward the picture window. "T-ball's over at seven-thirty."

"Then we've got about forty-five minutes to lay this out," Stoner says.

"Can we make it less?" T.J. asks.

Stoner folds his arms. "Normally, I'd let Robbie go on about how you have no balls, but since we all live in mortal terror of your wife, I think we should move this along."

I'd be amazed if we were able to do that. We've been here twenty minutes and we've already used up time dealing with Wayne's objections over no beer, Mike not being allowed to turn on the TV and Robbie's attempts to mate two Susie Madison dolls. Stoner, rather than taking control of the situation, spends most of his time exchanging texts with the woman he met at the coffee shop. Meanwhile, T.J. runs around like he's in charge of the world's shittiest daycare center.

"What about a sandwich?" Wayne asks, "I'm starving."

"No," T.J. says, blocking the door to the kitchen, "Hunter will know if any sandwich meat is missing."

Wayne's eyes bug out. "Jesus, she keeps track of that shit?"

"She keeps track of everything. I might have to air out the house after you guys leave."

My head drops into one hand. If T.J. was allowed out of the house, we wouldn't have the meeting here in the first place. Mike, shockingly, is the one who gets us back on track.

"All right, listen, you assholes," Mike says, "Unless we want Wayne's corpse—or portions of it—to end up floating in the river, we've got to focus. Wayne, that seem more important than a sandwich to you?"

Wayne bobs his head and mutters: "Yeah, it is. But less important than a beer."

"Fine," Mike says, "Stoner, from the bottom of my heart, fucking get on with it."

Stoner slips the phone into his pocket as Wayne mopes back into the living room and sits in the easy chair. T.J's visibly pained that one of the pillows are crushed. Stoner waits until he's got the room's undivided attention.

"I did a little research on this," Stoner says, "And here's what we're looking at: Frankie Ace keeps his stolen stuff in a lot behind The Iron Gate Bar, a place he owns on Rice Street."

An uncomfortable stir goes around the room. Rice Street isn't a high-end part of town, so we've got a pretty good idea what kind of place Frankie Ace is running. Stoner is undaunted.

"From what I gather," he says, "The back is surrounded by a chain link fence with a heavy-duty iron gate. It's not a simple matter of picking the lock, so we're going to have to get ahold of the keys. And we're going to have to do that under the nose of Frankie and his crew. Oh, and we're going to need to move what Wayne assures us is, conservatively, a shitload of merchandise." Stoner gives the room another look. "So that's what we're up against. Anybody want out, now's the time."

Glancing around the room, it appears T.J. is the only one who'd like to leave, but he lives here. Stoner nods.

"All right," he says, "Then follow me."

He reaches behind one of the chairs and comes out with a rolled-up piece of drawing paper; the kind you find in art classes you sign up for just to see the female models naked. (Not that, uh, I know anything about that…or that it ever backfired horribly.) Stoner walks into the tiny dining room and unfurls the paper across the dining room table. T.J. winces, probably wondering if there's anything he needs to cover up. Stoner ignores him.

"Okay, stage one," Stoner says, "We need something to move the merchandise. Robbie, I assume your uncle still has the big truck?"

Robbie squirms. "Yeah, but he won't let me borrow it. He's still pissed about me puking in his swimming pool last Fourth of July. I tried telling him it was the bad shrimp and not the fourteen beers, but he wouldn't listen."

Stoner is unfazed. "Not a problem. There's a pretty easy remedy."

"We rent a truck?" T.J. asks.

"No, we're going to steal Robbie's uncle's truck."

Robbie slaps the table. "Damn straight."

T.J. wipes the table where Robbie smacked it. "Wouldn't it be easier just to rent one?"

"And if something goes wrong?" Stoner asks, "How are we going to explain any damage up to and including bullet holes? And if the cops get involved, a rental might be traced back to one of us. Worst that's going to happen with Robbie's uncle's truck is that he'll never speak to Robbie again. And what with the pool-puking, that's probably going to be the case anyway."

"Fine by me," Robbie says.

Stoner returns his focus to the paper on the table. "Robbie, you and T.J. will be in charge of stealing the truck." Stoner glances at Robbie. "You can handle that, right?"

Robbie scoffs. "Please. You think it'll be the first time I stole that damn thing? He keeps trying to Robbie-proof it, but no luck."

Stoner slides his finger to another part of the paper. "Once you guys have the truck, give us a call. Mike, that'll be your cue to move in. Frankie's been trying to make a deal with an out-of-towner named Denny Laine to move the stuff. You're going to pose as Denny Laine."

Mike frowns. "I don't know anything about this Denny Laine."

"Neither does Frankie," Stoner says, "They've been talking through their crews. Frankie hasn't met this guy and doesn't know what he looks like. Frankie's a reasonably smart guy. Problem is: his crew is the biggest collection of troglodytes ever to walk the Earth. And keep in mind I've known Robbie for fifteen years."

"Fuck you, Stoner!"

Stoner ignores his best friend/eternal nemesis. "We don't have to worry about the crew. Frankie's the one you need to keep an eye on."

"What am I supposed to do?" Mike asks.

Stoner fixes him with a look. "Mike, you really don't need me to tell you how to craft a line of bullshit, do you?"

Mike sits back, chastened. Stoner moves his fingers further down the list while T.J. throws another anxious look toward the picture window.

"Joe, I've got two jobs for you," Stoner says, "You're going to play Mike's henchman. And you're going to need to find an excuse to get outside. We need a little coordination between the distraction and the actual robbery. Bring your cell phone. Now, as a further distraction, we're going to have someone fake a heart attack. Create a little chaos. Since none of us are prime heart attack candidates—at least for another five years or so in Robbie's case—"

"Fuck you, Stoner!"

"I've taken the liberty of hiring an actor I know. He's a good guy. Older. Very subtle. Very thorough. Does a lot of research."

"How do you know this guy?" T.J. asks.

"Mutual friend recommended him. I've used him on a few disability cases."

I shake my head, as if to clear it. "Why are you involved in disability—?"

Stoner holds up a hand, stopping me. "Joe, please. Can we focus on the task at hand?"

He's right, of course. It's a policy I've pursued since college. The less I know about my friends' extracurricular activities, the better. Stoner moves to the next item on the list.

"Robbie, you're going to be in charge of getting the keys from the guy at the gate."

"How do I do that?" Robbie asks.

"You think I'd ask you to do anything that would require cleverness or finesse?"

"So you want to me to knock him out?"

"Just nothing lethal, okay?"

"Works for me, man."

Stoner glances at me. "Once that's done, Joe, you're going to need to get outside and help with moving the stuff. Say you're going to wait for the ambulance or something. The only guy who's smart enough to question that is Frankie. And Mike, you're going to distract him. Once the stuff is loaded, Robbie, Wayne and T.J. will get in the truck and get the hell out of there. Joe, you call Mike and then you guys get out of there as well."

"What are you going to be doing?" Wayne asks.

"I'll be keeping an eye on everything. I'm the wild card. Trust me."

Well, we've trusted him so far. But when you're stealing the stolen possessions of Chechen gangsters from a thug and his henchmen, the term *wild card* doesn't inspire confidence. Stoner isn't concerned. He rolls up the paper and looks around the room.

"Everything goes into action tomorrow night," Stoner says, "Be ready."

Everyone looks at each other, awkwardly. Wayne scratches his neck.

"Feels like we ought to have a drink or something," he says, "It's what The Rat Pack would do."

T.J. waves his hands, frantically. "No, no. I'd have to wash out all the glasses and re-mark the liquor bottles. And there's still a chance Hunter would find out."

Mike looks at me and mutters: "Yeah, we can't exactly pull off The Rat Pack."

***

The first difficulty I run across, as befits anyone walking into a life-or-death situation, is what to wear. I'm not sure if I'm supposed to go with the formal gangster look one finds in *The Godfather* (I'm a fedora short of making that work) or the more casual *Sopranos* look. (In which case, I'd have to buy a tracksuit.) Ultimately, I go with a cross between the two, throwing a black sport coat over a button up shirt and jeans. Thankfully, Mike's gone with the same look.

"You talked to this guy yet?" I ask, pulling my Saturn away from Mike's building.

"Yeah. When I set up the meeting. Sounds a little gruff. But then, it's not like he's in a people business." He checks his reflection in the window. "Do we have the truck?"

"Robbie called and said they were able to steal it from his uncle. We're still on track."

"For better or worse. But almost certainly worse."

The Iron Gate Bar and Lounge (more bar than lounge, it seems) is on the north end of Rice Street, near Larpenteur Avenue. As shitpile neighborhoods go, this isn't the worst one in St. Paul, but it's in the running. I find a parking space near the front door. Mike takes a quick breath.

"All right, let's get into character," he says.

Mike leads the way inside. A set of rickety steps brings us up to the bar proper. It isn't much to look at it. There's a long bar along the back wall with a cracked mirror and various dusty bottles of booze behind it. Most of the tables are high-tops with seventy-five percent of the legs even. The hardwood floors were swept promptly at Ronald Reagan's inauguration. The lighting is dank, but you can still see the dust particles floating in the air. There are four or five knuckle-dragging patrons and I'm guessing they're all on Frankie Ace's payroll.

Frankie himself is at a high-top halfway across the floor. At first glance, he could pass for a member of our gang. He's in his early thirties, thin, with slicked-back black hair. His nose is bent and his chin is weak, but the keen look in his eyes gives him a formidable appearance. He glances up from his phone and gives us a nod of recognition, but no smile.

"Denny Laine?" he asks.

"The same," Mike says.

"Have a seat."

Frankie shows no suspicion about Mike or his assumed name. Mike loosens a button on his suitcoat and sits down. Frankie sets his cell phone aside, folds his hands on the table.

"What do you got for me?" he asks.

"I understand you're the man I talk to if I want to move some stuff."

Frankie inclines his head by way of acknowledgement. "I have been known to distribute peace and tranquility at reasonable rates to deserving clientele."

"As long as the deserving clientele aren't the rightful owners?"

Frankie chuckles. "Rightful owner. What does that even mean? Some guy's driving in a lane of the freeway, does he own the thing? No, he's using it for his own convenience. Everything else in life? Same thing. That's my philosophy. *You* got one?"

"Make money, get laid, leave a beautiful corpse."

"Works for me. Let's do business."

Mike lays out a bullshit story about some stuff he came into when a colleague was sent to Stillwater. He needs to move it and was told Frankie Ace was the man. Frankie seems flattered but doesn't gush with gratitude. The dude is all business.

Before Frankie gives him a response, though, the door to the bar opens. I glance back, expecting to see the actor Stoner hired. Instead, I see a tall woman with poofed-up blonde hair and more makeup than strictly necessary. She wears a blue dress that stops just below hoo-hah level and accentuates the ample curves in her body. She balances carefully on her high heels and flutters her fingers toward Frankie.

"Hey baby," she says, her voice bubbly and high-pitched.

Frankie gives her a small wave. "Hey Joy. Wait for me at the bar, would you, babe?"

"Sure thing."

Joy sashays to the bar, drawing admiring looks from the troglodytes. The effect on Mike, though, is more pronounced. His body jackknifes and he tosses a spoon he'd been holding. He gives Frankie an apologetic nod and leans over to retrieve the spoon. As he does, he draws me into a whispered conversation.

"Holy shit snacks," he says, "I know that broad."

"What?"

"I know her."

"No, I'm back on *broad*. Are Sammy and Dean-o waiting for us down at the Sands?"

Mike gives my arm a sharp rap with the back of his hand. "You want to focus, please? I'm telling you I dated this woman."

"How long?"

"About three hours. An hour longer than needed, really. And she didn't handle the breakup too well. I'm assuming. I disconnected my home phone and changed cell phone carriers. Point is: this chick could recognize me. And if she does, our little swindle is going up in smoke."

Frankie raps his knuckles on the table. "You guys got a problem or are we gonna do business?"

Mike turns back to the table, looking like he'd just as soon as hide under it as transact business. But he puts on a determinedly cheerful face.

"Sorry," he says, "Trouble with the hired help. You know how it is."

Frankie throws his head toward the troglodytes near the bar. "I do. Believe me."

They go back to talking business. Mike throws furtive looks toward Joy. She enjoys a fruity cocktail and seems blissfully unaware of Mike's presence. My phone buzzes in my pocket. I sneak a look at it. It's Robbie.

Truck's here. So's Hunter.

Holy shit. T.J.'s wife is on the scene? My thumb goes into overdrive as I send a message back to Robbie.

What the hell is she doing here?

She thinks T.J. is cheating on her. You need to get out here.

Before I can send Robbie an answer, Frankie's taken notice of me. "Your boy seems a little distracted."

Mike turns to me, thoroughly annoyed. I hand him the phone and nod toward Frankie.

"Sorry, Mr. Ace," I say.

"Just call me Frankie. Ace ain't my real last name."

"No?"

"No. You think they had Aces on the fucking *Mayflower?*" He focuses on Mike. "This gonna be a problem?"

Mike's eyes bug out like a bullfrog's. He returns the phone to me, his back turned slightly to Frankie. He's barely able to disguise the pants-shitting panic on his face.

"Never a problem," he says, "Just need a second." Mike turns to me. "You remember that thing out in the car?"

I have no idea what he's talking about. "That thing?"

"Yeah, the thing."

"In the car."

"The car. Yes.

Mike looks ready to burst a blood vessel. He flicks his eyes toward the door. It suddenly dawns on me.

"The car!" I say, "Yes, of course. The car."

I start toward the door, but Frankie's voice stops me. "Hang on a sec." He snaps his fingers at the troglodytes. "Hey Billy! Walk this guy out to his car, would you?"

The tallest of troglodytes heads my direction. He's a beefy guy whose chest looks ready to burst out of his black t-shirt. He narrows his eyes as he looks at me.

"Sure thing, Frankie," Billy says.

I'm wondering if *Walk him out to his car* is slang for making sure I don't come back. Billy's beady eyes are firmly on me. Mike returns his focus to Frankie.

"Should we get back to it?" Mike says.

I start toward the door, Billy right behind me. I only get a few steps when I hear a voice coming from the bar.

"Joe Davis!" Joy shouts, "You lousy son of a bitch!"

I stop and look back. Joy has gotten off the bar stool. She's gripping her drink glass so hard, it might explode. Her eyes are wide and hateful. I'm trying to figure out what I did. Joy points at Mike.

"Joe Davis, you lousy son of a bitch!" she says, "You screwed me and didn't call!"

I look to Mike. He says out of the corner of his mouth: "I might have told her I was you."

Great. Like there aren't enough women in this city cursing my name. For the moment, though, there's the matter of Mike's cover and the way it's currently being blown. Frankie stares hard at Mike.

"Joe Davis?" he says, "What the fuck is a Joe Davis?"

Before Mike can answer, Joy stalks over to the table and slams her drink glass down. "Frankie, I want you to kill this son of a bitch."

Joy puts her hands on her hips. Mike looks ready to dive under the table. I hope the infarction I'm about to suffer doesn't blow our cover before Joy can.

Speaking of infarctions, the door opens and a guy comes in. He's half-a-head taller than me and has a rather hefty mid-section spilling out of his tan suitcoat. His face is red and crinkled with pain. He's sweating and his breath comes in gasps. One large mitt is clutching his chest.

"Help me," he says, his voice both deep and weak at the same time.

He collapses over the railing and through a table. Joy screams. Frankie slides his chair away from the table. Mike and I are frozen in place.

"CPR!" Joy says, "Anybody know CPR?"

Absolutely nobody responds to that. Stoner's actor has done his job. I need to do mine. I run toward the door.

"I'll get help," I say.

I bolt out the door. Unfortunately, Billy the goon follows me. I have to lose this guy. I look down the alley to the back of the bar. The gate is visible from where I'm standing. The sounds of an argument are audible. Son of a bitch. In all the excitement, I forgot about T.J.'s wife being here. The shouting not only gets my attention, but Billy's as well.

"The fuck's going on down there?" Billy asks.

I shake my head. "No idea."

Billy heads down the alley. This time *I'm* following *him*. When we get to the gate, I'm greeted by the sight of a confab involving Robbie, T.J.'s wife and another of Frankie's henchmen. None of them look up as Billy approaches.

"What the fuck is going on?" Billy asks.

Robbie glances briefly at Billy, but immediately goes back to T.J.'s wife. The henchman is visibly relieved to see Billy on scene.

"You gotta do something," the henchman says, "This woman here showed up, yelling and screaming about her husband. I don't know what the hell is going on."

"Who's her husband?" Billy asks.

"Some guy named T.J."

Yep, I've got front row seats to the screwing of this particular pooch. Meanwhile, the situation does a half-gainer from the frying pan to the fire.

"Who's this guy?" Billy asks, pointing at Robbie.

The henchman looks over, as if noticing Robbie for the first time. "No idea. Maybe he's this T.J. guy."

But the opportunity to ask isn't about the materialize. Mrs. T.J. is dominating the conversation and using most of the oxygen supply in the general area.

"I want to know where T.J. is," she says, "He said he was going to talk to your uncle, Robbie. But he's not there."

"How do you know that?" Robbie asks.

"I followed him! You think I don't know what's going on?"

Bullshitting isn't necessarily Robbie's strong suit, but he gives it a shot. "What, uh, what makes you think he's cheating on you?"

"Oh, you think I don't know what goes on with T.J.? The time he spends in the basement. The way he keeps looking at his phone. The way he's so quick to close down his laptop and erase his browser history? And tonight, he lies about going to see your uncle. Why would he do that, Robbie?"

Robbie's lips flap as he tries to sputter out an explanation. He's silly enough to think he can take on T.J.'s wife and live. Fortunately, Frankie's idiot crew decides to intervene.

"Hey lady," Billy says, "You need to move it along."

Mrs. T.J. turns to Billy. Fire's about to come shooting out of her eyes. Even Robbie has the sense to back away. T.J.'s wife speaks very, very slowly.

"What…did…you…say…to…me?"

Sadly, Billy doesn't read the situation. "I said you need to move it on down the line. This is a place of business, not— what was it?—Melrose Place. Take it back home to the kids."

I should turn and run; get as far away from the blast radius as possible. But there's a morbid curiosity. I've never seen anyone ripped limb from limb. Still, the delay in dealing with this is making our night *more* rather than *less* complicated.

I'll confess it's a relief when Stoner shows up.

Stoner's got a certain calm (or at least he's doing an admirable job of faking it) that the rest of us don't. He steps over to Billy and claps him on the shoulder.

"Looks like you got a situation here," Stoner says.

Billy inclines his head, agreeing, then shoots at look at Stoner. "Who the hell are you?"

"I'm Stoner. Nice to meet you."

"Um, okay. Nice to meet you, too. Stoner."

"Appears to be a problem with the young lady."

Billy shrugs. "Says she's looking for her husband. Some guy named T.J."

"Yeah, that'll happen. You gonna let her slap you around like this?"

"Well, it's…wha…what do you think I should do about it?"

Stoner shrugs. "I don't know. It's totally up to you. Guys look to you to make decisions. They need to know you have their backs. Unless a really, really angry woman comes along. Then I guess they're on their own."

Billy throws a look at Stoner, who gives him nothing in return. He doesn't read anything unfriendly in what Stoner said, but he's clearly stung by it. He marches over to T.J.'s wife.

"Last time I'm telling you, sweetie," Billy says, "Run along hom—"

And that's as much as Billy gets out before a thunderous uppercut separates his brain from consciousness. He crumbles to the pavement like someone clipped a marionette's strings. The henchman drops the keys to the gate and runs down the alley, never to be seen again. T.J.'s wife stands over Billy's carcass, her cheeks puffing and her fingers forming claws. There's half a chance she's about to recreate the final scene of *The Day of the Locust* right in front of us. Stoner's voice stops her.

"Hunter! May I call you Hunter?"

"No!"

"Hunter, listen to me: I appreciate your willingness to test T.J.'s faithfulness—after all, what is faith without proof?—and to beat the living hell out of a large man in the process. But you're missing the bigger picture here."

T.J.'s wife downgrades her look from murderous to annoyed. I hope my faith in Stoner is justified. We're one case of "mansplaining" away from a mass murder.

"What is the big picture, Stoner?" she asks, "What are you even doing here?"

"I've been asking myself that same thing. Here's the deal: T.J. is going *way* out of his way to plan the greatest birthday present you've ever received."

"My birthday isn't for three months yet."

Stoner waves his hands around. "So you can see the size of the thing he's planning. If he's had to start this far out."

Mrs. T.J.'s claws retract and she steps away from Billy's possible-corpse. She folds her arms across her ample chest and her mouth tightens. Stoner's talked her all the way down to skeptical. If he pulls this off, he has my eternal gratitude. I might even buy him a beer.

"How do I know you're not covering for him?" she asks.

"You think we'd go to this much trouble just to cover for T.J.? If he's so foolish as to throw away his beautiful wife and family for some cheap, but no doubt spectacular, nookie, we're not going to defend him. Right, Robbie?"

Robbie, who's been hiding behind a dumpster, pokes his head out. He's got the same startled expression one gets when discovered on the toilet. He looks from Stoner to T.J.'s wife and clears his throat.

"Um, yeah. That's, that's exactly what I was saying."

"You see?" Stoner says, "Robbie always talks about your marriage to T.J. and the devotion to it and his own jealousy. Or words to that effect."

"Sure," Robbie says, "Something like that."

"Can I ask you to let us get back to this thing?" Stoner asks, "If I promise to get T.J. back, safe and chaste, to you?"

T.J.'s wife tries to decide between believing Stoner or pulling his larynx out through his earhole. Finally, she steps back, though she keeps her eyes on Stoner.

"You guarantee he's not cheating on me?" she asks.

"Absolutely," Stoner says.

"Good. Because if he is and I find out about it? After I'm done with him, I'm going to come for you. And after I'm done with *you*, you're going to be able to accomplish every guy's dream of blowing yourself."

"That sounds swell," Stoner says.

T.J.'s wife gives Stoner the *Who Farted?* face. But she walks away, disappearing down the alley. Stoner brushes his hands.

"Well, our work here is nearly done," he says, "Robbie, you can stop cowering in the shadows now."

Robbie pops out, trying to regain his swagger. "I wasn't cowering. I was lying in wait."

Stoner nods. "In a puddle of your own urine. Clever. She never would have suspected."

"Fuck you, Stoner!"

The van starts down the alley, getting us all back on track. Robbie retrieves the keys and opens the gate. Stoner and I drag Billy out of the way, allowing the truck into the enclosed area. Everyone works like hell to get the stuff loaded on the truck. Nothing's too heavy or difficult to move. I've never been particularly good at packing, but the other guys have played enough Tetris to master the process. Within about five minutes (and at least thirty instances of T.J. saying, "C'mon, you guys, hurry up") we've got the damn thing loaded.

"I wonder what's happening inside," Robbie says, as we hop off the back of the truck.

We get our answer in the form of two troglodytes coming out the backdoor. They get one look at us and freeze like their mom caught them masturbating. One of them points at us and shouts, "What the fuck?"

Stoner looks at the guys and says, "Hi there. Did you get Frankie's message?"

The troglodyte is stopped cold by thinky pain. "Frankie didn't send me no message."

Stoner clucks his tongue. "My point exactly."

"What fucking point?"

"You just said it yourself. When you used the double-negative. Frankie didn't send you no message. The *no*s cancel each other out. Therefore, Frankie sent you a message."

The troglodyte's eyes narrow as he thinks. "What the fuck are you talking about?"

"Nothing, really," Stoner says, "I'm just distracting you while my friend Wayne sneaks up behind you."

In the second it takes for the troglodytes to figure that out, Wayne has laid them both out with a baseball bat. He tosses the bat aside and runs back to the truck.

"For the record," Wayne says, "I didn't know what the fuck you were talking about, either."

The truck pulls into the alley. Stoner hangs back and walks with me. I throw my head back toward the truck.

"You aren't going with them?" I ask.

"No. There's half a chance they'll get arrested or shot. I try to avoid that kind of thing."

"Where are you going then?" I ask.

"Any place that will give me plausible deniability."

I grab Stoner's arm. "What about Mike?"

"He's a big boy. He'll find a way out. Unless he's dead, in which case, he's already found a way out. See you around."

Stoner walks away, whistling. I follow the truck out of the gate and watch it round on to Rice. I head back for the bar. I'm almost at the front door when Mike comes flying out and nearly runs me over.

"You're going to want to get out of here," he says, "Or we're fucking dead."

"Frankie figured it out?"

"Good guess."

Mike pushes past me and hauls ass to the Saturn. He gets behind the wheel, clearly not trusting my driving skills. (No objection here. We need our best, most reckless man on this.) Mike's just turned the key when someone else comes flying out of the bar. Joy moves with an alacrity one doesn't normally associate with a woman in high heels. She dives into the backseat. Mike doesn't stop, though he does take the time to be annoyed.

"What the hell are you doing?" he says.

"I'm getting the fuck out of here," she says, "My job is done."

"What job?" I ask.

"To distract Frankie," Joy says.

Mike does a U-turn and shoots past the bar. Again, the door to the place opens and Frankie comes out, followed by two of his troglodytes. They hop into a nearby car. I look toward our new passenger.

"Joy, what are you—?" I say.

"My name's not Joy," she says, "It's Denise."

It takes a second for it to hit me. "Denise? You're the one who screwed over Wayne."

Denise looks offended. "Wayne screwed himself. And if that's what he's telling people, he'll be doing a lot of that in the future."

"Wait," I say, "You were there to distract Frankie? What about the actor Stoner hired?"

Denise sticks her poofy head into the front seat. "Stoner's actor cancelled on him, so he hired me. Don't ask how the hell he found me. He said I needed to help Wayne."

Mike glances into the rearview mirror. "Then who the hell was the guy in the bar? The heart attack guy?"

Denise shrugs. "He was a guy having a heart attack."

Here's hoping Frankie's goons saved him. They don't appear to be doing much for us, beyond being in hot pursuit. Mike comes right up behind the van and that's as far as we can go. Frankie and his guys keep coming.

"Do we pass the van?" I ask.

"We'd be leaving them to the mercy of those guys," he says. "So yeah, it's tempting."

Mike swings into the other lane, maybe giving the passing-the-van idea a test run. We almost go nose-to-nose with an oncoming car. Denise screams. So does Mike. He throws the Saturn back behind the moving van. I hear firecrackers. Then realize those are gunshots.

Both Denise and I drop down. Mike moves the Saturn in a zig zag pattern to avoid the bullets. Things seem to be going smooth until Mike shouts: "Ah, fuck my mother!"

I pop my head up. The van has narrowly avoided a bit of road construction (which is as rare as mosquitos during a Minnesota summer). Mike is heading straight for it. The Saturn swerves. I'm nearly thrown into Mike's lap. Somehow, Mike clears the construction.

Unfortunately, so do Frankie and his guys. Up ahead, the moving van weaves through a couple of cars. No idea how the hell T.J. did it. It's like a herd of buffalo went through a turnstile. Mike and Frankie follow. More shots. I drop down again. Denise screams again.

My phone buzzes. Who the fuck would be calling me now? I scoop it up. It's a text message. From Stoner.

Tell Mike to slow down.

"Stoner wants you to slow down," I say.

"Why?" he says.

"Mike, we're in the middle of a highspeed chase with some fucking gangsters. You think I'm going to play Twenty Questions over text? Just fucking slow down!" Mike looks unsure, so I add: "He's gotten us this far."

Frankly, *this far* isn't as far from death as I'd prefer. But Mike takes his foot off the gas. It creates a little distance from the moving van. And a lot of closeness with Frankie and his crew. The Saturn gets a love tap. Mike fights to maintain control. The Saturn stays on course. A shot comes through the back window.

And then we hear sirens behind us.

I look back and see a cop car positioned behind Frankie's car. My phone buzzes. Again, it's from Stoner.

Pull over.

"He wants you to pull over," I say.

Mike looks uncertain. He's not a big fan of cops. But Frankie hasn't endeared himself to us, either. "I hope Stoner knows what he's doing," Mike says.

He and Frankie both pull over. One cop goes to Frankie's window while the other, a balding, mustachioed dude getting thick through the middle, comes to the Saturn. Mike fumbles for his driver's license. The cop doesn't seem particularly interested.

"You realize you got a taillight out?" he asks.

"No," Mike says, "I'm not sure how that happened."

Denise tries to fix her hair. "Must have been all those gunshots." Mike and I look at her. Denise shrugs. "What? Like they couldn't see the front and back windows?"

She's right. Both windows are spider-webbed with bullet holes (and it's not like bullet holes look like anything other than bullet holes). The cop gives it a flip of his hand.

"Looks like you got enough problems with the window," he says, "Hope insurance will cover it."

Mike nods, vacantly. "Uh, yeah. Me, too."

"Good luck with that," the cop says. He looks toward his partner, a dude in his twenties who appears to spend most of his off hours in the gym. "Hey Freddie, how's it going?"

"Damnedest thing," Freddie says, "They've got a taillight out."

This is followed by the sound of breaking glass, signaling, I'm guessing, a newly-broken taillight on Frankie's car. The cop talking to us shakes his head.

"You better ask them to step out of the car," he says, taking the gun out of the holster, "And surrender their weapons and get on the ground."

Frankie and his guys get out of the car. The cops are on them faster than I (or they) would have expected. A second later, Frankie's crew is on the ground and the cop strolls back to us.

"You folks have a nice night," the cop says, "Tell Stoner we said hi."

There's a stunned silence before Mike gets it together. The Saturn pulls back on to Rice Street and hauls ass out of there. Denise leans into the front seat.

"What the hell was that?" she asks.

Mike takes a brief glance in the mirror. "That? That was a clean getaway."

***

The Tav is, as always, the place we celebrate. Mitch, the owner, finds us a booth near the back, far away from the customers and the breakables. We start with a round of shots and quickly move on to pitchers. Thankfully, I've got the option of staggering home to my own bed. Which I'll still be alive to sleep in.

Robbie is the first to raise his glass. "This hurts like a son of a bitch," he says, "But here's to Stoner. He fucking pulled this off."

Everyone drinks to that. Stoner sips his beer, nonchalant. Just another day in the life. But the rest of us are in a mood to cut loose. We've survived and helped out an old friend. With the return of the stuff (accomplished before we hit The Tav), Wayne is home and dry. Not to mention bombed and staggered.

Wayne leans toward Stoner, bleary-eyed. "That was a hell of a thing with the cops. How did you pull that off?"

"Cops are like anybody," Stoner says, "They make an occasional mistake and need someone to help them out. When that happens, they might feel they owe that person a favor. And if *you* are that person, you just need to call that favor in."

Wayne blinks, looking like someone just explained the Theory of Relativity to an ermine. "So…you just, uh, bought those cops off?"

"In a manner of speaking, yeah."

Mike gently moves Wayne out of the way. "Speaking of buying someone off. What was up with Denise? She could have gotten us all killed."

Stoner bats the idea away. "I didn't know you two had been a thing. Really, Mike, you need to be more discreet."

I take up a position on the other side of Stoner. "What about the heart attack guy?"

"Lucky break," Stoner says. Seeing the look on my face, he adds: "I called 9-1-1. And I checked with the hospital.

The guy's going to be fine. Well, as fine as a guy with a serious heart condition can be."

Wayne tries to pour himself another beer. He sloshes a lot of it on the table. "No way I can keep working for Icon. Those dudes are nasty."

Stoner smoothly takes the pitcher and pours himself a refill. "I may be able to help you out there. Part of my deal with Denise was that I help her find new work. I've got a contact at an electronics company. I found some work for Denise in the clerical department. I might be able to help you out as well."

Wayne is as close to tears as I've ever seen him (or ever hope to see him). He claps a hand on Stoner's shoulder. "You are the fucking best, Stoner. I love you, man."

Stoner returns the gesture. "I love you, too, Wayne. We'll discuss my finder's fee later."

I should have figured Stoner's help would come at a price. Oh well. Unfortunately, not everyone's in a mood to celebrate. T.J. stares glumly into an almost-full beer. I snap my fingers to get his attention.

"What's the story?" I ask, "It's a party, right?"

T.J. pushes his beer glass around. "Yeah. Except I've got two months to figure out a giant surprise for Hunter."

"You'll do it," I say, filled with booze and bonhomie (but mostly booze), "Everything will be fine."

T.J. is not comforted. "Easy for you to say. You're not going to be sleeping on the couch if this gets screwed up."

Once again, Stoner comes to the rescue. "Not a worry, Teej. I can plan the whole thing for you. Just need a weekend to focus."

T.J. looks like he's been thrown a lifeline. "Seriously?"

"Absolutely. We can discuss my planning fee later."

T.J. gives Stoner a small toast. We order another couple pitchers. I can see some cabs in our future. Meantime, Wayne slaps his mug on the table.

"I might have an idea," he says, "This electronics stuff? There might be a little money to be made on the side. All sorts of spare parts hanging around. I find a way to get that stuff moved and, Stoner, you might get your finder's fee back sooner than you think."

I look at Mike, who's nothing short of chagrined. "What do we do?" I ask.

Mike shrugs. "We could kill him."

I shake my head. "No, give him a little bit. He'll probably get that job done on his own."

DEATH AND THE GENTLEMAN'S GENTLEMAN

From the Diary of Reginald Squigglesworth, gentleman's gentleman
15 July

Three days now and no change to Master Joseph's condition. He is still in the grip of what he refers to as a "summer cold." While he remains attentive regarding feedings and litter box maintenance, his strength has clearly been sapped. He spent much of the afternoon lying upon the davenport with an afghan blanket wrapped about his person. On these occasions, I feel it best to take up position nearby, lest my assistance be required. Leonard, however, chooses to approach the master and burrow under the blanket. This has only resulted in Master Joseph ejecting him from the arrangement on multiple occasions.

For not the first time in our acquaintance, Leonard has disappointed me.

The manor was somewhat drowsy in the early part of this afternoon, but, as always, perfectly shipshape. This, sadly, was disturbed by Master Joseph's acquaintance from downstairs.

Mr. Lars entered, as is his custom, without knocking. While this did not perturb Leonard, it startled Master Joseph. (He's accustomed to these disturbances from Mr. Lars, so I have to assume his senses were dulled by the ague.) I leapt to a protective position on the main chair, lest Mr. Lars get the impression he was welcomed to stay.

He made his way into the kitchen and retrieved a bottle of lemonade from the icebox. "Still under the weather, brother?"

Master Joseph sat up on the davenport and kept the afghan wrapped around him. "Buried under it."

"Sorry to hear that. Summer colds are the worst. Absolute misery."

Mr. Lars took a seat at the breakfast bar. I was dismayed by his obvious intention to stay, but I said nothing and showed less. A gentleman's gentleman must know his place. Mr. Lars finished most of his lemonade in one drink and made a spectacle wiping his brow.

"I don't have it easy, either," Mr. Lars said, "I've been helping the Anchor sisters get moved out."

"I was wondering what all that crashing and banging was about. I didn't know they were moving."

"It came pretty much out of the blue. I mean, who the hell moves in the middle of the month? *And* there's somebody moving in there tomorrow."

"In the middle of the month?"

"This is what I'm saying."

From the snatches of conversation I've overheard during my time with Master Joseph, I have deduced that the Anchor sisters occupy the dwelling across the hall from Mr. Lars. Their names, I believe, are Gladys and Irene (one likes to stay informed but does not wish to pry). They are between the ages of eight and ten (fifty to sixty in human years) and have, in the opinions of some, a profound distaste for Mr. Lars. (I do not know this as a fact and do not wish to engage in idle gossip.) Still, they have occupied the dwelling for such a length of time that their sudden departure seems untoward. Particularly since, of late, Mr. Lars has been on what passes for his best behavior.

"They give you a reason?" Master Joseph asked.

Mr. Lars finished his lemonade with a loud smack of his lips. "They just said they're moving in with their sister in California."

"There's a third Anchor sister?"

"At least. I get the idea it's a pretty big family. And at least one brother. Gladys threatened to call him and complain about me. Ex-Navy. Vicious S.O.B. I'm told."

"But they didn't say *you* were the reason they were leaving?"

Mr. Lars seemed befuddled. "Why would I be?"

Master Joseph had the tact to not pursue that line of inquiry. Instead, he gave himself over to a brief coughing fit. Ever present, I placed myself on the master's lap in the event he needed assistance. He asked nothing of me, but the method in which he scratched my ears conveyed his approval.

"What about the guy moving in?" the master asked, "You know anything about him?"

Mr. Lars shook his head. "Not a thing."

"Really? You're the superintendent."

"The paperwork is handled by management. I just do the maintenance and help out where I'm needed. I got the guy's name and when he's moving in. That's it. I'll tell you: he's lucky. Last week, management called to ask if there were any openings in the building. I told them no. Boom. Two days later, the Anchor sisters are giving their notice."

There was a contemplative way in which Master Joseph wiped his nose. "You know the new guy's name?"

"Neil Hanna. And that's about all I know. Except he doesn't need my help moving in."

The master said nothing, but I could discern from the look on his face that he regards *help* to be a rather specious term for what Mr. Lars provides. He adjusted his position on the davenport, letting me know I was no longer needed. As such, I took up a new position near Leonard at the arch windows. Mr. Lars left his lemonade glass on the counter, paining myself and, I'm sure, the master. He moved to the front door with that peculiar sashay of his.

"I don't suppose you can give me a hand?" Mr. Lars asked.

Master Joseph responded with another brief coughing fit. "Lars, I barely have the energy to feed myself. I don't know how the hell I'm going to get a column written. There's no way I can move chintzes and knick-knacks and tea cozies and whatever the hell else the Anchor Sisters have down there."

Mr. Lars raised a hand as he opened the front door. "Not a problem, brother. Get well. Plenty of vitamin C. Maybe a shot of bourbon."

"Bourbon? Will that help?"

"Does it ever hurt?"

With that perspective granted, Mr. Lars removed himself from the apartment. Master Joseph looked wistfully toward the drinks cabinet but opted to remain on the davenport.

I thank heaven for small favors.

16 July

Another day and the master's ague has not abated. He was able to take up position at his desk, though the afghan remained wrapped about his person and his typing was reduced to aimlessly picking at the keyboard with one finger (a method he describes as "hunt and peck"). I was again close at hand, frequently urging the master to rest himself. He responded to these attempts by saying, "Sorry, Squigs. Up against a deadline."

Though I have no intimate knowledge of it, the master's progress appeared to be sluggish at best. By the middle of the day, I wasn't sure that he hadn't fallen asleep in his chair. I was about to check on him when there was a disturbance downstairs. Nothing greatly concerning, but a certain banging which indicated activity. It seemed to rouse Master Joseph, who rose from his chair and opened the front door to check on the matter. I positioned myself at his side.

A gentleman appeared to be moving into the dwelling recently vacated by the Anchor sisters. He was attempting to get a rather sizeable desk chair through the front door at the time of our arrival. Though the struggle did not show him in his best light, he appeared to be rather formidable. He was a few inches shorter than the master, but several human years older. Though he had a bit of a paunch (and what proper gentleman does not?) there still appeared to be a certain hardness about him. He had dark hair and a dark complexion. When he glanced up the stairs, a pair of blue, possibly malevolent eyes, were clearly visible. Master Joseph temporarily abandoned the afghan and started down the stairs.

"Hi there," the master said, "My name's Joe Davis. I'm your new upstairs neighbor."

The gentleman looked thoroughly nonplussed and grunted only, "Neil Hanna."

I could tell from the master's body language he was a bit thrown and yet he remained undaunted. "I'd shake your hand, but I've got a little bit of a—"

"That's fine."

"Can I give you a hand with the chair?"

"I got it. Thanks."

"Well, if you need—"

"I said I got it. All right?"

Master Joseph seemed uncertain as to a reply. He remained still while Mr. Hanna continued his struggle with the chair. The gentleman took notice of me standing at the top of the stairs but didn't appear to be at all pleased.

"That your cat?" Mr. Hanna asked.

Master Joseph saw me standing just outside the doorway. Instantly, I felt shame, as I know the master does not approve of either myself or Leonard leaving the grounds of the estate. Master Joseph took a step my direction and I retreated into the entryway. Rather than pursue me, the master turned to Mr. Hanna.

"Um, yeah, that's Squiggy," Master Joseph said.

"He one of these cats that wanders all over the building?"

"No, no. I usually don't let him out of the apartment."

"Good. I don't feed cats and I don't return them to their owners. You keep him out of my hair, okay?"

It took only a single look at Master Joseph's visage to see he was not pleased with this statement. After a few moments that could only be described as awkward, Master Joseph started back up the stairs.

"Um, if, uh, if you need anything," the master said, "I'll be right upstairs. I'm home most of the time."

Mr. Hanna's concentration remained on the chair. He said only: "Great."

I, for one, questioned the sincerity of that statement.

19 July

The master's cold is progressing and not for the better. He is now the possessor of a rather nasty cough in addition to his other ailments. He remains in a weakened state and continues to struggle with work.

Sadly, the issue of our new neighbor has similarly deteriorated. Not in the area of disturbances, as nothing has been heard from Mr. Hanna since his arrival a few days ago. The hindrance comes in the form of the obsession Mr. Lars has developed regarding Mr. Hanna. Earlier this evening, as Master Joseph struggled with his ague, Mr. Lars decided to pay a call. When he arrived, I was curled up at the master's feet, lest he need my assistance. Leonard made his way from the arch windows to the feet of Mr. Lars. (Though I do not take it upon myself to lecture him, there are times I wish Leonard had some pronounced good taste.)

"There's something up with that Hanna guy," Mr. Lars said, making his way to the refrigerator and helping himself to one of Master Joseph's fine ales.

"What makes you say that?" the master asked, not rising from the davenport.

"I've been keeping an eye on him. Believe me, something is hinky."

Master Joseph sat up on the davenport. "Can you cite any specific hinkiness?"

Mr. Lars scooped up Leonard and made his way to the adjoining chair. Leonard immediately made his home in Mr. Lars' lap. (Sigh.)

"There's barely any furniture in the place," Mr. Lars said, "I stopped over to see if he needed anything—"

"And to be nosey."

"A little of that. Yeah. But I got a look around. He has a TV, a mattress and a chair. That's it. I've seen squatters with more stuff."

Master Joseph didn't seem overly-concerned. "Maybe he's waiting on the rest of his stuff. He could be from out of town or something. Did you ask him about that?"

"I did. Have you tried talking to this guy? He's Johnny Tight-Lips himself. I don't think he uses more than five words in a sentence."

"I gathered that. I offered to help him move in, but he shut me down pretty quick."

Mr. Lars leaned forward in his chair, waving his bottle of ale and causing Leonard to hold on for dear life. "Yeah, well, I can understand that. You're known all over the building for being anti-social. But I have a reputation for being avuncular and loveable."

"Where did you hear this?"

"They say it to my face. People like to talk to me."

Master Joseph rolled his eyes and appeared as dismissive of Mr. Lars' claim as I was. "What else have you noticed?"

"I think he was breaking into Melissa Danen's place."

"Breaking in? Seriously? You didn't lead with that?"

"I have a sequential mind. Things have to go in a certain order."

Master Joseph seemed ready to upbraid Mr. Lars but was overcome by a coughing fit. He *did* manage several less-than-friendly gestures. For his part, Mr. Lars was frozen in position, allowing the master to have the floor.

When he finally recovered breath, Master Joseph said, "What do you mean he was breaking into Melissa Danen's place?" (I will confess to a feeling of anti-climax with such a simple question following the bronchial display.)

Mr. Lars set Leonard aside and began to pace the room. "I got home from having lunch with my buddy, Chuck. Y'know, I told you about that clown-themed restaurant we're planning?"

"The one where the *customers* dress as clowns?"

"That's the one. I think it's going to be big. It's—"

"But regarding the break-in?"

"Huh? Oh right, the break-in. Anyhoo, I'm coming up the backstairs and I'm about to pass Melissa's place, when I see this Hanna character sneaking out of it. He doesn't see me, so I back up and take a position where I can see everything."

"Sneaking? You sure he wasn't just leaving?"

Mr. Lars shook his head. "No chance. He was backing out, all sneaky-like. Making sure he re-locked the door. Then he left her deck and went back to his place."

"You didn't say anything to him?"

"You know me. I don't like to be a buttinski."

Strange. While I'm not entirely familiar with the term *buttinski*, it's the one most frequently used regarding Mr. Lars. Master Joseph clutched at the afghan.

"Okay, so the guy was coming out of Melissa's place," the master said, "Maybe he's, uh, involved with her. Or something."

Mr. Lars dismissed this with a flit of his hand. "No, they're not involved. Melissa's just getting out of a long-term relationship. She doesn't want to get involved with anyone."

"How do you know this?"

"I'm the superintendent. It's my business to know what's going on. You should see what I have on you."

Master Joseph let that pass without comment. I personally have witnessed many of Mr. Lars' gossip sessions and am aware he is a font of information regarding the goings on within the building. Apparently, his view of what is and is not his place as superintendent is something of a moving target.

"Let me guess," the master said, "You're not going to just ask this guy what he was doing at Melissa's place?"

"You've met him. I don't like asking how his day is going, let alone accuse him of anything."

Mr. Lars finished his ale and left the empty bottle on the counter rather than placing it in the recycling bin. Again. I feel for Master Joseph, whose pained look had nothing to do with his bronchial condition. Mr. Lars moved to the door and paused after opening it.

"Just keep an eye out, brother," he said, "This guy might be bad news. Building management should really be more careful about who they let in here."

"You don't say?" Master Joseph replied, in his driest tone.

Mr. Lars was oblivious to the sarcasm (as he frequently is). I, however, took the warning seriously. I moved further up the davenport and took up guard duty on the master's lap.

One can never be too careful.

20 July

A banner day today, as Master Joseph allowed me to accompany him to the storage unit in the basement of the building. The master was in search of an older book he wished to re-read and I lent him what assistance I could, though he seemed preoccupied with making sure I remained within the limits of the storage unit. (The master is fair but controlling.)

Master Joseph was locking the storage unit when Miss Danen emerged from her own unit, located on the other side of the basement. She stopped suddenly, let out a small gasp and dropped something she was holding.

Master Joseph held out a cautioning hand. "I'm sorry. Didn't mean scare you."

Miss Danen quickly scooped up the dropped item. "Don't apologize. It's just me. I guess I'm a little jumpy."

"This basement will do that do you."

We could have safely moved on, but the master chose to linger. It's entirely possible this was related to Miss Danen's physical appearance. She's petite, with long dark hair and very blue eyes. She had what appeared to be a nervous habit of tucking said hair behind her ears. While the wiles of the human female are lost on me, I have to confess being drawn to a certain vulnerability in the young lady.

The master gave her a small wave. "Joe Davis. I live up on the third floor."

The young lady returned it. "Melissa Danen. I've seen you around the building." She looked toward me and knelt down, offering her hand. "And who's this little guy?"

"That's Squiggy."

"Squiggy?"

"His brother Lenny is back up in the apartment."

She met this information with a light laugh. "Cute." She began scratching me behind the ears. A bit forward of her, but I felt denying her would be a social faux-pas. I may have purred, but only to be polite.

Master Joseph cleared his throat and said, "Sorry again about startling you."

Miss Danen ceased scratching my ears and stood up. "No, no. It's fine. Like I said, I've just been jumpy."

"Something making you nervous?"

"Um, no, it's just, just work stuff. Y'know. Really no big deal."

I would've liked to believe the young lady, but she was continually threading the object in question through her fingers and steadfastly refusing to make eye contact with Master Joseph. The item she had dropped was a silver necklace with a charm at the end. Some sort of paste diamond, if I don't miss my guess. After an awkward moment, the master wished her a good day and we started up the staircase leading from the basement. Miss Danen quickly went about locking her storage unit. Master Joseph paused on the stairs.

"If you need anything," he said, "I'm just up on the third floor, couple doors over."

Miss Danen didn't quite look toward us. "I appreciate it. Nice meeting you. You too, Squiggy."

I gave her a simple nod and the master and myself continued up the stairs. Master Joseph seemed troubled, but any train of thought he may have had was undone by a coughing fit.

Still, a banner day.

21 July

Miss Carol arrived early in the afternoon, bearing a pot of homemade chicken noodle soup. I've always found she brings a certain lightness to the manor, a better atmosphere than that created by Mr. Lars or Mr. Michael. Master Joseph, still ailing, was more than willing to accept the gift of the soup.

I took up a position on Miss Carol's lap as a show of hospitality. She displayed her appreciation by scratching my ears in a delicate manner. Master Joseph did his best to entertain, but seemed a tad preoccupied. When Miss Carol asked him about it, Master Joseph related the recent events, beginning with the arrival of Mr. Hanna. Miss Carol listened attentively.

"You don't know anything about this guy?" she asked.

"No. I'm guessing management knows, but they haven't shared anything with Lars."

"Why wouldn't they?"

"You've met Lars, right?"

Miss Carol sipped her overly-sweet coffee as she contemplated this. "But with all of this going on, it's at least worth checking out, isn't it?"

Master Joseph focused on his soup. "From what I understand, the building is owned by a group that has a bunch of properties around the Cities. They probably don't know any more about this guy than his name, application and financial information."

"What are you going to do?"

The master fetched the coffee pot from the kitchen and poured refills for both himself and Miss Carol. I often feel remiss in my duties when I cannot provide this service, but the pot is nearly my size. And I've not been gifted with the physical acumen to perform such activities. Still, I keep my shame to myself. Stiff upper lip and all.

"I don't know there's much I *can* do," he said, returning the pot to the kitchen, "I need to stay out of this guy's way."

"You think you can do it?"

"Avoiding people is my mission in life."

Master Joseph settled into the large chair. I sensed he and Miss Carol were ready to move on to more pleasant topics when the front door opened and Mr. Lars entered the manor.

"Something's going down," Mr. Lars said, "Melissa Danen's disappeared."

Master Joseph tossed aside his afghan while Miss Carol turned suddenly, dislodging me from her lap. I did not enjoy the disruption, but unlike Leonard, I hid my annoyance.

"Disappeared?" the master asked.

Mr. Lars paced the room as he spoke. "She didn't show up for work this morning. For some reason, she listed me as her emergency contact. They called me and I went over and checked her apartment. There's nobody there."

"Did she clear out?" Miss Carol asked.

"No. All of her stuff is still in the apartment, but her car's gone from the parking lot. I didn't see a suitcase or an athletic bag in the apartment, so she might have packed up a few clothes. Or she doesn't own any luggage."

"What adult doesn't own luggage?" Miss Carol said.

Mr. Lars stopped and focused on her. "I don't own luggage."

"What do you use when you go on vacation?"

"Shopping bags do the trick and I have no emotional investment in them."

Master Joseph waved his hands, trying to get the attention of the room. "Getting back to the point: do you have any other contact information for Melissa?"

Mr. Lars resumed pacing. "Her mother's in San Francisco. I called her, but she hadn't heard from Melissa. I didn't tell her anything else. I didn't want to worry her."

The master glared at him. "Yeah, you called her up and said her daughter's missing. I'm sure she's having cocktails on the lanai as we speak."

"Well, she promised to call me if she heard anything from Melissa."

Master Joseph rose and stepped toward the front door. "You mind if I take a look at Melissa's place?"

"I believe I did a rather thorough job," Mr. Lars said, "But if you really feel the need to check it out…" Master Joseph was out the door before the sentence could be finished.

Miss Carol was last out and left the door ajar. While I normally adhere to Master Joseph's dictum to remain in the manor unless obtaining his approval, I felt these were extraordinary circumstances. I tried to remind Leonard of this when he followed me out of the manor, but he was, as usual, incorrigible. I pursued the master and his associates to Miss Danen's residence. I did my best to keep them in sight, as I was not entirely sure of the route back to the manor. Master Joseph was looking over the residence when Leonard and I arrived.

"Nothing out of order," he said, "You sure she isn't playing hooky for the day?"

Mr. Lars waved his hands in denial. "She would have at least called into work. I think she's that responsible."

The master seemed on the verge of giving up the search. I took it upon myself to look over the room, not out of any lack of faith in Master Joseph, but merely in the spirit of being thorough. Miss Carol offered me a suspicious look. I'm sure she's aware of Master Joseph's policies restricting myself and Leonard the freedom of the building. Fortunately, she said nothing. Feeling the urgency of the situation, I leapt upon the desk. This brought my presence to Master Joseph's attention. Unfortunately, he seemed more annoyed than intrigued.

"Squiggy, what are you doing here?" he said, "Get off there."

Before I could reply, he ushered me off the desk with a gentle sweep of his arm. As he did so, something caught his attention. It was a slip of paper. He picked it up and read the contents aloud.

"*Vince M, now in town*," the master said, "What the hell does that mean?"

Mr. Lars shrugged. "Maybe her old boyfriend. Maybe she's with him."

"Really? You have a lot of ex's you'd skip work to hang out with?"

"Well, I have my share of—"

"Imagine you're someone normal."

"Oh, in that case, no. I don't."

Master Joseph continued to look over the desk but found no additional information he deemed useful. He finally left the residence, offering only a brief glance to Mr. Lars.

"Let me know if she turns up," he said.

"Hopefully safe and sound," Mr. Lars said.

The master sighed. "Yeah, that would be nice."

22 July

The master seemed pensive today. Clearly, the disappearance of Miss Danen was weighing on his mind. I remained close at hand, ready as always to assist. He made an aborted attempt to work on a column. A combination of his illness, as bad as ever, and his supreme distraction proved his undoing. He gave up and laid on the davenport.

He looked toward me and said, "Any ideas, Squiggs?"

I thought the next step to be rather obvious and told him so. He didn't react and for a moment I feared that he either disagreed or was willing to ignore me. However, he began to nod and rose from the davenport. Normally, the master is very careful in making sure neither Leonard nor myself have access to the hall. But he was clearly preoccupied and left the door ajar. Again, given the extraordinary circumstances, I felt it best to pursue him. His path took him one floor down, to Mr. Hanna's residence. I maintained a respectful distance but was at the ready if Mr. Hanna should turn ruffian. Personally, I had hoped Mr. Hanna would not respond to Master Joseph's knock. Sadly, this was not the case. He opened the door and appeared thoroughly annoyed at the interruption.

There was a rather awkward moment of silence and then Master Joseph said, "I was hoping we could have a chat."

"About what?" The hope Mr. Hanna would remain civil was becoming somewhat remote.

"Um, Melissa Danen."

Mr. Hanna remained froze in position. His stare was disquietingly penetrating. "What about her?"

Master Joseph certainly seemed disquieted but was undeterred. "She, uh, she disappeared. We think."

"Who's 'we'?"

"Me and the management."

"The management?"

"Well, the superintendent."

Mr. Hanna looked repulsed. "That idiot?"

"Yeah, that one. Listen, I'm just wondering if she said anything to you? Anything that might give you an idea where she was going?"

"Why would you think I'd know anything?"

Master Joseph cleared his throat. "The, uh, the super thinks he saw you coming out of her place a few days ago. I thought, maybe, you knew her. Know her. I mean, there's no indication that something terrible has happened to her. Yet."

"What the fuck are you babbling about?"

The master was not thrown by Mr. Hanna's vulgarity. "Did you know Melissa Danen?"

"No."

Mr. Hanna started to close the door, but the master blocked its path. Unfortunately, he used his own body for this task and the door made rather unfortunate contact with his testicles. Master Joseph kept his foot in the doorway, even as the rest of him clearly suffered.

"Get out," Mr. Hanna said.

I moved closer to Master Joseph, ready to offer what support I could. However, something caught my attention, momentarily distracting me. The master must have spotted it as well, as his head quickly turned toward it. The necklace which had once been in Miss Danen's possession was now sitting on the breakfast bar of Mr. Hanna's dwelling. Master Joseph pointed toward it.

"Where did you get that?" he asked.

Mr. Hanna, however, chose to ignore the question. He placed a hand on Master Joseph's chest and moved him back into the hallway. I retreated halfway up the stairs. I briefly considered engaging Mr. Hanna in fisticuffs, but the absence of my claws made me reconsider. Mr. Hanna closed the door behind him and stooped slightly so his face was fully even with Master Joseph's.

"Nothing in my apartment is any of your business," Mr. Hanna said, "And nothing I do and no one I talk to is any of your business. You and that idiot super leave me the fuck alone. We clear?"

"We very clear."

"Good." With that, Mr. Hanna returned to his dwelling and slammed the door behind him.

Mr. Lars opened the door of his apartment and took in the scene. He appeared thoroughly annoyed. "Will you keep it down?" he said, "I got company in here."

Master Joseph slowly, painfully, made his way up the stairs. He said nothing about my being outside the manor. I remained close at hand. Clearly, the master needed my assistance.

23 July

We've reached the end of the third day and still no sign of Miss Danen. The matter weighs on Master Joseph. Miss Carol came by to visit and did her best to engage the master in conversation. Sadly, she received very little response. Finally, her patience wore thin (and I can't say that I blame her).

"Am I boring you?" she said, in a clearly annoyed tone.

Miss Carol was sitting on the davenport while Master Joseph was reclined in his desk chair, staring out the window. Leonard remained in his usual slothful position near the arch windows. It was left to me to entertain Miss Carol and I was duly rewarded with a head scratching. The master turned slightly toward Miss Carol.

"What was that?" he said, his tone more distracted than usual.

"Am I boring you?"

"No, that's Lars' job."

Miss Carol felt it necessary to remove me from her lap and approach Master Joseph. "What is up? Is this about that neighbor of yours?"

"It's about a couple neighbors of mine," the master replied. He proceeded to tell Miss Carol the entire story regarding Miss Danen, her disappearance and the strange translocation of her necklace to Mr. Hanna's apartment. At this, Miss Carol's objections faded. She lapsed into a thoughtful silence of her own.

"Have the police been called?" she asked.

"Lars just called them this morning," Master Joseph said, "Without any evidence of foul play, we had to wait forty-eight hours before the police would consider her missing. Lars stayed up the whole damn forty-eight hours, hoping she'd come home."

"He didn't need to do that."

"That's what I told him. But he said it was easy. After twenty-four hours, he was in a groove and now he *can't* get back to sleep."

Miss Carol merely sighed. "And did the police say anything?"

"Not really. They just took statements from me and Lars, didn't ask too many questions and told us to call them if Melissa suddenly turns up."

"Alive, I'm assuming?"

"Well, I assumed that, too, but…"

Miss Carol paced the floor, concerned, obviously, with Miss Danen's fate. She asked some further questions about Mr. Hanna, but the master had no information to offer. I maintained a discreet silence, ever vigilant.

Finally, Miss Carol turned to Master Joseph, an idea clearly forming in her mind. "Have you had a chance to check out this guy's apartment?"

"Check out in what sense?"

"I mean, look around. See what's there."

"Snoop, in other words."

"In other words."

Master Joseph dismissed the notion with a simple shake of his head. "I'm not sure when the guy is there and when he isn't. And I'm not exactly suicidal."

"But if you knew he wasn't there?"

The master considered it but offered only a non-committal bob of his head. "I might think about it."

"How 'bout I do it?"

Master Joseph seemed taken aback, perhaps even appalled. I moved quickly to his side, rubbing against his leg in a show of solidarity. He made no move to acknowledge it, but I sensed his appreciation. He waved a hand toward Miss Carol.

"Are you insane?" he said, "You have any idea what that guy will do if he finds you?"

"Do you?"

"Well, no. But my imagination is pretty good."

Miss Carol was unmoved. "Listen, all we have to do is come up with a plan. This shouldn't be hard. Lars lives across the hall. He'll know when the guy is there and when he isn't."

"What? Are you saying Lars has nothing better to do than listen at the door and know when this guy…you know what? Disregard. Go on."

"And Lars is the super, so he has the keys to the place. You can keep an eye on the front. Lars can keep an eye on the back. And I'll sneak in and check it out. Nothing to it."

Master Joseph seemed anything but convinced. All eyes in the room, save Leonard's, were upon him, awaiting his decision.

"I think this is a terrible idea," he said, "Maybe I should be the one who checks out the apartment and you keep watch."

Miss Carol approached and laid a hand on the master's cheek. "That's a nice thought," she said, "But I'll do it. You're still sick. And you're kind of a pussy."

I certainly had no objection to the term Miss Carol used, but the master seemed taken aback. I must confess: the man has my undying loyalty, but there are times when I simply don't understand him.

23 July (Supplemental)

A truly frantic night. I find my nerves nearly shattered by the events. Even Leonard, normally indifferent to anything but his own appetites, appears profoundly shaken. I can only hope we all recover. I shall recount the events as best I am able.

The evening began with Miss Carol's ill-conceived plan to invade Mr. Hanna's dwelling. The gentleman (and I use that term in its broadest possible sense) left his domicile at roughly nine in the evening. Mr. Lars promptly notified Master Joseph and Miss Carol of the event and took up his position observing the back of the building. Master Joseph made one final, ultimately fruitless, attempt to dissuade Miss Carol before he began his watch at the front window. As always, I remained close at the master's hand. Leonard chose this time to take an evening nap in the master bedroom. (I will certainly take up the matter of his indifferent behavior with him at a later date.)

Miss Carol left the apartment and, for a few moments, her footsteps could be heard on the stairs. Master Joseph gave a concerned look toward the front door, then resumed his watch. I'm certain only a handful of minutes passed, but in the thick tension filling the manor, it seemed like hours. There was nothing visible out the front window, save for the occasional pedestrian, stumbling to or from one of the local pubs. It is certain that none of the residents entered or left the building during this vigil.

We were in this position when something caught the master's attention. I confess it caught mine just a moment earlier (my hearing being a tad more acute than the master's) but Master Joseph seemed to have recognized its threat earlier than myself. It was a noise coming from just outside the manor, perhaps down on the landing next to Mr. Lars' dwelling…and Mr. Hanna's.

The master raced to the front door. I followed and nearly found myself bowled over by the door as Master Joseph heaved it open. He froze in place and, a moment later, I understood why. Mr. Hanna was on the landing, unlocking the door to his domicile.

There was no evidence Miss Carol had vacated the premises.

"Hi," Master Joseph said, suddenly. The outburst appeared to have surprised even him.

Mr. Hanna looked our direction and grunted something that resembled, "What?"

"You're home already," Master Joseph said, still looking as if he were attempting to find his footing in this conversation.

"How the fuck did you know I left?" Mr. Hanna said.

"I, uh, I didn't. I was just, y'know, thinking…hey, there you are."

I have the greatest respect for Master Joseph's talents, particularly his way with a sly *bon mot*. But improvisational deceit is, to state this mildly, not his forte. Particularly when he is concerned about Miss Carol's well-being. Mr. Hanna simply looked at the master—and I hope I'm not out of my place in stating this—as if he were a gibbering buffoon.

"Yeah, great," Mr. Hanna said, "Fuck off." With that, he disappeared into his dwelling.

Master Joseph ran down the stairs as quickly—and as lightly—as he could manage. He opened the door to Mr. Lars' dwelling without stopping to knock (a practice Mr. Lars frequently performs, but never Master Joseph). I followed him into Mr. Lars' residence and discovered—to my chagrin—it was exactly as I'd imagined it. I will not dwell on its tackiness and simply state Mr. Lars was found on the deck at the rear of the domicile. And that he was soundly asleep.

The master shook him awake. "Lars, what the fuck are you doing?"

Mr. Lars seemed somewhat disoriented, looking about and rubbing his eyes. "I, uh, I must have fallen asleep."

Master Joseph decided to forgo upbraiding Mr. Lars for this dereliction of duty and instead concentrated on the well-being of Miss Carol. He raced back through the dwelling and returned to the landing near Mr. Hanna's door. Working, I imagine, from instinct, he quickly knocked. Mr. Hanna simply glared at the master once he answered.

"What?" Mr. Hanna said.

"I, uh, I had a question for you."

"What?"

The master did not appear to have an immediate answer to this question. In his defense, he was a tad preoccupied with looking past Mr. Hanna's shoulder and into the residence. I joined him in this activity, desperately searching for an indication Miss Carol was safe.

"I was wondering," Master Joseph said, "I was wondering…if you have…a cup of…sugar. I could borrow."

Mr. Hanna's face best resembled the look one gets after Leonard has used the litterbox. "Sugar? No, I don't have any sugar. There's a convenience store around here, isn't there?"

Before Master Joseph could answer, we spotted Miss Carol slipping out of the hall closet. She attempted to quietly close the door behind her. The hallway in question would lead her to the backdoor and an escape route. But only if Mr. Hanna did not take notice of her. Both the master and I sensed the urgency of otherwise occupying the ruffian.

Master Joseph casually threw his weight against the door, stymying Mr. Hanna's efforts to close it. "Y'know, the convenience store is so far away. It's the thing about this neighborhood that's always bugged me. You can't throw a rock in any direction without hitting a bar or restaurant, but you have to go blocks and blocks to find a gas station or a grocery store. You noticed that?"

I will never know if Mr. Hanna is aware of this quirk of the neighborhood because he didn't seem inclined to answer the question. Rather, he preferred to close the door on Master Joseph. Mr. Hanna having an advantage in the area of brute strength, there seemed little doubt he would succeed. If he did, he would turn back to the apartment and couldn't fail to notice Miss Carol. It was time for me to spring into action.

Fortunately, the necklace Mr. Hanna purloined from Miss Danen's residence was sitting on a table next to the door. The string of the necklace dangled in the same sort of tantalizing way the master dangles string when providing exercise for Leonard and myself. I dove toward it and took the necklace in my mouth. The action had the effect of bringing down both the necklace and the table. I only narrowly avoided the falling furniture. Mr. Hanna's reaction can best be described as apoplectic.

"What the fuck?" he screamed, making a failed grasp for me, "Can't you control this fucking thing?"

The master gave a quick glance toward the closet and noticed Miss Carol making her way down the hallway. He then made a show of turning his wrath on me.

"Squiggy!" he shouted, with as much conviction as he could muster, "What are you doing? Bad kitty!"

Master Joseph scooped me up and removed both of us from the dwelling just before Mr. Hanna brutally slammed the door. As we ascended the stairs, the master dangled the necklace from his opposite hand.

"Good boy, Squiggs," he whispered, "We'll get this back to the rightful owner. If we ever see her again."

It is the small moments such as these that make my work gratifying. However, our triumph was to be short-lived. Miss Carol returned to the manor, slightly shaken but none the worse for wear after her ordeal. Mr. Lars also put in an appearance, though he looked somewhat chastened. Master Joseph supplied adult beverages for everyone.

Miss Carol drank something called a vodka press with particular alacrity. "I'm lucky he didn't come in his backdoor. How did he get to the front without you guys noticing?"

"He must have come in the backdoor of the building," Master Joseph said, "We might have spotted him if Captain Narcolepsy over there hadn't passed out."

Mr. Lars opened his mouth as if to say something but chose to forego reply. Miss Carol gave him an unflattering look, but quickly moved on to the subject of what she discovered.

"He definitely had the necklace," she said, "You got ahold of that. And I managed to find this." She brandished a slip of paper she had previously stored en décolletage, "I'm guessing Hanna wrote it."

Miss Carol handed the note to Master Joseph, who glanced at it while Mr. Lars peeked over his shoulder. While not wishing to appear unduly curious, I took up a position on the back of the davenport in order to get a look at the paper myself. It was merely two lines, saying, *Harris Motor Inn, St. Paul Park, Room 122. V. McCauley*

"I don't know who V. McCauley is," Miss Carol said, "But if this is a St. Paul Park location, I'm guessing the hotel is a shithole."

Mr. Lars snapped his fingers. "Maybe that's where they're holding Melissa."

Master Joseph didn't seem convinced. Before he could state his objections, however, the sound of a door closing was heard in the hallway. Having grown familiar with the noise, I knew immediately it belonged to Mr. Hanna's apartment. The others appeared to be of a similar mind. Miss Carol ran for the backdoor.

"We can follow him to the hotel," Miss Carol said, "Find out what's going on."

Mr. Lars abandoned his previous lethargy and was quickly on Miss Carol's heels. "Sounds great. I'll drive."

Master Joseph moved to follow them but was overcome by a coughing fit. "Wait a minute. Why don't you just call the cops?"

Miss Carol paused before the backdoor. "And tell them what? The creepy guy downstairs has a note?" Before the master could offer further objection, Miss Carol added: "We'll just watch from a distance. Call the cops if anything happens."

"Maybe I should go with you," Master Joseph said, before collapsing into a longer coughing fit.

Miss Carol and Mr. Lars were unsuccessful in hiding their distaste for the master's condition. Miss Carol was able to phrase it diplomatically. "Maybe you should stay here. I mean, the two of us can handle it."

"Besides," Mr. Lars added, "I don't really want to get snotted on."

Master Joseph was still attempting to recover himself when the others abandoned the manor. He simply shrugged and looked my direction.

"Well, Squiggs, I suppose we should see if there's anything on TV."

Whatever charms the television possesses are lost on me, but Master Joseph enjoys it. If I'm to take what I've overheard in conversation as the gospel, it's largely how he is able to support us. While I find myself indifferent to the medium, I never object to the master's willingness to indulge. He seated himself upon the davenport and I took up position in his lap. He stroked my head absent-mindedly while staring at a presumably older program called *Star Trek*. He could have only watched the program with a cursory eye because he was soon attempting to engage me in conversation.

"V. McCauley," he said, "And there was a note in Melissa's place about a Vince M. That can't be coincidence."

I meowed my agreement. Setting me aside, Master Joseph moved to the desk and began searching the internet. I leapt on to the desk but kept a respectful distance. (Leonard will often stroll over the keyboard in a bid for attention, one that invariably results in his being ejected from the desk area.) The master finally sat back and read his findings aloud.

"Vince McCauley. One of the guys suspected in a jewelry heist in Chicago. Former resident of St. Paul Park." He looked over various articles. "There were pictures and names for all of the suspects. You know who I didn't see, Squiggs? Neil Hanna."

The master rose from the chair and began to pace. While Leonard ran into the kitchen, thinking Master Joseph was going to feed us, I remained close by, knowing his thoughts a tad better. He must have sensed this because he continued to consult me.

"If Neil Hanna isn't part of the gang that did the jewelry heist, then who is he?" The master asked. He stopped his pacing and added: "Unless…"

Leaving that thought unfinished, he raced to the backdoor and stepped out on to the deck. I was anxious to be at the master's side, but his policy of neither Leonard nor I ever appearing on the deck is absolute. I waited as patiently as I could until he returned.

"Hanna's car is still in the parking lot," he said, "If he's not heading out, then…"

Again, Master Joseph persisted in this habit of not completing his thoughts. Instead, he brushed past me and headed out the front door. I followed his path down to Mr. Hanna's residence. The master was in the process of knocking when I arrived. He had not received a response.

"Something's wrong," he muttered.

Master Joseph tried turning the doorknob and, to his obvious surprise, discovered the door unlocked. We rushed into the residence and found Mr. Hanna lying face down upon the floor, his body splayed out as if the fall had not been his undertaking. Master Joseph hastily checked Mr. Hanna's condition and discovered he was merely unconscious. Mr. Hanna was coming around just as the master arrived but was groggy in the extreme.

"McCauley…necklace…look out…"

Master Joseph could not get any more out of the man. He looked around the room and discovered what appeared to be a billfold laying near Mr. Hanna. The master picked it up (perhaps fearing Mr. Hanna had been the victim of a robbery). What Master Joseph found inside the billfold caused him some distress. He dropped it back on to the floor. From my position, I could make out what appeared to be a silver shield.

Feeling the urgency of the situation, he simply told Mr. Hanna, "Stay here." (An entirely unnecessary request, as Mr. Hanna didn't appear to know which area code he was in, let alone where to find the exit.) The master bolted from the apartment with me close on his heels. When we returned the manor, Master Joseph sought out his mobile phone and placed a call to Miss Carol. He was forced to leave a message with her answering service.

"Carol, it's Joe. We got this all wrong. Hanna's a cop. I think he's trying to catch some thieves. I'm going to call 9-1-1. You do the same when you get this. Something's going down."

Master Joseph was quick to ring off and begin his call to the authorities. He hadn't said anything before we heard the backdoor open. And an intruder entered.

The intruder was an emaciated man of about forty. His short, dark hair was swept back and he sported a graying goatee. Even under the loose black t-shirt and jeans, it was apparent his frame was hard and coiled, as if ready to strike.

He was holding a long hunting knife in his gloved right hand. His cold eyes glared at Master Joseph as he made his way down the hall.

"You got the necklace?" he asked, his voice gruff and uncouth.

The master stood his ground, but the bobbing of his Adam's apple was rather pronounced. "Vince McCauley?"

"Yeah, genius. You got my fucking necklace?"

Master Joseph stepped toward the desk made no move to collect the necklace. "You kidnapped Melissa?"

Mr. McCauley did not appear in a mood to answer questions. "She's my woman."

"Was it her idea to leave?"

"No."

"Well, the rest of us call that kidnapping."

Mr. McCauley's response was to grab the hall table and hurl it toward the kitchen. Both Master Joseph and myself winced. The cleanliness of the manor is paramount to both of us. So much so, that it temporarily superseded our concern for our own well-being. Mr. McCauley, perhaps to his credit, was quick to return us to the point of his visit.

"This is the last time I'm asking," he said, "I want that fucking necklace."

Master Joseph remained pinned against the desk. Mr. McCauley was blocking the only two exits out of the manor.

Unless one considered the window an escape route and I doubted that the master did so. He was possessed of no guarantee he would land upon his feet. We were caught between the proverbial rock and hard place. Leonard, of course, was nowhere to be found and I confess to wishing I was with him. However, it was now Master Joseph and myself against this blackguard. While I sensed a certain indecisiveness on the part of the master, I felt the choice was clear.

I leapt upon the desk, took the necklace in my mouth and did a bunk for all I was worth.

The chaos created by this action was immediate. Master Joseph, disagreeing with my actions, attempted to grab me, but came up empty. Mr. McCauley, shouting uncouth profanities, was also in pursuit. I found a temporary haven under the davenport. It lasted only as long as it took Mr. McCauley to reach about with the hand (thankfully) not containing the knife.

"Give me that fucking thing!" Mr. McCauley shouted.

I managed to get clear of his hand and flee down the back hallway. With no ability to open the backdoor (nor permission to exit even I possessed such an ability) my options were limited. I had just passed the bedroom entrance when Leonard chose to make an appearance. His timing (for once) was impeccable. Mr. McCauley tripped over Leonard and became a virtual whirling dervish. His gyrations ended with him narrowly avoiding me and hitting his head against the lower step leading to the backdoor. He was rendered senseless and, as soon as Master Joseph caught up to him, weaponless. The master had just obtained the hunting knife when sirens could be heard approaching the building.

Master Joseph slumped against the wall and looked at the two of us. Leonard had retreated to the bedroom and was cautiously looking out. I still had the necklace dangling from my mouth, an appearance I fear seriously compromised my dignity. The master, however, smiled and shook his head.

"Thank God I'm a cat person," he said.

To which I could only heartily agree.

27 July

The household is, thankfully, back in order and a sense of calm has been restored to the building. All of Master Joseph's possessions have been returned to their regular positions and the manor is once again shipshape. Even the master's cold appears to be on the wane.

He came through the backdoor earlier this afternoon. Leonard and I were awaiting him in the hallway, as is our custom. The master greeted us by calling out, in a sing-song voice, "Daddy's boys!" His standard greeting. I find it demeaning, but Leonard seems to enjoy it. He breezed past us and greeted Mr. Lars coming through the front door.

"Heard you come in," Mr. Lars said, "Can you give me a hand with something? The Anchor sisters are moving back in. You can see the moving van out front."

Master Joseph glanced out the front window. "So it is. I'm guessing the whole move to California was a ruse?"

Mr. Lars nodded. "They were doing a favor for the St. Paul Police Department. The cops needed an apartment to keep an eye on Melissa, in case this McCauley guy showed up. We didn't have one available, but The Anchor sisters were willing to cooperate."

"Nice of them. I wonder why the cops didn't just go question Melissa?"

"They did. She hadn't heard from McCauley. Didn't *want* to hear from him. She'd been hiding out ever since she left him."

"Why didn't she hand over the necklace?"

"She didn't know she had it," Mr. Lars said, "McCauley had stashed it with her. After the police questioned her, she looked through her storage unit. When she found it, she panicked a little, thought she'd lied to the police. So she just stayed quiet."

"And then McCauley showed up."

Mr. Lars pointed at Master Joseph. "He wanted to get the necklace, but Hanna had grabbed it by that point. So McCauley grabbed Melissa and took her to a hotel in St. Paul

Park. Held her there. He thought maybe he could swap her for the necklace. Don't know if you gathered, but the dude isn't right in the head."

Master Joseph retreated to the kitchen and began making a pot of coffee. "When did you talk to Melissa?"

"This morning. She's doing fine. A little shaken up."

"Good thing you and Carol called the police."

"We didn't have time to wait until we got to St. Paul Park. Carol and I got there in time to see the whole gang surrender. Apparently, once they saw a fleet of police cars in the parking lot, they folded immediately."

Master Joseph turned on the coffee maker and slumped against the kitchen counter. "McCauley wasn't much better. He was in la-la land when the cops got here."

Mr. Lars smiled, impressed. "Taken down by two cats. Who'd have thunk it?"

The master gave me a warm look and said, "I would have. They're good boys."

With that, Master Joseph left to assist Mr. Lars in handling the Anchor sisters return. Leonard dozed next to the window, oblivious to the heat and radiating in the sunlight. Seeing the manor back in order, I chose to join him.

Certainly, one has earned a rest.

DEATH IS HARD-BOILED

I think it's time we all come to a certain realization: at some point, our parents simply outlive their usefulness.

Yes, of course we still love them. And I'm sure even Descartes still had useful advice for his kid when he got older. But for most of us, our parents' advice is largely, "Yeah, you shouldn't do that" and other pearls of wisdom we could have figured out for ourselves. So, we're left with these people who provide no basic necessities or words of wisdom and yet we're required to have them in our lives. Because nobody really has an alternative to how these relationships should work.

My name is Joe Davis. My parents hate to know I make my living writing stuff like that.

I'm not sure my friend Carol would agree with that assessment of parents. Whenever she talks about her folks, it's generally in a positive context. Although I've always thought it strange that I've picked up more about her father from the internet than I have from his daughter. So, I'm rather surprised when a conversation with Carol starts like this:

"I need your help with my dad."

I'd like to tell you Carol interrupted me in the middle of my work. And if I were a slightly-crappier mood, I might alter the facts to support that accusation. But I'm *working* only in the broadest possible definition of the word. I'm on the sofa, sipping a beer and tapping at the keyboard every few minutes while also watching a football game. The fact I was willing to take Carol's phone call tells you where I'm at, creatively.

"What's going on with your dad?" I ask.

"I have to pick him up at the airport. His driver's dead."

This is the point where I should explain a thing or two about Carol's dad. The man's name is Walter Ryan and while I've never met him, I've read all his books. He writes hard-boiled mysteries set in the Forties and chockfull of two-fisted detectives, sap-wielding cops and gum-cracking molls. It's the kind of stuff that caused my college professors to turn up their noses, but certainly makes the hours on an airplane or a car trip shoot by. Carol's a little embarrassed to be the child of a celebrity. And more-than-a-little embarrassed she doesn't like her father's books and, beyond giving his first book a cursory glance, hasn't read any of them.

That, of course, doesn't address the whole *Driver is dead* thing.

"He has a driver?" I ask.

"Yeah. Look, I can explain in the car. Can you just meet me in front of your building in about five minutes?"

I'm a little torn. I shouldn't be getting involved in a thing based on a few vague bits of info. But I can't pass up the opportunity to meet Walter Ryan.

"I'll be out front," I say.

Five minutes later, I'm sitting on the front steps of my building. Fall is closing in, but it's not quite jacket weather yet. My black long-sleeve tee and a pair of jeans are all the protection I need. The leaves are turning, creating halos of gold in the streetlights on Summit Avenue. This would be a very pleasant night under normal circumstances. Carol's green Lexus pulls up to the curb. She's focused on the street when I slide into the passenger seat.

"To the airport, Jeeves!" I say, tapping the room like it's a hansom cab.

Carol's mouth is tight. "Thank you for coming along."

"No problem. You mind filling me in on what's up?"

It's a quick run down Ramsey Hill to Highway 35E. The airport is about ten minutes away. Carol brushes a hair off her forehead and checks herself in the mirror.

"My dad's driver was named Matt Ellison. They were in the army together. He'd volunteer to drive dad around whenever he came to town."

"And now he's no more?"

"He is not. And what's worse, I think he was murdered."

My head swings away from watching the pretty lights on the freeway. "What makes you say that?"

"Dad said something was fishy and he was going to get to the bottom of it."

Jeez. Am I living one of Walter Ryan's novels? "When did this Matt guy die?" I ask.

"A couple days ago."

I pull out my phone and Google Matt Ellison's name. There's not a plethora of information, but I get the basic facts. Matt was found in his apartment. Cause of death not released, but police have reason to believe it's a homicide. Asking the public for any information that might lead to the apprehension of the perpetrator.

"Looks like you're right about the murder part," I say, slipping the phone into my pocket.

"Maybe Dad's just trying to find information."

"You sound like you're talking yourself into that."

Carol starts to say something, then bites her lip. All she'll give me is, "We'll see."

We don't say any more before we get to the airport. Carol's tense and I'm not sure if it's from the issue with her dad's friend or her dad himself. As I said, I've never known Carol to say a bad word about her father. Mike, on the other hand, lived in mortal terror of the man while dating Carol. A text message tells us Carol's dad is waiting at baggage claim in the Humphrey Terminal, the decidedly smaller of the two terminals at the Minneapolis/St. Paul Airport. Carol's tension grows as we get closer to the place. I take my life into my hands and ask her about it.

"Is there something you're not telling me?" I ask.

Carol bobs her head as she considers this. "Matt was willing to do anything for my dad. I always appreciated that. My dad's not the easiest guy in the world to get along with."

"But..." I say, because I sense there's one coming.

"But Dad liked Matt more than I did. Let's leave it at that."

Carol's dad is standing in the concourse as we approach. His bag is in one hand and his coat is tossed over the other arm. Carol greets him a hug. Walter Ryan, I have to say, looks just like the author pictures in his books. He's in his later fifties, roughly my height (about six feet tall) and getting a tad thick about the waist. He's got Carol's piercing blue eyes (or I should say, she has his). An unlit cigar hangs from one corner of his mouth and a black fedora sits atop his round head. He accepts Carol's hug and glares at me.

"This your friend, sweetie?" he asks, voice filled with gravel, "The one that's friends with Griffin?"

I'd love to think Mr. Ryan calls everybody by their last names, but something in the way he pronounces *Griffin* makes me wonder. It's the same tone one would use to describe hemorrhoids. Only nastier.

"Joe Davis," I say, throwing my hand out, "It's a pleasure to meet you, Mr. Ryan."

Carol puts a hand on my arm. "You can call him Walt."

Mr. Ryan glares at me. "When you've known me for a few years. Meantime, Mr. Ryan will do nicely."

Carol rolls her eyes, clearly not impressed with her dad's gruffness. Mr. Ryan tosses his bag to me (if I had to guess by the weight, it contains a warthog stuffed with bowling balls) and offers his arm to Carol. They start down the concourse while I struggle to keep up and ponder the hernia the bag is giving me.

"What happened with Matt?" Carol asks.

Mr. Ryan shakes his head. "Whole thing's a queer business. He went tits up two days ago and the coppers haven't done a thing."

I nearly walk into a support beam. I've always loved Mr. Ryan's dialogue, but I assumed that's all it was: dialogue. This is what I get for not looking him up on You Tube.

Carol is unfazed. "How do you know the police haven't done anything?"

"Two days and nobody's been arrested. You think the coppers got the whole thing under control? Forget it. They're throwing snake eyes."

Carol takes a breath, trying to keep her voice even. "What do you want to do?"

Mr. Ryan takes the unlit cigar out of his mouth and waves it around. "Simple. I'm going to find the son of a bitch who snuffed Matt and I'm going to cancel his check."

He spends the rest of the trip to Carol's car moodily chomping on the cigar. Mr. Ryan slides into the front passenger seat, letting Carol do the driving. I deposit his bag in the trunk. Once Mr. Ryan is settled in, Carol comes around to the trunk and lowers her voice.

"Clearly, I need your help," she says.

"I'm not certain *you're* the one who needs help."

Carol levels a look at me. "It's just part of his persona. He's been doing it so long, he doesn't realize what he sounds like."

I finally get the bag in the trunk and stop to take a breath. "In wrestling, they call it living your gimmick. But he's not really going after whoever murdered his friend, is he? He's a writer, not a detective."

Carol folds her arms "Really, Joe? You have any idea what you sound like?"

"Um, the pot calling the kettle black?"

"I was going to say a hypocritical horse's ass, but you say tomato…"

I start to close the trunk, but realize that would expose us to Mr. Ryan, who'd want to know what we were—I don't know—*gabbing* about, or however he'd put it.

"Fine," I say, "What do you need me to do?"

Carol puts a fingertip to her lips as she thinks. "What about that cop friend of yours? The one who arrested Mike?"

"Sergeant Pike? You'd call him a friend?"

"He isn't?"

"In the sense he'd like to see me buried up to my neck in a mound of fire ants, yeah, we're quite tight."

"Can you at least call him? Maybe he can let my dad know what's going on. Maybe Dad will drop the whole thing."

That's a few more maybes than I prefer, particularly when dealing with a cop who hates me—well, not me, just my guts—but I have a hard time saying no to Carol. She's one of the few level-headed friends I have. I have to take an active role in this idiocy. Huh. Wonder if this is what Carol feels like when she gets dragged into *my* latest act of idiocy?

I pull out my cell phone. "I'll give him a call."

Carol goes back to the car to stall for time while I make the call. Sergeant Frank Pike's number is still in my phone, stemming from the last time I had to deal with him. I'm sure he'd just *love* to know I have him on speed-dial.

Pike's answer conveys his enthusiasm: "Pike." (Then again, he'd probably answer that way if his mother was calling.)

"Sergeant Pike? It's Joe Davis."

He lets out the kind of sigh that tells me he regrets picking up. "What can I do for you, counselor?" (The *counselor* nickname stems from the first time I dealt with Pike; when Mike had me posing as a lawyer. Don't ask.)

I explain the whole thing. He doesn't say much, beyond letting out disgusted little breaths here and there. Only when I mention the name of Carol's father does he suddenly perk up.

"Walter Ryan?" he asks, "The mystery writer?"

"You've heard of him?"

"I've read all his books."

"You read?"

"During my rare down time when I'm not taking dipshit phone calls. Yes, counselor, I like to read."

I suppose I could've done a better job buttering him up. "Anyway, do you know who's working on this case?"

"Intimately. It's me."

I'm trying to decide if this is a lucky break or not. "Is there any chance you'd be willing to meet with Mr. Ryan? Just to set him straight on what's going on with the investigation?"

Pike considers it and then: "I can spare about ten minutes. You know where Glacier's coffee shop is?"

"Do you know where your left hand is? Of course I know Glacier's."

"Good. I'll be waiting." And that's how he ends the phone call.

Going to have to talk to the SPPD about their public relations.

***

Glacier's is just down the block from The Tav, my favorite neighborhood watering hole, and like The Tav, pretty much functions as my home away from home. (Or my home away from my home away from home. I've lost control of this metaphor.) It's a converted café with checkerboard tile floors, straight-back chairs and picture windows. It has the kind of cozy atmosphere chain stores spend millions to replicate and never achieve. And the espresso drinks are damn good.

Sergeant Pike is at a small table near the door, a to-go cup of coffee sitting in front of him. He's small, slim and balding. His sad bulldog face sports a pair of wire-rim glasses perched at the end of his nose. He's wearing a rumpled gray suit and a permanent frown. He musters the closest thing he's got to civility for Carol and respect for Mr. Ryan. I get the usual back-of-the-hand treatment.

Pike looks almost obsequious when he says, "I'm a big fan of yours, Mr. Ryan."

"'Preciate it. But I ain't here to gas on about that. I need the skinny on what happened to my pal."

Pike briefly looks at me and Carol. I give Pike a slight nod, as if to indicate *Yes, he actually talks like that.* They sit at the table while Pike explains the case and I go to the counter to fetch some coffees. Pike's concluded his remarks by the time I return. If we were holding out hope this would satisfy Mr. Ryan, it's dashed before I can even hand out the coffees.

"Matt was found tits up in his apartment," Mr. Ryan says, "And you got no suspects?"

"We have a few persons of interest," Pike says, keeping his voice even.

"Such as?"

"I'm not at liberty to share that information with you. As I said, we're looking into it. We're going to find who murdered your friend."

Mr. Ryan isn't impressed. "And when will that be?"

"Soon."

"You ain't much of a detail man, are you?"

Pike takes a large breath of air through his nose. He stands and offers his hand to Mr. Ryan. "It was a pleasure meeting you, sir."

Mr. Ryan takes it but doesn't look at Pike. "You too."

Pike points at me and throws a nod toward the door. I follow him over. Pike sticks a finger in my chest.

"I'm warning you," he says, "Stay out of this."

"Stay out? I never wanted *in*."

"Just keep him out of trouble. I didn't want to tell him this, but his friend was a bad guy. Mixed up with other bad guys. One of them probably killed him. I don't want Walter Ryan's next book to be posthumous."

Pike disappears out the door. Strangely, he and I are on the same page. Yes, I'm curious about what happened to Mr. Ryan's friend, but I'm not anxious to get caught up in anything dangerous. On top of that, I don't want Sergeant Frank Pike investigating *my* homicide. (Of course, he's likely to be the cause of it, so...)

I rejoin Carol and her father at the table. He ignores his mug of coffee (dark roast, black) and stares at the picture window. If the look on his face means anything, he's not enjoying the view of Cathedral Hill. Or even particularly noticing it. Carol and I let him have the moment, sensing we'd only interrupt his train of thought.

"All right," he says, "I guess it's up to me."

Carol's eyes widen. "You? What do you mean 'you'?"

"I mean me, sweetie. That cop's useless. I gotta find out who did in Matt."

So much for Carol's plan to use Sergeant Pike to keep the peace. (I could have told her that was a mistake. Wait, I did.) She attempts to talk her father out of it, but even Stevie

Wonder could see it's not going to work. I sip my cup of decaf and wait for things to run their course. Carol sags, defeated.

"Can we at least help you?" she says.

Mr. Ryan finally sips his coffee. "Long as you stay out of my way."

"We're getting a lot of that tonight," I say.

Carol kicks me under the table before saying, "Where do we start?"

Mr. Ryan shoves the mug aside and stands. "We'll start with the place Matt stepped out of the canoe. His apartment on Payne Avenue. You know where that's at?"

"I can find it," Carol says.

"Good. Grab your boyfriend and let's go."

Mr. Ryan starts for the door. Carol scrambles after him, trying to explain I'm not her boyfriend. I bring up the rear and contemplate a night that's got me heading for Payne Avenue, AKA the armpit of St. Paul.

This is what I get for answering the phone.

***

Matt's apartment is in a squat, two-story building. The brickwork is faded and splotches of paint cover the fine work the taggers have done. The glass on the front door is cracked and the windows in the apartments look like they haven't been cleaned since the Johnson administration. The Andrew Johnson administration. Beyond that, it's a complete shithole.

The building doesn't have a landlord (at least not one onsite). It *does* have a superintendent. Her name is Rachel and she doesn't seem thrilled we took her away from whatever reality show she's got on the tube. Her face is a mess of lines and crags, made all the worse when she's scowling, which I'm guessing is most of the time. Her hair is covered in a scarf and a cigarette hangs out of one corner of her mouth. She stands in the doorway of her first-floor apartment and blows smoke at us.

"Yeah, of course I know where Matt's place is," Rachel says, "You think we have a murder around here every week?"

Looking around, I wouldn't rule that out, but I keep the thought to myself. Carol wrinkles her nose, probably trying to figure out the odd smell. (It's urine, but I keep *that* thought to myself as well.) Mr. Ryan tucks his hands in his coat pockets.

"I need to check the place out," he says.

"You cops?"

"I'm Walter Ryan." As if that explains the whole thing.

Rachel shrugs. "Okay. Why do you want to look at the place?"

"Matt was a pal. If someone offed him, I'm going to find the sucker. You gonna get on board with that, toots?"

"Toots?"

Carol steps past her dad, giving Rachel the best smile she can muster (and at the moment, it isn't much). "My dad would just like to take a look. I'm sure the police have found everything they need, but it wouldn't hurt to have another set of eyes on it, right?"

Rachel shakes her head. "They got crime scene tape up. I let you in, the cops'll have my ass. Might even go after me for—what do you call it?—tampering with a crime scene or something like that."

Mr. Ryan looks at Rachel from under the brim of his fedora. When he speaks, he points at her with the cigar still wedged between his fingers.

"How long you been seeing Matty?" he asks.

Rachel's eyes bug out and her jaw works for a few seconds before any words come. "I didn't...that's ridiculous...I didn't..." And she realizes her reaction has given the game away. She says, "How did you know?"

"Known Matt a long time," Mr. Ryan says, "Know the type of dame he goes after. I'm guessing you didn't tell the cops you were seeing each other?"

Rachel suddenly looks tired. She steps into the apartment and comes out with what I'm assuming are the master keys for the building. She heads down the hallway, Mr. Ryan walking beside her and Carol and me bringing up the rear.

"I didn't say anything to the cops," Rachel says, "I'd appreciate it if you didn't either. The owners would throw my ass on the street if they knew I'd been seeing a tenant."

Mr. Ryan points at her. "Long as you're straight with us, we'll be straight with you. Capice?"

"Yeah, whatever."

"You were the one who found him?"

"Yeah. He was supposed to pick me up and we were gonna go to the movies. He never showed. I figured he had somebody up at his place. That's the kinda shit Matt used to do. Cat around, no matter who he was seeing. Fucking prick. God rest his soul."

Matt's former apartment is on the second floor. As expected, it's not exactly the kind of apartment Will Smith would purchase in Manhattan. More like the kind of place DJ Jazzy Jeff would purchase. There's a main room with a few pieces of dilapidated furniture, a less-than-inspiring bedroom at the back and a kitchen so tiny it could fit in a backpack. A few chairs have been overturned and the coffee table seems to be out of place (unless Matt actually wanted it at an angle perpendicular to the sofa). Everything is grungy and fading, which I'm guessing is the apartment's natural state.

"Where'd you find him?" Mr. Ryan asks.

"In the bedroom." Rachel gives an involuntary shiver. "It wasn't pretty. His eyes were bugged out. His tongue was hanging out. He'd shit his pants. It was awful."

"What'd you do?"

"I screamed and ran out the room. Started crying. Got hysterical. I felt awful for Matt."

I step next to Rachel. "I thought you didn't like him."

She shrugs. "He was good for a laugh. Great in the sack."

I sneak a look at Carol, who's on the verge of throwing up. Mr. Ryan strolls over to the bedroom. I fall in behind him, consigned to playing the role of sidekick. The bedroom consists of a single bed, a nightstand and a good handful of porno mags. I nudge one of them with my toe.

"*Asses and Jugs*," I say, looking at the cover.

Mr. Ryan looks away. "Matt was a man of appetites."

We leave it at that and inspect the room. For a crime scene, it's surprisingly clean. The bedclothes are a mess (again, I'm guessing that's normal). The only thing a bit untoward is the drawer of the nightstand hanging open.

Mr. Ryan nods toward the drawer. "Matt always kept his cell phone in there. Never knew why. Pain in the ass. I'd call him and he couldn't hear the damn thing."

The drawer contains only a small bottle of hand lotion. (Swell.) "It's not there now."

Mr. Ryan paces the room, his mouth twisted to one side as he thinks. He closes one eye and holds up his hands, framing the room.

"Okay, here's how it went down," he says, "Matt's in here, asleep. The guy comes up on Matt before he can wake up. He does the deed and, in his rush to get out, he knocks over the furniture."

I clear my throat. "Or—just spitballing here—he drags Matt out into the living room and knocks over the furniture as he strangles him."

"Other possibility," Mr. Ryan says, "He surprises Matt, drags him out into the living room and knocks over the furniture as he strangles him."

He looks at me like I'm supposed to shout out *You've hit it. Good show, Holmes!* I nod in agreement. I mean, I *do* like the theory, no matter who came up with it. (But we know it was me, right?)

Mr. Ryan leads the way back into the main room. He rubs his chin, putting together some kind of theory in his head. I step past him and examine the front door. I open it and look over the frame. Carol joins me.

"What are you looking for?" she asks.

"A sign of forced entry," I say, "I'm guessing Matt kept his door locked?"

Rachel scoffs. "This neighborhood? If he had the sense God gave a green turnip, he did."

Mr. Ryan points toward the front door, cigar wedged between two fingers. "Meaning the killer used a lock pick of some kind."

"Or Matt let him in on his own," I say

"Another possibility," Mr. Ryan says, "Is that Matt let the killer in on his own."

I look to Carol, as if to say, *You're seeing this, right? I'm not the only one doing the Laurel and Hardy routine?* She pats me on the arm but doesn't look at me. For Carol's sake, I'll stay patient. Until I can't.

Mr. Ryan strolls around the room, chomping his cigar as he thinks. "So obvious conclusion is that this joker ran some kind of ruse on Matt. Pretended he was a neighbor or a traveling salesman."

"Or Matt knew him in the first place," I say.

"Or Matt knew him in the first place," Mr. Ryan says, as if I didn't even speak, "It's a long shot, but I may have to go with that last theory. Who did Matt know and why would they kill him?"

"A lot of people wanted Matt dead," Rachel says, "It was just a matter of who was going to do it."

Mr. Ryan lets out a breath that runs close to a growl. He sticks the cigar back in his mouth and stares at the cracks in the wall. He does it for so long I'm getting the impression he has no idea what to do next. I turn to Rachel.

"Is there anything else you didn't tell the police?" I ask.

Rachel is impatient with the question but is at least willing to think about it. Mr. Ryan also glares at her, maybe trying to encourage her along. After several seconds, something comes to her.

"He was going to The Saloon a lot," she says, "The place over in Frogtown. There were three or four different times in that last week when I called him up to do something and he said he couldn't, he was going over to The Saloon. I'd never heard him talk about the place before and all of a sudden he's a regular."

"He didn't tell you why he was going over there?" I ask.

"Nope. And I didn't ask."

Mr. Ryan suddenly turns to me and takes the cigar out of his mouth. "We're going to check out this Saloon place." He steps over to Rachel. "Thanks for letting us in, toots. You did me a solid."

Rachel blushes and toys with the collar on her shirt. "It's my pleasure. I hope you find who did this."

Mr. Ryan gives her a surprisingly disarming smile. "You can count on it. These bums don't stand a chance."

He winks at Rachel, then turns to me and Carol and jerks a thumb toward the door. Rachel flutters her fingers at Mr. Ryan in a school-girlish manner and I have to say: it kind of makes me sick. When we get to the car and Mr. Ryan has hopped in, I take out my cell phone and pull Carol aside.

"Just give me a minute," I tell her, "I need to get some information on The Saloon."

"You're calling the cops?"

"Think the other end of the food chain."

Carol's eyes widen. "You're calling Mike?"

"You mind stalling your dad for me?"

While Carol hops into the car with the greatest alacrity, I hit the *Send* button and a few seconds later, Mike is on the other end of the line.

"What's going on?" he asks. Judging by the lazy tone in his voice and the faint sound of a football game in the background, he must be flopped in his beanbag chair, staring at the TV.

"I need your help with something."

"What?" he says, slowly. Fifteen years I've known Mike and every time there's even a hint of me asking a favor, he gets a suspicious quality to his voice, like I'm about to ask him to go undercover in Blofeld's organization.

I ignore the tone and plow bravely forth. "I'm working on something and it's kind of an emergency."

"Is it a column?"

"No. It's something with Carol's dad."

"Is he dead?"

"No!"

"Oh." And he sounds disappointed.

I wish this phone call wasn't necessary. But it is. While he left his (rather weenie) criminal days back in college, Mike still enjoys hitting pool halls and disreputable taverns. He fits in with that crowd a little more easily than I'm comfortable with. Regardless, it's given him an extensive knowledge of St. Paul's underground. If there's something untoward about The Saloon, Mike would know it.

"You know The Saloon, over in Frogtown?" I ask.

"Hung out there a few times."

"Imagine you're a smalltime hustler. You've got something going that's not exactly legal. Would you have any reason to go to The Saloon?"

"If I was dealing with Jack Spencer, sure."

"Who's Jack Spencer?"

"He owns The Saloon. Also runs a crew over in Frogtown."

Eep. Frogtown. The *other* armpit of St. Paul. (Yes, the two armpits are right next to each other, but this is St. Paul. Nothing about the layout makes sense.)

"Frogtown, huh?" I say.

"Yeah. The guy's bad news. Has some, uh, anger management issues. Especially when it comes to his wife."

"He's a wife-beater?"

"No, no, nothing like that," he says, "You've never seen this lady, have you?"

"No, Mike, I don't hang out with a lot of mob wives."

"About five-eight, red hair, built like a brick shithouse. Looks like the flute chick from *American Pie*, but with an actual set of tits."

You can see why most of my conversations with Mike don't involve philosophy or the arts. I hold the phone away from my ear, as if the conversation will infect my brain.

"I take it Jack Spencer's the jealous type?" I ask.

"Jealous-and-a-half, yeah," Mike says, "Word on the street is he and the Mrs. fight like hell, usually because he's gotten jealous and had some poor bastard's ass kicked. Or he's done it himself. He gets squirrely if a guy even looks at his wife with a little appreciation."

"Doesn't sound like a healthy relationship."

"From what I gather, only two things keep them together: they love making up and Jack needs her for his business. Probably not in that order."

"What does she do for his business?" I ask.

"Runs the books. She's a smart lady. Jack would still be doing liquor store holdups if it wasn't for her."

Well, it's interesting as background on Jack Spencer. Doesn't really tell me anything useful yet.

"You know anything about a guy named Matt Ellison?" I ask.

"Heard the name. That's about it. Small-timer, right? Sleaze bucket?"

"That's what I'm gathering. He have any dealings with Jack Spencer?"

"You're going to have to ask Jack about that," Mike says, "If you really want to."

"I don't. But I may not have an option."

"Why?"

I give him the rundown on what my evening's looked like. Mike's quiet until I get to the end. He starts chuckling.

"Carol's dad is insane," Mike says, "You know that."

"Well, y'know, creative types. They always walk that sane/insane line."

"Aren't you a creative type?"

"Only when I'm trying to impress a girl," I say, "You think Jack Spencer would be at The Saloon right now?"

"There's a good chance. He hangs out in the upstairs bar. Avoid the downstairs bar. It's like *Mean Streets.*"

"I'll do my best, but I'm not entirely in control of the situation."

That gets an out-and-out laugh from him. "I'd ask you to tell Walter I said hi, but he doesn't want to hear from me.

Son of a bitch never thought I was good enough for his daughter."

"*Nobody* thought you were good enough for his daughter."

"Yeah, but they had the decency not to say anything."

"*I* told you that on a daily basis."

"I know. But your opinion doesn't mean anything."

Well, contempt of Mike is now something Mr. Ryan and I have in common. I ring off and hop into the car. Carol's Googled the address and she gets us on our way to The Saloon. Mr. Ryan looks over his shoulder at me.

"How's Griffin doing these days?" he asks.

"The same."

"Too bad."

***

It takes about ten minutes to get to The Saloon. The place is a two-story operation, tucked into a cruddy neighborhood. Once you go through the door, you have two options: the downstairs bar, filled with florescent lighting and scar tissue, or the stairs to the upper bar, containing mood lighting and a dancefloor. We head up the stairs.

We can already hear the band plowing their way through a cover of *Crossroads Blues*. The patrons are at the tables grouped around the dancefloor. A few hearty souls are dancing. The bar itself is through an archway off the dancefloor. Neon lights run the length of it. The bartender is a tall, dark and handsome dude in his late twenties, wearing his finest (strategically) ripped black t-shirt and (carefully groomed) stubble. Carol's nostrils flare when she looks at him. (Cripe.) The bartender's on his cell phone as we approach.

"No, I was just thinking, like, an afternoon at Fleur de Lis, something like that…I don't care who'd see…" Then he notices us standing at the bar. His lips purse and he mutters, "I gotta go." He slides the cell phone into his pocket and says, "What can I get you?"

"I'm looking for Jack Spencer," Mr. Ryan says.

The bartender glances down the bar, toward the offices in the corner. He hesitates before saying, "Don't know who you're talking about."

"Really?" Carol says, "Because it kind of looked like you did."

"Nope. No idea. You guys gonna order something?"

Mr. Ryan reaches across the bar and grabs the bartender by the shirt, hauling him into a nose-to-nose face-off. "Listen, bucky, you can rummy all you want. We both know you know who Jack Spencer is and where he's at. Now you spill before I decide to smack you around a little."

The bartender lays his hands on the bar. Suddenly, there's no sense of hesitation or nervous energy in the guy. His eyes narrow.

"Listen, old man," the bartender says, "I'm busy enough without having to knock you on your ass."

"I'm shaking like a leaf over here."

"Last warning."

"Go piss up a rope."

Five minutes later, we're at a table in the downstairs bar. Mr. Ryan is nursing a scotch-and-soda and a black eye. Carol stares into a weak beer (having first knocked back a shot of whiskey). I'm looking at the patrons, wishing I had either a stun gun or less money in my wallet.

"That son-of-a-bitch," Mr. Ryan says, "Sucker-punched me. I didn't even see it coming."

I mumble to Carol, "Yeah, I hate it when someone warns me twice before they go ahead and slug me. I mean, where's the etiquette?"

Carol hushes me, but it's clear she agrees. "You should be careful, Dad. We're not going to get answers out of these guys if we try muscling them."

Mr. Ryan waves this off. "I know how to get answers, sweetie."

"Dad, please don't call me 'sweetie.'"

"I was talking to your friend over there. Thanks for the backup, candy ass."

I don't usually argue with the designation *candy ass* since I so often fit the description. In this case, I can't help being annoyed. *I'm* not the horse's ass who picked a fight he couldn't win. I don't see how also getting my ass kicked was going to improve the situation. While we're contemplating this, someone approaches our table.

"How you folks doin'?"

The guy is tall and thin to the point of being gaunt. He's got shaggy hair hanging past his ears and he looks to be in his early fifties. The crow's feet highlight a pair of eyes that are hard and wary. He's making an effort to seem casual, but the tense body language betrays him. He points at the drinks in front of us.

"Those are on me." He waves a hand toward the bar. "So's the next round. My bartender was out of line."

Mr. Ryan gives the guy a wary look out of his good eye. "You're the owner?"

The guy offers his hand. "Jack Spencer. Understand you wanted to talk to me."

Huh. He's friendlier than Mike described. Still, appearances are often deceiving (Mike frequently being a good example). Mr. Ryan takes the hand and they exchange what appears to be a bone-crusher.

"You gonna fire the bartender?" Mr. Ryan asks.

Spencer shakes his head. "Can't. My sister's kid. She'd have my ass. He's a dunce, but he's family. You know how it is."

"You gotta keep an eye out for the feebs."

"That is the case."

I sneak a glance at Carol, who's the most politically correct person here. Her fingernails claw the table, but she says nothing. This is good. The bar and all the people in it don't scream *sensitivity*. Spencer keeps his focus on Mr. Ryan.

"What did you need to talk to me about?" Spencer asks.

Mr. Ryan sets his scotch aside. "Got a buddy of mine used to come in here. Name's Matt Ellison. You know him?"

If the name causes Spencer any panic, he conceals it beautifully. He looks away for a half-second while he tries to place the name and nods when he does so. "Yeah, I think I remember him. Skinny, short, ugly. Kind of a small-timer."

"That's our Matty," Mr. Ryan says.

"Seen him in here. That's about all I can tell you."

"You never did any business with him?"

"Not that I know of."

Mr. Ryan is temporarily flummoxed. It's up to me to keep the questioning going. "When Matt was in here, did you see him talking with anybody?" I ask.

Spencer barely glances my direction. "Nobody special. I get a lot of people in here. I don't keep track of everybody. Your friend used to hang out in the upstairs bar. That's about all I can tell you."

And about all I can ask. Frustrating as it is, I'm not getting any odd feeling off Spencer. I genuinely believe he saw Matt but took no further interest. Not exactly worth the beating Mr. Ryan took.

Jack Spencer moves on, again signaling the bar for another round. Nobody at the table speaks. One corner of Mr. Ryan's mouth hangs particularly low, which is as close to downtrodden as I've seen him. Eventually, the silence gets too much for even me, a born introvert.

"If Matt wasn't doing business with Jack Spencer," I say, "Why was he coming here?"

Mr. Ryan shrugs. "He wasn't a music guy, so it wasn't for the band. He could find cheap liquor closer to his house." He glances around. "And it sure as shit wasn't the ambiance."

"Don't suppose we want to try the upstairs bar again?" I ask, "That's where he hung out."

"Why?" Mr. Ryan asks, "You gonna sack up and actually do something this time?"

That puts me off the whole idea. It's not that I'm afraid of doing Mr. Ryan's version of "sacking up" (although, I am) but more that I'm afraid of what Mr. Ryan might get us into. He's like an ill-tempered four-year old with a bulldozer. You don't know what he's going to do, but you know it's going to create damage. He buys me some time by ambling away from the table, announcing he needs to "hit the head."

Carol runs both hands through her hair. "This seems like a lot to go through for someone as scummy as Matt."

"That reminds me: what is it you have against this guy? I understand disapproving of your father's friends. My dad has a poker buddy named Butch that even my mom won't allow in the house. But I'm sensing a personal thing with Matt."

Carol looks around, making sure no one can overhear us (although I don't know who the hell would want to). "When my parents moved away, Dad was worried about me. I mean, I was twenty-six and had an apartment and a full-time day job, but you know how parents are."

"You were daddy's girl?"

"Oh God, don't put it like that. But yeah, more or less. Anyway, Dad asked Matt to keep an eye on me, make sure I was doing alright. Be there if I needed anything. Well, Matt's idea of keeping an eye on me extended to putting his hands on my ass."

"Ouch."

"That's what he said. Right after I clocked him one."

Carol's *playfully* punched me on the arm and it hurt like a son of a bitch. I can only imagine what it's like when she hits with intent.

"Did you tell your dad about any of this?" I ask.

"No. I didn't want to create trouble. Matt was a scumbag, but he was a friend of my dad's. There was no sense in ruining that. Matt and I came to an agreement: I wouldn't tell Dad about the pass if he stayed the hell away from me."

"And he held up his end?"

"He did. And now he's holding it up permanently."

Mr. Ryan returns from the restroom. Our next—and hopefully final—round of drinks arrives. He moodily eyes his scotch before taking a good belt. He sets the glass back on the table with a little more force than necessary.

"I guess that's that," he says, "No idea what else we can do."

We let the gloom hang over us. I'm getting desperate to find a solution. Mr. Ryan hasn't exactly been a great guest, but for some reason, I don't want to let him down. I look toward the upstairs bar. A thought occurs to me. Just a little one, but the beginning of an idea is better than no idea at all.

"It looks like the offices are up there," I say, nodding toward the stairs.

"I suppose." Carol says. Then she sees the look on my face. "What are you thinking?"

I lower my voice, drawing in Carol and Mr. Ryan. "Matt was doing business, but not with Jack Spencer."

Mr. Ryan isn't intrigued. "You know who it was?"

"Not for certain, no. But the lovely Mrs. Spencer runs the books, right? Maybe Matt was coming here to meet her."

"About what?" Mr. Ryan asks.

"We could ask her and find out," I say.

The idea hangs there for a few seconds. No one's jumping up and down, but we lack any better ideas. Mr. Ryan rubs the stubble on his chin.

"Might as well check it out," he says, "Not like we got anything to lose."

True. Although we have plenty to gain. A beating and possible maiming, for example…

***

To those who believe crime does not, in fact, pay, I'm willing to present the home of Jack and Virginia Spencer as a counter-argument. It's a sizeable split-level house overlooking a tiny lake in Shoreview, a second ring suburb north of St. Paul. The fall colors lay a carpet of rust and gold over the grounds. Five bucks says the kids attend private school and the neighbors are willing to accept that Jack makes his money in "waste management". As long as the neighborhood stays quiet.

Our inquiries at the bar have led us to believe Virginia Spencer is at home. Carol ditches the car on the street about a half-block from the house. I'm worried Jack Spencer will come home and wonder what the hell we're doing in his house. Mr. Ryan looks annoyed to be here. I get the feeling he doesn't do well outside an urban environment. Or the Twentieth Century.

A curving front walk leads to a front door made of oak. Carol and Mr. Ryan leave me to press the doorbell. A few

258

seconds later, Virginia Spencer answers. I'm just glad she's not pointing a pistol at us.

"Can I help you?" she asks, her voice smoky and deep.

Yeah, she's every bit the knockout Mike portrayed her as being. She's not tall, even in the heels. But her body has all the advertised brick shithouse qualities, made all the more appealing by the wine-colored blouse opened one button too far for polite society. Her skin is smooth and there's no hint she's needed any work done. The green eyes flick from one of us to another, showing curiosity, but no sense of fear. Before I can find a polite way to explain our presence, Mr. Ryan steps to the plate.

"Pleasure to meet you, ma'am," he says, "Name's Walter Ryan. I write books."

The neatly-trimmed eyebrows go up slightly. "I've heard of you. *The Nothing Man* was yours, right?"

"It was."

"Good book. Read it straight through on a plane ride to Atlanta."

"Very kind of you. You mind if we come in for a minute?"

Virginia makes no attempt to move. "Can I ask why?"

"Friend of mine got killed. I'm trying to find out what happened."

"And you think I know something?"

"Shot in the dark. Maybe you can tell us something about Matt. Lead us to the killer."

Virginia still seems wary, but that's to be expected when mystery writers show up at your door, unannounced, and say they're going to ask questions about a recent murder. Having two nervous-looking geeks in tow probably doesn't help. Still, she's a good enough sport to let us in. (It's more than I would've done in her position.)

Virginia leads us up to the living room, which has a picture window overlooking the lake. She mutes a giant flat-screen TV showing some variety of (ironically-titled) Real Housewives program. The three of us settle into one corner of a sectional couch that's a tad smaller a train car. Virginia situates herself nearby, practically posing, her drink glass held out in space while she scrutinizes us.

"What friend are you talking about?" she asks.

"Matt Ellison," Mr. Ryan says.

Something flickers across Virginia's face. It's too fast to get a solid read on, but it certainly seems uneasy. "Not sure who you mean," she says, carefully taking a sip of her drink.

I lean forward, past Mr. Ryan. "He's kind of a small-time hustler. Scumbag."

Mr. Ryan looks back, as if to say, *Hey, this was a friend of mine.* I hold up a placating hand and shrink back, giving Virginia the floor.

"Why would I know somebody like that?" she asks.

"Because he did a lot of business at your husband's watering hole," Mr. Ryan says, "The Saloon. From what I hear, you're the brains behind that outfit."

Virginia gives him a shy smile; more an attempt at modesty than actual modesty. "I just handle the books."

"Your hubby has a lot of trust in you. I can see why."

She holds the glass up in a little toast. Mr. Ryan tips his hat in return. This is sweet and all, but it's not getting us anywhere. I already get the feeling Virginia's going to stonewall us. Unlike her husband, she knows who Matt Ellison was. Probably had dealings with him. That little flash of something gave it away. But what does she know and how do I get her to tell me?

Virginia sets her drink down on the glass coffee table. "I'm sorry about your friend, but I don't think I can help you. I handle the books at The Saloon, but my husband deals with the, uh, people who come in. If he didn't know anything about—Matt, was it?—I'm afraid I don't know anything."

Yep, she's stonewalling us. There's no joy in being right about this. It just means another dead end. And I have *no* idea where to go from here. I have to hope Mr. Ryan will finally accept *The police will handle this* as an answer.

An uncomfortable silence falls over the room. We're going to get the bum's rush in another minute. It's not like we have drinks to finish up or anything. I prop my chin in my hand and focus on the doorway to what seems like a gigantic study. There's a beautiful roll-top desk propped against one wall. What I wouldn't give to have something like that as my writing area. Maybe I should have become a gangster after all. Carol, meanwhile, finds something of her own to envy.

"I love your nails," she says.

Virginia's face lights up. She holds out one hand, showing off the blood red nails. "Thank you. I have a gal at Fleur de Lis who does them. She's the best."

It's clear—to me, at least—that Carol is stalling for time, maybe hoping I'll get a brainstorm or something. Not that Carol's above the girly delights of a salon trip, but she wouldn't bring it up under these circumstances. She's desperate. But she's also in luck. I just got a brainstorm.

Things are going pop-pop-pop in my head. *Fleur de Lis.* I've heard that name before. The bartender at The Saloon. He was talking on the phone. Matt's a hustler. He's got something going at The Saloon. He let his killer into his apartment. His cell phone's missing.

I look toward Carol and mumble, "Distract her."

For once, Carol does something without asking me to explain. She slides off the sofa and approaches Virginia to get a better look at her nails. While they dissolve into girlish glee, I lean toward Mr. Ryan.

"Do you have Matt's phone number?" I ask.

He looks at me like I'm nuts (which is becoming rather chronic). "'Course I do. Why?"

"Call it. Now."

Mr. Ryan decides to cooperate. A lucky break, as this really isn't the time for a discussion on the subject. He takes out his cell phone (one of these times, I'm going to have to talk to you about how amusing I find it that every crusty, anti-technology guy in the world will *still* own a smartphone) and punches in the number.

A few seconds later, we hear Matt's phone ringing.

The entire room comes to a halt. Virginia's hand is resting in Carol's while Carol examines her nails. Mr. Ryan stares at his phone. I'm looking into the study, where the ringing is coming from. We sit in these positions like we've been frozen in carbonite. I sneak a glance toward Virginia. She gives me a small smile.

"Well," she says, "Shit."

A second later, we're both on our feet, running toward the study. It's really no contest. I've got a straight line, I'm younger and I'm faster. Matt's cell phone is lying on top of the desk. I scoop it up and turn around, expecting to see Virginia standing right behind me or at least a few steps back. But she's given up the chase. She's halfway across the living room when I step out of the study.

I hold up the phone. "What did Matt have on here?"

Virginia folds her arms. "You don't really think I'm going to tell you, do you?"

Since I'm guessing matters of finance are not Matt's specialty, there has to be blackmail of some kind on this thing. First place to look is in the photos. And it doesn't take long to find what I'm looking for.

"Holy mother…" I mumble, staring at the phone.

The bathroom to this place is down the hall, but this photo already tells me the layout. It looks to have been taken from a nearby tree, likely the nice maple I saw on the way in here. There are two people in the photo, both of whom I've already met.

"This is the bartender from The Saloon," I say.

A corner of Virginia's mouth tightens. "He's Jack's sister's kid."

"And if I'm picturing the family tree correctly—and I think I am—that would make him your nephew."

"If I wasn't married to Jack, we'd be strangers."

I take another look at the photo. "Well, you don't look like strangers here. The kid's what? Twenty-seven? Twenty-eight? A bit old to be giving the little tyke a bath, isn't it, Aunt Virginia? And why aren't *you* wearing anything? And does he really need help washing *that?*"

Virginia stamps one of her feet. "Are you finished, you drooling pervert?"

"Are there any more pictures like this?"

"No."

"Then I'm done."

Mr. Ryan holds out his hand. I pass the phone over. His eyebrows go up. He uses his index finger to push back the brim of his hat.

"Great googly-moogly," he says.

I leave Mr. Ryan ogling the picture and take a few steps toward Virginia. "Let me see if I put this whole together right. You and Mr. Bartender there—"

"Raymond, okay?" Virginia says, "His name is Raymond."

"Hey, that's the tops," I say, "Anyway, you and little Raymond are photographed doing the nasty. Matt, knowing your husband's rather homicidal views on marriage fidelity, starts blackmailing you. Since blackmail is the sort of thing that doesn't really have a statute of limitations and Matt seems like the kind of guy who can't be trusted, you decide he needs to be taken out. Since Raymond's your partner in the first crime, why not make him the partner in the second? How am I doing so far?"

"You're an asshole."

"Must mean I'm getting it right. Since, as Mr. Ryan can attest, Raymond can handle himself and since he's related to your husband, I'm guessing the fruit doesn't fall too far from the poisoned tree. He's the perfect one to take Matt out."

Virginia looks away, putting on an air of being only half-interested in what I have to say. "Raymond was being used as the go-between. Matt wouldn't think anything was odd when Raymond showed up at his apartment. Once we had the cell phone, I figured the rest of it would go away. Nobody was going to miss Matt."

Mr. Ryan looks up from the phone. "Nobody really did. Except me."

Virginia picks up her purse from the glass coffee table and fishes out a pack of cigarettes. "Fine," she says, "How much is it going to take?"

Mr. Ryan and I look at each other, confused. He does the talking. "What do you mean?"

Virginia pulls a cigarette from the pack and digs around the purse for a lighter. "It's not a hard question. How much is it going to take to make you idiots go away? You leave me the cell phone, collect your money and nobody has to know anything."

I can't help but laugh. It's not that I couldn't use the money, but there's no way I'm taking this deal. Morals aside, I've seen how Virginia treated the last guy to whom she paid hush money. I have no desire to end up the same way. Mr. Ryan has his own set of objections.

"I don't need your money, sister," he says, "I'm just getting a square deal for my pal."

Virginia keeps digging for the lighter. "That's very commendable of you."

The next few seconds play out very quickly. Virginia's hand flies out of the purse. She's not holding a lighter. She's holding a very small gun. (Likely referred to as a *hooker's gun* but I haven't faced off against a lot of hookers, so I can't say for sure.) She swings behind Carol, grabs her around the neck and sticks the barrel of the gun into Carol's jaw. Mr. Ryan and I gape at the two of them.

Virginia speaks quickly, but clearly. The tone of her voice is ice cold. "Here's what's going to happen. You're going to set the phone down on the coffee table. Then the three of you are going to get out of here and not say anything to anyone about this. Ever. Because if you do, I will find you and I will fucking kill you."

Mr. Ryan chuckles (and I'm *really* hoping that's nervous laughter). "We both know it ain't gonna work that way, sister. Sure, maybe you'll let us walk out of here, but sooner or later, you're gonna get to worrying. Because there are three people out there, knowing stuff you don't want them to know. And then you're gonna send your little boy toy after us and we go tits up just like my pal, Matt."

Virginia jams the gun farther into Carol's jaw. It's not a particularly powerful, but at this range, it doesn't have to be. I'm afraid to move for fear Virginia will pull the trigger. Carol grimaces from the pain. Virginia's eyes bug out and she shakes Carol as she speaks.

"That's the offer on the table," she says, "Take it or leave it. You got five seconds."

Mr. Ryan sticks the cigar in his mouth. "*This* is the offer on the table: you take that peashooter out of my little girl's face and put it on the table. Then we walk out of here. Cut and dried. That is it. You do that or else."

Virginia laughs. "Or else what?"

The next few seconds go *very* quickly. Carol drives an elbow into Virginia's midsection. The gun slides away from Carol's jaw. In the same motion, Carol's arm swings up, her knuckles hitting Virginia's forehead and snapping her whole head back. Carol grabs Virginia's hair and flips her over her shoulder. Virginia crashes through the coffee table, glass flying in all directions. Only Mr. Ryan doesn't recoil.

"Or else that," he says.

***

It's past midnight before we find ourselves in the bar at the Ambassador Suites. Mr. Ryan is springing for a celebratory round before retiring to his room. The place is quiet, as St. Paul usually is. Mr. Ryan pops a new unlit cigar into one corner of his mouth.

"You did good work, kiddos," he says, holding up his scotch in a toast, "Even if that cop didn't seem too grateful."

I swirl the Oktoberfest in my glass. "Sergeant Pike and I have a complicated relationship."

Carol laughs into her Cosmo. "He hates your guts. What's complicated about that?"

"Yeah, but deep down—"

"He *really* hates your guts."

Carol's got a point. Sergeant Pike's cup of gratitude didn't exactly runneth over. I gave him a courtesy call while Carol called 9-1-1. The Shoreview police had already arrived by time Virginia regained consciousness and they were ordered by Pike to hold her until he arrived. Raymond the Bartender was grabbed at The Saloon before his shift ended. Pike told me Jack Spencer looked stricken when told about everything that went down. It probably had less to do with his wife ordering someone's death and maybe even less to do with her messing around on him and *a lot* more to do with her knowing enough to destroy his whole crew if she cuts a deal. But none of that is my concern. Mr. Ryan knows who killed his friend and the rest of his visit, I hope, can proceed peacefully.

In fact, he comes close to smiling when he says, "Don't think I ain't grateful. You did me and my little girl a solid. Almost makes up for you being friends with Griffin. Almost."

I join the toast, accepting what passes for praise. "I've got to hand it to Carol. She really took care of herself."

Carol leans toward her father. "I told you those judo lessons were going to pay off."

Mr. Ryan waves his hand, a more fluid version of the *erasing a blackboard* gesture I've seen from Carol. "Yeah, yeah, yeah. Just knowing that is going to make your mother feel better. Of course, we're both smart enough not to make her wise to any of this."

"You've got my word," Carol says.

She turns to order another drink. Mr. Ryan leans toward me and drops his voice to a whisper.

"You pulled my fat out of the fire tonight," he says, "Don't think I don't appreciate it. If Matty were here, he'd thank you to." He clears his throat and glances away. "Good to know my little girl has good people in her life."

I try not to blush (because I'm pretty sure he'd slug me for it). I fumble for the words. "That means a lot coming from you, Mr. Ryan."

He twists his mouth to one side. He lets out a breath, as if coming to a difficult conclusion. "You can call me Walt."

"Oh. Well, thank you, Walt."

"Every now and again. Don't abuse the privilege."

It's Walt's turn to order another drink. Carol slides back to her seat, holding a new Cosmo. We clink glasses in a little toast. Yeah, I didn't want to be dragged into this and it raised my blood pressure more than the average evening. But to do a favor for a friend like Carol? It's worth it.

After all, she's a hell of a broad.

DEATH CAN'T BE TRUSTED

All of us, I believe, have a friend we completely trust. Even when we don't want to.

Here's what I mean: there's always one person in our circle of acquaintance we could live without. But sometimes this person is the most trustworthy one of the bunch. He's the person who will plow out your driveway after the big blizzard. The one who's only a phone call away if you're in trouble. The first one to respond if you put out a call for help on Facebook. The person who forces you to end your every rant about them with the words, "Yeah, but so-and-so would be there for me, no matter what." You have to appreciate that.

The miserable ass.

My name's Joe Davis and I've got one of those friends. It's my buddy, Lars.

Lars isn't the first person you'd think of as reliable. In fact, he's probably not the five-hundredth person you'd think of. But somewhere beneath his veneer of slackerism is a shockingly honest person. Abe Lincoln honest. (If Lars thinks Abe proved his honesty by confessing to chopping down a cherry tree, well, that's more rank ignorance than dishonesty.) He's proven his worth, lo these many years, as treasurer of my fantasy football league.

I've had the league for about eight years now. While I enjoy being the commissioner, I've always hated the money aspect: trying to get entry fee money out of various deadbeats, explaining to the winners that I don't have all their winnings yet (due to the aforementioned deadbeats). Still, I was a bit dubious when Lars offered to be treasurer. He treats money as the disposable entity it is, but it's more disposable in Lars' hands than in others. He has a tendency toward various get-rich-quick schemes that leave him poorer than when he started.

But I have to admit: Lars has been a great treasurer. He has a knack for staying on people until they cough up the entry fee. He holds the money throughout the season without a single thought (near as I can tell) to using it for personal gain. And his payouts are always prompt and accurate. Much as it pains to me say: I don't know where I'd be without Lars removing the *one* aspect of fantasy football I don't enjoy.

So, it's disconcerting when he shows up at my apartment and says: "Joe, I've lost the fantasy football money."

I should have sensed something was wrong when Lars knocked on my door. Lars *never* knocks. If he finds my place locked, he simply uses his master key to let himself in. So, I was off-balance even before Lars delivered his opening line.

"Lost?" I say, gripping the doorknob, "Lost how?"

"It was in its usual place last night. Today, it isn't there."

I'm doing my best not to slam the door into Lars' head and watch him tumble down the stairs. Instead, I step back and wave him into my apartment. Lars slinks past me and ambles around the living room. The day is otherwise lovely, what with the sun shining in the arch windows, the fall colors visible all along Summit Avenue and the smell of pumpkin spice coffee in the air (up yours, haters!). Lars' news has pretty much shot the atmosphere to hell.

I sit at the breakfast bar. "Maybe you ought to give me the whole story."

Lars puts his hands in the pockets of his khaki slacks. "Okay, I had a couple of people over last night for a business meeting. Robbie, Chuck and T.J. I had a proposal for them."

I take my Charlie Brown mug to the coffeemaker for a refill. "What kind of business?"

Lars glides to the breakfast bar. "You remember the idea I had for a food truck?"

Nausea creeps into my stomach. "Is this the Squidburger thing?"

"Indeed, yes! Squid: the cow of the sea. It's the coming thing in cuisine. Believe me."

I don't believe him for a second, but that won't stop him. The first time he told me this idea, we were at a party and I had to find an excuse to get away before the mere idea made me vomit. I was hoping this, like most of Lars' ideas, would disappear as soon as he sobered up. No such luck.

"You sure people are going to flock to a thing like that?" I ask, hoping the smell of pumpkin spice will keep my stomach steady.

"Absolutely. The delicious flavor of ground squid? What's not to love?"

Gorge…rising…but still: "You sure a squid can be ground?"

He laughs it off, as if the suggestion came from a mere child. "If you can jerk a chicken, you can grind a squid."

Okay, that's as much of that subject as I want to cover. "I understand Chuck being there. Why did you need Robbie and T.J.?"

"Nuts and bolts. Robbie's uncle owns a moving van. Remember? You and Mike used it when you had that thing with the Chechen gangsters."

"How can I forget?" I say, though God knows I'm trying.

"I thought Robbie's uncle might be interested in selling—or better yet, donating—the van to a good cause. It seemed logical to run it by Robbie first."

"Why was T.J. there?"

"From what I understand, Robbie has a difficult relationship with his uncle," Lars says, "Made worse by the thing with the Chechens. But I hear this uncle gets along well with T.J. Hence, his presence at the meeting."

I have a hard time imagining Robbie and T.J. going along with a plan this goofy but I'll let Lars figure that out on his own. Meantime, I'm still waiting for part about the theft.

"It was just the four of you there?" I ask.

"At first. It was a business meeting. A dry affair we masters of industry indulge in."

"Uh-huh. And how many beers did you guys have?"

"Before or after the chicks came over?"

I pinch the bridge of my nose, dealing with the headache Lars frequently gives me. In other circumstances, I might be disappointed Lars didn't invite me to the party, but I was on a date last night. Which provided its own disappointment.

I take my coffee back to the breakfast bar. "Which chicks were these?"

"Cyndi and Penni. They're in 3B. I run into them frequently out on their deck."

"The sunbathers?"

"Penni is, yes. Cyndi, not so much."

I've seen the two of them out there. Penni is slim and small, with flowing blonde hair and mysterious eyes. When sunbathing, she wears a white bikini that shows off her huge…tracts of land. I don't have a handle on what Cyndi looks like. When she joins her roommate, she wears only slightly less covering than the Invisible Man.

"What were they doing over at your place?" I ask.

"I invited them. They seem like lovely young ladies and I want to get to know them better. In a physical sense, of course."

"Of course."

"I thought it might be a good time. For a while, it was."

I step around the breakfast bar and wander toward my desk. "Okay, so you had the whole gang over. They leave. You go to bed. You wake up this morning and the money's gone."

"That's the fact, Jack."

Quoting Bill Murray will get you somewhere with me. "How did you know the money's missing?"

"It's in an envelope I keep on the shelf, right next to the tribal mask."

"It was just sitting out in the open?" I ask, "Where just anybody could steal it?"

He laughs. "The envelope is marked *Bea Arthur, nude photos*. Believe me, nobody's going to take a look in there."

Son of a bitch. Five years of trusting Lars with the fantasy football money and I discover the shocking part is that it wasn't stolen sooner. I dig around the desk and find a notepad. I walk back to the breakfast bar, toss the pad down and scribble *Timeline* at the top of the page. Lars peers over my shoulder.

"What are you doing?" he asks.

"We're going to put together a timeline of where people were and what they were doing last night. Figure out who stole the money." Lars plunks down next to me at the breakfast bar. We focus on the notepad. "Okay, what time did everyone get together?" I ask.

"Eight o'clock."

I scribble down *Eight pm: business.* "What time did the business meeting end?"

"Around nine. I didn't have a full commitment from the guys, but I thought it appropriate to toast the occasion. Start the venture on a classy note."

"What did you toast with?" I ask.

"Jagermeister."

"Classy."

"I thought so," Lars says, "After a few shots, I thought we should invite the girls over. They were agreeable. Came over right away."

I write down *Nine pm: party starts*. "And what was the last thing you remember?"

"I remember passing out on the couch," Lars says, "And being angry."

"About what?"

"That I don't remember. I must have had an argument. Or overheard an argument."

"What time did you pass out?"

He puts a hand over his eyes, as if trying to focus on some vision. "I remember looking at the clock and thinking, 'Hey, it's almost one o'clock'. I remember being mad, so this must have been after whatever it was that ticked me off."

I write *1am* and then two lines below it, add *Lars passes out*. On the line between, I write *Argument?* The whole thing looks pretty sketchy.

"Was everyone there when you passed out?" I ask.

"No," Lars says, "Cyndi left pretty early on. And T.J. left early, too. Said he was tired. Robbie and Penni were still there. They'd spent most of the night talking. They really hit it off. Can't deny feeling a bit cock-blocked there. And I don't remember when Chuck left"

I scribble their names in the margin, figuring I can fit them in later. I tap the notepad with the pen. "Anything else you can remember?"

Lars bounces off the stool and paces the living room, his head down in intense concentration. Finally, he kicks at the futon (and misses).

"I don't!" he says, waving his arms like straw in the wind, "That's the maddening part! I can remember little images, but none of them significant. And none of them involve someone spiriting away the league's loot." He runs a hand through his quasi-pompadour, which is sagging and looking rather pathetic. "What am I going to do? As soon as the guys find out the money's gone, they're going to kill me."

I put a hand on his shoulder, trying to calm him. "The guys will understand. We're all friends, right?"

"Not when money's involved," he says, "They turn into a collection of jackals. You watch. There will be blood."

"I doubt that."

"Oh yeah? Give Mike a call. Tell him what happened."

I could debate Lars, but it would be faster to show him he's wrong. I take out my cell phone and punch in Mike's number. He picks up on the third ring, sounding a tad hungover (not an unusual condition for him).

"What do you need?" is how he answers.

"I'm just wondering something," I say, "You know how Lars holds on to the money for the fantasy league?"

A note of trepidation creeps into Mike's voice. "Yeah, I do."

"Well, what if—and I'm just spitballing here—Lars lost the money. What would—?"

Mike's voice can be heard by Lars and most of the surrounding neighborhood. "The stupid son of a bitch lost our money? I'll kill his ass! He put it in one of those bullshit schemes of his, didn't he? The stupid pile of shit! When I get my hands on him, I'm going to—"

I ring off, figuring the point has been made. Lars sinks on to a stool and drops his head in his hands. "You see now why I have to leave town and change my identity," he says. Then he claps a hand on my shoulder and says, "Been nice knowing you, Joe."

"You are *not* leaving town," I say, "We'll get the money back."

"How are we going to do that?"

"By finding out who took in the first place. The only people who could have done it were at your place last night: the two girls from 3B and the guys at the business meeting. It's a start, right?" I head for the front door. "Let's go talk to Cyndi and Penni and see what they know."

Lars heaves a sigh and joins me at the front door. He gives me a fleeting smile. "You're a good man."

"Thank you."

"A foolhardy man, but a good one."

Funny, I could say the same thing about him.

***

Cyndi's and Penni's apartment is on the third floor, in another section of the building. I knock on the front door and wait until the door opens a crack. Penni (the one generally in the bikini) peeks out.

"Can I help you?" she asks, in a voice more commanding than I expected.

Before I can answer, Lars sticks his head in front of mine. "How ya doing, Penni? This is my buddy, Joe. You got a minute?"

Penni looks back and forth between us. Finally, she flips the door wide and stands aside. "Come on in," she says.

The apartment is a mirror image of mine, with the door and the breakfast bar and such on the opposite side. It's like stepping into the Bizarro World. Lars, of course, is right at home. He drops on to the sectional sofa and stretches his arms across the back.

"Hell of a party last night, eh?" he says.

"Um, sure," Penni says, "Can I get you guys some coffee or something?"

"Coffee would be great," I say, hanging near the door.

Penni pads into the kitchen. She's wearing a sweatshirt over a pair of boxer shorts. (Her sleepwear, by my guess.) Her flowing blonde hair is tousled and her eyes are a tad puffy. She hasn't been awake long. She returns and hands me coffee in a slightly-chipped University of Minnesota mug. She gives me a wan smile.

Lars cranes his neck. "Where's Cyndi?"

Penni sits at the breakfast bar and cradles a cup of her own coffee. "At work."

"That's right," Lars says, snapping his fingers, "She's an architect?"

"She does data entry."

"I knew I was close." He looks back at Penni. "What about you? No work today?"

"I work nights."

"English teacher?" Lars asks.

The coffee cup stops short of Penni's lips. "I'm a receptionist at a health club."

Actually, *I* was close on that one. Don't ask me why (and the reasons are probably sexist) but I pegged Penni as either a health club receptionist or a server at a sports bar. She just seems to fit the mold. (I guess you can remove the *probably* from *sexist*.)

"We're here because Lars…lost something last night," I say, "We're asking the people at the party if they saw anything. Figured we'd start here."

Penni looks at Lars, confused. "What did he lose?"

"Some money," I say, "He's holding it for our fantasy football league. It was in an envelope and now it's missing."

"And you think I did it?" Penni says, eyes narrowing.

I hold up my hands. "Not at all. But the odds are pretty good that someone at the party did. We just want to know what people were up to and what they saw." Penni relents slightly, so I press forward. "From what Lars says, you and your roommate came to the party around nine?"

Penni bobs her head as she thinks. "Sounds about right."

"And your roommate left early?"

Her face tightens into a classic stinkface. "She had to get up early. She's a real tight-ass."

"What time did she leave?"

"I don't know. Probably nine-thirty."

"And what time did you leave?" I ask.

Penni hastily sips her coffee. "A little after one. Like one-fifteen, I want to say."

"You spent most of the night talking to Robbie?"

"Yeah, he's a nice guy," she says, staring into her coffee cup, "We hit it off. Too bad I got a boyfriend. For him, I mean. For Robbie." Another quick sip of coffee.

"Was Robbie still there when you left?" I ask.

"Yeah, he was. We didn't leave together. It was just me."

I look to Lars, hoping he can verify this. He just nods, serenely. Sadly, his drunkenness last night limits his usefulness.

I make a mental note of the time, figuring I'll add it to the timeline later. I'll have to double check the time—among other things—with Robbie.

"Do you remember Chuck?" I ask.

Penni wrinkles her nose. "The weird guy? No, he left by then."

Another couple mental notes to add to the timeline. I take a decent sip of the coffee, which is lukewarm and a little bland compared to the pumpkin spice back in my apartment (again, suck it haters).

"Did you see anyone getting into an argument?" I ask.

"Nope. Nothing like that," Penni says, "Wish I could be more help."

I finish the coffee and thank Penni for her time. I head for the front door while Lars glides over to Penni. He puts his hands in his pockets and takes on a shy air.

"So, this boyfriend of yours," he says, adding a little chuckle, "This is a serious thing?"

Penni leans away from him. "Yeah, it is. He's a good guy. And a bodybuilder. And an Army Ranger. With anger management issues."

Lars nods, considering this. "But in the sack…?"

I grab Lars and haul him out of there before Penni can damage him, sans boyfriend. Lars gives her the *call me* gesture as I'm dragging him out the door.

I might be better off letting the guys get ahold of him. It would be more humane.

***

After leaving Penni's, we stop for a quick breakfast at The Tav. I've added Penni's arrival and departure times to our timeline. It looks like Robbie was left alone in the apartment after Lars passed out. That would make him my top suspect. There's the possibility the money was stolen before Lars passed out, but in a room full of people it would be hard to pull off. Unfortunately, questioning Robbie is impossible at the moment. He's at work and incommunicado. (Any attempts to roust him at work may result in physical violence.) Instead, our next stop is in Roseville and a little office building housing the workplace of our buddy, T.J.

It's the best, if not the only, place to question him. Last night's excursion aside, T.J.'s rarely allowed to leave the house, thanks to his loyalty to (see also: sheer terror of) his lovely wife. T.J. takes lunch around noon and the cafeteria in his building is open to the public.

Said cafeteria, like the rest of the building, isn't particularly large. There's a lunch counter and a salad bar with a handful of tables and chairs beyond them. T.J. sits at a small table, eating a wrap with one hand and using a paper napkin to dab his lips with the other. Some paperwork is stretched out in front of him. It could be work-related or fantasy football league-related. Lars waves a hand toward the lunch buffet.

"I'm going to grab myself something," he says.

"You just ate," I say.

"That was hours ago."

"It was forty-five minutes ago."

"Let's not dwell on the past. I need grub."

He strolls off to the counter while I make my way over to T.J.'s table. T.J. looks up, startled, as I arrive. He quickly stuffs the paperwork into his briefcase. (That tells me it's fantasy football-related. If it was work-related, I wouldn't care.) I slide into a chair across from him. He straightens his glasses.

"Hi, Joe," T.J. says, his voice reedy as ever, "What, uh, what are you doing here?"

"I'm here with Lars. We wanted to talk about the party last night."

"Wha…what about it?"

I fold my hands on the table. "Lars lost the fantasy football money."

T.J. goes white. He nearly drops his wrap. "Lost? Did he already invest it in that disgusting food truck?"

"No, Lars wouldn't do that. Someone at the party took the money. We're trying to find out who."

Before T.J. can respond (and likely offer a denial), Lars strolls up, carrying a tray with a mushroom burger and fries. He sits next to T.J., who doesn't quite look at Lars.

"How's it going, Teej," Lars says, hoisting his burger, "Hell of a party last night."

T.J. chuckles, nervously. "Hell of a party. No doubt."

I find myself picking a fry off Lars' plate. (Seriously, we *just* had breakfast. And it was good.) "Like I said, we need to find out what went on last night. See if we can find the money."

"Well, I…I don't know anything about it," T.J. says.

"I understand you had to leave early," I say.

T.J. gives me a sharp look. "Where did you hear that?"

"Lars," I say, tilting my head toward Jughead Jones over there, "And the girls. Well, Penni, anyway."

T.J. straightens his glasses. "Ah. They were…they seemed really nice. Not as nice as Hunter, but very, very nice."

I've met T.J.'s wife and while I can think of a lot of words to describe her, *nice* isn't among them. Unless she's standing right in front of me, in which case I'd be only too glad to call her *nice*. While holding my hands over my junk.

"I haven't had a chance to talk to Cyndi yet," I say, "But Penni seems nice enough."

"Yeah, Robbie really seemed to like her," T.J. says, "*Really* seemed to like her."

"I heard he was hitting on her."

T.J. nods. "He had that look in his eyes. Same one he'd get in college on Nickel Beer Nights at Boomtown."

I remember that look. I'd pity any girl who got it. It meant they were going to be afflicted with Robbie's company until it was stopped by either a boyfriend or a restraining order.

"Too bad for Penni," I say.

"I don't think you need to feel bad for her," T.J. says, "She didn't seem to mind."

Huh. I wonder how Robbie views that flirtation? I'll be interested to hear his take (which will be a novel experience after I've spent most of my adult life tuning Robbie out). Meantime, Lars turns to T.J.

"You given any more thought to the project?" Lars asks, "I could use your support."

T.J. gets interested in his wrap. "I've, I've given it some thought, yes. And, uh…I really don't think it's a good investment."

Lars sets his burger down. "You're kidding. What possible objection could you have?"

"Well, leaving aside how disgusting I find the cuisine," T.J. says, "You'll need money to remodel the van. Assuming Robbie's uncle even sells it to you."

"*That's* why I need investors," Lars says, "I'm letting you guys in on the ground floor."

"I don't have the money to invest. I've got children and Hunter devotes her time to raising them. There just isn't any money left over." Then he mutters: "Especially not lately."

Lars slaps the table. "You're being short-sighted. A little pain now, a lot of gain later."

T.J. fumbles with cleaning his glasses on his shirt. "Actually, if Hunter found out, there'd be a lot of pain *now*." He slips the glasses back on. "I'm sorry, but I'm going to have to say no. I think Robbie's in the same position. I know his finances aren't any better."

Lars, disgusted with the loss of his enterprise, pointedly turns away from T.J. and resumes eating. T.J. looks more relieved than anything. At least I have the floor with him again.

"Is there anything else you remember?" I ask, "Anything that might help us figure out where the money is?"

"I don't remember much," he says, "I had to leave kind of early. I've been working a lot of overtime. I get tired pretty quickly."

"Pretty busy around the office?" I say. I'll be honest: I have absolutely no idea what T.J. does for a living. Nor do I really care.

"Just keeping the nose to the grindstone," he says, "You know how it goes."

"I do," I say. Truthfully, I have no freakin' clue. I'm a single guy in his thirties with two cats. I work for rent, cat food and booze. Not necessarily in that order.

There's a faint buzzing sound. T.J. pulls his cell phone out of his pocket. His brows knit. He pops to his feet, hastily grabbing his briefcase and abandoning his wrap.

"I've, uh, I've got to take this," he says, "It was good seeing you guys. Hope you find the money. Good, uh…luck."

He walks away from the table and disappears past the lunch counter. I wait a few seconds, then signal Lars to follow me. I lead the way back to the lobby. Lars is just a step behind me, having not only grabbed his burger, but also commandeered the rest of T.J.'s wrap. We find T.J. standing next to one of the high-top tables scattered about the lobby. From the look of things, it might be all that's holding him up. He spots us and shakily turns away. Feeling I'm not going to get anything out of him, I head for the front door.

"I wonder what that was all about?" I ask, as soon as we've cleared the lobby.

Lars is sulking. "That was about T.J. blowing the opportunity of a lifetime."

I'm about to correct him but what's the use? I doubt he's going to feel for T.J., a guy with a life so miserable that a common-sense decision like not throwing money at Lars' latest jackass scheme is considered a victory.

Mental note: use T.J. as a case study the next time my mom pesters about me not being married.

***

The next stop is the home of my buddy, Robbie. His house is a few blocks off Dale Street, just a stone's throw from the State Fairgrounds. (On those rare occasions when I go to the State Fair, I park at Robbie's.) It's a tiny little rambler with a couple of bedrooms and one bathroom. Not splendid, but more than enough for a single guy with a small child who's only around part of the time. The exterior is well maintained and the lawn is tiny, but pristine. And the neighborhood is quiet. A decent place to raise a part-time kid. (Well, she's a kid full-time, but…you know what I mean.)

Robbie's Prius is in the driveway when we pull up. We stroll up to the front door and I ring the bell. No one answers. I try the bell again. Finally, Robbie's face appears in the little diamond-shaped window in the door. He frowns (not that he's Mr. Happy-Happy Joy-Joy at the best of times).

He opens the door a crack. "What do you want?" is his greeting.

"Just wanted to talk to you," I say, "We've got a situation."

"What kind of situation?" he asks, not moving the door.

"With the money for the fantasy football league. Can we come in? It's only going to take a second."

"Can't do it," Robbie says, "Marissa's here."

As if on cue, a little girl's voice can be heard. "Daddy, are you coming back? Everything's getting cold."

But I'm not going to let a little girl stop me. "It's important. Trust me."

Again, Marissa's voice: "Da…ddy!"

Robbie deflates. He pushes open the door. "Fine. Come in."

He steps aside, allowing Lars and me into the entryway. In the middle of the living room floor is a small table, probably produced by Fisher-Price. It has a tea set and a couple of Twinkies on paper plates. Marissa, a lovely little girl of about six, sits at one of the chairs. She's wearing a pink dress and her mass of blonde curls is done up.

Robbie, wearing a frilly apron over his beer gut, puts his hands in his back pockets. "Sweetie, these are daddy's friends," he says, in a tone of voice I've never heard him use and didn't think he was capable of producing.

Marissa takes this in her stride. She gives us a gap-toothed smile and waves. "Do you want to have tea with us?"

I look toward Robbie. He says nothing, but the look in his eyes tells me I will never speak of this if I wish to have a long life. I look toward Marissa and nod.

"That would be lovely," I say.

Marissa points toward two of the chairs. "You can sit there."

The three of us join Marissa at the little table. It's built for someone Marissa's size, so the three of us are sitting with our knees up around our ears. Marissa pours us each an imaginary tea and splits the two Twinkies so they'll go around. I sip my imaginary beverage, making sure to point my pinkie.

Robbie holds the little cup like someone put a small turd in his hand. "What, uh, what is it you guys want to know?"

"We're wondering what you saw at the, uh, business meeting last night," I say, "What you remember."

"Why do you want to know?" Robbie asks.

"Because the fantasy football money is missing," I say.

Robbie starts to get up but stops out of a) consideration for Marissa and b) the realization that weight gain and bad knees have this move impossible. "What the fu…fu…for heaven's sake, guys, how did that happen?"

I wave my cup toward Marissa, letting her know I enjoy the "tea". "Someone at the little gathering must have taken it."

Marissa gives that a *tsk-tsk*. "That's naughty."

"Indeed, naughty is the exact word for it," I say, "Lars and I are piecing together what happened and trying to identify the exact, uh, naughty individual who took the money."

Robbie looks at me, quickly, and says: "It wasn't me."

"Never thought for a second it was," I say, lying my ass off for the sake of the child, "I'm just piecing stuff together. I know the meeting was at eight. I know the, uh, post-meeting festivities started around nine. What time did you leave?"

"Around one," Robbie says, squirming in the tiny chair, "That's when I left Lars' place."

Something in the phrasing intrigues me. Before I can figure it out, Lars jumps in. "Where was Marissa?"

"I was at Mommy's," Marissa says, with the habitual annoyance kids get when they're talked about as if they're not in the room.

Robbie smiles (though it could also be cramps) and says, "Bailey dropped her off this afternoon."

Implicit in the smile is the notion we should not, under any circumstances, go into detail about Robbie's, uh, interpersonal activities from last night. Bailey, Marissa's mother, has never gotten over the relationship with Robbie and usually calls up with all sorts of threats, both to Robbie and herself, when she finds out he's dating someone. Or really, doing anything with someone. Marissa, like all children, is an unfiltered conduit of information. Obviously, we don't need to feed gossip to the darling little rat bastard.

"You left at one," I say, "You sure it wasn't one-fifteen?"

He shrugs his broad shoulders. "Might have been. You'd have to ask…Lars' friend. The one who lives in the building."

"Ah yes," Lars says, "The one you were hitting on."

Robbie's meaty hands start to come up. Fortunately, before he can strangle Lars, Robbie catches sight of Marissa and tamps down his anger. Marissa gives him a quizzical look.

"What's 'hitting on'?" she asks.

Robbie gives that a nervous laugh. "It means playing around. Kind of."

"Like with dolls?"

"Sure. Why not?" Robbie turns his attention to me. "Penni and I left together. I thought I should walk her to her front door. Y'know, be a gentleman."

"You just went as far as the front door?" I ask.

Robbie scratches the back of his head. "Maybe a little farther than that."

Marissa pipes up. "Did you tuck her in?"

"No, I didn't, sweetie." Then he mumbles, "Not for a lack of trying, I'll tell you."

Lars clucks his tongue. "Too bad. She's really hot."

Robbie's face is turning red. I'm checking the mental database to see if I'm equipped to handle a stroke. (No such luck.) I somehow manage to stand up from the table (guess all those squats at the club weren't a waste of time, after all.)

"Hey Robbie, I need to use the bathroom," I say, "All this tea. You think you could show me where it's at?"

Somehow, the subtext of my message pierces both Robbie's anger and his native stupidity. He manages to get up, though he nearly upsets the table in the process.

"It's down the hall," he says, "I'll show you."

Robbie and I excuse ourselves and walk down to the back bedroom. It's replete with threadbare carpeting and paneling on the walls. (Robbie's kept the place clean but has absolutely no eye for interior decoration.) He closes the door behind us.

"I'm safe leaving Marissa out there with Lars, aren't I?" he asks.

"She'll be fine. Lars is only a threat to women eighteen and over." I lower my voice. "Okay, I know you were hitting on Penni all night. She claims she left at one-fifteen and you were still at Lars'."

"Horseshit. We went back to her place and rolled around on the couch for a while. I thought I was getting somewhere but then she got an attack of the guilts about her boyfriend. So I left. Probably around two." He rubs his eyes. "My ass has been dragging all day."

"Were you the last two to leave?"

"Yeah. Lars was passed out on the couch. Him and Chuck had some kind of fight, so Chuck stormed out. T.J. and, what's her face…Penni's roommate. They both left early."

"What was the fight about?" I ask.

"Not sure. It wasn't exactly my highest priority, you know what I'm saying? I think it was about money, but don't take that as the gospel."

"You know what time Chuck left?"

Robbie hums as he thinks. "Maybe fifteen, twenty minutes before we did. After the fight, Lars passed out the couch. Penni and I decided to take the show on the road." Robbie glances in the direction of the living room. "Lars really lost the fantasy football money?"

"Somebody stole it. We'll get it back."

He mumbles: "I ain't holding my breath."

I don't blame him (though that doesn't stop me from being annoyed by him). I thank Robbie for his time and tell him we'll leave him to his tea party. Just as I'm opening the bedroom door, he grabs my arm.

"Do me—and yourself—a favor: don't tell Stoner about this."

I can his point. Handing this kind of information to Stoner, Robbie's archenemy and relentless tormentor (also his best friend and Marissa's godfather), would be like giving him the nuclear codes.

"No worries," I say, "I won't tell Stoner a thing."

"Thank you."

"I'll buy a billboard and let that do the work."

***

The next step, unfortunately, is talking to Lars' friend, Chuck. Lars contacts him, since I have neither Chuck's number nor a desire to talk to him any more than necessary. We arrange a meeting at Glacier's, my favorite neighborhood coffee shop.

Lars and I get there first. Glacier's is a converted café with checkerboard tile floors, straight-back chairs, brass rails and picture windows. It's currently in the grip of an evening lull. A few regulars hang about and some wannabe writers spend more time on their phones than their manuscripts. Lars and I find a table near the window.

"Now, you have to handle Chuck with kid gloves," Lars says, "He hates having his honesty impugned. He is a figure of extreme rectitude."

"You're saying he shouldn't be a suspect?" I say.

"Well, he's also an opportunist, so let's not rule anything out."

Chuck strolls through the door a second later. He's a slightly flabby dude with swept-back blonde hair and deep-set eyes. While Lars hails him as a creative genius, I've seen little evidence of it. He just strikes me as suspicious and constipated.

He sweeps into the seat across from me and glares at Lars. "What's this all about?" is how he greets us.

Lars places his hands palms down on the table. "Chuck, the envelope where I kept the fantasy football money was empty this morning."

Chuck doesn't bat an eyelash. "So?"

I, on the other hand, bat Lars on the arm. "You told Chuck where the fantasy football money was kept?"

Chuck scoffs. "Please. I figured it out before he told me. If he *had* nude pictures of Bea Arthur, you think he'd just sit on them?"

"Besides, Chuck's my business partner," Lars says, "There's two people you tell everything to: your business partner and your priest."

"What about your significant other?" I ask.

"No, you hide everything from them," Lars says, "It's the secret to a good relationship."

Given that neither Lars nor I have been married—or even gotten close, really—I'm not going to debate him. Meantime, the business partner returns to the subject at hand.

"Okay, the envelope was empty," Chuck says, "What's that got to do with me?"

"We're trying to piece together the events of last night," Lars says, "And I understand you and I had a little argument."

Chuck's eyes are hooded slightly by the lighting. "You telling me you don't remember?"

"That is what I am telling you, yes," Lars says.

Chuck sits back and holds his hands up in mock surrender. "Fine, then. I won't hold you responsible for what was said."

Lars offers Chuck his hand. "That's a huge relief. Thank you, brother. I knew you were the forgiving sort."

"No worries," Chuck says, shaking Lars' hand, "We go back too far to let a few words get between us."

They seem content to let it go at that. I'm tempted to quit this whole operation and let the guys tear Lars limb from limb. But I'd be out fifty bucks (I might be anyway if my receiving corps doesn't get its shit together) and I wouldn't know which of my fellow league members is a damn thief. I guess it's up to me to question Chuck. (Because this is *exactly* how I hoped my evening would go.)

"I'm surprised you're so forgiving," I say, "From what Robbie said, the argument was pretty intense."

"Surprised he'd notice," Chuck says, "He was wrapped up in chasing that broad."

"Was the, uh, *broad* still there when you left?" I ask.

"Yeah, I think she was. I wasn't paying much attention."

Given I've never seen or heard of Chuck being with a woman, I'm not surprised by his lack of interest. Still, we've established Robbie and Penni were still at Lars' by the time Chuck left. I mentally tick off another box in the timeline.

"And T.J. left early, right?" I say.

Chuck nods. "Yeah, that didn't surprise me. He seems like a bit of a delicate doily."

No argument there. Speaking of which… "What were you guys arguing about?" I ask.

Chuck glares at me and then says, "I suppose I can tell you. Long as Lars apologized."

Lars holds up both hands, as if he's giving a runner the stop sign at third base. "To be clear: I didn't apologize. I just said it was magnanimous of you to let things go."

"Which implies you were in the wrong," Chuck says, "And you were. Because you're a fucking cheapskate asshole."

The two of them face off across the table, their noses only inches apart. I look around, wondering if anyone's going to step in or perhaps call the cops. No one's paying attention. I grab the sugar shaker for protection. Lars slides up the sleeves of his flannel shirt.

"Listen, I am the money man in our operation," Lars says, "You're a visionary, Chuck. I will never dispute that. But sometimes—and I'm sorry to be the bearer of bad tidings—you need a little adult supervision."

Chuck puffs up like he's about to explode. "There's no use being a visionary if some goddamn tightwad isn't going to fund the venture. This idea is solid and you know it!"

Lars waves him off, like he's erasing a blackboard. "In the long term…maybe. Believe me, I love the idea of starting a private streetcar line. But first, private ownership of public transportation just isn't done anymore."

"Really? You taken a taxi lately?"

"You can't pull it off on this level."

Chuck flips his hand. "Just gotta grease the right politicians. They're all for sale."

"Still, with the outlay for the tracks, the rolling stock, the employees, the electrical lines, you're running into an enormous expense."

"It's a tall task. But with the right fundraising—"

"It would take years!" Lars says.

"Hey, you're the money man. If you can't raise the money, what good are you?"

Lars sticks a finger in Chuck's face. "You're the one who—" He stops. "This is what we argued about last night, wasn't it?"

"You're goddamned right it was!" Chuck says, getting the attention of the coffee shop dwellers, "I'm tired of having my work hampered by small-minded penny pinchers like you!" He stands and tucks his coat around him. "Gentlemen, have a good evening. And go fuck yourselves." He throws his head in the air and strides out.

I look toward Lars and say: "That went well."

He shrugs. "Chuck's a man of passion. It occasionally gets the better of him."

"I'm impressed you could see the impracticality of the streetcar plan."

"I could," Lars says, stroking his goatee, "But let's not rule anything out."

***

It's been nearly twelve hours and we're right back where we started: lounging in my apartment. Lars is stretched out on the couch (with his shoes still on, even though I've asked him a hundred times not to do that). An opened bottle of Grand Brewing Oktoberfest is on the floor beside him (without a coaster in sight). I'm at the breakfast bar, nursing an Oktoberfest of my own. My cats, Lenny and Squiggy, are on the window ledge, staring at Lars and wondering, no doubt, when he's going to leave. I tap the beer bottle on the counter.

"Doesn't feel like we got far," I say.

"We did not," Lars says, "My plans to leave town and start a new life remain unchanged. I can shave the beard, change my wardrobe, go by the name Hans Pfaffenberg again."

I shoot him a look. "Again?"

"It's an identity I've used in the past."

"I didn't know that."

"I have a——"

"Life outside of me. Yes. That I *do* know." I look over the timeline on the notepad sitting in front of me. "Not a lot to see here. Party commences at nine. Cyndi leaves around ten. T.J. leaves around ten-thirty. Chuck left around twelve-forty-five. Penni either left alone or with Robbie at around one-fifteen. You were passed out shortly after Chuck left. We know the money was in the envelope before the party started and gone by the morning." I tap the notepad with a pen. "The only thing we haven't done is talk to Cyndi, the roommate. I wouldn't get your hopes up. She left pretty early."

"Oh, believe me. My hopes are anything but up."

We finish our beers and trudge out the backdoor. It's a nice enough night to approach Penni's and Cyndi's place from the deck. We make our way through the erector set and, to our surprise, Cyndi is outside. She's got short dark hair and a pinched face. She wears a baggy gray sweatshirt, faded jeans and a pair of sandals. She sits at a green plastic table with a hammered glass candle and a bottle of red wine on it. She doesn't seem entirely pleased to see us.

"Penni's not here," she says, sipping her wine out of an old fruit jar.

"That's okay," I say, "We're actually here to see you."

"What about?"

"The party last night," Lars says, "Some weird, wild stuff went down and we need to know what happened."

She folds her arms. "What do you mean by 'weird, wild stuff'?"

I tell her about the missing fantasy football money. As I do, Lars joins Cyndi at the table. She looks like someone just cut one (I get the feeling she frequently has that look on her face). Lars slings an ankle over a knee.

"So you see the urgency here," he says, "The money needs to be returned before the guys in the league hang me up by my thumbs and do unspeakable things to my person."

"What sort of unspeakable things?" Cyndi asks.

"Let's not speak of them," Lars says.

I hover over Lars' shoulder. "I know you left the party early. But did you see anything unusual going on? Anything suspicious?"

Cyndi shakes her head. "Just a bunch of louts becoming drunken louts. Not the sort of thing I wanted to hang around for. I had to work early." She yawns, as if to stress the point.

Shazbot. We've talked to everyone at the party and there isn't a smoking gun, so to speak. Robbie is still my top suspect, since he may have been alone with the money at some point. The only useful question I can ask Cyndi is a rather delicate one.

"I heard your roommate hit it off with our buddy, Robbie," I say.

Cyndi groans. "God, he was the worst of the bunch. I can't believe Penni brought him home with her."

Ah ha! I have an answer to the *Did Robbie fool around with Penni* mystery! Which means…he was never alone with the money. And can't be considered a suspect. Bugger.

"So Robbie and Penni *did* come back to your place?" I say.

Cyndi's stinkface goes up to eleven. "Yes. She's already dating a complete troglodyte and now she feels the need to bring home strays. I think she just likes the drama." Disgust laces every syllable. "They woke me up when they came in. They were talking like they were in a club. Then they were…making out." I cringe, having been in that situation once or twice (having a dorm room next to Robbie was no picnic). Cyndi continues. "I wound up coming out here, just to get away from the noise. If it had been any warmer, I might have slept out here. It was peaceful, at least. Only one I saw was your friend T.J."

My head swings her direction. "T.J. was out here?"

"He was coming up the back stairs over there," Cyndi says, waving a hand in the general direction of Lars' place, "I assumed he was going back to the party. Why, I don't know." She looks at Lars. "Didn't you see him?"

Lars scratches the back of his head. "I was not in a condition to see anyone at that point."

I ask Cyndi to confirm once more that it was T.J. She does, sounding thoroughly annoyed. I thank her for her time, then grab Lars and haul him off the deck. He tries to keep up as we navigate the path back to my apartment.

"Does T.J. know where your spare key is kept?" I ask.

"I think so. I keep it a close-guarded secret. It's only shared by the two of us, Mike, Carol, all the people in the fantasy league and my graduating class from high school."

"Right. So, just you, me and the rest of Western Civilization."

He stops to catch his breath as we arrive at my deck. "Why do you ask?"

"Because I think T.J. has our money."

***

I text T.J. and ask if we can talk. He texts back to let me know he isn't home, which is a relief because I didn't want to confront T.J. in the presence of his wife. Not when there's half a chance the confrontation ends with her pulling T.J.'s still-beating heart out of his chest and chanting *Kali ma! Kali ma!* T.J.'s meeting someone at a place called Norman's Steakhouse, near Rosedale Mall. I let the correspondence end without telling him he's likely to see me soon.

Norman's Steakhouse is, like most retail near Rosedale, a cookie-cutter restaurant vying for stylishness. There's a sizable fireplace and a sort of faux-deco aesthetic. A series of picture windows provides a lovely view of the parking lot and the big box retail stores beyond.

Lars and I slip past the hostess' stand and head into the bar area. It's crowded with customers waiting for tables. We find T.J. at the end of the long mahogany bar, nursing a martini larger than his head. Lars and I take up positions on either side of him.

"How you doing, T.J.?" I say, "Fancy meeting you here."

T.J.'s head swivels about. He glances, goggle-eyed, past us, toward the restaurant entrance. "This really isn't a good time…"

Lars taps the bar. "We know, we know. You've got a meeting. We only need a few minutes. Maybe less."

"Okay, but, but make it quick," T.J. says.

"No worries," Lars says, "We'll be the peak of efficiency." Then he turns to the bartender and orders a stinger.

I'm left to take over. "T.J., we came for the money."

His eyes widen (and I didn't think they could get any wider). "The…the money?"

Lars leans in from the other side. "The fantasy football money. You took it, Teej."

T.J. shakes his head, a little too emphatically. "I…I didn't. It…"

I wave him off. "We have a witness who saw you go into Lars' apartment after everyone else had left. You snuck back and took the money out of the envelope, didn't you?"

T.J. sputters, trying to find an excuse. Finally, his shoulders sag. "Yeah, I took the money. I'm sorry, Lars. I've never done a thing like this before. And I wouldn't do it now if I wasn't totally desperate."

Lars lays a hand on T.J.'s shoulder. "My investment opportunity? Can't miss, huh?"

"No, no. There's no way Hunter would let me…" His jaw drops. "Oh dear God, you didn't tell Hunter I took the money, did you?"

"We haven't talked to her," I say, "And we won't if you give it back."

"I can't!" T.J. says, grabbing my arm, "If I give back the money, I'm a dead man."

"T.J., what the hell is going on?" I say, "Maybe we can help."

"No, forget it," he says, "You guys would be out of your lea…then again, we did take on a bunch of Chechen gangsters, didn't we?" He draws me and Lars into a huddle. "I've got a gambling problem."

"An addiction?" I ask.

"No," T.J. says, "Like I'm horseshit at it." He runs a hand through his hair. "Let me start at the beginning. Hunter and I have money problems. With a couple of kids and a mortgage and what my job pays, we can't make ends meet. I brought up the idea of her getting a job, but…well, she made it clear if I want to get through this life with both of my testicles, I'll never bring that up again."

I could argue the ship has sailed on the no-testicles thing, but it wouldn't get us anywhere. "That's why you took the fantasy football money?"

"It's a little more complicated than that. Robbie's uncle mentioned this floating card game he knew about. Said anyone who's halfway decent could make a little side money. I though that sounded like a good idea. So I got involved."

Ugh. I know where this is headed. T.J. fancies himself a good card player. As does everyone in our college gang. But that's only because we're all equally horseshit.

"How did it turn out?" I ask.

"I lost a ton of money," T.J. says, staring into his drink, "And I borrowed to stay in the game. You know how it is. You keep telling yourself you'll get it back. You just need one big hand. It didn't happen. And these guys need their money. I had to get some cash, quick. When I was at your place last night, Lars, it dawned on me that you kept the fantasy football money. I wasn't sure where, but I figured I could come back later and look. That's what I did."

"You caught a lucky break," Lars says, "With me being passed out and all."

"Not really," T.J. says, "Way you were drinking, I could see that one coming."

Lars sips his stinger. "It's a fair cop."

"The worst part is it won't even pay off the debts," T.J. says, "These guys claim I owe them interest. The fantasy money is only going to buy me time."

Oh boy. I feel like I should lecture T.J. on the stupidity of his actions. But the time for that is long past. Best to deal with the disaster currently impending.

"Who are you meeting here?" I ask.

"Guy's name is Rich," T.J. says, "He runs the game. Typical thug. All smiley and nice when you first meet him. Then the second you owe him money, he turns into a shark."

I've met the type a few times and was careful never to get into any kind of debt with them. Man, T.J. has thoroughly screwed the pooch here, but I'm trying to be understanding. Yes, I've had money problems, but they could be solved by a call home to my parents. I've never had little kids to care for or a wife breathing down my neck. But that understanding only goes so far.

"You got the money on you now?" I ask.

T.J. slips an envelope out of his pocket and holds it up. I snatch it out of his hand and stick it in my coat pocket. T.J. looks stunned, as if waiting for me to hand it back.

"What the hell are you doing?" he asks.

"Taking the money back," I say.

"But…but it's mine!"

"No, it's not," I say, "That's kind of the point here. You can't pay off your gambling debts by stealing money from the league. And you certainly can't let Lars take the blame for it. That's not how this works. That's not how any of this works."

T.J. grabs me by the coat but lets go when the bartender stops by to take my order. The sweat on T.J.'s face makes his glasses slide down his nose.

"You don't understand," he says, "This guy will fucking kill me."

Lars claps a hand on T.J.'s shoulder. "We'll talk to him." His tone, as always, conveys an unwarranted confidence.

T.J. is not comforted. "This guy won't be reasoned with. He's—"

I look past T.J. "Here right now."

The guy walks toward us, his eyes lasered in on T.J. He's short, his face craggy, his eyes malicious. He keeps his hands in the pockets of his black windbreaker. He's clearly unhappy to see Lars and me. (We're getting a lot of that today.)

T.J. smiles, weakly. "Hi, Rich."

Rich's greeting: "Who the fuck are these guys?"

Lars throws his hand out. "My name's Lars. I'm a friend of T.J.'s and a—"

"Great. Fucking good for you." Rich is still focused on T.J. "You got it with you?"

T.J. looks at me, desperate. My expression tells him where I stand. "Well, yes and no," T.J. says, "Mostly no."

Rich is not thrilled with this answer. He looks ready to throttle T.J. This would seem to be a good time for me to step in.

"T.J. tried to get the money," I say, "But he got it by stealing from our fantasy football league."

"And who the fuck are you?" Rich asks.

"I, uh, I represent the league," I say, realizing how completely lame that sounds.

Rich concurs. "Yeah, fucking good for you, too. I don't give two shits how you get the money, T.J. I need it. Now."

Lars pokes his head between Rich and T.J. "There might be room to negotiate here."

Rich pushes Lars' head out of the way. He reaches into his pocket and takes out his cell phone. He rests the hand holding it on the bar.

"Last chance, T.J.," Rich says, "You got the money or no?"

T.J. looks back at me. I shake my head. T.J. turns to Rich but can only give him a defeated shrug. Rich punches a number into the cell phone and waits for an answer.

"Have it your way," he says, "I got guys at your house right now. You don't want to give us our money, we're going to talk to your family about it."

T.J. hops off the stool and reaches toward Rich. "You can't do that. Rich, please."

"You had your chance," Rich says, "Now we're doing business my way." He speaks into the phone. "Move in. Keep me on the line."

T.J. bounces from one foot to the other, frantic but powerless. A living nightmare. Lars vigorously rubs his beard, something he does when trying to think up a quick idea (something I can tell you from experience he's horseshit at). I slip my cell phone out of my pocket and start to dial 9-1-1. I only get to the first "1" before Rich speaks to me.

"Wouldn't recommend that," he says, patting his jacket pocket to indicate he has a gun.

Oh great. Armed thugs. I would have preferred facing the guys after telling them the fantasy football money is gone. Of course, my agonies are nothing compared to T.J.'s. The dude looks like he's going to dissolve into a puddle right before our eyes. He spins toward me.

"Joe, just give him the fucking money," he says, "Please. We can figure out what to tell the guys."

Before I can answer, Rich gives T.J. a light punch on the arm. "Don't bother with that shit," Rich says, "We'll get our money. But you need a little lesson in cooperation." He speaks into the phone. "Put a scare into them."

T.J. looks like he's ready to cry. Rich holds the cell phone a few inches from his ear. It's not on speaker but the volume is just loud enough for the four of us to hear what's going on. Over the phone, there's a crash that may be a door getting kicked in. A few seconds later, a woman's voice comes in, faintly. It's T.J.'s wife and she doesn't sound happy.

"What the hell are you doing?" the tinny voice says, "Who are you?"

One of the thugs responds: "We got a little message for your husband."

Then all hell breaks loose. Crashing, banging, screaming. T.J. drops his face into his hands. Rich smirks. Over the phone, we hear a loud thud. Then things get strangely quiet. After that, we can hear T.J.'s wife screaming.

"My family! You motherfuckers come here and think you're going to do something to my family! I will fucking kill you!"

That's followed by another crash. Then what might be a door slamming. Things get quiet again. Rich looks confused.

"What's going on?" he says into the phone.

A thug's voice comes over the line. "Rich, we, uh, we got a little situation here."

"What fucking situation?"

"This, uh, this woman you sent us to scare? I don't think she's a woman. Matter of fact, I don't think she's human."

Any trace of a smirk is gone from Rich's face. "Where are you right now?"

"I'm hiding in a closet. Tony got knocked out by a chair. Phil got thrown through the coffee table. Freddie wound up in the front yard. I...I don't know what happened to Brian."

Rich hops off the stool and lowers his voice. "I sent five of you guys over there."

"Yeah," the guy on the phone says, "You needed to send a hell of a lot more."

There's a sound like a door being ripped open. More screaming, from both T.J.'s wife and the guy on the phone. Then the line goes dead. Rich stares at the phone. He slowly puts it back into his pocket.

"All right," he says, "That didn't work out like I hoped."

Strangely, I feel for Rich's thugs. They didn't know what they were getting themselves into. T.J. edges away from the bar.

"I'm sorry about your guys, Rich, but…"

Rich is not having it. He takes out the gun and sticks it in T.J.'s ribs. No one notices. Lars and I are accidentally screening them from view.

"We're going outside," Rich says, flicking looks at me and Lars, "You two idiots are coming with us. You're going to hand that envelope over to me and then we're going to take a drive to your house, T.J. We'll see what happens from there."

Lars leans toward Rich. "Listen, I think we can negotiate here…"

"Fuck you," Rich says, "That's my negotiation."

"Well, there's no real counter offer I can make to that," Lars says.

T.J. starts to raise his hands, but Rich bats them down, not wanting to make the scene obvious. T.J. starts across the bar area. Rich nods for me and Lars to follow. We have no choice but to do it. If we get to the parking lot, we're in deep trouble.

Turns out we don't have to worry about it.

As T.J. is squeezing past a two-seater table, he trips over the corner of the table and sprawls to the floor. Lars, who has been staring at a blonde in one of the booths, trips over T.J. and hits the floor as well. Rich comes to a halt, unaware that without T.J. in front of him, the gun is now visible. It takes all of a second for a customer to spot it and cry out.

And all hell breaks loose.

Everyone in the bar starts screaming. Rich looks around, trying to figure out what to do. A waiter carrying a tray comes to a sudden halt, nearly tripping over T.J. The tray slides out of his hands and crashes to the floor. Along the way, it slams into Rich's hand, knocking the gun to the floor as well. (We're lucky the damn thing doesn't go off. The gun, not the…you know what I mean.) Rich kicks the tray aside and tries to fall on the gun like it's a fumbled football.

Lars dives at the gun and gets there just before Rich. Rich falls on Lars, which he wants significantly less than the gun. He throws a couple kidney punches, but Lars is curled around the gun and not letting it go. Rich pops to his feet and runs for the exit. I'm about to give chase, but there's no need. Rich trips over T.J.'s carcass and hits the floor himself. When Rich gets to his feet again, he finds a large guy with a buzzcut standing in his path.

"Roseville PD," the guy says, "I suggest you don't move."

***

Twenty minutes later, we're in the parking lot, hanging out by T.J.'s car. The police have carted off Rich and a call to 9-1-1 by T.J.'s wife has corralled the (beaten and battered) thugs. T.J. leans against his car, looking as close to happy as he's every likely to come. I slip my hands into the pocket of my coat.

"Hell of a break," I say, "An off-duty cop being here."

T.J. smiles, slyly. "Not entirely a break. Meeting at Norman's was my idea. They offer free steaks to any Roseville cop, on duty or off. I figured if Rich was going to get out of hand, I might be protected."

Lars rubs his hands together. "It all worked out in the end. The league got its money back. T.J.'s off the hook. And I found some investors for my food truck."

I snap him a look. "Who the hell would that be?"

"That off-duty cop," Lars says, "When I talked to him, I couldn't help noticing his 'Get the hell out of here' lacked a certain conviction."

I let Lars have the delusion. We've got the money back and his physical safety is guaranteed (for the time being). If his disgusting food truck is doomed to fail, hey, it won't be the first failure he's experienced. I pat my jacket, where the fantasy football money is stored.

***

"Just remember, T.J.," I say, "If you get into money trouble, don't steal from your friends. Tell us about the problem and we'll help you out."

"You really believe that?" T.J. asks.

"Not particularly. No."

He nods, understanding. "Well, I don't think I'll be getting into that kind of trouble again. I've learned my lesson."

I step away. "In that case, we'll let you get home to the wife."

T.J.'s face freezes. "My wife."

He suddenly realizes what's waiting for him when he gets home; the explanation he's going to have to provide his wife. His face has the look of someone who's fondest wish is a quick and painless death. Lars claps a hand on T.J.'s shoulder.

"Been nice knowing you, Teej."

DEATH IS OLD SCHOOL

I will be the first to admit: there are a lot of reasons to hate social media. Politics, of course, is a great one. Religion fits the bill. (I've not seen any discussion of The Great Pumpkin, but I'm sure it's only a matter of time.) There's also the echo chamber of opinions, the insecure people needing validation and the pissing on other people's interests simply because you don't share them. And, of course, the endless stream of cat videos.

But there's an upside. Once upon a time, if you thought of an old friend, you had to wonder, "Whatever happened to so-and-so? He/she was a decent person. I hope things turned out well for him/her." Now, there's half a chance you're friends with him/her on Facebook and you know how things turned out. Ideally, they're perfectly fulfilled people with lives that make them happy. Rather than gun-toting rednecks who think this country would be going along swimmingly if we hadn't elected that damn Muslim A-rab Obama.

My name's Joe Davis and I'm currently distracted by Facebook.

My lack of focus shouldn't be confused with a lack of ambition. I really do want to finish this article and send it off to *The Daily Bugle* so I can return to a rich, full evening of goofing off. But apparently I've made goofing off the priority.

I'm in my favorite place for writing: Glacier's coffee shop on Cathedral Hill. There's snow falling outside the window and a cup of peppermint hot chocolate next to my laptop. A perfect atmosphere for writing.

Instead, I'm chatting on Facebook.

But I'm not anxious to get out of it. The person I'm chatting with is Lisa Cleary. She's a reporter for Metro Communications, a big syndicated media service (once upon a time, those were called *newspapers*). She was in the national spotlight a few years back for exposing an energy company that had been raiding its employees' retirement accounts to subsidize shady investments. She was a celebrity for about a minute and could've landed a permanent spot as a talking head for various news channels. But she rejected all that. She's a reporter, first, last and always; a working stiff who goes after that sometimes-nebulous thing we call *the truth*. That dedication was one of the things I admired about her back in high school.

That, and her taste in music. When she was my high school girlfriend, she introduced me to some kickass bands.

Her end of the conversation is taking place in a hotel room in Washington. I'm guessing she's either not busy or, like me, ignoring her actual work for this Facebook chat. But if she's fine with it, I'm fine with it.

How's the column? she asks.

Still paying the rent, I tell her.

No fans stalking you?

No such luck. Any spies about to kick down your door, Ms. Bond?

Not that I know of. I COULD go for a vodka martini. But it's a little early.

Six o'clock here. It's not THAT early.

I need to pace myself. Hey, what's this I hear about you solving a murder?

How did you hear about that?

I'm an intrepid reporter, Joe. You want to me bother with the whole chain of events or do you just want to tell me about it?

It wasn't much. Just a thing with my friend. They had the wrong guy, so I had to get him out of jail.

Congrats. Was it like the thing with Mr. Jacobson?

Oh wow. You still remember that?

Are you kidding me? Are you going to tell me YOU forgot about it?

How could I?

No, that's a thing I'll never forget. As I reach for my peppermint hot chocolate, my mind drifts back to my junior year in high school. Seventeen years and a lifetime ago.

***

It was December and I was still a few months shy of my seventeenth birthday. But I had my driver's license and my first car; a pile of crap Ford Taurus that my brother Kevin couldn't wait to divest himself of when he went off to college. My parents figured car ownership might teach me responsibility. This particular morning, for example, we'd gotten the first decent snowfall of the year and I learned my father would wipe the snow off *his* car, but not mine. (My dad's a good guy, but he never missed an opportunity to push the little birdies out of the nest.) Warmed by righteous indignation and a bowl of my mom's oatmeal, I managed to get to school on time, even finding a parking space near the Seventh Avenue entrance. I fought my way through the falling snow with only a light dusting covering me by the time I got inside.

Porter's Bay High School was built back in the twenties, when iron ore was booming and being shipped out of the bay and across Lake Superior to points east. It was a four-story brick and marble building that covered a city block. The main entrance was in the front, off Twenty-First Street, and there were side entrances off Seventh and Ninth Avenues. I dropped down a small stairway and took a left, heading down the cavernous hall toward my locker. The kids were gossiping more than usual and there was a sort of excitement in the air. I chalked it up to an episode of *Friends* I had missed the night before. Sam and Andy were waiting at my locker.

I'd known Andy Clark since kindergarten at Cobb-Cook Elementary. He lived four blocks away from me and during summers we were inseparable. He was thin and dark-haired, with a big set of teeth and a goofy grin. Sam Nelson was a later addition to the gang; his family having moved to town when we were in junior high. He was a little on the small side but made up for it with a large personality. He had near-total recall of every decent comedy bit and standup routine from the dawn of *Saturday Night Live* to the present day. So you'll understand if I took the first thing Sam said to me that day with a grain of salt.

"Mr. Jacobson's dead."

Of course Sam would say a thing like that. Get a rise out of me. He'd been doing it so long, I wasn't going to bite.

"Yeah, right," I said, ignoring him and doing the combination on my locker.

Sam got wide-eyed. "Joe, I'm serious."

Which, of course, is *exactly* what someone says when they're trying to put one over on you. I tossed my rapidly soddening letter jacket into my locker and collected my books.

Andy's face appeared over Sam's shoulder. "Joe, he's actually serious. You didn't see the ambulance and the cop cars out front?"

I stopped grabbing my books. If Andy was involved, there was more credibility. But what if the two of them had dreamed this up? Andy was a good guy, but not above the occasional tomfoolery.

"Mr. Jacobson's dead?" I asked, skeptical tone still in place, "What happened?"

Andy shrugged. "Nobody knows. They found him in his classroom. Maybe a heart attack."

I glanced at the clock over Miss Gilles' room across the hall, weighing how much time I had to go to the front and see if the ambulance and the cop cars were still there. Before I could do that, the principal's voice came over the P.A.

"Students, please report to your first hour class at this time."

Mr. Reynolds, our principal, had to make the announcement a second time before the kids, reluctantly, started filing toward their classrooms. Sam fell in with the herd.

"Going to be an interesting day," he said.

***

It turned out there was *no* day, school-wise. Everyone reported to their first hour class and after the expected twenty minutes of chattering and rumor-mongering, the principal came on the PA and announced that school would be cancelled for the day. He further announced that grief counselors would be made available for the students. With that, everyone raced out to enjoy the snow day we felt we should have gotten in the first place.

You're probably thinking I was a little hard-hearted, but I wasn't alone in how I viewed the situation. Truth is, nobody particularly liked Mr. Jacobson and nobody was mourning his passing. The idea that he'd—even unintentionally—sacrificed himself to get everybody a day off made him more popular than he'd ever been in life. I had sat through his classes and he was every bit as boring as he was condescending. His voice didn't have any inflection and I couldn't shake the suspicion it was more out of a desire to drive his students crazy than a habit he couldn't control. So I wasn't exactly gripped with grief.

The morning paper and the news reports from Duluth (where our TV stations originated) confirmed Mr. Jacobson died of an apparent heart attack. No one had any reason to believe otherwise. When we all reported back to school, Mr. Jacobson had been replaced by Mrs. Nyland, a perfectly nice substitute teacher who had a habit of misplacing her class list, making her classes eminently skip-able. It looked like the entire affair would quickly be consigned to the mists of history.

That afternoon, I followed one of my usual afterschool rituals and dropped by the offices of the school newspaper, *The Bay Breeze*. (Don't look at me. I didn't name it.) I had my own column in the paper (called *My Thoughts*…yeah, I didn't come up that one, either). I was toying with the idea of writing a column about death and how people handle it differently. It was going to have a satirical bent (most of my stuff did) and I wanted to run it by Mr. Somrock, the newspaper's faculty advisor. The offices for *The Bay Breeze* were in a little-used corner of the school's oversized library. I had just walked in when Mr. Somrock looked up from his desk and offered me a sheet of paper.

"Joe, I want you to write Mr. Jacobson's obituary. I'm going to need it by Monday."

Frankly, I was crushed. I had always thought Mr. Somrock and I had a good relationship. He had given me my column and had always supported me in a way that encouraged my talent but not my ego. And in English class he read *Edward, Edward* in a killer Scottish accent. How could a guy so cool give me a jackass assignment like this?

I asked the question that immediately springs to every sixteen-year old's lips: "Why me?"

Mr. Somrock flapped the paper and said, in a patient voice, "Because I'm assigning it to you, Joe. Please hand it in by Monday."

"What about my column?"

"You've got the weekend. I'm sure you've got time to write both of them."

I opened my mouth to protest, but Mr. Somrock raised his eyebrows slightly and I knew protesting would be a waste of time. There was nothing particularly intimidating about Mr.

Somrock. He was a tad shorter than me and his round face and high forehead didn't exactly look badass. But there was a formidable quality to the man; a firmness that said he would be patient and courteous but brook no nonsense. (I thought, at the time, that was a shame. Nonsense being one of the things I did best.) I took the paper from him, trying to infuse the gesture with as little attitude as possible.

"What is this?" I asked.

"It's a fact sheet on Mr. Jacobson. It should give you a lot of what you need to write the article. I recommend talking to teachers, getting some more information. I think you know better than to bother his family right now."

"I do."

"Good. I look forward to reading it." Mr. Somrock clapped me on the shoulder and strolled out of the office.

Yeah, I remember thinking, talking to a bunch of teachers on an assignment I don't want about a guy I never liked in the first place. I'm sure there won't be a dry eye in the house.

The newspaper office was a fairly simple affair. There was Mr. Somrock's desk and a few scattered tables; some empty, some covered with paperwork. The room was glass enclosed and would've felt a fishbowl if anything noteworthy went on inside or if anyone outside cared. I plunked down at the nearest table and gave Mr. Jacobson's info sheet a split-second of my time. I tossed it aside and let out a cluck of disgust. Only then did I notice someone else in the room.

"You don't like the work?" she said.

I knew her name was Lisa Cleary. I knew her family had moved to Porter's Bay the previous summer. I was vaguely aware that Lisa threw herself into every activity that interested her: yearbook, speech, drama, school newspaper, what have you. The cumulative effect was that she was already as popular as I was (not that the bar was set particularly high there). At that moment, her bright blue eyes were looking through a pair of wire-rim frames at a sheet of copy. Her wavy black hair was corralled into something resembling a ponytail, with stray hairs still dropping over her eyes. She was wearing a plaid shirt over a white long-sleeved tee, a pair of ripped and faded jeans and a simple pair of white sneakers.

Lisa had never talked to me before. For a second, I was too stunned to reply. Three months of working together on the paper and the yearbook and I didn't recall her even looking my direction. Only when she glanced up from the paper did I get my act together.

"I don't mind the work," I said, "Just not sure what to write."

"I thought that's why Mr. Somrock gave you the sheet."

"Yeah, I just…" I thought she might let me get away with trailing off lamely, but she kept her eyes on me. I had to come up with something. "I guess I didn't like Mr. Jacobson very much. Not nice to say, I know, but…"

Lisa looked at her paper again. "Never had a class with him."

"You didn't miss much."

Looking back, confessing my disdain for Mr. Jacobson didn't show me in my best light. But I wanted to keep the conversation going and I was saying whatever came into my head. (I haven't gotten much better over time.)

Lisa bobbed her head to one side. "Speaking of which, you realize you might be missing the biggest part of the story?"

That shook me. I didn't realize there *was* a bigger part of the story. A teacher found dead in his classroom in a small town in northern Minnesota certainly qualified as pretty big. I didn't think it could be topped.

"What, uh, what part of the story is that?" I asked.

Lisa set the paper aside. She moved over to my table and sat across from me. I folded my hands, probably so she couldn't see they were shaking.

"Mr. Jacobson was found in his room, right?" she said, "On Mondays, his first class wasn't until second hour. He *never* got to school before first hour was half over. Why was he so early that day?"

"Um, I don't—"

"On top of that, he was wearing jeans and a flannel shirt. I didn't have a class with him, but I'm guessing he usually dressed better than *that* for work."

She had a point. Mr. Jacobson wasn't a vision of sartorial splendor, but he was at least presentable. Until he was found dead. Before I could comment, Lisa had her next item.

"And there's the thing with his coffee cup."

"Wha, what about—"

"It was always on his desk. He kept it at the school. It was nowhere to be found yesterday morning. The police still don't know where it is."

"Well, I, I don't—"

Lisa ran back to her book bag. She pulled out a notebook and paged through it as she returned to the table. When she found what she was looking for, she set it in front of me and stabbed one of the notes with her finger.

"Mr. Jacobson died of a heart attack, right?" she asked.

By this point, I was willing to think Johnson set Kennedy up for a hit. Or that I was adopted. I wasn't sure of anything I supposedly knew. "That's what I hear," I said.

"Then how come he didn't show any symptoms of heart disease? Why have all his yearly checkups given him a clean bill of health, including the latest one? Why is there no family history of heart disease?"

Lisa was looking at me as if I might have the answer. Her eyes were fierce and I felt like she'd pound me into the earth if I didn't give her the right answer. I could only shake my head.

"How, uh, how do you know all this?" I asked.

Lisa slid the notebook aside, as if it had outlived its usefulness. She took a sudden interest in her thumbnail. "Just did some research."

"Seriously?" I asked.

"Yeah." She gathered up the notebook and spun in her chair. "I know. I'm a freak."

My voice stopped her before she got up. "No, not at all. I was just impressed you did all that."

A corner of Lisa's mouth rose. "You were?"

"Yeah, of course. Just…wondering why you did it."

She regarded me for a few seconds, maybe gauging how much she could trust me. She swung back around, facing me again. "Because the whole thing seems strange, doesn't it?" she said, "I thought something seemed off. So I did a little research."

I wasn't sure what to say to that—she'd done more research in a day than I'd done in a lifetime on *any* subject—so all that came out was, "Wow."

Lisa looked down, the half-smile still in place. When she looked up again, the intense look in her eyes was back. "So do you see where I'm going with this?" she asked.

I thought I did, so I offered her the sheet of paper Mr. Somrock had given me. "You want to write the article on Mr. Jacobson?"

Lisa flinched and I knew immediately that was the wrong answer. She slid the piece of paper to one side. "I want to write an article on Mr. Jacobson. I just don't want to write the article Mr. Somrock wants *you* to write."

I'd never felt dense until I met Lisa. It was the product of being the smartest (or at least the one who's allowed to think of himself as the smartest) person in your group of friends. But here I was, sitting across the table from this very driven, very intense girl and I didn't have a clue what in the hell she was talking about.

And I didn't pretend otherwise. "What, uh, what article do you want to write?"

Lisa lowered her voice. (I began to wonder if the room was bugged.) "I think Mr. Jacobson was murdered," she said, "That's the article to write."

I had no idea how to respond. I had a brief instinct to laugh, but I was certain she'd never speak to me again if I did. (Sometime later, Lisa admitted, yes, that would've been a deal-breaker.)

I pulled the paper back to me. "Have you talked to Mr. Somrock about this?"

"No. I already know what he's going to say. 'I can't print it until you have proof. And I don't think you're going to get proof.'"

"Has he said this to you before?"

"Yeah. Before I busted the parking lot attendant for taking bribes to let in kids without parking permits."

I remembered that article. Not because I read it in the paper (I confess: I only read my column) but because everyone was up in arms that the school had replaced a perfectly corrupt parking lot attendant with one who made cheapskates like me park on the street.

"That was you?" I said.

"Yeah. Uh, Mr. Somrock didn't put my name on the article. He thought kids would want to kill me."

"They did."

I didn't make it sound harsh. More a statement of fact, one Lisa seemed to accept and even like.

"When I first brought that to Mr. Somrock, he asked me to get proof," she said, "So I did. And he'll tell me the same thing about this Mr. Jacobson deal."

"So you're going to prove he was murdered?" I ask.

"Yes. Will you help me?"

If Lisa had grown a second head—an alien head at that—I wouldn't have been any more surprised. I had to remind myself she was my age. It was like Nellie Bly had suddenly reincarnated in front of my eyes. And the strangest part was that she wanted my help.

"Me?" I asked, "Why me?"

Lisa's eyes dropped toward the table and she traced a pattern with her finger. "Because Mr. Somrock told you to talk to the other teachers and students. If you walk around asking questions, wanting to talk to people, nobody's going to think it's weird."

"And what are you going to do?"

"I'll go with you. We'll just say I'm helping you out."

If I had been honest, I would've told her the whole thing was ridiculous. A couple of high school juniors acting like The Hardy Boys. Who the hell were we kidding?

You can imagine my surprise when I found myself saying, "Yeah, that sounds good."

Lisa smiled and reached for my forearm. Then she stopped and just tapped the table. "Good. We should start by talking to Marcy Carter. She was Mr. Jacobson's student assistant. She's the one who found him."

The school had a student assistant program for kids interested in becoming teachers (probably to head them off before they got into a poorly paid, thankless line of work).

"Sounds good," I said, "Where do we find her?"

Lisa grabbed her backpack. "She's supposed to be down in the student assistants' office. We can probably catch her."

I stumbled toward the door, pulled along in Lisa's wake. Five minutes ago, I was gliding along, blithely writing my rather blithe column and now I was caught up in something I hadn't planned for.

Turned out to be the story of my life.

***

The student assistants' office was on the ground floor, in a hallway near the locker rooms. It wasn't particularly large, housing just one desk and a filing cabinet. The most prominent feature was a wall of cubby holes in which correspondence to and from teachers was placed. Marcy was sitting at the desk when we arrived. She adjusted her glasses and brushed some of her short, dark hair off her forehead. Her gaunt face took on a wary expression when she asked if we needed something. Lisa quickly put her at her ease, assuring her we were there for an article on Mr. Jacobson. Marcy took a breath in through her nose and looked down. After a moment, she regained her formidable composure.

"What can I help with?" she asked.

Lisa gave me a quick look, but I simply nodded; letting her know she was more than welcome to run the show. "We're just looking for names of people we can talk to. Since you knew Mr. Jacobson better than any of the other kids, we thought you could help us."

Marcy tapped a pencil against her hand and stared at the wall as she thought. "Well, for students, you can talk to Staci Morgan and Ryan Becker. They needed some extra help with science. They were about the only kids who saw Mr. Jacobson outside of class." Lisa made a note in her notebook. "For teachers," Marcy continued, "You could talk to Mrs. Bendix. She used to have coffee with Mr. Jacobson during their office hours."

Lisa made another note. "Speaking of coffee, I heard Mr. Jacobson always kept the same coffee mug on his desk."

"It was an oversized mug from Terzich's," she said, "I always brought him coffee."

"But it wasn't there when you found him?"

Marcy's eyebrows went up. "I didn't notice that. It wasn't the first thing I was looking for. How did you find out?"

Lisa waved her hand, nonchalant. "Something I heard. When you found Mr. Jacobson, he was wearing a flannel shirt and jeans. That wasn't what he normally wore to school, right?"

"No, not at all," Marcy said, "He spent a lot of weekends at his cabin. Sometimes he came straight from there to school. But usually he changed clothes."

"Any idea why he wouldn't have changed this time?"

"No." Marcy tilted her head. "Is that something you're going to put in the article?"

"No. Just trying to find out all the information I can. You know?"

Immediately, Marcy defrosted. "Oh sure. What else do you want to know?"

Lisa guided Marcy through a series of background questions on Mr. Jacobson. All of it was information we already had, none of it interesting. But it removed any last trace of Marcy's suspicion. In fact, she was downright friendly by the time we were ready to leave.

"Mr. Jacobson was a good man," she said, "I hope you write a nice article about him. He, uh, he deserved it."

Lisa looked to me, reminding me I was, in fact, the one who was supposed to be writing said article. I took on what I imagined to be a serious reporter-like demeanor.

"I'll do the best I can," I said. (I was trying to sound like Tom Brokaw and I probably wound up sounding like Screech from *Saved By The Bell*.)

We said our goodbyes to Marcy and walked to the huge marble steps at the front of the building. Lisa paused when we reached the doors.

"Do you know Staci Morgan or Ryan Grant?" she asked.

"I went to elementary school with Ryan. I haven't talked to him much since sixth grade. Staci and I had Mr. Schultz for Creative Writing last year, but that's about it."

Lisa's gloved hand rubbed her chin as she considered that. "I'll figure out how to get ahold of them. Are you going to be around tonight?"

"Probably." I figured *definitely* would sound pathetic, although I knew I would *definitely* be around the house.

"I'll call you if I find something out."

With that, she hoisted her backpack over her shoulder and hightailed it out the front door. I watched her go. Just as she reached the plaza at the front of the school, Lisa looked back and gave me a little finger wave. I put up a hand to wave back.

I remember thinking: *that seems like a good sign.*

***

When I was in school, my parents encouraged me to get my homework done as soon as I got home from school (usually after stopping at Arthur's Diner to grab a burger with Andy and Sam). If I headed up to my room, put on some music and dove right into my homework, I'd have it done by the time my mom put dinner on the table and then I'd have the evening to relax. It was an approach that served my brothers Kevin and Owen very well during their school years.

If only I had ever tried it.

341

Instead, I tended to goof off until an hour before bedtime and then divide my homework into what could be done before bed, what could be done before school and what could be quickly crammed during study hall. This particular evening, I was up in my room, staring at the ceiling and thinking about my next column when my brother Owen called up the stairs.

"Joe?" he said, "There's a girl on the phone for you."

See, this wasn't quite pre-cell phone days. A lot of people had them. But the idea of giving them to high school kids hadn't occurred to anyone yet. It sure as hell hadn't occurred to my parents (I sometimes suspected my father viewed color television as a passing fad). So if someone called me, they reached the one phone in our house. Which meant if I got a call from a girl, particularly in the post-dinner hour when most of the family was home, I had to walk the gauntlet of stares on my way to the phone. (Not that this had been a big issue to that point.)

I knew it was Lisa even before I got to the phone. "Staci Morgan can talk to us tonight," she said, "Do you have time to go over there right now?"

I made a show of mentally checking my (in reality, totally clear) schedule. "Yeah, I think I can swing it. Do you want me to pick you up?"

"Would you? I don't have a car. Let me give you the address."

I barely scribbled down the address before Lisa gave me an "Okayseeyouinaminutebye" and hung up. I hastily put on my boots, letter jacket and scarf while my parents watched. My father went so far as to set aside his paper and fold his hands over his paunch.

"Going somewhere, Joe?" he asked.

I looked at him, startled. In my haste, I'd forgotten I wasn't yet old enough to leave the house without letting my parents know where I was going. (I'm still not, come to think of it.)

"Oh, sorry," I said, wrapping my scarf around my neck, "That was a girl from school. I'm doing an article on Mr. Jacobson and she's helping me out."

My mother looked up from her knitting. (Yes, she knit. Still does.) "That was nice of her. Who is this girl?"

"Lisa Cleary. Her dad's—"

"The new dentist," Dad said, "I have an appointment with him next week."

I pulled on my stocking cap and realized they were still staring at me with sort of an expectant look. I jerked a thumb toward the door.

"Is it okay if I go?" I asked.

Mom looked to Dad, as she always seemed to. His response, as usual, was to pick up the paper and start reading again. Mom looked back to me.

"Please be home by nine," she said.

"No problem," I said, already half out the door, "This shouldn't take long." Although, truthfully, I had no idea.

Lisa was waiting on the front porch when I pulled up. She dashed down the front walk and skidded the last few feet to the car. Her head was covered with a stocking cap that seemed ready to burst with the effort of holding in her hair. She hopped in and nodded, giving me to okay to go.

"How'd you swing a chat with Staci?" I asked.

"I found her phone number and called her. I gave her the story about us doing an article on Mr. Jacobson."

"Is that a story? I thought that was the truth."

"It's the truth. The *kind* of article we're going might be the story."

There was a ring in her voice, like she was getting away with something. I had to smile. What does a high school kid love more than the feeling of getting away with something?

Staci Morgan lived near the edge of town, in a slightly rundown neighborhood near Bennett Park. It was a thin, two-story house, stacked next to similar houses on a tiny street. I studied the peeling paint around the screen door while we waited for someone to answer our knock. Staci's mother, a woman with wide hips and a stained white t-shirt, greeted us. She looked nonplussed while Lisa explained why we were there. Then she shrugged and shouted for Staci without inviting us inside. A few seconds later, Staci appeared at the front door.

Staci had flowing black hair and sharp, suspicious eyes like her mother. But she was thin in every place that her mother was wide. She was also nervous and timid where her mother seemed disengaged and uncaring. Looking back on it, I'm sure it was just a matter of time before Staci turned into her mother. But at that moment, she was her own, unformed person.

Lisa reeled off the story about us writing an article for the school newspaper. She seemed to have an innate talent for putting people at their ease. Staci stepped toward us, taking the conversation fully out to the front porch.

"I'd meet with him a couple times a week," Staci said, "Just for extra help."

"Were you supposed to meet with him the morning he died?" Lisa asked.

"Yeah. Our usual meeting."

"How was Mr. Jacobson before that morning?" Lisa asked, "Did it seem like anything was on his mind? Was he okay, physically?"

Staci nodded. "He was fine. He was like…he usually is. Was. Whatever."

Lisa's eyes narrowed slightly. She got the same feeling I had: Staci wasn't telling us something.

"So you got along with Mr. Jacobson?" Lisa asked.

Staci started chewing one of her fingernails. "I guess. I mean, we didn't have any problems. Really."

Lisa looked at me and then her eyes cut toward the street. I wasn't good at picking up signals from girls, so she had to do it a second time before I get the message. I cleared my throat and stepped off the porch.

"I, uh, I think left something in the car," I said.

I managed to get off the porch without falling ass-over-teakettle into the snow. I got in the car and watched Lisa and Staci. The conversation got a little animated but didn't seem argumentative. It went on long enough to give me the feeling Lisa was getting somewhere. Finally, she hopped off the porch and ran to the car.

"Sorry about that," Lisa said, "I didn't think Staci would open up with a guy there."

"Not a problem," I said, "Did she open up?"

A sour look came over Lisa's face. "Yeah. Turns out, she got along just fine with Mr. Jacobson. He was helpful and understanding and he came on to her."

The last part left me feeling sucker-punched. "He came—"

"On."

"On?"

"To Staci. Exactly."

I shook my head, as if to clear it. "Why, why would he do a thing like that?"

"Simple. He was a scumbag."

Having had little experience coming on to high school girls, I was willing to believe Mr. Jacobson had maybe done something Staci misinterpreted. Those things happen, right?

"How…I mean…maybe…"

Lisa put on a patient tone of voice. "He started rubbing her back and told her he had a cabin and was wondering if she'd like to go there with him some weekend. She told him no and he kept pushing it. When she tried to get out of the room, he told her to think about it. That if she said no, he wouldn't help her anymore and it might affect her grade."

Yep, so much for the misinterpretation. "You're right. He was a scumbag."

"Anyway, that was the last time Staci saw him."

"When was this?" I asked.

"The Friday before he died. She was practically sick the whole weekend. Wasn't sure how she was going to face him on Monday morning. Turned out not to be an issue."

I let out a long breath. "Did she tell anyone else?"

"She said she didn't. She thought her parents would freak. And she didn't want to take a chance on rumors getting out. You know what people are like around here."

Yeah, in a small town, gossip spreads like a gas fire and is just about as damaging. In fact, I was surprised Mr. Jacobson would do a thing as stupid as that, given the possibility that word could get out. Apparently, he was willing to take a chance.

"Did she talk about the morning Mr. Jacobson died?" I asked, "What she was doing? An, an alibi? Or something?"

"She said she was hanging out in the cafeteria when she heard kids talking about it. Do you know anyone who hangs out in the cafeteria in the morning?"

"Yeah. My friends Andy and Sam have breakfast there. They'll know who Staci is."

"Are you sure?"

"She's a female they see during the day. Trust me, they've committed her to memory."

Lisa waved a hand forward. "All right, Woodward, let's be on our way."

"Gotcha, Bernstein." I stopped to think. "Wait, which one was played by Robert Redford?"

"Woodward. You're the good looking one."

My face got warm. I looked away to hide it.

***

I checked with Andy and Sam the next day. They remembered Staci, but they didn't remember her being in the cafeteria that morning. For a minute, I doubted their memories, but they had such total recall of her various outfits and what her bookbag looked like that I had to take their word as gospel. I met up with Lisa in *The Bay Breeze* offices that afternoon. She listened passively while I gave her the report.

"So we've got someone who was, uh, propositioned by Mr. Jacobson and wasn't where she said she was the morning he was killed," I said, "We might be on to something."

Lisa held up a hand, slowing me down. "We still aren't even a hundred percent certain how Mr. Jacobson died. He had to be poisoned. It's the only way I can think of. But how would Staci find poison? How would she get it to Mr. Jacobson?"

I felt a tad deflated. She was right, of course. "What do we do next?" I asked.

"We should talk to Ryan Becker. Mr. Jacobson tutored him, too."

"You know where to find him?"

Lisa looked through her notebook. "He's in a floor hockey league. Plays in the gym most nights. Starts at seven."

"Maybe we can catch him before it starts. Or after."

"Let's try before. You want to meet here at six?"

"Sure."

Lisa patted my hand and headed out of the office. I was suddenly in the odd position of hoping Mr. Jacobson *had* been killed. Lisa was so filled with determination, I wanted her to be rewarded for it. And maybe me, too. But my reward would come later.

***

We met promptly at six, but Ryan Becker managed to get by us. He must have used another entrance to get into the gym. I was willing to wait until afterwards, but Lisa was afraid we'd miss him again. She had another suggestion.

"They have to change for this, right?" she said, "Shorts, tennies and tees are required. He must change in the locker room."

"Unless he changes at home."

"Would you wear shorts in this weather?"

She had me there. While not all of my classmates got with the program, northern Minnesotans are, in general, ruthlessly practical when it comes to cold weather. Just living up there is proof you're tough. You don't need to make an idiot of yourself to prove it further.

"He's probably in the guys' locker room," Lisa said, "Go in there and talk to him."

Yeah, strolling into a locker room and striking up conversation was a precarious business. It was less appealing when you consider I didn't belong to the floor hockey league

350

and had no real business being in there. And if you threw in the fact I had to ask the guy about a possibly murdered teacher and his possible involvement, it became *really* unappealing.

But I couldn't look like a wuss in front of Lisa. I agreed to do it.

I headed downstairs and into the locker room. It was a reasonably large room, used for the football and basketball teams. About thirty guys were changing into shorts and t-shirts. Several of them looked up when I strolled in, clearly wondering what the hell I was doing there. If I had been a better athlete, they might have thought I was being brought in as a ringer. (Trust me, there was no concern about that.) Ryan was in a far corner, his back to me. I strolled past and pretended to use the urinals. Everyone had gone back to getting ready by the time I returned. I practically ran into Ryan as he rounded the corner, heading for the stairs to the gym. He mumbled something resembling "Excuse me" and started to step past.

"Ryan," I said, "You got a minute?"

He shot me a quizzical glance. Beyond his laughing at the time I brained Rick Rue with the "E" section of the World Book Encyclopedia in sixth grade, we hadn't had much interaction over the years. Not only was he probably wondering why I had chosen *now* to break the ice, he was probably wondering why I had chosen the boys locker room as the place.

"Yeah," he said, slowly, "A minute's probably all I got. What's up?"

"I wanted to talk about Mr. Jacobson."

Ryan threw a look back toward the other floor hockey guys. Nobody seemed to notice my remark, though I was still getting a few sidelong glances for being there in the first place. Ryan nodded toward the stairs leading out of the locker room.

"Out there," he said.

I followed Ryan up to a hallway. If we went right, it would lead us to the gym. If we went left, it would lead to the football field. Ryan led me to the left, keeping us out of the flow of traffic of guys heading up to the gym. He leaned on his plastic hockey stick.

"Okay, what do you want to know?" he asked.

I gave him the standard spiel about the article I was working on with Lisa. When I mentioned talking to Staci, Ryan noticeably stiffened.

"What did Staci tell you?" he asked

I could pussyfoot around the whole subject or I could come clean and risk getting a plastic hockey stick upside my head. I decided to take my chances and be honest.

"She told us Mr. Jacobson got out of line," I said.

Ryan took deep breaths through his nose. In one quick motion, he picked up the hockey stick like a tomahawk.

Fortunately, he aimed at the wall and not me. After a second, he lowered the stick to the floor.

"Miserable motherfucker," he said.

I don't know why I didn't put it together sooner. Probably the complete lack of interest in Ryan's life before the last day or so. But it suddenly hit me.

"Are you and Staci going together?" I asked.

He nodded, barely. "Since the start of the year. She started getting help from Mr. Jacobson first. Said I should start doing it. I was having trouble in science."

"And you got along with him? Until the thing with Staci?"

He mumbled. "Yeah, I suppose."

"Where were you when you found out he died?"

If Ryan thought I was fishing for an alibi, he didn't show it. "I was at my locker. Talking to Staci. Then we went to first hour and I heard the news. Nothing much to it."

According to Lisa, Staci hadn't said anything about hanging out with Ryan that morning. It seemed a better alibi than her hanging out in the cafeteria (which she *wasn't* doing anyway). But I let it go. I asked Ryan a few more questions about Mr. Jacobson, but his answers weren't any more enlightening or any less bitter. Finally, he looked over his shoulder toward the gym.

"You need anything else?" he asked.

"No, I, uh, I guess not. Have fun."

His eyes narrowed as he backed away. "Thanks. Good luck with the article."

Ryan ran down the hall, catching up with the other floor hockey players. I got the hell out of there, lest I turn into a guy who was just hanging around the boys' locker room.

Lisa was waiting for me outside the gym. I gave her the rundown on my chat with Ryan. Her eyes widened when I mentioned his dating Staci. But she didn't have a theory as to why Staci didn't tell us about that or her hanging out with Ryan the morning Mr. Jacobson was found.

"We've still got Mrs. Bendix to talk to," she said, "She'll meet with us tonight."

I must have looked like I'd been told Christmas vacation was cancelled. "She, uh, she will, huh?"

My hesitation was more than just the thought of visiting a teacher after hours. I had heard Mrs. Bendix could be very nice, but I hadn't seen any evidence. She was the coach of the school's speech team and in that capacity displayed a competitiveness that would have made Mike Ditka shit his pants. There was no doubt she was successful. For a little town in northern Minnesota, we had one of the best speech teams in the state. But the threat of her killing us always hung over the team. Lisa, though, didn't seem daunted by the task.

"I already called her from *The Bay Breeze* offices," she said, "While you were talking with Ryan. She can give us a minute, but we have to come right away."

You may be wondering how Lisa could have gotten into *The Bay Breeze* offices (let alone the library) after hours. Well, it was an open secret in the school that Dino, our alcoholic janitor, never locked any door behind him. He'd do his rounds in the afternoon and then take a flask of vodka down to the custodian's office by the gym. He'd be there until his shift ended, assuming he didn't pass out in the meantime. Since people generally liked Dino and there'd been no incidents of teachers' possessions being stolen, nobody said anything. While Lisa was new to the school, I wasn't surprised she'd already figured out that bit of info. I followed her out the front door, into the driving snow that coated the cement steps.

"Mrs. Bendix is actually willing to talk to us?" I said, "How did you pull that off?"

"It was no big deal," she said, "She and I get along just fine in Communications."

"And you don't, uh, find her intimidating?"

Lisa shrugged. "She doesn't find *me* intimidating. Why should I find her intimidating?" Then she stopped and looked at me. She bit a corner of her lip and her voice got soft. "Do *you* think I'm intimidating?"

"Only when you drink ale from the skulls of your enemies."

To this day, I have absolutely no idea why I said that. Apparently, my instinct to meet every question with a smartass remark was finely honed even then. I tried to hide my chagrin. Then I heard a snicker, followed by full-on bubbly laughter. Relief flooded my chest.

It was the first time I ever made Lisa laugh.

"You've got it all wrong," she said, "It's grog. I drink grog from the skulls of my enemies. Remember that."

"Got it."

We headed down the steps and out to my car. I had to work to avoid skipping.

***

Mrs. Bendix's place wasn't far away. She answered the door herself, smiling toward Lisa and nodding at me. She was in her early thirties, which often translated to a teacher being more relatable. Mrs. Bendix, though, was as stern as a schoolmarm. And her countenance at home apparently wasn't any less stern. We could hear her husband playing with the kids in the den, probably under orders to clear out while she chatted with us. Lisa and I were on the sofa while Mrs. Bendix sat in a nearby chair and fixed me with a look that always left me wondering if I'd prepared properly for the speech meet (and it wasn't even speech season yet).

"What did you need to know?" Mrs. Bendix said, skipping any small talk.

I cleared my throat. "You were friends with Mr. Jacobson?"

Mrs. Bendix bobbed her head as she considered this. "I suppose you could call us friends. We had the same open hour, so we'd see each other in the teacher's lounge. We'd chat."

I took longer than necessary to write that down, not only because my handwriting is terrible, but because I was stalling to think up another question. Lisa, thank the gods, took over for me.

"What sort of hobbies or interests did Mr. Jacobson have?" she asked.

With Lisa doing the talking, Mrs. Bendix unbent a little. She answered the question about Mr. Jacobson's interests, which were primarily fishing, hunting and his cabin. Maybe watching the occasional TV show. (Hunting shows and family comedies. Apparently, Mr. Jacobson's hobbies were no more interesting than he was.) Mrs. Bendix was polite, but I got the feeling she tolerated her conversations with Mr. Jacobson more than she enjoyed them. I scribbled down the information, though after a few minutes I got bored and started doodling stickman pictures of me committing various forms of suicide.

Lisa twisted her stocking cap in her hands and I got the feeling she was about to move into a more dangerous line of questioning. "Did anything seem off with Mr. Jacobson? Like something was bothering him?"

Mrs. Bendix looked more confused than concerned. "Not that I'm aware of. Why would you want to know that?"

Lisa faltered, having lost the chummy feeling she was getting from Mrs. Bendix. (Well, the closest thing you could get to a chummy feeling with Mrs. Bendix.) I picked up the slack.

"It's just one of those things when someone has a heart attack," I said, "You start to wonder about what kind of stresses they might have had, stuff that was concerning them."

Lisa followed my lead. "It never hurts to get as much information as you can. At least that's what Mr. Somrock teaches us."

Mrs. Bendix nodded, thinking about it. "I can't say he really had anything on his mind. He was thinking about buying a boat. Something he could take out on the big lake."

The *big lake,* in the parlance of my hometown, was Lake Superior. You didn't exactly take your little fiberglass boat out on the largest freshwater lake in the world. A boat you can take out on the big lake means serious money. It was a conclusion both Lisa and I were quick to reach. But this time I got the first word in.

"That would have cost him a decent chunk of change," I said.

Mrs. Bendix inclined her head to one side. "I suppose it would have. But I'm not sure it's relevant to your article. I think Mr. Somrock would agree with that."

He certainly would have. I made a show of looking over my notes and snuck a look at Lisa. She gave me the slightest of nods, telling me we were done here. I flipped my notebook shut and thanked Mrs. Bendix for her time. She promptly guided us to the front door. Lisa and I thanked her and scurried out into the cold. The porch light was out by the time my car pulled away from the curb. Lisa threw a look back up the street and let out a nervous laugh.

"I thought for sure she was going to bust us," Lisa said, "If she figured we're up to something, she'd go to Mr. Somrock."

"You think we fooled her?"

"I think we did." Lisa gave me an appreciative look. "You're a pretty decent liar."

I wasn't sure how to take that. "Actually, I'm a terrible liar. I don't know I pulled it off."

"Well, you did good."

I soaked that in for a second before I asked, "What do we do next?"

She thought about it as I drove her home. We were almost there when she let out a breath, as if she'd made some kind of decision. "I have an idea," she said, "But it's not the most...well, *ethical*."

"What does it look like?"

"Mr. Jacobson's visitation is tomorrow night. Over at the Cease Funeral Home." (Yeah, it was really called the Cease Funeral Home. Still is. Family business. Don't get me started.)

I was trying to put on a brave face, but I didn't like where this was going. "You want us to go to Mr. Jacobson's visitation and start asking questions?"

Lisa quickly waved that off. "No. Nothing like that."

"Oh, good."

"I want to break into his house while his family's at the visitation."

"Oh. Good."

It was like the old Egyptian headache cure, where somebody stomps on your foot and you forget all about your head. Suddenly, going to Mr. Jacobson's visitation and asking a bunch of questions didn't seem like the worst idea I'd ever heard. In fact, it was running a distant second.

Lisa sensed my hesitation. She straightened her glasses (a gesture I would come to realize meant she was insecure). "What do you think?"

"Um, do you know anything about breaking into houses?"

"No. But I'll figure out a way."

"What if someone sees us?"

"The neighbors will be at the visitation. Who's going to see us?"

Yeah, even then, I knew there was *always* someone who could catch you. But I didn't want to shoot Lisa down, either.

"I don't know," I said. And that was as much hesitation as I felt I could show.

Lisa didn't get angry, but she seemed a tad exasperated. "Look, Mr. Jacobson was saving up to buy a boat that, unless we're missing something, there's no way he could afford. It's not like I can walk into a bank and demand his records and there's no way we can talk to the family. If we're going to find something, we're going to have to get…creative."

These days, I tend to use *extra-legal* rather than *creative* as the metaphor for taking actions I really ought not to. But I could see Lisa's point. It wasn't like we were full of options.

"C'mon," she said, gently slapping my leg, "It'll be an adventure."

Those were the same words Sam used the night he talked us into TP-ing Mr. Harms' house; the night we discovered Mr. Harms had a large gun collection and a rather indiscriminate view toward using it. To this day, Sam insists he didn't shit himself and he's the only one who believes him. So, a call to adventure wasn't likely to sway me. But it gave me an idea.

"What if we have a couple of lookouts?" I asked, "If my friends Sam and Andy come along, I'll feel better about it."

"Do you think they'll do it?"

"Sam might ask us to TP somebody's house as payback, but that won't be for months."

Lisa laughed; the one where she threw her head back and her mouth was wide open, but the sound that came out was lilting instead of harsh. The one I would become oh-so-familiar with. The one that puts an ache in my chest when I think about it.

"I'll see you tomorrow night," she said.

She patted my arm one more time and was off. I sat in the car and watched her run through the falling snow.

***

I picked up Andy and Sam just after dinner. Neither of them was pleased to be along on this mission. Sam only liked breaking the law when there was very little chance of getting caught and Andy didn't like breaking the law at all. They didn't seem mollified when I told them they'd only be *abetting* someone breaking the law.

"And you're doing this for a girl?" Sam asked.

"I am doing this so we can find out if someone killed Mr. Jacobson," I said.

"I thought his heart killed him," Andy said.

"I don't have to explain this whole thing to you again, do I?" I asked.

Before Andy could say anything, Sam jumped in. "Okay, riddle me this: if this Lisa wasn't involved, would you even care what happened to Jacobson?"

I opened my mouth, ready for a rebuttal, but closed it when I realized I didn't have one. Instead, I went into a largely-faked coughing fit and dropped the subject. Lisa was standing on the front porch when I pulled up. I did some quick introductions and everyone seemed to be on their best behavior. It felt a tad weird. It wasn't like Sam and Andy were the *only* people I hung out with, but I didn't cultivate a huge social circle outside of them. It felt like worlds were colliding. Fortunately, Lisa got us on track.

"There's a front door facing Fourth Street," she said, "And a backdoor facing the alley. If someone can keep an eye on those, we should be all right looking through the house."

Neither Andy nor Sam were overjoyed with the plan. Lisa was too focused to pay any attention and, truthfully, it would be a year before she knew Andy and Sam well enough to pick up on their moods. I gave them a glance and shrugged an apology.

We parked a few blocks down from the house. Since none of us owned a cell phone, the plan was for either Sam or Andy to drive by the house and honk the horn if someone was coming. (I've got to say: breaking and entering is so much more efficient these days.)

Lisa and I slipped down the alley. A light snow was starting to fall, the umpteenth in the last few days. It covered up the tracks we were leaving. The Jacobsons' backyard was enclosed by a wooden fence roughly as tall as me. Nothing was visible beyond it and the yard light was not on. I had to hope the Jacobsons didn't own a dog. Lisa stopped in front of the back gate. There was a gleam in her eyes. I was reasonably certain she'd gotten into a fair bit of mischief in her life. There was definitely a thrill junkie lurking in there somewhere. The same could not be said for me, as going home and watching TV was now my fondest wish. Lisa opened the back gate and winced as it creaked. She paused, waiting for one of the neighbors to come out. But the street was quiet.

The backyard was about the size of a postage stamp and bisected by a cement walkway. Whoever tended the yard had missed a few snowfalls, shoveling-wise, but it wasn't impassable. Lisa led the way to the back steps. She knelt down and started swiping at the snow. A rock garden was revealed. She picked through a few of the rocks before finding what she was looking for. She cracked one of the rocks in half.

"They have the spare key hidden inside," she said, pulling it from the rock.

"How did you know about that?" I asked.

"Just did some research. You ask around, you find things out."

Lisa said it like it was no big deal. The girl was a born reporter. Or petty thief. But I'm glad she chose reporter.

The key got us in the backdoor. There was no worry about a security system, since nobody in Porter's Bay dreamed of having one. (Even today, they're considered a fad.) We found ourselves in a kitchen with an amazingly small amount of counter space. (I'm remembering it that way. It didn't make that much of an impression on me at the time.) The basement door was right in front of us. The dining room was visible to the left and the living room to the right. Lisa took a penlight out of her coat.

"Try not to break anything," she said.

Our search didn't take long. The main floor of the house was essentially one big circle and there was nothing interesting to find. The upper floor wasn't much better. Two bedrooms and a study, also devoid of anything interesting beyond a few filthy magazines lying in the bottom of Mr. Jacobson's sock drawer.

"Gross," Lisa said, quickly closing the drawer.

"We should get those out of here," I said, "You don't want Mrs. Jacobson finding them."

She leveled a look at me. "Is this your way of telling me you're a perv?"

"No! Not at all. But we should give Sam and Andy *some* reward for helping us out."

I reached for the drawer, but Lisa gently slapped my hand. "Sorry," she said, "No dice. Just in case Mrs. Jacobson knows they're there, we need to leave them alone."

"Sam and Andy are going to be disappointed."

"You're going to tell them about porn they don't know exists?"

"You're right. I could never be that cruel."

Lisa smiled slightly, like she didn't quite know what to make of me. For a second, I forgot we were standing in a house we hadn't obtained legal permission to enter.

"We just have one place left to look," Lisa said, "Might as well try the basement."

I've never been a fan of basements. Ours was unfinished from the time I was a kid. My brother Kevin delighted in telling me stories about the various boogeyman that inhabited the place. As a result, basements have always given me the heebiest of jeebies. (That said, I'm still going to build a Batcave if I ever own a house.)

The basement at the Jacobson's place fit right into my nightmares. An uneven set of wooden steps descended into the gloom, stopping at barely paved floor. A giant octopus of an old furnace dominated the room. Lisa ran the penlight over a collection of boxes against the wall.

"You suppose there's something in one of those?" she asked.

"Might as well take a look."

We worked quickly, opening and rifling through the boxes as fast as possible. Ultimately, it wasn't what was in the boxes that got our attention. It was what was behind them. I noticed it first, while Lisa was going through one of the boxes. She stopped and looked at me.

"What's going on?" she asked.

"The wall looks funky," I said.

She swung the penlight toward it. There was a discoloration in the wall, barely noticeable. Lisa slid toward it, moving a box out of her way. She felt around.

"Part of the wall's been taken out and replaced," she said.

Lisa put the penlight in her mouth and did some more digging. Sure enough, a panel came loose in her hand. There was a cubby hole tucked behind it.

She took the penlight out of her mouth. "Just looks like a duffel bag."

Lisa pulled out the gray duffel and set it on the floor between us. She opened it and discovered it was filled with blocks wrapped in plastic and sealed with masking tape. I picked one up and my eyes bulged when I realized what I was looking at.

"It's money," I said.

She took the block from me and her head bobbed as she came to the same realization. "Twenties," she said, "How much do you think is here?"

"Offhand? A shitload."

"And there are other bags in the hole. It's got to be tens of thousands of dollars."

Before Lisa could say anything else, the faint sound of a car horn could be heard in the distance. Andy's and Sam's warning signal. Lisa and I looked at each other, eyes wide.

"What are the odds that's a car alarm?" I asked.

"I don't want to hang around and find out."

We hastily stuffed the bag back into the wall and returned the boxes to their original positions. Lisa led the way upstairs, dousing the penlight. We spilled into the kitchen as the distant sound of footsteps were audible on the front porch.

"I thought you said they were going to be at the wake," I whispered.

"Really? You think now's the time to second guess the plan?"

"Mea culpa." (Yes, I used the phrase *mea culpa* when I was in high school. It's probably why I didn't get more dates. That reason and no other.)

The only escape was the backdoor. Lights were coming on in the living room and footsteps were headed our direction. I led the way out, vaulting the steps and landing on the back walk. And slipping on the fresh snow and landing on my ass. I stifled a scream as my tailbone felt like it caught fire. I had just gotten to my feet when Lisa started rummaging through the rock garden.

"What the hell are you doing?" I whispered.

"I've got to hide the key! And stop swearing at me!"

"Sorry." (I still count that as our first fight. It's one of the few we ever had.)

I led the way down the back walk. We were just about at the gate when Lisa grabbed the back of my letter jacket. She put a finger to her lips and beckoned for me to follow her. She slid over to the back of the garage. I followed, both of us trying to simultaneously catch and hold our breath. I was dying to ask Lisa what was going on, but I didn't think speaking was a good idea. I got my answer a few seconds later.

"You see something, girl?"

The jingling of a leash and the panting of a dog told me exactly what caused Lisa to stop. Footsteps were closing in on the back gate. A light came on in the kitchen. All someone had to do was turn on the yard light and we'd be clear as day. In fact, there was half a chance the guy walking his dog would spot us if he stepped into the backyard.

Whoever built the backdoor to the garage built it with a recessed entrance. We had just enough room to get out of sight. As long as nobody looked too closely, we could remain hidden. I slipped into the recessed area and pulled Lisa along with me.

We sat there, huddled into that little recess. I'd like to tell you I was terrified for my life. But Lisa was pressed against me and breathing into my neck and I was fighting the natural, uh, *biological* reaction that comes upon a teenage boy in that situation. I *was* vaguely aware of someone coming through the back gate. Just past Lisa's head, I could see people strolling around the kitchen. I was praying the dog wouldn't get our scent or that her master wouldn't notice the footprints leading this direction. Someone inside the house glanced through the window. The backdoor opened and a middle-aged woman looked out.

"Is that you, Jerry?" she asked.

"Yeah," the dogwalker said, "Is that Vanessa?"

"It is. Marjory forgot something, so I ran back here to get it for her."

"She's at the visitation? How's she holding up?"

"Well as can be expected."

"Ali and I are going to stop over in about an hour. Just had to walk the dog first."

"I'll see you then."

"See you then."

Fascinating conversations we had in Porter's Bay. If I hadn't been fighting both abject terror and an impending boner, I would've rolled my eyes. The dogwalker exited into the alley and the middle-aged woman headed back into the house. After about thirty seconds, the light in the kitchen went off and I could hear, faintly, the sounds of the front door opening and closing. Nearly a minute passed and all was clear.

And I noticed Lisa hadn't moved.

Not that I wanted her to (having gotten my, um, *self* under control) but with an opening to get out of there, hanging around the backyard didn't seem to be a particularly good idea.

"I, uh, I think the coast is clear," I said.

Lisa's head snapped up so quickly the top of her head brushed my chin. She flinched and reached for my chin by way of apology. She stopped short and looked around.

"We should probably go," she said.

"Yeah, that's, that's a good idea."

We dashed out the back gate, checking to make sure the alley was clear. Lisa was no longer pressed up against me and I was somewhat relieved for that. It was the only time I can remember that being the case.

***

Sam and Andy had disappeared, probably freaking out and following the instinct to run. Lisa and I were forced to walk through the falling snow, heading in the direction of home. It would be a long walk, but a makeable one. We talked about the money we found in Mr. Jacobson's basement and what to do about it.

Lisa grimaced as she thought. "The right thing to do would be to tell the police."

"And how do we explain how we found it? I think we have to sit on that until we have proof that somebody killed Mr. Jacobson."

Lisa ran a hand through her hair, brushing away some of the snow that was caking there. It wasn't all that cold, but you don't have to spend a lot of time outside before it starts to get to you. Still, I had no particular desire to go inside. Even at sixteen, I had a habit of thinking about some other thing I wanted to be doing, some other place I wanted to go. With a brain that won't sit still, it's a wonder I ever became a writer. At that moment, though, I was content to be where I was at and doing what I was doing.

But there was still work to be done. An idea came to me. "What about the cabin?" I asked, "Maybe there's something up there."

"Like what?"

And that's as far as that idea could travel. "I don't know. But it's someplace we haven't checked out yet. Y'know, no stone left unturned and all."

Lisa was warming to the idea. "You know where the cabin is at?"

"No. But you seem pretty good at finding out that kind of stuff."

She laughed. "All right, I can check it out."

"Okay if I bring Sam and Andy along for backup?"

"Definitely. You think they'll be okay with it?"

"Why wouldn't they be?"

And of course, that's when Sam finally found us. The car pulled up and the window came down. "Hi kids," Sam said, "You need a lift?"

"Mom told me not to accept rides from strangers," I said.

"Consider this a citizen's arrest," Sam said, "I'm going to bring you kids home."

I looked toward Lisa, who seemed almost giddy with relief. She said: "I think I've had enough law-breaking for one night."

I waved a hand toward the car. "Your chariot awaits."

Sam snorted as he rolled the window up. "You call this thing a chariot?"

Yeah, Sam made a lousy wheelman on a number of fronts.

***

Mr. Jacobson's cabin was on Mirror Lake, about an hour outside Porter's Bay. It wasn't a heavily populated area in general and less so in the winter. The best time to go was after dark on Saturday night, since we could stay out later. (Yes, we could all go to a remote cabin and risk life and limb investigating a possible murder…but we had to make curfew.)

Andy and Sam agreed to go but were not thrilled. The idea of being a collective third wheel while I ran a possible fool's errand to the middle of nowhere with a girl they barely knew but had shown a troubling proclivity for getting us into hairy situations was not appealing.

We piled into my car around four o'clock and took Highway One out of town, heading northwest. We passed a handful of Podunk towns, each one a tad podunkier than the one before it. We made it within an hour thanks to my early tendency to treat the speed limit like a guideline rather than an actual law. The cabin was at the end of a winding road about a half-mile long. We kept a careful eye on the lot numbers until we reached the cabin belonging to the Jacobsons.

It wasn't awe-inspiring, but then I didn't really expect it to be. It was one story and looked to have about three bedrooms, at most. A path led down a small hill, ending at the front door. A set of steps led from the back of the cabin to what I imagined was the lake (it was too dark to get a good look). I wedged my car into a parking space that had been cut out across the road. Nobody moved for several seconds. Finally, Lisa pulled a flashlight from her coat.

"Shall we?" she said.

Sam and Andy gave me dirty looks before we all piled out of the car. Lisa and the flashlight led the way. The whole scene was creepy as hell. The silence. The cold. The desolation. If Lisa shared my hesitation, she didn't show it. She marched up to the cabin, the rest of us slipping and sliding to keep up. When we got there, everyone stared at the front door.

"How do we get in?" Sam asked.

Lisa frowned. Her flashlight (one of those big security flashlights) was held loosely in her hand. There was a screen door covering a main door with a couple small windows.

"I guess we only have one choice," Lisa said.

She opened the screen door and used the flashlight to smash one of the small windows. It was a swift move; over, in fact, before I even realized what was happening. Lisa pushed her hand through the broken window and felt around for the doorknob. When she found it, she unlocked the door and flipped it open.

"How are we going to explain the broken window?" I asked.

A corner of Lisa's mouth curled up. "Probably some damn teenagers."

She headed inside. Sam looked at me, a smile of his own in place. "I think I like her."

A little thrill ran through me; that feeling you get when someone tells you, *You two would make a cute couple.* Then I had to remember I was in the middle of nowhere, breaking into a cabin I didn't own (not that breaking into a cabin I *did* own was more acceptable.)

The place was a simple affair. The three bedrooms bordered a large main room that was living room, dining room and kitchenette all in one. A picture window looked out over the lake. There was a fireplace in one corner. A cabin right out of central casting.

Lisa, Sam and Andy each searched a bedroom while I looked around the main room. It wasn't a long search or a particularly enlightening one. The refrigerator had been turned off. The stove wasn't in operation. The pantry had been cleared. According to Lisa, Sam and Andy, the bedrooms had been packed away, all linens stripped from the beds and nothing resembling entertainment left around (no reading material, no DVDs, nothing). I had to admit: Mr. Jacobson had done a sterling job of closing down his cabin for the winter. There was a distinct bit of frustration in the air when we gathered in the main room.

"Was this a waste of time?" Lisa asked.

I was about to, hesitantly, agree when something occurred to me. "The place is closed up for the winter."

Sam's eyes rolled toward the ceiling. "Yeah, we can see that."

"But Mr. Jacobson was coming up here on the weekends. If it's closed up for the winter, what was he doing up here?"

Nobody had an answer, though we could agree it was strange. But there was nothing in the cabin that was going to give us an answer. Lisa glanced toward the front door.

"We can look over the grounds," she said, "There's two buildings left to check. The outhouse and I'm guessing the other is a woodshed."

Sam and Andy spoke at practically the same time. "Let's check out the woodshed."

The search of the grounds was, like the search of the cabin, brief and uninteresting. I was getting pessimistic. Not only was I on the verge of having recommended a waste of time and feeling like an incompetent boob in front of Lisa…but my feet were getting cold.

"Sorry," I said, "I was hoping we'd find something."

She patted my shoulder. "It's okay. You were right. No stone unturned."

That removed the weight from my chest. Then Andy's voice cut through the air.

"Hey guys? You might want to take a look at this."

Lisa and I ran to the woodshed. Andy and Sam had just stepped out. Lisa pointed the flashlight toward one corner, where Andy and Sam had apparently taken apart a pile of wood. Lying there was a plastic bag filled with oregano. Or what closely resembled oregano. And there were other goodies inside. My jaw dropped.

"Is that…?" I said.

"Ganja?" Sam asked, "Yep, that's a mess of ganja."

Lisa picked up the bag. "Is that all it is?"

Sam took the bag and rummaged through it. "There's other stuff, too. Pills, powder, crystals. It's like a little drugstore. And for some reason, there's a couple copies of *The Underground* in here." *The Underground* was the high school's oh-so-cleverly-named underground newspaper.

I'll confess to being shocked and not about *The Underground*. I'd heard rumors about this person or that person being into drugs and what sorts of goings on one would find in the less-savory portions of Porter's Bay. But I knew everyone well enough to know those rumors for what they were: utter horseshit. Yes, there was probably some illegal activity going on, but it's not like we were Pablo Escobar's vacation spot. Apparently, though, there were a lot of drugs in

Porter's Bay. Because most of them were sitting right in front of me.

"I guess we know where the stash of money came from," Lisa said.

There was a momentary thrill. We were able to connect a couple of dots. But it didn't tell us why Mr. Jacobson was killed (didn't, in fact, prove that he'd *been* killed) or who would have done it. Before we could consider that, though, there was a voice outside the shed.

"Okay, whoever the fuck is in there, you can come out right now!"

Lisa instinctively doused the flashlight. It didn't do us any good. With the door to the woodshed hanging open and my car parked across the road, the jig, as it were, was up.

"What do we do?" Sam whispered.

No one had any idea. Andy was the first one to speak. "We need to get out of here."

"Yeah, no shit," I said, "You see a backdoor to this place?"

The voice called to us again. "I said, come out!"

The voice in question was harsh and grinding; the sort found among some working class (read: redneck) folks in northern Minnesota. We had no choice but to face the music. I led the way, with Lisa right behind me and Sam and Andy slowly bringing up the rear. The first thing I saw was a shotgun pointed at me. Granted, the guy was up on the road and a decent distance away, but a shotgun's still a shotgun. The guy holding it looked like he was eighty percent flannel and twenty percent beard.

"Who the hell are you?" the guy shouted.

Nobody had an answer. Lisa called over my shoulder. "We're friends of Mr. Jacobson!"

"Dammit, I talked to him about having more of you damn kids up here! I'm gonna kill that son of a bitch."

Sam, unable to help himself, mumbled, "Too late."

But Lisa seized on the other sentence. "He's had kids up here before?"

The guy looked a little wary and confused. (Then again, maybe he always looked like that.) "Yeah. Hasn't happened for a few weeks, but he's had them up here. They aren't loud, but that don't make it right."

It occurred to me we were four teenagers with a bag of drugs in our possession. We weren't going to dispel whatever myth the guy had created in his head. Lisa stepped around me.

"We're actually working on an article for the newspaper," Lisa said, "We're checking out Mr. Jacobson's background. We heard there's, uh, some suspicious stuff going on. We wanted to come up and check it out. Is there any way you can help us?"

I had to give her credit. She'd barely lied (stretched the truth more than anything) and she'd started to turn the guy in our favor. If he was suspicious about something, why not give his suspicions credence and let him know we were on his side? The guy lowered the gun, slightly.

"What do you need to know?"

Lisa inched forward. I was tempted to grab her arm, lest she get too close to the nice redneck with the shotgun. "How often did Mr. Jacobson have kids up here?" she asked.

"'Bout every couple of weeks."

"Was it a lot of kids? Like a party or something?"

The guy shook his head. "Nah. Just a couple. Same ones as always."

"I don't suppose you got any names?"

"Nope. It was a couple of guys. Never actually talked to them."

"Do you remember what they looked like?"

The guy didn't seem interested in giving it any thought. "I don't know. Tall. Skinny. One of 'em had dark hair. They were teenagers, y'know?"

Yeah, we did. We went to school with about eight hundred of them, half of them boys and most of them fitting the description the guy just gave us. It wasn't exactly a revelation. Lisa, though, was more diplomatic.

"That's a big help," she said, "Thank you. Do you want us to send you a copy of the article when it comes out?"

The guy waved off the idea. "No. That's okay. Long as that Jacobson fella stops bringing teenagers up here, I'm fine."

"Fair enough. Is it okay if we go?"

"Um, yeah." The guy cleared his throat, maybe trying to get back some air of authority. "But don't let me catch you kids around here again. You understand?"

We didn't have to be told a second time. Everyone quickly fled the scene. Even as I had the car going down the road, Sam and Andy ducked down, taking no chances.

"Did you remember the drugs?" Lisa asked.

Sam patted his jacket where he'd stashed the narcotics. I let out a breath I'd been holding the last five minutes. We hadn't found a murderer, but we were coming back with a crapload of drugs. And the trip wasn't a waste of time. Oh, and *Did you remember the drugs?* is a catchphrase I use to this day.

***

Sunday, though, felt rather bleak. There was football on and that's never a bad thing. But my article was due the next day and, while I had enough bland background info to write a serviceable obituary, the major story Lisa and I wanted to break had not come together. There was an outside chance I could put off Mr. Somrock for a day, but that was as far as I could go. I was thinking about this as I sat on the couch, keeping half an eye on the football game and listlessly looking through a copy of *The Underground* when the phone rang in the front hall. A few seconds later, Owen poked his head into the living room, looking thoroughly sullen.

"Joe, that girl's on the phone for you. Again."

In Owen's defense, he was in eighth grade at the time. He had developed a large interest in girls and was simultaneously terrified of them. One of the few things he and I shared was an inferiority complex to our brother Kevin, who left behind roughly three thousand ex-girlfriends when he went off to college. If *I* was now getting the attention of a girl, Owen would be the sole loser in the family. I grabbed the phone and shooed Owen away.

"We're running out of time," is how Lisa greeted me.

"I was just thinking that. I don't know what to do."

"Mr. Jacobson had a couple of kids up at his cabin on the weekends. They were either his suppliers or his dealers. Either way, I'm guessing they're from Porter's Bay."

"But we don't know who they are."

She let out a sigh. "No, we don't. And that's what's got me tripped up."

I didn't have an answer. Then I spotted the copy of *The Underground* on the sofa. "I might have a way for us to get the word out," I said, "You know *The Underground*?"

"Yeah, we found a couple copies at the cabin."

I looked around, making sure Owen wasn't eavesdropping. "I know the guys who run that. Well, I don't know them, but I have a way to get to them. If we planted a story in *The Underground* about how we had the drugs, maybe we could flush out whoever's dealing."

Looking back, it was something of an idiot plan. Given Lisa was smarter than me, it was a mark of how desperate she was that she agreed to go along with it. I told her I'd get ahold of her as soon as I knew. I rang off and put in a call to Sam.

"I need to talk to Beans," I said.

"About what?" Sam asked, probably still half-watching the football game.

"The new issue of *The Underground* comes out tomorrow, right?"

I now had Sam's undivided attention. His tone of voice was hushed, like I'd just asked to have The Unabomber over for cookies.

"Are you out of your mind?" Sam said, "I wasn't supposed to tell you Beans runs *The Underground*. If he finds out you know, he'll kill me"

"He's going to have to find out because I need to talk to him. I wouldn't ask if it wasn't important."

"Is it about the thing with Mr. Jacobson?"

"Yeah. Can I meet him later? After the Vikings' game?"

Sam hemmed and hawed. "I'll call him and find out. I can't promise anything, though."

We hung up and I loitered around the phone. Owen peeked in on me, but since I wasn't talking to anyone, there was nothing to hold him there. I was thankful my parents had gone over to the Seavers to watch the game. They would have found me suspicious and may have dragged the truth out of me. With them absent, I was free to do suspicious things, such as grab the phone on the first ring when Sam called back.

"Beans will meet us at Rudi's Pizza," Sam said, "And it better *just* be us. He was pretty clear on that."

"Sounds good. I'll pick you up after the game."

"By the way, this makes us even for the time we broke into your parents' liquor cabinet."

"What do you mean? I was the one who had to clean up your puke."

"I wouldn't have gotten sick if you hadn't let me talk you into breaking in there."

If you haven't figured it out by now, Sam was the dry run for my friendship with Mike.

***

Beans Madden was a year ahead of us, meaning he was about seven months from being freed from the gulag he considered high school. He didn't care a hell of a lot about school and was going to care significantly less as time went on.

Beans had worked for *The Bay Breeze* once upon a time. But his need to insert his opinions into every article, including things as bland as the rearranging of the school trophy case, led to multiple clashes with Mr. Somrock. After a particularly unpleasant interview with Vice-Principal Cooper, it was agreed Beans should probably follow his own muse.

The Underground first appeared toward the end of the previous school year. Looking back, it probably wasn't as radical as we all wanted to believe. It was largely a collection of sophomoric jokes (some of them written by actual sophomores), largely at the expense of teachers and certain popular kids. But this being the days before social media, it was the first kind of organized resistance many of us had ever seen. As such, it was wildly popular among kids who wanted a subversive thrill. The school administration, of course, was less thrilled. All copies of *The Underground* that could be found were confiscated, but new issues kept popping up like that gopher that won't die in *Caddyshack*. While I find it impossible to believe that Mr. Somrock didn't know who was behind *The Underground*, he never said anything. It was tacitly understood, though, that anyone involved in *The Bay Breeze* would have nothing to do with *The Underground*. So I was taking my own chances on this little scheme.

Rudi's Pizza was a hole-in-the-wall joint about two blocks from the high school. Since we had open lunch in those days (yeah, I know, it's shocking) it was a popular noon hour hangout. It had a stainless-steel counter, a drink fountain and two tables next to the window. That was it. It was decidedly a grab-it-and-go kind of place. Perfect for lunch and perfect for Rudi, who probably didn't want a mob of teenagers loitering around. Beans was sitting at one of the tables, sipping a soda and working on a slice of pepperoni when Sam and I arrived. He didn't look particularly impressed as we pulled up chairs.

"You took me away from the game," he said.

"The Vikings game is over," I said.

"I like the Cowboys, too."

"We got you out of the house, didn't we?" I said.

If you can't tell right off the bat, I never had the best relationship with Beans. From the time I met him in junior high, he struck me as a bit of a dink. He was a pudgy kid with a smirk that conveyed a confidence his physical appearance and intellect didn't warrant. I'm sure these were assets later in life (I've heard he's doing well selling medical supplies) but they were just irritating at the time.

"Why am I here?" Beans asked.

I told him my plan for an announcement in *The Underground*, saying something had been found at Mr. Jacobson's cabin and offering a number to call if someone wanted the items back. Beans screwed his pudgy face into a scowl.

"That sounds like a want-ad," he said, "We don't do that kind of thing."

"It's not," I said, "It's a message I need to send to someone who reads your paper."

"Like a love note?"

I was trying very hard to stay patient. "No. It's part of an article I'm writing. And it's big. If it works out, I'll make sure you get credit."

Beans held up his hands like I'd just pulled a gun on him. "No way. I don't want anybody knowing who's involved in my paper. I didn't even want *you* to know." He glared at Sam. "Problem was, not everybody could keep their mouths shut."

Sam lowered his head, looking not unlike a whipped puppy. I kept trying to reason with Beans, which I was pretty certain was a waste of time.

"The point is," I said, "I need this done and it's got to be done tomorrow."

Beans worked his next sentence around a rather large bite of pepperoni. "Yeah, see, that's the problem. I already got it pretty much laid out. It's too much work to change it now."

"For fuck's sake, Beans," I said, all patience gone, "The fucking paper is four pages long on a *good* week. You telling me you can't find a spot for a little two sentence announcement?"

"Hey," Beans said, looking a tad offended, "You're telling me you're working an article for the school newspaper. Somrock kicked me *off* that paper. Remember?"

"Because he wouldn't let you call Vice Principal Cooper a *corrupt tool.*"

"No, *Vice Principal Cooper* wouldn't let me call him a corrupt tool. He made that clear when he was throwing me out of his office. But that's just the thing. What you do at *The Bay Breeze* isn't journalism. You're doing what the stiffs in the office tell you to do. Why should I help that out?"

"Because I know you run *The Underground.*"

Beans laughed. "I'm one guy. There's a bunch of us working on the paper. You take me out, it ain't gonna matter. *The Underground* will still go on. Besides, you got no proof."

He had me there. I could practically hear Mr. Somrock reminding me an accusation was not a fact. I didn't have a lot of operating room with Beans and he didn't seem inclined to help. I did, however, have an ace in the hole.

"You heard of Lisa Cleary?" I asked.

Beans stopped masticating. "Word on the street is she's the one who busted the parking lot guy."

"She is," I said, "And she's working with me on this."

There was a flash of panic in Bean's eyes. "That so?"

"And if you won't help us, I'll let her know what *I* know about *The Underground*. And if I do that, I don't care what you guys do or how you think you can protect yourselves, it's just a matter of time until you're busted."

I was afraid Beans was going to choke on his pizza. He looked to Sam, checking whether or not I was bluffing. Sam tilted his head, as if to say, *You don't know the half of it.* Beans swallowed his pizza.

"This thing you want," he said, "Just two sentences?"

***

The next twenty-fours played out the way I hoped. Mr. Somrock wasn't thrilled about giving me an additional day and seemed a tad suspicious. He made it *very* clear he expected the article on his desk by the end of the day on Tuesday, along with my usual column (which I had completely forgotten to write). Beans was good on his word, putting the little two sentence missive at the top of page three, above an article making fun of Mike Swenson's breath. The number I left was my own and I hovered around the phone after school, drawing curious looks, but no questions, from my mother. Finally, the phone rang. I grabbed it ASAP.

"You're the one with the stuff from Jacobson's cabin?" a gruff voice said. If I had to guess, someone was holding a sock or something over the phone.

"Yeah, I am. You want them back before I turn them over to the police?"

"How much?"

"We can talk about that tonight," I said, "Seven o'clock. Mr. Jacobson's classroom."

The caller hung up. I caught my breath and called Lisa. Per her orders, I picked her up just after dinner. We were quiet on the drive over to the school, but it was more anticipatory than uncomfortable.

Mr. Jacobson's room was on the third floor. As expected, it was unlocked and completely empty. I led the way inside and closed the door. We each sat on the top of a desk, our feet dangling near the floor.

I glanced up at the clock. It was five to seven. I had no idea what we'd do when the rightful (if that's the word I'm looking for) owner of the drugs came through the door. I'm not good at thinking two steps ahead *now*. I really wasn't good at it then. We were quiet for several seconds. Lisa cleared her throat.

"I really like your column," she said.

I nearly fell off the desk. "Wha?" And I asked it like that. Couldn't even add the "t". Just "Wha?"

"I like your column. You're really funny. I, uh, I don't think I've told you that."

There was a flutter in my stomach. "Thank you," I said, "I'm looking forward to staying up half the night writing it."

"Does it take you that long?"

"Not usually. But I'm hoping we have a big story to work on here."

She smiled. "Me, too. I mean, we've worked pretty hard on it."

"And taken a few chances."

"Yeah." Lisa slipped me a look. "But it's been fun."

We'd been threatened with a shotgun, chased out of a house we'd broken into, looked at crossways by teachers and students we barely knew and risked whatever small standing we had with the school newspaper. But I had to agree with her. It *had* been fun.

Whatever moment Lisa and I were having was interrupted by the sound of footsteps in the hallway. They were heavy, likely a guy's. And there was only one set. It was a small relief knowing we outnumbered whoever was about to walk through that door.

I leaned toward Lisa. "You ready?"

She answered by hopping off the desk and facing the door. I followed suit. There was a little tap on the door. "Come in," Lisa said.

The door opened. I stood there, heart in my throat, fists clenched, suddenly wishing I'd brought a weapon. Wishing I even *owned* a weapon. Lisa drew in a quick breath. She might have been having the same thoughts.

And Ryan stepped into the room.

He looked up quickly, startled at who he saw. Then the air seemed to go out of him. We stood there, nobody quite knowing how to start this conversation.

"You got the drugs?" Ryan asked. (Sadly, *that* never became a catchphrase.)

Lisa patted her pocket where the drugs were located. (Well, where they *would* have been located if she had brought them.) "If you want them, you're going to have to talk to us."

Ryan hung his head. "I figured as much."

Lisa started firing facts at him. "We know about the drugs up at the cabin. We know Mr. Jacobson had high school kids up there. We know about the huge stash of money at his house. We know he was saving up for a boat. And because you're here, you've confessed to knowing about the drugs."

Ryan was sweating. "You gonna go to the cops?"

"It depends," Lisa said, "Do you want to talk to us?"

Ryan wrestled with the situation. His eyes darted, as if looking for a way out of the room. "He found out I was dealing. At first, he just wanted a cut of the money. Y'know, so he wouldn't tell anyone. Then he started dealing himself. Some people up by his cabin were customers."

Well, *there* was something big. A teacher accepting drug money as a blackmail payment *and* dealing on the side. At least we were going to be able to deliver on that promise to produce a decent article. Lisa narrowed her eyes as she thought.

"How did Mr. Jacobson find out?" she asked, "That you were dealing."

Ryan took an involuntary step back. "He just, uh, y'know, he's a teacher. Was. Anyway. They find stuff out."

You didn't have to be the most observant person (and I wasn't, believe me) to see that Ryan wasn't telling us something. Lisa hit him with the big question.

"Did you kill Mr. Jacobson?" she asked.

Ryan wiped his forehead. "N…no."

"But he *was* murdered, right?" Lisa said.

"Yeah, it…" And he stopped right there; clamming up like he was on the verge of saying something he shouldn't have.

Then he ran like hell.

Ryan was gone before Lisa and I could even react. By the time we got out of the classroom, he was already starting down the steps.

"We're going to lose him," Lisa said.

"No, we're not," I said, "Just try to keep me in sight."

Confession: I was never an athlete. I tried my hand at various sports, but I couldn't skate well enough to be a hockey player, never developed the love for getting hit that a decent football player needs and the less said about how my hand-eye coordination torpedoed my Little League career, the better. But I've always had one thing going for me: I run *really* fast.

And I didn't have the fear of death one should have when running down a flight of marble stairs. I had no idea where Ryan was going, but he wasn't going there without me. The sound of our shoes slapping against the steps echoed throughout the building. I wasn't gaining on him, but I wasn't losing him, either. If I could keep him in sight, I was golden.

I assumed he was heading for the front entrance. Instead, he took a zig-zag path to the ground floor. He ducked down the hallway leading to the locker rooms. Weird choice, I figured, but there he was. I followed him.

And found the hallway empty.

I stopped for a quick "Son of a bitch." He couldn't have reached the locker rooms. He wouldn't have got there before I spotted him. I slowly walked down the hall, trying to catch my breath. There were offices on both sides of the hallway. He had to be in one of them. I slipped to my right and hugged the wall.

Someone tapped me on the shoulder. I spun around like The Flash after sucking down a Red Bull. Lisa recoiled, having gotten a bigger reaction than she probably expected. I let out a huge—but quiet—sigh of relief. She held a finger to her lips and pointed to the office across the hall. It was the student assistants' office.

And then it all came together.

The missing coffee cup. Someone who could feed Mr. Jacobson information. Someone who was giving Ryan his marching orders. I mouthed it out.

Marcy.

Before Lisa could stop me, I marched across the hall and whipped open the office door. Two people were visible, even in the low light. I flipped the light switch.

And there was Marcy. Holding a knife.

Ryan was behind her, cowering in a corner. Before I could shout out a warning, Lisa followed me into the office. She let out a little gasp when she saw the knife. Marcy's eyes narrowed as she regarded both of us.

"Close the door," she said.

Lisa hastily complied. The knife Marcy was holding was long and serrated. At the time, it looked to be the size of a javelin. Marcy's lip curled into a sneer.

"I should've figured," she said, "You were going to follow the whole thing."

I looked over at Lisa. Her face was pale and her glasses were slightly askew. She looked scared. And that scared *me* more than anything. Lisa tried to catch her breath.

"You killed Mr. Jacobson?" she said.

Marcy nodded and said, very quietly, "He had it coming."

Lisa and I were on edge. Marcy seemed awfully comfortable with the knife.

"You put something in his coffee, right?" I said, "That's why the cup was missing."

"Yeah. A nice amphetamine cocktail. All he could handle. And maybe a little more."

"It killed him that fast?" I said, "That morning?"

"It killed him the night before," she said, "I told him I knew something about Staci, something he needed to know. So he met me at the school. Didn't even think about the coffee I brought him. The coffee I *always* brought him."

That's why he wasn't dressed for school. But there was a bigger question to ask: "Why?"

Marcy didn't say anything. Her mouth tightened with bitterness. She had been as forthcoming as she was going to be. And then there was a voice from the corner.

"Because he made a pass at Staci," Ryan said.

Marcy spun around and waved the knife. "Shut up!"

Ryan's words tumbled out in a rush, as if he'd been dying to get this off his chest. "Marcy's been coming on to Mr. Jacobson all year."

"Shut up!"

"She even cut him in on the drug deal," Ryan said, "*That's* how he knew. And then he hit on Staci and—"

The next thing I heard was a scream. There was a flash as Marcy ran at Ryan. He went down, clutching his leg. Lisa screamed and it's possible *I* screamed. Marcy, holding the now-bloody knife, stared at Ryan with a detached, glassy look in her eyes. I grabbed Lisa's hand and pulled her out of the office.

Once we reached the hallway, though, Lisa went right toward the front door of the school and I went left toward the locker rooms. Since we were holding hands, we immediately came to a halt. We looked at each other for a split-second, silently trying to come up with a coherent plan. And then we became aware of Marcy standing in the hall with us.

Again, she had the drop on us. We moved to the left, but she started to go with us. We moved to the right but got the same thing. We could have separated and she could have only gone after one. But that thought didn't occur to us. There were several long moments where we stood there, not sure what to do. I was running a silent clock in my head, hoping like hell my backup plan would work.

"We should call an ambulance for Ryan," Lisa said.

Marcy barked out a laugh. "Fuck him. He had that coming."

"Just like Mr. Jacobson?" I said.

"Yes," Marcy said, practically snarling, "I did anything he asked me to do. Anything. He talked about this boat he was dreaming of. But he didn't have the money. I knew what Ryan was doing. I got Mr. Jacobson cut in on the whole thing. And how does he repay me? He goes after Ryan's fucking girlfriend!"

I'll be honest: it wasn't until I met Stephanie Brucker, years later, that my first impression of someone would be *this* far off. Marcy was lightspeed insane. And she had a weapon. Her voice got quiet again.

"What are you going to do?" she asked.

Lisa didn't hesitate. "We're going to tell the truth."

Marcy nodded. "That's a real shame."

I held out a hand, cautioning her. "Look, Marcy, you don't want to do this." She raised the knife. I dropped the hand. "But I can see you're warming to the idea."

Marcy was awfully decisive in that rather awful moment. "I guess this is how it goes."

The next couple seconds seemed to unfold in slow motion. Marcy had been so focused on us, she hadn't seen Sam and Andy coming. Sam grabbed her around the chest (of course he did) while Andy went for the knife. I stepped in front of Lisa, shielding her. Andy and Sam tackled Marcy to the floor. Andy got possession of the knife and held it as far away from his body as possible. Without the knife and clearly outnumbered, Marcy went limp. Lisa stepped around me, her jaw dropping slightly.

"Nice work, guys," she said, shell-shocked.

"Yeah," Andy said. He seemed surprised himself.

Lisa looked toward me. "You planned this?"

"Figured we needed a backup plan," I said, "Just needed the guys to keep us in sight."

"Good thinking."

Sam sat up so that he was, in fact, sitting on Marcy. "Glad you appreciate it," he said, "You think maybe you should call 9-1-1?"

It was enough to jolt Lisa into action. She ordered Andy to look in on Ryan then started toward the main hallway.

"There's a phone in *The Bay Breeze* office," she said, "We can use that."

Neither of us spoke until we reached the office. Lisa made the call and seemed earnest enough to overcome the operator's skeptical tone. She hung up and looked at me, her eyes slightly wild, as if the adrenaline was still pumping.

"We did it," she said.

"We did."

"We pulled it off. I mean, we *actually* got the story."

"We did."

Lisa suddenly threw her arms around me and we both laughed. A few minutes earlier, we had been wondering if we were even going to be alive and now here we were, ready to write the biggest story ever to hit Porter's Bay. For a high school newspaper. It was crazy and absurd and wonderful all at the same time.

And then we realized we'd been hugging for nearly a minute.

Lisa broke away, her face slightly red. She laughed again, a little strained. I suddenly found my shoes very interesting. After a second, Lisa regained her usual air of command.

"We need to get downstairs," she said, "We're going to have to talk to the police. Then we can get started on the article."

I let out a sigh. "Gonna be a long night."

Lisa patted me on the shoulder. "We'll go to The Hub Diner. We can stay until midnight before they kick us out."

"I don't think my parents will let me do that."

"Tell them what you're working on. Maybe they'll change their minds. Besides, I could use a cup of coffee. How about you?"

"I, uh, I don't even like coffee."

Lisa laughed. "I'll have to cure you of that." Then she gave me a last look and headed out the door.

∗∗∗

I sip my coffee and stare out the window of Glacier's. I think about that night. With Lisa driving us, we got the article finished, even though I was drowsy the whole next day.

For a few minutes, we were a big deal. The story shocked Porter's Bay. It was safe to say nothing like it had happened before. The fact it was broken in a high school newspaper by a couple of sixteen-year-old kids added to the interest. It got us attention from the Duluth newspapers and then the Twin Cities papers. As with all scandals, it faded from peoples' memories pretty quickly. I doubt anyone in the Cities now connects Joe Davis: intrepid teen reporter with Joe Davis: guy who writes artful dick jokes. Certainly, Porter's Bay, a city whose tourism trade relies on its rustic charm, was anxious to disassociate itself from the situation. So things died down as fast as they started.

Ryan recovered from his leg wound and managed to avoid any serious time in juvie by giving up the names of the people who were supplying him. Though he didn't graduate with the rest of us, he did clean himself up. Last I heard, he was managing a convenience store in Two Harbors. Marcy was sent to the state mental health facility. I assume she's been released from there, though I haven't followed up and don't really know for sure.

Mr. Somrock was a little hesitant to publish the article, but when the local paper threatened to scoop him, he went ahead and ran it. He was surprised at the content of the article, but not surprised Lisa and I were working on something. He seemed to suspect it all along. Looking back, he was a better observer of people than I gave him credit for. When Lisa and I started dating, he seemed happy, but hardly surprised.

You still there?

I snap a look at the laptop, realizing I've let my mind wander and I'm still in the middle of a chat with Lisa.

I'm fine. Just got distracted by something. Sorry.

It's okay. I've got to get going anyway. I'm interviewing the HUD Secretary tomorrow.

Sounds cool.

Actually, he's a colossal bore. But it pays the bills. You going home for Christmas?

Planning on it. I'll say hi to Andy and Sam for you.

Do that. I'll have to get back there some day.

Lisa's parents moved to Madison about ten years ago. It eliminated any chance of me running into her in Porter's Bay. She missed our ten-year high school reunion (and probably missed preventing Paula Kipling from using me to get back at Troy Samuels for dumping her after the senior prom). I haven't seen Lisa in person in fourteen years.

It was nice (virtually) talking to you. Take care. Stay out of trouble.

Shouldn't I be saying that to you?

Ha! Merry Christmas.

Merry Christmas.

A second later, she's logged off. There's a moment where I think about going back to work on the column. Then I close the laptop and pick up my mug of coffee.

It's dark outside and the snow is falling. Nostalgia, particularly nostalgia about Lisa, is a thing I work to keep at bay. When I feel it come upon me, my mind leaps away from it at warp speed. But right now, I don't feel like avoiding it. Maybe later I'll have a martini, wipe away whatever feelings I'm having. But just for this moment, I'll let them have sway.

I think about the old days. My friends. The kid I was then. The person I am now. I feel warm and empty all at the same time.

I watch the snow fall. Watch it accumulate and drift away on the wind. Picture Lisa running through it, heading for her parents' front door.

THE END